About the Authors

Nicole Helm grew up with her nose in a book and the dream of one day becoming a writer. Luckily, after a few failed career choices, she gets to follow that dream – writing down-to-earth contemporary romance and romantic suspense. From farmers to cowboys, Midwest to *the* West, Nicole writes stories about people finding themselves and finding love in the process. She lives in Missouri with her husband and two sons, and dreams of someday owning a barn.

Using actual Texas settings and realistic characters, this *USA Today* and *Publisher's Weekly* bestseller, creates stories with characters who put everything on the line. **Angi Morgan** is an eleventh generation Texan who lives there with her husband and 'four-legged' kids. Find her at AngiMorganAuthor.com

Joss Wood loves books, coffee and travelling – especially to the wild places of Southern Africa and, well, anywhere. She's a wife and a mum to two young adults. She's also a servant to two cats and a dog the size of a small cow. After a career in local economic development and business, Joss writes full-time from her home in KwaZulu-Natal, South Africa.

Friends to Lovers

Friends to Lovers:
One Kiss

NICOLE HELM

ANGI MORGAN

JOSS WOOD

MILLS & BOON

First Published in Great Britain 2024
by Mills & Boon, an imprint of HarperCollins*Publishers* Ltd,
1 London Bridge Street, London, SE1 9GF

www.harpercollins.co.uk

HarperCollins*Publishers*
Macken House, 39/40 Mayor Street Upper,
Dublin 1, D01 C9W8, Ireland

ISBN: 978-0-263-32333-7

MIX
Paper | Supporting
responsible forestry
FSC™ C007454

ISOLATED THREAT

NICOLE HELM

For those who've learned to ask for help.

Chapter One

In the dark of his apartment, Brady Wyatt considered getting drunk.

It wasn't something he typically considered doing. He stayed away from extremes. If he drank alcohol, it was usually two beers tops. He'd never smoked a cigarette or taken a drug that wasn't expressly legal.

He was a good man. He believed in right and wrong. He believed wholeheartedly that he was smarter, better and stronger than his father, who was currently being transferred to a maximum-security federal prison, thanks to a number of charges, including attempted murder.

When Brady thought of his twin brother nearly dying at Ace's hands, it made him want to get all the more drunk.

Brady wished he could believe Ace Wyatt would no longer be a threat. His father wasn't superhuman or supernatural, but sometimes...no matter what Brady told himself was possible, it felt like Ace Wyatt would always have a choke hold around his neck.

Once he could go back to work, things would be fine. Dark thoughts and this sense of impending doom would go away once he could get out there and do his job again.

The fact he'd been shot was a setback, but he'd taken his role as sheriff's deputy for Valiant County, South Dakota, seriously enough to know being hurt, or even killed, in the line of duty was more than possible.

He'd been shot helping save his soon-to-be sister-in-law. There was no shame or regret in that.

But the fact the wound had gotten infected, didn't seem to want to heal in any of the normal ways no matter what doctors he saw, left him frustrated and often spiraling into dark corners of his mind he had no business going.

When someone knocked on his apartment door, relief swept through him. A relief that made him realize how much the darkness had isolated him.

Maybe he should go stay out at his grandmother's ranch. Let Grandma Pauline shove food at him and let his brother Dev grouse at him. Being alone wasn't doing him any favors, and he was not a man who indulged in weakness.

He looked through the peephole, and was more than a little shocked to see Cecilia Mills standing there.

Any relief he'd felt at having company evaporated. Cecilia was not a welcome presence in his life right now, and hadn't been since New Year's Eve when she'd decided to kiss him, full on the mouth.

Cecilia had grown up with the Knights, on the neighboring ranch to his grandmother's. Duke and Eva Knight's niece had been part of the fabric of Brady's life since he'd come to live with Grandma Pauline at the age of eleven—after his oldest brother had helped him escape their father's gang, the Sons of the Badlands.

While Brady had been friends with all the Knight girls, Cecilia was the one who'd always done her level best to irritate him. Not always on purpose either. They were just…diametrically opposed. Despite her job as a tribal police officer on the nearby reservation, Cecilia bent rules all the time. She saw gray when he saw black, and even darker gray when he saw white. She was complicated and they didn't agree on much of anything.

Except that their fundamental function in life was to help people. Which, he supposed, was what had made them good friends despite all their arguments.

Until she'd kissed him and ruined it all. She hadn't even *tried* to pass it off as a joke when he'd expressed his horror.

Still, he opened the door to her, even if he couldn't muster a polite smile.

She was soaked to the bone, carrying a bundle of blankets. The blankets let out a little mewling cry and Cecilia shoved her way inside.

Not just blankets. A baby.

"Close the door," she ordered roughly.

He raised an eyebrow but did as he was told, if only because there was panic underneath that stern order.

Her long black hair was pulled back in the braid she usually wore for work, but she wasn't wearing her tribal police officer uniform. Her jeans and T-shirt hung loose and wet and her tennis shoes were muddy and battered. Even with the panic on her face, and the casual clothes, there was an air about her that screamed *cop*.

He should know.

"What's all this?"

Goose bumps pricked visibly along her arms and she quickly began unbundling the baby. It was warm outside, even with the all-day rain, so he had the air conditioner running. He moved to turn it off.

"You got anything dry for him?" she asked.

Brady wanted explanations, but he could see just how wet they both were. So, he walked into his room and rummaged around for dry clothes for Cecilia, and a few things to wrap around a small infant. He grabbed some towels from the bathroom and headed back to his living room.

He handed the towel to her first. She knelt on the floor, placing the baby gently on the rug. She spoke softly to the child, unwrapping the wet layers, and even the diaper. Brady winced a little as she wrapped the baby's bare butt in the towel he'd given her, rather than a new, dry diaper, though she didn't appear to have any baby supplies.

"You need to get out of your wet clothes too," he insisted once the baby was taken care of.

She looked up at him, an arch look as if he was coming on to her.

Heat infused him, an embarrassment he didn't know what to do with. He did not *blush*, being a grown man. He was probably just feverish from this damn infection he couldn't kick. Again.

"I'm not going to jump you," Cecilia said in that flippant way of hers that always set his teeth on edge. "That ship has sailed. So unclench."

He had never appreciated Cecilia's irreverence for the rules of life. Or at least, *his* rules of life. One of which was nothing romantic between him and any of the Knight girls. Maybe some of his brothers had crossed that line, somehow made it work, but Brady had his rules. If there'd been a brief, confusing second on New Year's Eve when Cecilia's surprise kiss had made him wonder why, it was a moment of weakness he wouldn't indulge.

Cecilia didn't follow the letter of the law. She often advocated for wrong as much as right. She had *kissed* him. On the mouth. Very much against his will.

Then had had the nerve to laugh when he'd lectured her.

"Just go to my room and change," he grumbled. "I'll watch..." He gestured at the baby.

She looked back at the wriggling infant she was crouching over. Pain clouded her eyes, and fear was etched into her face.

"This is Mak." She stroked his cheek with the gentleness of a mother, but Brady knew Cecilia had not secretly been pregnant or given birth to a child. He saw her too often for that to be possible.

He sighed, sympathy warring with irritation. "What's going on, Cecilia?"

CECILIA COULD FEEL the shivering start to spread. It had been hot outside in the rainstorm, but Brady's apartment was cold. Pretty soon her teeth would chatter, no matter how hard she fought against it.

And she would fight against it. Showing weakness in front of Brady Wyatt wasn't something she could afford right now. She had to be in charge if this was ever going to work. If she was ever going to convince by-the-book Brady to go along with it.

"I'll go change. You can leave him there or pick him up. He can roll over though, so keep an eye on him."

She grabbed the stuff he'd brought out, helped herself to his room, and then once the door was closed, slumped against it.

She'd been a tribal police officer for seven years. She'd been afraid, truly afraid for her life. She had struggled to understand the right thing to do in the face of laws that weren't always *fair*. It was hard, stressful, at times painful work, and she intimately knew fear.

But this was new. Bigger and different.

She didn't want to die, so she feared for her own life when she had to at work. But she'd also accepted that she *would* die to save someone. That was why she'd gone into law enforcement, or at least something she'd accepted as she'd taken on a badge.

Now she had a *specific* someone. A tiny, defenseless baby. Poor little Mak. He didn't deserve the stress and panic of being on the run, and yet she didn't know what else to do. If Elijah got a hold of him…

Cecilia shook her head.

She needed help. She needed…

God, she did not need Brady Wyatt, but she didn't have any other viable options in the moment. And the moment was all there was.

It was that lack of options that forced her to move. She stripped off her wet clothes, then put on the dry, too-big ones that were Brady's. She paused at that. Brady had worn these clothes on his body.

And washed them, you moron.

She couldn't help the fact she had the hots for Brady. Couldn't help that the New Year's Eve kiss hadn't helped dissipate them any. Luckily the memory of his stern lecture afterward always made her laugh.

He was just so *uptight*. He drove her crazy. Yet, there was this physical thing that also drove her a different kind of crazy. She believed deep down it was just her dualistic nature. Of course she'd be attracted to someone whose personality made her want to pull her hair out.

That was her lot in life.

But that lot was way in the background now. Her only concern was finding a way to protect Mak. Cecilia had been trying to help her friend Layla through postpartum depression for the better part of six months, but a suicide attempt had landed Layla in the hospital with the state preparing to take Mak away.

Layla had begged Cecilia to hide him. The state would only take him to his father, who was rising in the ranks with the Sons of the Badlands.

The fact Ace Wyatt's gang had begun to infiltrate the reservation Cecilia worked and lived on, the place she'd been born, filled her with a fury that scared her.

So, she'd focus on this. Keeping Mak safe until Layla was given a clean bill of mental health.

Elijah had already threatened to take Mak, maybe more than once. Layla wasn't always forthcoming with what went down with Elijah, since there was still a part of Layla who believed she could save the man she loved from the wrong he was doing.

Cecilia didn't believe. She knew the world was gray— that black and white were illusions made by people who had the privilege to see the world that way—but anyone who moved up the ranks in the Sons was too far gone to change for the better.

She would save the innocent baby who'd had the misfortune of a terrible father and an emotionally abused mother.

She'd been that baby, more or less, and her aunt and uncle had saved her. Showed her love and kindness and taken her in when her mother had died. She'd been six years old. Aunt Eva was gone too now, but she still had Uncle Duke, and the four other women he'd raised who were her sisters regardless of biological ties.

Cecilia tied the sweatpants tight around her waist. They were too long by far, but she cuffed the ends, then did the same with the sleeves of the sweatshirt. She took the bundle of wet clothes with her as she stepped back into the living room.

She stopped short. Brady held Mak, cradled easily in his good arm. Brady wore a T-shirt, so she could see a hint of the bandage that was on his opposite shoulder.

Recovery from the gunshot wound he'd received when saving Felicity had been complicated.

There were six Wyatt brothers, any of whom she could get help from. Easier help. All of them understood, to a point, you had to bend some rules to save people from the Sons.

Brady was the one who didn't, or wouldn't, accept that. He was also the one who currently couldn't work. Who lived alone. Who could hide a baby.

Elijah might think to look at the Wyatt Ranch for Mak, but he wouldn't think to look into Brady individually. Not at first anyway. Not while she came up with a plan.

"Can I throw these in your dryer?"

Brady inclined his head, gently swaying Mak's body back and forth as if Brady had any practice with calming babies.

She'd spent some time in Brady's apartment. Not much. They'd all helped him out here over the past two months, trying to give a hand with chores that might hurt his shoulder. She'd come over with Felicity and Gage one night and made him dinner. She'd delivered some food courtesy of Grandma Pauline a few weeks ago when he'd been doing laundry, and despite how little she wanted to be alone with him when everything about him made her body *react*, she'd insisted on helping him move the clothes from the washer to the dryer.

She did so now, tossing her own clothes in the dryer. She wouldn't have time for them to get completely dry, but it would help. Hopefully the rain would stop so it wouldn't be a completely futile gesture.

She hesitated going back into the living room. Much as she wanted Mak in her own arms where his warm weight gave her a settled purpose, she knew she couldn't go back to Brady without a clear sense of what she was going to say.

She'd practiced on the way here. She'd just go with that. *Brady. I need your help. I know you won't approve, but you're the only one who can keep this innocent child safe and away from the Sons. I know you'll do the right thing.*

Simple. To the point.

But as Cecilia stood on the threshold of his small, stark living room, watching a big man holding a tiny baby, she could only say one thing.

"His father is a member of the Sons."

Brady's expression did that thing that had always fascinated her. It didn't chill. It didn't heat. It was like something inside of him clicked off and he went perfectly blank.

She envied that ability.

"His mother is in the hospital," she continued. "The state is going to award him to his father. I can't let that happen."

"It's not up to you, Cecilia."

He said it so coolly, so *calm*. She wanted to scream, maybe give him a good punch like he'd once taught her to do when she'd been thirteen and a boy at school was bothering her.

But rage and punching never got through to Brady Wyatt. So, she had to be harsh. As uncompromising as he always was. "Would you send this baby to survive *your* childhood?" Because Brady had spent eleven years stuck with the Sons, surviving his father—the leader of that terrible gang.

There was a flicker of something in his eyes, but his words and the delivery didn't change. "He isn't Ace's son."

"He could be," Cecilia returned, trying to match his lack of emotion and failing. "Ace is gone. Elijah is trying to move up, take over. He's recruiting people at the rez at a rapid rate."

"Elijah Jones," Brady said flatly.

The fact Brady knew him didn't soothe Cecilia's nerves any. "Yes. You know him?"

"Of him," Brady replied, still so blank and unreachable. "He has a record." Brady's gaze lifted from the baby to her. "The state wouldn't put a child with someone who—"

"You know what? Forget it." God, he infuriated her. After everything he'd seen as a police officer, everything he'd survived as a boy, he could believe the state would do the right thing. She marched toward him. "I don't need your help. I don't need you and your rigid, ignorant belief in a system that does not work. Hand him over." She held out her arms.

But Brady simply angled his body, keeping Mak just out of her reach. "No," he said firmly.

Chapter Two

Brady had seen Cecilia angry plenty of times. She was a woman of extremes. Completely calm and chill, or…this. Fury all but pumping off her in waves. If he hadn't been holding a baby, he was certain she would have decked him. Possibly right in the gunshot wound.

"You brought him here for a reason," he said in a tone of voice he'd learned and used over the years as a police officer. Calm, but not condescending. Authoritative without being demanding. It often soothed.

Not with Cecilia. "Yes, and boy was it a stupid reason," she returned through gritted teeth. He could practically see the wheels in her head turning as she tried to figure out how to get the baby away from him without hurting Mak.

"Why don't you calm down and—"

She bunched her fist and he winced because he'd made a serious tactical error in telling her to calm down.

"I swear to God I will—"

The baby in his arm began to cry. Brady blinked down at the little bundle wiggling against his arm. He'd dealt with babies before—not often, but he'd held them. Calmed a few after a traffic accident or during a domestic case. Babies weren't new or strange to him.

But little Mak was so tiny. His face wrinkled in distress as he cried, clearly disturbed by the sound of raised voices. He had a patch of dark hair, and spindly little limbs that reminded Brady of a movie alien.

Cecilia held out her arms, gave Brady a warning look, but Brady simply bounced the baby until he calmed, nestled closer. There was something comforting about the weight of him. Something real and…heavy, even though the child was light. Brady had been adrift for weeks, and holding Mak felt like a weight tethering him to shore.

Cecilia frowned, her forehead wrinkling in much the same way Mak's had. But she didn't argue with him any more. There was a kind of anguish on her face that had his heart twisting.

Brady nodded to the couch. "Sit. Tell me the whole story," he ordered quietly.

"I don't want to sit," she returned, petulantly if he had to describe it.

She would not have appreciated that characterization. She folded her arms across her chest and began to pace.

She was tall and slender and like a lot of the female cops he knew, played down everything that made her look too feminine. Her hair was simple—straight, black, braided. She wore no makeup, and the jeans and T-shirt she'd shown up in were on the baggy side, as if she might have to put her Kevlar on underneath.

Cecilia could flip the switch when she wanted to. Put on a dress, do up her face in that magical way women seemed to have—like she had on New Year's Eve, all glitter and smoke and fun. She even seemed to enjoy it. Or maybe she'd just enjoyed knocking him off his axis.

With Cecilia, he'd bet on the latter.

"His mother's in the hospital. She…" Cecilia hugged

herself tighter, then finally sat on his couch. "She's one of my oldest friends on the rez. She's been wrapped up in Elijah Jones for years now. I couldn't come out and say he was bad news, you know?" She looked up at him, an uncomfortable amount of imploring in her eyes. "If you say they're bad, it only makes some people want to hold on even more. Fix them even more. Some people don't understand that not everyone is fixable."

Brady nodded. He'd worked enough domestic cases to know that people of both sexes were often blinded by what they thought was love. Enough to believe they could change the worst in someone else.

Cecilia seemed to find some relief in his understanding. "So, I tried to be subtle. I tried to make it more about her. What she should have. What she *could* have if she only gave up on holding herself back." Cecilia shook her head. "Anyway, she was ecstatic when she got pregnant. Elijah stuck around more. He had plans. But they all involved the Sons." Her tone turned to acid. "Layla had the baby, and Elijah told her he'd be back once the kid was out of diapers so he could take him. *Make* him."

Cecilia popped back up onto her feet. "Take him. As if that boy was a peach that had to ripen before he ate it. Take him, as if he had any right." She shook her head vigorously. "Layla had already been struggling a bit, but that really sent her over the edge. I helped out, but I urged her to talk to her doctor. Something wasn't right. Finally I took her down to her doctor myself and wouldn't leave until she told someone how she was feeling. They said it was postpartum depression."

"Common enough."

"Sure. Sure. Since then I've done my level best to help her out. To do what I could to help Mak. I took her to her appointments, but we had a hard time scheduling them. Her insurance is terrible and she was already struggling financially. She didn't have any supportive family, and I tried to be that for her, but…"

"You're only one person, Cecilia." It came out gentler than he'd intended, and the look of anguish she sent him made his chest too tight.

She collapsed back onto the couch. "One person or ten, it doesn't seem to matter. The night I came to the hospital to talk to Felicity and Gage, that night you were shot? She took a bunch of pills. She called me. Told me, so I called an ambulance and it got there in time, but—"

"You know better than to blame yourself."

"Do I?" she snapped.

"You should," he replied, keeping his voice gentle even though he wanted to snap right back. She should know better, and she shouldn't be sitting here making him feel sorry for her. She didn't want his pity any more than he wanted to give it.

"Yeah, well *should* can bite me. I do blame myself, and I will," Cecilia replied with a sneer, though it quickly faded. "I also know if it weren't for me, she would have had no one to call and she would have died. So, maybe it evens out. I don't know. They let me see her and she begged me to take Mak. He was with a neighbor and Layla didn't trust the woman not to hand him over to the state or Elijah." Cecilia blew out a breath. "She just needs help. She needs to get through this. She won't if Mak is with Elijah. Or gets shipped off into foster care."

"Cecilia, there are laws and rules and—"

"I had to. I *have* to do this for her. I know you only care about your precious laws and rules, but—"

"Those precious laws and rules are the difference between people like us and people like Elijah." And Ace. Though he didn't say that aloud, he had the uncomfortable feeling she heard it anyway.

"Except when those laws are going to hurt an innocent baby," Cecilia insisted. "If they give Mak to Elijah, being abused by the Sons is all that boy has to hope for. Is that what you want?"

Of course it wasn't. He didn't want that for anyone. It wasn't that he thought the law was infallible, that people didn't fall through the cracks of it. No rule could possibly apply to everyone in every situation, but this wasn't so much about following the letter of the law as it was about consequences.

"We could both get fired for this. You far more than me, but it risks both of our badges. We are sworn to uphold and protect the law, even when we don't agree with it."

She closed her eyes, then buried her face in her hands. Brady was rendered speechless and frozen in place for a good minute as Cecilia began to cry.

He'd never seen her cry before. She'd broken her arm falling out of a tree when she'd been thirteen and she hadn't cried. She'd yelled and cursed a blue streak, but she hadn't actually cried. At least not while he'd stayed with her and Gage had run to get help.

"Stop that," was all he could think to say.

She looked up at him dolefully, her face tearstained and blotchy. "You're such a comforting soul, Brady," she replied, her voice scratchy.

He didn't know what to say to that, since usually he *could* comfort people. Usually he knew what to say, how to calm and soothe so the work could be done. If she was anyone else he would have sat next to her on the couch and patted her shoulder, or leg or something. He would have known what to do with her tears.

But when it came to Cecilia, all those options seemed dangerous, and he didn't want to figure out why. He wanted to keep his distance.

"I'm sorry," she said on a sigh.

"You don't have to apologize for crying."

She rolled her eyes, wiping her cheeks with her palms. "I'm not sorry for crying. I'm sorry because I shouldn't have brought this to your doorstep. It's just, I had to think of the place Elijah would be least likely to look for Mak. He's going to suspect I had something to do with Mak's disappearance—Layla's neighbor will no doubt tell him who took him even though I bribed her not to. So, he'd know to look at the ranches, and I thought Nina and Liza made them too obvious," she said, speaking of her foster sisters who each had a child in her care—Liza her young half sister and Nina her daughter. "But you're just a bachelor in an apartment."

"Just a bachelor in an apartment," Brady repeated, surprised at how much that appraisal hurt.

"You know what I mean. Besides, you're hurt. He'd think less of you because of it. He'd think I'd want Mak with someone…"

"Who could actually protect him." That feeling of everything that had gone wrong since the gunshot wound settled deeper. He nodded toward his bad shoulder. "I *can't* protect him."

Cecilia stood again. Though the traces of tears were still on her face, there was something powerful about the way she stood, the way she angled him with a doleful look. "I'd take an injured Wyatt over just about anyone else. You'll protect just fine."

Brady didn't want that kind of responsibility thrust upon him when he was so… Things weren't right inside of him, and if he looked too closely at it, he had to believe it had begun even before the gunshot wound.

"Now, I have to get going. I don't think Elijah would have tracked me, but the longer I stay here, the more chances there are. I have to get back to the rez."

"You're just going to leave the baby with me?"

Her expression went grim, but it softened when her gaze landed on Mak's sleeping form cradled in Brady's arm. "Unfortunately, I'm a liability to him right now. I have to leave him with someone I can trust."

"They could track your car."

She shook her head. "We walked."

"You…walked. In this rain?"

"I had to. I had to." She cradled her head in her hands again, though she didn't cry, thank God. "I didn't want to tell you this. I didn't want to… It isn't fair, but I can't worry about that when Mak's *life* is in my hands."

She looked up at him—desolate, apologetic. His heart twisted, though he tried to harden himself against that. Against her.

"Elijah idolizes Ace. He worships him. He wants to *be* him, and not in that Sons way where they'll do whatever Ace did just for power. In a real way. In a real, dangerous way. He wants to take Ace's spot, and he'll do anything to get there."

Brady felt no surprise, no hurt. He should be feeling both of those things, but he couldn't manage it with a soft baby curled up against him. He could only tell her the truth. "I know."

"You know?" Cecilia blinked at Brady, at that harsh, final way he said those two words. "How do you…"

His jaw was set, and that blankness he'd perfected enshrouded his whole being. But his eyes told a different story. There was anguish there. Had she ever seen anguish in Brady?

"I've had run-ins with Elijah for the past eight years," he said, not offering any explanation as to what *run-in* might mean.

"Eight years," Cecilia repeated, just barely keeping the shriek out of her voice, and only for Mak's sake.

"It was happenstance. The first time."

"The first… Brady. What is this?"

"I arrested him. My first arrest actually. When he realized I was a Wyatt…it became something of a game to him. To poke at me. To try and get arrested by me specifically. I assume to prove he could get away with things—and out of jail over and over again. Nothing serious, obviously, but he made it pretty clear he was the next iteration of my father and there was nothing I could do to stop it."

"How come none of you ever told me?"

He turned away from her, Mak still sleeping cradled in his arm like the baby belonged there. "I'm the only one who knows. I didn't think it'd ever touch anyone else."

"Brady." She was utterly speechless. He had a secret from his brothers. She hadn't thought it possible. Oh, there were emotional scars they all kept from each other, anyone who'd grown up in the midst of them knew that. But not actual…secrets.

She'd thought.

"What do you mean—"

"It isn't the point right now. The point is if you really don't want anyone to know you stole this baby—"

"I didn't steal—"

"Then you can't stay. Do you have anything for him? Diapers? Food?"

"Not yet, but there's a plan in place."

"A plan?"

She looked at him for a second, trying to wrap her brain around what was happening. What she was asking, and what he was saying. She'd known Brady would have to go along with some of this because he understood what it was to be a child in the Sons.

But she'd had no idea he had a connection to Elijah. That her life, which had just taken the most complicated turn, would be even more complicated by the man in front of her. She'd always considered him pretty uncomplicated.

"You can't tell me there's something you've never talked to your brothers about, that ties to this child, and then change the subject."

"Except I just did."

"Were you *born* this frustrating or did you have to work really hard at it?"

"Says the woman who brought me a stolen infant."

"He is not stolen," Cecilia replied through gritted teeth. She'd done the right thing, knew that with an absolute certainty that had no room for doubt, and yet he made her feel shame for not finding a legal way to do it. "What would you have done differently, Brady?" she asked, though she was half-afraid he'd have an answer, and a good one.

He looked down at the sleeping baby for the longest time, then finally sighed. "I don't know."

Thank God.

"What's the plan for baby supplies?"

"Felicity and Gage are going to bring you dinner... but it won't be food in the take-out bags."

"And you didn't take the baby to them because...?"

"Felicity has already had her Sons run-in. Besides, she..." Cecilia trailed off. She was usually an expert at keeping secrets, but that one had nearly slipped out.

Brady raised an eyebrow, waiting for her to finish that sentence.

"She has a job. They both do. I know you'd love to be back at yours, but you can't. Trust me, if I could leave him with Liza or Nina, I would, but I think Elijah would expect that. He's going to look at my sisters harder than he looks into the Wyatts, what with it being my friend's baby and all."

Brady's face was impassive. "He'll look at us too."

"Maybe he will, but I don't trust anyone else." She hated being so baldly honest with him, hated the fact she'd cried in front of him. But she would do it over and over again if it kept Mak safe.

And Mak *looked* safe in Brady's arm. Sleeping against Brady's chest. Brady was too noble not to do everything in his power to keep Mak safe. She had to believe he'd bend some rules for *this*, if nothing else.

"I have to go. Gage and Felicity should be here soon. I'll be in touch." She moved for Brady and Mak. She looked down at the baby she loved and thought about Layla's desperate pleas. All that responsibility weighed heavy.

This small, helpless life was in her hands, and the only way to ensure his safety was to leave him in someone else's.

They were capable hands, though. She looked up at Brady, whose face was way too close for comfort. She'd had a few drinks that night she'd kissed him. Still, she remembered the kiss far more clearly than she remembered the rest of the night. The impulse, the need.

That split second where shock had melted into response before he'd firmly taken her by the shoulders and pushed her a step back. He'd looked furious.

But there had been that moment. It had scared the life out of her. Just like all the things jangling in her chest right now, looking up at his hazel eyes and knowing he'd take all of what she put on his shoulders.

She stepped back and then turned and headed for the door. She couldn't let herself look back, or even go back to the dryer and get her damp clothes. She had to keep moving forward until Mak was safe. For good.

Chapter Three

Cecilia was right. Felicity and Gage showed up not too long after she left and disappeared into the night. Brady opened the door, keeping the sleeping baby in his arm out of sight.

Gage and his fiancée stood on the threshold. It was still weird. His twin brother and Felicity. Engaged.

It wasn't all that long ago Felicity had had a crush on *him*. Brady had never seen Felicity as more than a little sister. He respected Duke Knight too much to look at any of his foster daughters and see... Whatever it was people saw in each other that made them want to get married, apparently.

Gage had no such qualms. It hadn't taken more than a few months for him to settle into being with Felicity, to propose marriage.

"We brought you dinner," Felicity said, smiling as she held up the bag. They both stepped inside, carefully closing the door behind them.

Without hesitation, Felicity moved across the room to the counter that ran between his kitchen and his living room. She pulled things out of the bags.

"Diapers. Formula. Bottles. We've got some more

stuff in a bag in the car. We'll go down and get that later when I leave."

"You mean, when you both leave."

"Nah. I'm bunking," Gage said, settling himself onto the couch easily. "You don't expect to care for an infant on your own, do you?"

"I'm not sure I expect the two of us to do it either."

"We'll figure it out," Gage said, all smiles. Gage liked to lighten a situation with a joke, but this smile was more than just that. It was aimed at Felicity. It was love. "Go on now," he said to her.

"You should," she replied, clasping her hands together.

Gage patted the seat beside him and Felicity went and sat there. They both looked up at him expectantly like he had any idea what they were doing.

"What is with you two?" Brady grumbled.

Gage slung his arm across Felicity's shoulders. "We're going to have a baby," he announced, grinning. Not Gage's typical grin meant to hide everything going on inside his head. No, this was a true smile. True happiness.

Brady blinked. It took a while to realize his brother had not spoken in a foreign language, but had in fact delivered a clear, concise sentence in English. "A baby."

"Real as the one you're holding."

"But… You aren't married yet."

Gage snorted out a laugh and Felicity smiled indulgently.

"Did you need a lesson about the birds and the bees?" Gage asked, with a smirk.

"No. I… A baby. Congratulations."

"I hope you'll be able to say that and mean it at some point," Felicity said gently.

Brady stepped toward them. Irritated with himself for not handling this the right way. "I *am* happy for you. I'm just shocked. It's been a day," he said, looking down at the baby he held. Who wasn't his, but was now his responsibility.

Mak began to squirm, fuss, then cry. Felicity popped off the couch, holding out her arms.

"Can I?"

He handed off the fussing baby and rolled his shoulders, trying not to wince at the pain in his injured one. Felicity rocked and crooned to Mak and Brady looked at his twin brother. They'd shared everything, or close to it. Not everything. Not the separate ways their father had tortured them.

Not Elijah Jones.

"You're going to be a father," Brady offered helplessly.

"Not a word I've ever cared for, but I'll make it mean something different."

"I know you will." It was a strange thing, since Brady wasn't this infant's father, but Gage's news and words crystalized what Brady had to do.

He'd grown up in the Sons. Thanks to his oldest brother's belief in right and good, Brady had come out believing in right and good, as well. Jamison had sacrificed a lot to get Brady and Gage out of the Sons together. He'd given them the gift of hope, and the gift of each other.

So, Brady believed in laws and rules—the following of them, the enforcing them. Believed in good. In doing the right thing. Always. Because of Jamison's example. Because of Grandma Pauline and the privilege he'd had to escape from the Sons and grow up in a real home, with real love.

But if he truly believed in Jamison's example, it couldn't be just about upholding the law. It had to be about keeping this innocent life out of the Sons. Which meant accepting that he'd bend some rules to do it.

"Gage. I've been keeping a secret," Brady announced.

Gage's eyebrows went up. "What kind?"

"The Sons kind," Brady said grimly.

CECILIA WAS BEING WATCHED. She could feel it, and see the signs of it. Still, she went about her workday. Answering calls. Patrolling the rez. She kept her body on alert, ready to fight off whatever was watching.

But she didn't stop doing what she loved to do. Being a tribal police officer was everything to Cecilia, and even being watched wouldn't stop her from handling her responsibilities.

She didn't remember her early years here with her mother. Vaguely, in a misty kind of way, she remembered her mother. Mostly, she thought, because Aunt Eva had made sure of it.

But Aunt Eva had moved Cecilia off the rez and onto the Knight ranch after Mom had died. Cecilia had been loved, she'd had sisters, and the kind of stability her mother had never been able to give her. Aunt Eva had died a few years later, and that had been hard, but she'd had Duke and her sisters.

Still, she'd missed this feeling of community and belonging, of having a tie to her history. Maybe she spent an awful lot of time seeing the bad parts of the rez as a police officer, but she'd needed to figure herself out as an adult there. Right there.

She liked to think she had figured herself out, but this situation with Layla and Mak was testing everything she'd learned since joining the tribal police seven years ago.

No doubt she was being watched because Elijah knew she'd taken Mak. Which meant there was no hope of sneaking off to Brady's tonight and visiting him.

She'd be able to call, though. Elijah wouldn't be able to intercept that. So, she'd call and make sure Mak was okay and it would have to be enough for now.

It didn't feel okay. She'd left that sweet little boy with a stranger, and no matter how she knew that stranger was one of the best men on earth, Mak didn't.

Cecilia walked down the road toward her house. She waved at her elderly neighbor who liked to tell her stories about her mother. Cecilia wasn't sure they were true, but she liked listening to them nonetheless.

But when she saw her front door open behind the screen door, Cecilia didn't have time for neighborly chats. She hurried inside through the screen door, heart pounding in panic, hand on the butt of her weapon.

But it was no intruder. Cecilia's hands fell to her sides. "Rach?"

Rachel was in the kitchen, puttering around with making tea. She flashed a smile. "Hi. You're home early."

"What are you doing here?" It wasn't unusual for her cousin to visit, or to spend nights with her. Rachel was a teacher on the rez, and she split her time between here and the Knight ranch so she could keep an eye on her father when she wasn't teaching.

Normally, Cecilia loved having Rachel underfoot. She liked having company in this house. She loved her cousin, who'd been like a sister growing up.

But Rachel had been visually impaired since she was a toddler. Normally Cecilia didn't even think of it. Rachel knew how to get around. She'd dealt with the impairment since she was a child, and now she was an adult who could take care of herself.

Today, with someone watching Cecilia's every step, the last thing she wanted was Rachel here. She'd be vulnerable to whatever Cecilia had gotten herself wrapped up in, and more so because she wouldn't necessarily see an attack coming.

"Rach. I..." Rachel was Aunt Eva and Uncle Duke's only biological daughter. In some ways, Rachel and Cecilia had a closer connection because of that biology—cousins. Not because they didn't think of Eva and Duke's foster daughters as their sisters, but because the foster girls had always felt a certain kind of jealousy toward the biological relations.

It had never impacted their friendship, their love for one another. Cecilia would lay down her life for any of them, just as she knew they'd do the same for her. The four other Knight girls were her *sisters*. Luckily adulthood had smoothed over a lot if not all of those old resentments, but it didn't erase the special bond she had with Rachel.

Rachel was like her baby sister. She wanted to protect her. "You shouldn't be here today."

"Why not?"

Cecilia couldn't tell Rachel, no matter how much she wanted to. She'd already involved Gage, Felicity and Brady. Adding more people would be dangerous. For them.

The Wyatts and Knights had been through enough danger in the past few months.

And every time a Knight goes to a Wyatt man for help—what happens?

She shook that thought away. Liza had asked for Jamison's help, yes, and they were getting married and raising Liza's half sister. But they'd been together as teenagers.

Which was the same as Cody and Nina, who'd already eloped and were living in Bonesteel with their daughter after a teenage romance that had been broken up by the Sons, then rekindled again.

As for Felicity and Gage, well, that was a bit of a shock, and an odd pairing, but they made each other happy.

It was a parade of coincidences that had nothing to do with Cecilia and Brady.

"Cee, what's going on?" Rachel asked.

Cecilia forced herself to smile. "It's been a rough day." Rachel was already here, so sending her away wouldn't do any good.

"And you were hoping to be alone?"

"Yes. No. It's fine." Rachel was here. Whoever was watching Cecilia had seen her be dropped off and come inside. Cecilia just had to figure out a way to mitigate the situation.

She wanted to go to her room and cry. Or better yet, go home to the Knight ranch and hide from all of this.

But she wasn't weak—couldn't be, for Layla as much as for herself. She hadn't become a police officer because it was easy. She didn't want to help people only when it was comfortable.

Still, this was the biggest challenge of her career, of her *life*. Which meant doubts and fears and wanting to cry was normal. She just couldn't give in to those things. And she couldn't let on to Rachel that she felt them.

"You going to cook me dinner?" Cecilia asked, trying to infuse some levity into her tone.

"That's my lot in life," Rachel returned. "Cooking for a passel of helpless Knights."

"Helpless seems harsh. And not a word Sarah would appreciate." Sarah was the only one of the Knight girls who'd taken an interest in ranching, keeping her at home full-time. She was everything a ranching woman should be—tough, hardworking, and hardheaded.

"But it fits when she refuses to even learn how to make spaghetti. I won't be around forever."

A blip of panic bloomed in Cecilia's chest, but she kept her tone light. "Going somewhere?"

Rachel shrugged restlessly. "You got off the ranch. You have a life."

"You do too. You're here every summer and—"

"And driven by my daddy. Or my sister, which is fine. The rez isn't for me like it is for you. But maybe the ranch isn't either. Felicity is getting married and having a baby and I... Well, I'm never going to meet anyone the way my life currently is."

"Just get yourself into a life-threatening situation like Felicity did. Brady will follow in Gage's footsteps of falling for the damsel in distress and *bang*."

Rachel wrinkled her nose. "Felicity was hardly a damsel. Besides, Brady is so...stuffy."

"He's not—" Cecilia clamped her mouth shut. Defending Brady's stuffiness was not what she needed to be doing right now. Luckily, a knock on the door made the subject easy to change. It was probably Mrs. Eldridge wanting to share another story. "Be right back," Cecilia said, heading for the front door.

She opened it, expecting her elderly neighbor's face and finding no one. She looked around. No kids giggling in the bushes playing ding-dong-ditch. Just…quiet.

She began to close the door before she noticed the small lump of fur on the porch. Cecilia stopped short as her stomach heaved.

There was an arrow sticking out of it, though the prairie dog clearly hadn't been killed by an arrow. Cecilia swallowed, forced herself to look, to pay attention.

Worse than the fact it was a tiny dead prairie dog, there was a note attached to the arrow with three simple words written on it in capital letters.

See you soon.

She stared at the scrawled words until her vision blurred. She was only shaken out of her frozen state by Rachel's voice.

"Who is it?" Rachel called.

"Just a prank," Cecilia replied, swallowing down the bile in her throat as her fingers closed over the butt of her holstered gun. "I'll be right back." She stepped outside, closing the door behind her. She scanned the area—houses, a quiet street, no one skulking around.

Anymore.

She let her hand fall off her weapon. She'd dispose of the dead animal, and then get Rachel the hell back to the Knight ranch.

Then she'd play Elijah's game, she decided grimly. It was the only way to keep him off Mak's trail.

Chapter Four

Brady was bleary-eyed the next day. Since Mak had slept so much before Felicity had left, he'd spent most of the night up and fussy. Brady and Gage had a list of instructions on baby care, but it had still taken three tries and watching a how-to video online to get the diaper on right. Making bottles and feeding them to the kid was pretty easy, and Mak was mostly a happy baby. Still, Brady was glad Gage was here with him. He wouldn't have survived the night without help—at least not with his sanity intact.

Brady had filled Gage in about Elijah…to an extent. There were things he hadn't told his brothers. The reasons he'd had for keeping Elijah a secret still existed, so keeping some parts of his story to himself made sense. Giving them the truth didn't mean giving them *all* the truths.

It bothered him that he hadn't heard from Cecilia. Not even a text. Shouldn't she want to check in on the baby? What was he supposed to do all day? Gage would go in to work, and Brady couldn't keep having visitors. If someone was watching or looking into him, the trail of people would be suspect.

Not as suspect as it might be at another time in his life. People had been traipsing in and out of his apartment to help out for too long now. Maybe it wouldn't send up any red flags, but there was no reason to chance it.

Gage had smuggled up a foldable, portable crib thing in his duffel bag. Mak was currently sleeping peacefully, and Brady knew he should try to catch a few hours too. Maybe even wake the baby up in an effort to keep him on a correct day/night schedule.

But he couldn't bring himself to wake up the boy when he looked so peaceful, and Brady's shoulder was currently throbbing too much to sleep through.

He went to the kitchen and made coffee, took some ibuprofen and the last of his antibiotics—praying they worked this time. He was tired of hospitals and doctors and being poked at and *hmm*ed over.

Gage came out of the spare bedroom dressed in his uniform. It was the last week he'd be putting that particular uniform on. He was transferring from Valiant County to Rapid City PD to be closer to Felicity's job at the National Park, and Brady still hadn't fully grasped the reality of not working with his twin brother anymore.

"I know you miss it," Gage said, either not understanding the pain Brady felt, or purposefully changing the topic to another painful one.

Brady gestured at his bum shoulder, tried to sound nonchalant. "Not much I can do with this."

"It's not permanent."

"No." It felt it, though. He was *supposed* to be back at work by now, not sidelined by an infection. He was *supposed* to go back to work knowing Gage would be there, but Gage only had three shifts left before his life changed.

He'd marry Felicity, have a kid, be a cop somewhere else.

If Brady looked too closely at all that, he might find the source of the low feelings he'd been having before he'd been shot.

So he decided not to look closely. "Coffee?"

"I'll just grab some at the station. I want to check on Felicity before my shift starts. She's feeling a little off in the mornings."

"It fits, you know, you two. I wouldn't have predicted it. But it works." Brady didn't know what possessed him to say it, but there it was.

Gage grinned. "Yeah, I know." His smile dimmed. "This Elijah…" Gage sighed. "What do I tell the others?"

Brady loved all of his brothers—would fight next to, protect and die for every single one of them. But he and Gage had escaped the Sons together, thanks to Jamison. They'd been together from the very beginning, and no matter how old they got, there was a deeper bond or connection between them. They were twins.

The fact Gage was willing to keep part of the story a secret from their brothers only made Brady feel guilty that there were still things Gage didn't know.

Brady didn't like to deal in guilt—he refused to wallow in it. If a man was guilty, he needed to change his actions to not feel guilty anymore. Maybe there'd been reasons to keep Elijah a secret, but the reasons had lost their weight.

"I think I should tell them. Everything. Together. I don't think Mak and I should stay here. I think we should hide. I just have to figure out how I can get him somewhere without being seen—and making sure Cecilia is okay."

"Heard from her?"

Brady shook his head.

"I don't like it. I know she can take care of herself, but I don't like it."

"Same, but I also know there's no getting through to that hardheaded woman." Brady didn't know why she had to be contrary for the sake of being contrary, but he knew she would be. No matter what he said.

"Let's set up a family dinner. Cecilia comes and you come. We find a way to hide Mak. If everyone descends on the ranch and there's no baby—it'll throw anyone off the sent."

"But how do we completely hide the presence of a six-month-old?"

Brady looked down at the baby in the portable crib. Mak was still fast asleep, little fist bunched and tucked under his chin, knees bent but spread wide-open. Felicity had brought some clothes so he was wearing dinosaur footie pajamas.

Though he didn't say anything, Brady could tell Gage was thinking about his future as a father.

"I hate to bring anyone else into it…"

Gage fixed him with a stern look. "I think you know everyone else would be more than happy to help keep that or any child out of the Sons' clutches."

Brady nodded. He knew it was true, but it was still against that moral compass he'd always listened to. Don't bring more people than necessary into Sons danger. Especially innocent ones.

"Gigi has that doll she carries around. She was even pushing it around in a stroller last time she was at the ranch." Brady shrugged away the guilt that was already poking at him. Gigi was four, and though she'd spent most of those four years in the Sons' camps before Liza and Jamison had saved her, she didn't deserve to be dragged back into it.

"Mak's a bit bigger than a doll, but it's not the worst plan," Gage said thoughtfully. "Especially if it's just between apartment door and truck. I bet Cody could find us a truck with tinted windows." Gage rubbed a hand over his jaw. "I'll make the arrangements."

"I can—"

"You got a baby to take care of. You take care of him. I'll take care of getting him to the ranch."

Brady looked at Mak's sleeping form. Completely and utterly defenseless. Brady might want to protect him all on his own, but this child deserved everyone he had in his arsenal.

"Let's do it as soon as possible."

THE NICE THING about Rachel staying with her was that Cecilia was so worried about Rachel, she didn't have much worry left for herself. She spent a sleepless night checking and rechecking the doors and windows in her house to make sure they were locked.

Bleary-eyed the next morning, she subsisted off coffee—which she normally didn't drink—and as much sugar as one human could possibly stand. She did a quick walk around the house looking for any more dead animals or threatening notes.

As she stepped back inside, Rachel was shuffling into the kitchen with a big, loud yawn. Rach had never been a morning person. Cecilia didn't know why she'd taken a teaching job that required her to do most of her work in the morning, but she could only assume Rachel loved it.

When Rachel stayed with her, she usually walked to and from the school with her probing cane. Cecilia would feel better if she had a support dog, but Rachel had lost hers last year to old age and hadn't had the heart to go through the process of trying to get a new one.

"I'm going to drive you in today."

Rachel frowned as she deftly poured herself some coffee. "Why would you do that?"

Cecilia had prepared for that question, and still she winced. She hated to lie to Rachel. So she didn't lie... exactly. "There's been some stuff going on. Pranks most likely, but the kind that can escalate if given the opportunity."

Rachel's frown deepened. "That's vague."

"It's a vague kind of thing. You'd probably be fine walking, but it'd make me feel better if I drove you."

Rachel sighed a little, and Cecilia half expected her to press the matter.

"It's too early to argue," she said around another yawn. "But I'm walking back after my classes are done."

Cecilia tried not to snap that it wasn't an option. Compromise was the best bet when talking to a stubborn Knight woman—she should know. "Can you walk with someone? Maybe one of your older students?"

"If you really think it's necessary."

"I do."

Rachel shrugged and sipped her coffee. "I'll be ready in about twenty."

While she waited, Cecilia rechecked the house to make sure it was all locked up. She called in on her radio to start her shift, and drove Rachel to the school.

The morning was warm but with a hint of a chill. Fall was starting its slow unfurling, usually Cecilia's favorite time of year.

It wouldn't be this year with Layla in the hospital and trying to keep Mak from Elijah and the state.

Cecilia pulled to a stop in front of the school, tried to bite her tongue and failed. "Don't forget to have someone walk with you back to the house. Someone you trust," she said as Rachel got out of the car.

Rachel paused. "You're going to have to tell me what this is all about."

"When I've got more information, I will," Cecilia lied.

Rachel made a disbelieving sound, then closed the car door and walked toward the school. Cecilia watched until she disappeared inside.

Once she was sure Rachel was inside, she did her normal rounds. It didn't appear she was being followed today, which was only a minor relief. Someone could start at any moment.

After her first call of the day, a minor vandalism situation that had been solved by involving the mother of the teenage perpetrator, she almost felt relaxed.

Of course, that was when she noticed her tail. She tried to act nonchalant, to keep doing her job, but every hour it was harder to pretend to be unaffected. If they were watching her, was Rachel safe? If they were following *her*, would Rachel be left alone?

If they were following her in particular, what would they do if they found her isolated and alone?

Nothing, because you're a trained police officer carrying many weapons with which to defend yourself.

She wanted to believe that voice in her head, to feel

sure of it, but she also knew she was *one* police officer. She didn't know how many people were following her.

She got another call, this time a disturbance, and had to put her stalkers out of her mind while she tried to make peace between two neighbors fighting about property lines. It was an annoying, pointless screaming match—but it was her job to smooth it over.

It took a full hour, and her head pounded by the time she was walking back to her patrol car. People who couldn't—wouldn't—compromise always gave her a headache.

She glanced at her watch. Rachel would have walked to the house by now. Maybe Cecilia could drive by the house, just check in on her. Pretend like she'd forgotten her lunch and was grabbing a sandwich so Rachel didn't get unduly worried.

The pounding in her head stopped, as did her breath and perhaps even her heart when she saw a piece of paper tucked under her windshield wiper. It fluttered in the breeze.

It could be anything, but Cecilia knew what it would be. Another note—sans dead animal this time.

Or so she thought, until she stepped closer to her patrol car. Under the wheel was a dead raccoon. As if she'd run it over.

But she hadn't.

No, it was another sign. Another warning.

Steeling herself for another threatening note, Cecilia pulled a rubber glove out of the glove pouch on her gun belt. She picked up the note and read it.

She's pretty.

Cecilia didn't let herself react outwardly. Inside she was ice, her heart a shivering mass of fear and panic. But outside, her hands were steady and her gaze was cool. She slid into the patrol car and set the note carefully on the passenger seat, pulling off the glove as she did so.

She turned the ignition, calmly eased on the gas. Keeping her attention evenly split between phone and road, she clicked Rachel's name on her phone screen and called.

The phone rang. And rang.

"Pick up," Cecilia muttered, swearing when it went to voice mail.

She was tempted to increase her speed, fly through the rez to her house on the eastern edge.

The only *she* the note could refer to was Rachel. It was a threat against Rachel, and Rachel was alone. Cecilia should have predicted this. Should have insisted Rachel…

What? Not teach her class? Hide away? It wouldn't have been a fair demand, but Cecilia still knew she should have done *something*.

Cecilia drove within the speed limit, watching her surroundings in case it was a trap. An ambush. Because threatening Rachel was only about getting to her. Rachel didn't know anything.

Or would Elijah think she did?

Cecilia swore again, increasing her speed, though not enough to draw attention. She came to a screeching halt in front of her house. If anyone was watching or following, she'd broken her calm facade.

Since she already had, she raced inside, hand on the butt of her weapon. But Rachel was safe as could be, curled up on the couch, earbuds in.

She pulled one out and looked at Cecilia's form with raised eyebrows. "Everything okay?"

Cecilia let out a ragged breath. This couldn't go on. She knew Elijah was purposefully trying to scare her, and giving in to threats and scare tactics would give him what he wanted, but...

She couldn't risk Rachel.

"I have to take you back to the ranch."

"Cee, you're being super weird this week." Rachel's expression wasn't confused so much as concerned. "You're going to have to tell me what's going on."

"I know. I know. Look... I'll explain everything when we're home. With everyone." She had to fill everyone in on what was happening. It was the only way to keep Rachel and Mak safe. To make sure none of them were brought unwittingly into this.

Because Elijah was clearly ready and willing to threaten everything she loved. She didn't have to live with threats. She should act.

"Let's get to the ranch," Cecilia said. "I just have to call someone to take the last two hours of my shift."

"I can have Dad—"

"No. No, I'm taking you."

"This is really bad, isn't it?" Rachel asked, twisting her fingers together.

Cecilia didn't mind lying to the people she loved if it saved them from worry, but she wasn't sure she had that luxury anymore. "It could be, if I'm not very careful."

Rachel slid off the couch, crossed the room and took Cecilia's hands in hers and gave them a squeeze. "Then let's be very, very careful."

Chapter Five

Brady had faced unhinged people with guns, big men so high on drugs nothing short of severe use of force would subdue them, and a slew of other scary, life-threatening situations in his tenure as a police officer and EMT.

He had been shot trying to save Felicity from her father, had hiked the Badlands trying to find his brother before Ace killed him. At eleven, he and Gage had almost been caught escaping the Sons.

Yet none of those instances had ever made him as bone-deep *afraid* as the one he found himself in right now. Even in the moment he and Gage had been found by a member of the Sons. Brady had been sure they'd be dead, but instead the man had let them go.

He'd been murdered days later.

Why this was more terrifying, Brady had no idea. Liza was buckling Mak into the doll stroller Gigi had happily pushed into his apartment. Gigi was now holding the doll, making funny faces at Mak in an effort to make him laugh.

Brady couldn't say he'd been particularly welcoming when Liza had shown back up in their lives a few months ago. As the oldest brother, Jamison had gotten all of them out of the Sons before he'd saved himself.

When he'd saved himself, he'd brought Liza with him. The Knights had taken her in and Brady had always assumed Jamison and Liza would live happily-ever-after.

He'd had to believe it was possible. Then Liza had left, gone back to the Sons, breaking Jamison's heart. Brady had never let on how much that had affected him. He secretly wondered if they weren't a little cursed by the Wyatt name.

It hadn't helped when Cody's girlfriend Nina, another Knight foster, had also taken off. Not to the Sons but to no one knew where.

A few months ago, Liza had reappeared, needing Jamison's help to save Gigi, her half sister, from the Sons. A while after that, Nina had shown up, gunshot wound and all, needing Cody's help to keep their daughter safe.

And somehow, they were all back together and happy with it. Like the time in between didn't matter.

As an adult, Brady didn't know what to make of it. How to reconcile the things he'd begun to think were impossible, with what was in front of him. Possible and growing.

"It'll be fine," Liza reassured him, likely misreading the course of his thoughts. "Gigi will be gentle."

Brady had no doubt Gigi would handle this with the utmost care. Even at four, she'd dealt with more than most kids should ever handle. "He could make a noise."

"He could," Liza agreed, crouching to give Mak's belly a tickle. The baby gurgled appreciatively. "But Gigi and I will be chatting loud enough to cover any baby sounds."

Brady looked dubiously at Mak. He'd heard the boy scream pretty effectively for all manner of reasons, but he was freshly fed, changed, napped and seemed happy enough.

"I didn't want to drag you and Gigi into this."

Liza stood slowly, and she fixed Brady with a look. "I don't know why it's so hard for you hardheaded Wyatts to realize we were there too. Even Gigi knows what it's like in there. We'd always be part of helping someone stay far away from the Sons. No matter the risk. Because it's always worth the risk to get out."

Brady looked down at Gigi, who looked up at him solemnly. She was wearing a pink T-shirt that said *Girl Power* in sequins.

She knew too much for a girl of almost five. Brady knew, from his own experience, that escaping at eleven had given him a determination to *help*. And even as young as Gigi was, he saw that in her expression.

"All right. Let's go."

GIGI WAS GIVEN the stroller. Liza pulled the hood down so that it obscured all but Mak's feet.

Gigi took her job as pusher very seriously, slowly and carefully pushing it forward. Mak babbled in baby talk, but Liza started talking over it. She asked Gigi about some TV show Gigi liked and Gigi began a monologue on the merits of each character.

God bless her.

He and Liza worked to carry the stroller down the stairs, Gigi admonishing them to be careful with her baby.

They reached the tinted truck they'd borrowed for the occasion. Brady tried to search the perimeter without giving away that's what he was doing. He didn't spot anyone, but that didn't mean they weren't being watched.

"Now, you go on and get in your car seat," Liza said to Gigi, helping her into the back seat.

"Make sure you buckle my baby in," Gigi ordered sternly. She was an excellent actress, though she did give Brady a little wink as she scrambled across the back seat.

Liza sighed as if it were a silly request. "Dolls can't get hurt, sissy. It's a little silly to—"

"You *have* to buckle her in. Just like me," Gigi insisted.

Liza rolled her eyes and nodded and bent down to pick up Mak. He made a little squealing sound, but Liza had angled her body so that it would be almost impossible for any watcher to see what was supposed to be a doll actually wiggle.

Gigi started singing the ABCs at full volume, clearly obscuring Mak's noises.

Brady could only watch in awe as these two people managed to enact his plan even better than he'd imagined, and without a hitch.

"Hop in the passenger seat, cowboy," Liza said as she closed the back door.

"I can drive."

"No, you can't."

Brady scowled at Liza. "I've been cleared to drive." His shoulder was feeling moderately better. He hadn't even wanted to cut it off when he woke up this morning. It was possible the last round of antibiotics had worked.

Liza snorted. "My truck. I drive. Those are the rules, bud. Now, you can stay here, or you can come out to the ranch for some of Grandma Pauline's potato casserole."

She was still playacting, and continuing the argument would make it seem more important than it was.

So he had to suck up his control issues and go to the passenger side.

If he grumbled to himself a little bit while he did it, no one had to know. He slid into the seat and closed the door and then let out a long breath. They'd gotten through one hard part successfully, he thought. Mostly because of the precocious little girl in the back seat.

Brady twisted in his seat, though it hurt his shoulder, and gave Gigi a big grin. "Gigi, you're a star."

She beamed at him. "I like pretending. And I like Mak. We're going to keep him away from the bad men."

"Yes, we are." He turned back to face forward. From inside the truck he could do a better scan. Still no one. He blew out a breath, warning himself not to relax. There was a lot that could go wrong yet.

But one hurdle had been jumped.

Gigi entertained Mak in the back seat by talking and making faces. Mak happily gurgled and drooled back. Brady let himself watch that, reminding himself that he wasn't so much bringing Liza and Gigi into danger as letting them help an innocent child escape it.

They'd both crossed Ace, in a way, and so they were already living under that specter—no matter how many high-security prisons the man was put in.

Brady scanned the highway in front of them, then glanced in the rearview mirror. There was a lone Chevy truck. Something about it didn't sit right with Brady.

"Speed up," he ordered.

Liza raised an eyebrow, not taking her eyes off the road. "Tone, Brady."

Brady didn't have the patience to sweet-talk Liza. "Not crazy speed. Just enough so I can tell if this Chevy is pacing us."

This time she didn't make a snarky comment, she did as he asked. When the Chevy kept pace, Brady inwardly swore. He kept that emotion out of his voice when he spoke. "We have a tail."

"That doesn't mean he knows we have Mak," Liza said calmly, reaching across the console and resting her hand on his arm. "In fact, if we can convince him we *don't*, all the better."

Brady flicked a glance at Mak in the car seat. Gigi had reached across the space between their car seats and was holding his squirming baby hand in hers.

"Then I guess that's what we have to do."

CECILIA DROVE OFF the reservation, watching her rear-view mirror. She hadn't spotted a tail yet, but that didn't mean there wouldn't be one. Surely Elijah or his "buddies" hadn't simply stopped following her because she'd left the rez.

But she made it miles and miles down the mostly empty highway. If she saw a car, it usually passed her or was headed in the opposite direction. Cecilia knew she should relax as mile by mile they continued without being followed.

But she couldn't seem to let her guard down. Elijah wouldn't give up that easily, which meant he had something else up his sleeve.

If they made it home, she'd have help. Support. She didn't want to bring her family into this, but her family was already in danger. She might have felt guilty for getting involved in the first place, but all she could think of was Layla lost in the dark cloud that had become her life.

She'd begged for help. Begged for a chance to be a mother to her child.

There was no way Cecilia could have turned away from that, even to protect her family. And she knew, because of how her family was made up, because of what they'd been through, there was no way her family would have wanted her to turn away from Layla.

They'd *want* to be part of the fight too. So many of them had been impacted by the Sons. The Knights were not the kind to turn away from the dangerous just to save their own skin. The Wyatts even less so.

Thinking of it made Cecilia feel a little teary, so she focused on the road. On getting home.

When they weren't too far away from the turn off the highway to head toward home, both her and Rachel's phones chimed in unison.

Rachel sighed as she dug her phone out of her purse. "I really hate simultaneous texts. They're never good." She hit the button for her phone to read her text to her.

From: Gage Wyatt
Knight-Wyatt dinner at Grandma Pauline's. Everyone mandatory.

"Do they have to be so bossy?" Cecilia muttered. Then she frowned. "Brady can't go." How was he going to get out of "everyone mandatory"? Or would he try to bring Mak to the ranch? Surely not.

"Why can't Brady go and why do you know that?"

Cecilia didn't want to explain the whole thing yet. She only wanted to go through it once, hear all the disapproval once. And there was going to be some *serious* disapproval. "We'll get to that. Just text him that we're already on our way."

Rachel used her voice-to-text to send the reply.

Cecilia signaled the turn onto the gravel road that would lead them to the Reaves Ranch, Grandma Pauline's spread.

Instead of making an easy turn, Cecilia heard a faint pop, then the car rumbled and the steering wheel jerked. Cecilia almost lost her grip, but managed to tighten her hold at the last second. She braked a little too hard, fishtailing and tipping precariously into the gravel.

She managed to wrestle the truck to a stop, and quickly braked. She wasn't sure what had happened, but that pop she'd heard had sounded like a gunshot to her.

"Stay put," Cecilia ordered, heart hammering in her chest. Still, her voice was calm and authoritative.

She slid out of the driver's side, pulling the gun out of its holster but holding it behind her as she eyed the area. A big truck slowed to a stop on the highway a few yards away from where she stood.

She kept the gun out of sight as the driver leaned out of the window. "Need some help?" The man offered a pleasant enough smile. Cecilia was also certain she'd seen this same exact man come out of Layla's house with Elijah. It had been a long time ago, probably a year or two, but Cecilia rarely forgot a face. Especially one that ugly.

She fixed a grateful smile on her lips. "Oh, wow. That would be so great! I've got a spare in the back, but changing a tire can be such a pain."

The man smirked and shoved his truck into Park. It looked like there was potentially another passenger in the vehicle, but hiding. Cecilia pretended like she didn't notice. He slid out of the truck and there was a gun in his hand as a sleazy grin spread across his face.

Cecilia didn't pause, didn't hesitate. She kicked

straight out, landing the blow on the gun itself and knocking it out of the man's hands. She pivoted quickly, landing an elbow against his jaw. A nasty cracking sound whipped through the air and blood spattered.

Cecilia didn't have time to wince, she had to duck the returning blow. She didn't duck low enough and it clipped her head. Which probably hurt his hand more than her skull, all in all. But the satisfaction of missing most of that blow knocked her off-balance for the next, which hit her right in the cheekbone.

Pain flashed behind her eyes, but she could hear someone approaching. She didn't have time to even suck in a breath. She landed a knee to the man's groin and he let out a wheezing breath as he fumbled. She whirled to face the man, gun at the ready.

He had his own, so she shot, aiming for the arm so he'd drop the gun, ideally before getting off his own shot. She wanted both of them alive. They might have useful information after all, but if either of them went for Rachel, she'd shoot to kill.

The man howled and dropped his gun as the bullet hit him in the forearm. Blood gushed and he grabbed his arm and screamed.

The other man was crawling toward the dropped gun, still wheezing, but Cecilia quickly scooped it up off the ground. She held one gun on each man and eyed them with disgust.

"Elijah sent you."

"He'll keep sending more," the man she'd cracked in the jaw replied with a bloody smile.

"And I'll keep kicking their asses," Cecilia replied with a shrug. "Rach?"

"I already called Gage," Rachel said. Apparently she'd

gotten out of the truck during the fight, but Cecilia had been concentrating too hard on the men to notice. "He's not on duty, but he called dispatch for us."

The faint sound of sirens wailed in the distance, a sign that help was on its way. "Guess you boys are headed to jail," Cecilia said with a smile. "Anything you want to tell me about your buddy?"

The one she'd shot had stopped screaming, but he looked at her with cold eyes as he gripped his bleeding arm. "He's going to get you. He's going to make you pay. He'll only kill you if you're lucky."

A cold shiver went through Cecilia, but she didn't let it show outwardly. "He's going to try all those things, and he's going to fail. Just like you."

She tried to believe her own words, but the cold chill remained as she waited for backup.

Chapter Six

Brady paced the living room at Grandma Pauline's, Mak snuggled into his good arm. The boy cried if he tried to put him anywhere else or give him to anyone else. As it was, he wasn't sleeping. He was simply looking up at Brady with big brown eyes, a serious expression on his little face.

Brady didn't know what to do with *that*, or Gage currently coordinating officers to arrest the men who'd attacked Cecilia.

Brady didn't know if it was the same men who'd tailed him and Liza yet, but his tail hadn't approached them. They'd kept driving when Liza had turned off onto the gravel road to Grandma Pauline's.

Gage strode into the room, and Brady didn't even let him speak before he was peppering him with questions.

"Make and model?"

Gage's expression was grave. "Same as yours. They must have backtracked and waited for Cecilia and Rach."

Brady swore.

"It might not be such a bad thing."

At Brady's glare, Gage held up his hands. "You—the guy with the baby they're looking for—were deemed not as important. That means they don't know where Mak is."

"I don't think Cecilia and Rach being a target is a *good* thing."

"I didn't say that. I said it's not such a *bad thing*, because it means they don't know where the baby is. Based on the condition of the two men that tried to ambush Cecilia, I don't think we need to worry too much about her safety."

Brady grunted. He knew Cecilia could take care of herself. She was a fine cop, even if he didn't always agree with her methods. But it only took one second to be taken down. Since he was currently the one with a gunshot wound that wouldn't heal, he thought he had some perspective on the matter.

But it wouldn't do to argue with Gage over it.

"You want me to take him for a bit?"

Brady gave a shrug. "Seems to be happy here. Where are Cecilia and Rachel?"

"Should be any minute. Just finishing up giving their statements." As if on cue, they heard a commotion in the kitchen. Both men moved toward it.

Mak began to squirm in Brady's arms as he registered Cecilia's voice. Still, Brady stopped cold when he saw her.

Grandma Pauline was bustling around her while Duke Knight demanded to know what was going on. Sarah and Liza helped Grandma gather ice and towels, Tuck led Rachel to the table where Dev was already sitting with Felicity. Wyatt boys and Knight girls—men and women now—always working together to help each other.

"Well. Have that seat, right there." Grandma Pauline motioned to Cecilia, pulling an empty chair out from the table.

"I'm fine," Cecilia said, but she was already moving for the chair because God knew you didn't argue with Grandma Pauline.

Her eye was swollen. Blood was spattered across her shirt, but it didn't look like it was hers. When Gage had told him there'd been an incident, but Cecilia had taken care of it, Brady didn't realize "incident" meant fight and "taken care of it" meant gotten hurt in the process.

Something dark and vicious twisted inside of him. Brady couldn't say he fully understood it. He'd felt similar when seeing what his father or the Sons had done to his brothers—but this had a sharper edge to it. Not just anger. Not just revenge. Something closer to vengeance than he'd ever felt.

"You hand that baby over now," Grandma Pauline ordered Brady, already settling a bag of frozen peas over Cecilia's eye. "Nothing better for a few bumps and bruises than holding a sweet little boy."

It took everyone in the kitchen turning to stare at him to be able to move, to relax some of the fury on his face. To just…breathe. He met Cecilia's confused gaze past the bag of peas Grandma Pauline held under her one eye.

He had a flash of that ill-fated New Year's Eve kiss. Where she'd been laughing at him, poking at him. She'd kissed him out of some kind of…dare inside of herself, he'd always been sure.

But something had changed when she'd pressed her lips to his. A seismic shift inside him. An opening up of something he'd wanted closed. Maybe *that* was the moment everything had started to unravel for him.

It was all her fault, he was sure of that. If only he

could be sure of what was winding through him, tying him into knots.

Mak squirmed, started babbling somewhat intensely, breaking Brady from the moment. He looked down at the baby, then remembered what Grandma Pauline had told him to do. He moved to Cecilia's chair and had to kneel down so he could shift Mak into Cecilia's waiting arms. It required getting close, smelling her shampoo, brushing her arm.

Cecilia still looked at him, as if she could see into his thoughts. As if it shook her as deeply as it shook him.

He stepped away, shoved his hands into his pockets. He was losing it. Hallucinating due to lack of sleep. That was all.

That was *all*.

"I guess some of you need an introduction," Cecilia said softly, looking down at Mak. She took a deep breath, gazing down at him. "I had wanted to wait for..."

The door open and Jamison walked in with Cody and Nina and their daughter, Brianna.

"...the Bonesteel contingent," Cecilia finished.

If Brady wasn't totally mistaken, she seemed a little deflated everyone had shown up so quickly. But there was no more putting it off.

"You explain your end, then I'll explain mine," Brady said. Maybe it came out more like an order, but he wasn't feeling particularly genial or accommodating at the moment.

"Yours?" Cecilia asked, just enough acid in her tone to get his back up.

Brady'd kept one secret from his family, from Gage in particular, in his entire life. And it was this. Everything culminating with Cecilia needing his help.

Would he have ever told if she hadn't? If her problem hadn't connected to Elijah through this innocent child?

Would-haves didn't matter, because this—what was in front of him—was all he had. "Yes, my thing. My connection to Elijah, and why I think we need to disappear."

THE ENTIRE KITCHEN seemed to go supersonic. A cacophony of noises and arguments on top of arguments. Cecilia winced against the noise, then against the pain in her cheek.

Cecilia wouldn't admit it out loud, but a few of the jerk's blows had landed and left her feeling sore and achy. At least she'd taken the two guys out all on her own.

She had to admit, Grandma Pauline was close to being right. Mak in her arms didn't take away the pain, but it certainly shifted the pain to something bearable under a curtain of calm.

Mak was safe. No matter what happened today, no matter what would happen after today, Mak was safe. Maybe she should have brought him to both families in the first place, but she wouldn't beat herself up for what could have been.

He was here now, a large group of people ready and willing to fight for him.

Tucker had said, from his standpoint as detective, he thought the men she'd beaten up had followed Brady and Liza first. They'd given up on them and switched their gears for Cecilia and Rachel.

Which meant they didn't know Mak had been in the car with Brady the whole time.

She couldn't relax completely of course. Elijah would keep coming for her, and she was *here* now, which meant he or his men would be soon enough. But Cody had all sorts of security on the Reaves Ranch.

This was the safest place.

And Brady wanted to disappear? No way.

A piercing whistle stopped the competing voices. Grandma Pauline scowled at all of them. "Now. How are we ever going to know what to be mad about if we don't let them explain themselves? Boy—"

"Cecilia needs to go first," Brady said.

Usually it amused Cecilia that Grandma Pauline still called any of the Wyatt brothers *boys*, when they hadn't been that for a very long time. Even more amused that they answered to it without complaint.

But Cecilia couldn't find the means to be amused right now. Mak was in her lap, happily squirming and talking to her in his own language. His dark eyes were wide, trusting.

And she knew without a shadow of a doubt she'd have to leave him again.

But first she had to explain Mak and her dilemma to all the Wyatts and all the Knights. *Then* she'd have to figure out how to disappear...and lead Elijah away.

Which was going to be quite the challenge with *all* these voices in her ears.

"Let's start with the simple question," Grandma Pauline said. "Who's the boy?"

Cecilia explained who Mak was, and how she'd taken him to Brady because she thought he'd be protected there. "He was protected too. Elijah knows I took him, but he hasn't figured out where. So, that's our priority. Keep Mak a secret."

"We're all here. How much of a secret could it be?" Brady demanded.

There was a dark, edgy look in his demeanor that was so…not Brady. Brady was the even-keeled one who never lost his temper. When Dev or Cody raged, when Jamison got too high-handed, when Gage didn't take things seriously enough and Tucker was too quiet, there was always Brady ready and willing to bring the disparate parts together to create a unit. There wasn't a dark side to Brady.

She'd never thought.

But this was…uncomfortable. Like realizing you hadn't known someone at all. He was fierce, angry, and just barely tethering his temper…all completely visible in his expression and his demeanor. It was like he'd become someone else altogether.

"I needed to let everyone in on what's going on so Rachel isn't caught in the crosshairs—"

Rachel made a noise as if to interrupt, but Cecilia kept right on talking, not giving her a chance to object. "There was a vague threat at the rez. She wasn't safe there, and no matter who drove her here or picked her up, they were going to get a target too. Elijah knows I took Mak, and he might not know where, but everyone I care about is going to be suspect. So everyone needs to know what's going on, but I need to go back to the rez and my job. If Elijah wants to follow me there, he can go right ahead."

"No," Brady said, as if he had *any* say in the matter.

"I think I'll make my own dec—"

"No," Brady repeated.

Cecilia couldn't physically react what with holding a baby and Grandma Pauline holding the bag of frozen peas to her face. So, she could only do her best to come off as dismissive and haughty.

"And you have some big, bad reason for telling *me* no as if you have any right?"

Still, none of that darkness clicked off. There was no calm, blank demeanor like she expected. Brady Wyatt was visibly, unrelentingly *angry*.

Cecilia found that amazing fact undercut her own anger at his high-handedness. Had she ever seen Brady react to anything with this edgy fury? What was causing it? Why did it make her heart flutter?

"Elijah Jones is a sociopath," Brady ground out. "And a murderer, though I've never been able to prove it. He's Ace's protégé in every way, and he's spent the past eight years screwing with me, in particular, because I had the misfortune of being the first Wyatt to arrest him. My first arrest."

"You know this Elijah," Jamison said, his voice deceptively calm. Cecilia didn't believe that calm for one second. "A Sons member, who idolizes our father, targeted you. And this is the first we're hearing about it? Some eight years later?"

Brady was quiet for a long while, some of his normal stoicism clicking into place as he stood there. But his hand was still clenched in a fist at his side. "I think he would have settled for any Wyatt," Brady said after a while, purposefully ignoring Jamison's question. "I got lucky."

"How?" Jamison demanded.

"Pranks, mostly. Threats, sometimes. Nothing concrete and nothing dangerous. It was just like being taunted. It's why I didn't tell you. It was nothing. Just annoying."

"Why?" Tucker asked quietly. "What's the motivation? Ace is in jail. There's no need to win his favor by screwing with one of his sons."

No matter who asked the question, Cecilia couldn't seem to tear her gaze away from Brady.

"I couldn't say. If I understood it, I would have already dealt with it, or told you all about it," Brady said. With every word he was locking down those pieces of his usual calm. The fire in his eyes banked, the tension in his arms released. He was still intense, but the anger had disappeared. Or he'd hidden it.

"He hasn't visited Ace," Jamison said. "If he's some kind of protégé there hasn't been a connection since Ace has been in jail."

Cecilia sighed. "He's not looking to *be* Ace. He's looking to *replace* Ace. He wants to lead the Sons." She let her finger trace Mak's cheek. "If he's targeting a Wyatt, it's not for Ace so much as Wyatts are the Sons' enemy. You guys are the biggest threat to the Sons right now. You took down Ace and Tony. They've been scrambling."

"Eight years," Jamison said gravely. "That hasn't been true for the eight years he's been harassing Brady."

"True. Maybe there's something more to it. I can't speak to that. I didn't know he'd been harassing Brady either. What I do know is that Elijah wants to take over the Sons. It's why he started recruiting on the rez. The more people he enlists, the more power he has in the group itself."

"Why didn't he start his own?" Dev demanded.

"Why start your own when you can take over one of the biggest, most dangerous gangs in the country? I'm not saying it's always been his plan. I'm just saying things changed when Ace was arrested. Elijah's been different the past few months—around the rez, with Mak's mom. He's already got his own little group. It's not enough for him. He wants the Sons." Cecilia looked down at Mak in her arms. He'd started to doze there, immune to the tension around him. "But first, he'll want *his* son."

Which was why she had to leave. Any security could be breached if there was a constant, determined effort to get through. If Cecilia stayed, Elijah would only work on it until he breached it—which wouldn't just put Mak in danger, but Grandma Pauline, her sons, the Knights and any of the little ones.

Cecilia couldn't stick around. And she couldn't let anyone know she was getting out and leading Elijah away. They wouldn't let her.

But the sooner she disappeared, the better off everyone would be.

So, she let the Wyatts and the Knights argue it out, and she kept her gaze and her attention on Mak in her arms. If it was going to be the last time she saw him, held him, she was going to soak it all up.

"So, it's settled then," Jamison said, always the de facto leader. "Everyone stays put until we have a better read on what Elijah Jones is planning, or even better, until we can find a reason to arrest him."

Cecilia tore her gaze from Mak and found Brady's. The anger was back, but he didn't argue with Jamison. He just stared right back at her as if he knew what she was planning.

But he couldn't, and even if he did, he wouldn't stop her.

No one would.

Chapter Seven

"She's going to bolt." Brady found himself pacing. He'd already not felt like himself for months now, but these past few days had taken away all his usual coping mechanisms. All the filters and layers he put over his true feelings so he wasn't…

Well, his father.

This morning was worse. Everyone seemed content to just hang around Grandma Pauline's, pay extra attention to Cody's security measures, and wait.

They couldn't just *wait*. Cecilia would do something stupid. She was too rash. Too…her. She was going to try to lead Elijah away and Brady seemed to be the only one who realized it.

"Cecilia knows better," Tucker insisted, shoveling eggs into his mouth. He was sitting at Grandma Pauline's kitchen table dressed for his work as a detective. Slacks and a button-up shirt. Though he didn't live at the ranch, he would be staying close just like everyone else while they tried to protect Mak from Elijah.

"She most certainly does not," Brady returned. "Are you even listening to yourself?"

"She's a cop."

"She's a…" Brady didn't say "loose cannon" out loud

because it sounded like a bad line from some '80s action movie, but she was.

She always had been.

"I think you're underestimating her," Tucker said, with just enough condescension Brady ground his teeth together.

Still, he bit back the words he wanted to say. Because *no, you are* was childish, even if it was true.

If no one would listen to him, he'd have to take matters into his own hands. He gave half a thought to trying to lure Elijah away himself, but Brady didn't think Elijah would go for it. Cecilia had been the one to take Mak. Cecilia would be his target. Elijah was too smart to think Brady was doing anything except setting a trap.

Which meant Brady had to get Cecilia and Mak away from here—without Elijah being any the wiser.

"How's the shoulder?" Tuck asked around another mouthful of eggs.

"Fine," Brady replied without thinking about it. He gave it a little shrug. He had to admit, it hadn't been paining him as much lately. Maybe the third round of antibiotics had actually done what they were supposed to.

"When's your next doctor's appointment?"

Brady gave Tucker a puzzled frown over his sudden interest in doctor appointments. "Next week."

Tuck nodded. "Then I'd make sure you don't miss it," Tucker said blandly, moving away from the table. He took his plate to the sink and rinsed it, and left the kitchen without another word.

Brady frowned after him. It had been a subtle *don't go anywhere.* As if by being subtle, Brady wouldn't read the subtext and be irritated his younger brother was trying to tell him what to do.

Grandma Pauline breezed in, a basket of eggs hooked to one arm. She gave Brady a critical look. "You're not so peaked looking."

High praise, Brady figured. "I'm doing better."

"Good," she said firmly. "Now, when are you going?"

"Going?"

"Don't think I can't see through you, boy. And that hardheaded woman. You've both got it in your head to hightail it out of here. Neither of you can let the other do it alone. So. When do you sneak out?"

"I…" He could lie to his grandmother. He'd done it before. It just so rarely worked, and she seemed approving. "I was just going to stop her when she did, then convince her the three of us should—"

"No, you'll leave the boy here," Grandma interrupted matter-of-factly.

"But—"

"The safest place for that boy is here, especially if both you and Cecilia take off. Just like when we had Brianna while Cody and Nina were off."

"Only because they got ambushed on their way back from the jail, Grandma. They wouldn't have left Brianna by choice." When Ace had sent men to threaten Nina and Brianna, Nina had come to Cody for help. They'd been separated from their daughter and trying to survive Ace's men, but not because they'd chosen to be.

"They would have left her with me, and would still, if it was the best way to keep her safe," Grandma returned, as if that was just fact, not her opinion. "And Brianna was older. She could hide and be quiet. This little one can't do that. And you can't move fast enough carrying formula and diapers and a crib. Not if you're going to catch her."

"Catch her?"

Grandma Pauline rolled her eyes. "You don't think that girl is already making plans? She's not going to wait to skulk away under the dark of night. She would have done that last night, if so. My guess is she's going to come up with an excuse to run to town, make sure no one goes with her, and hightail it from there."

Brady stared dumbfounded for a moment, because of course that was exactly what Cecilia was going to do. He'd expected more subterfuge, but she hardly needed it when she was an adult woman who would need to do some things without supervision.

"Packed you a bag."

Brady blinked at his grandmother. "Why didn't you kick up a fuss last night? Tell them that their plan was wrong?"

"What's the point in arguing with all you fools? You're going to do whatever you want anyway. You take that truck Liza borrowed. Bag is packed with supplies. Don't you let that girl out of your sight. You can each take care of yourself, there ain't no doubt about that. But this is dangerous, which means you need to take care of each other. And trust us to take care of the little one."

It was hardly the first time in his life his grandmother had helped him, or seen through him or the rest of them. It was hardly the first time she'd known exactly what to say, and when to say it. He'd been blessed to have her for these twenty years he'd been free of the Sons.

Brady pressed a kiss to his grandmother's cheek. "I know you don't like to hear it, but we would have been lost without you. Lost. Separate. Maybe like him."

Grandma only grunted and shooed him away. "Not

one of you has got it in you to be like him, not truly. Be better off if you believe that. Now go."

TIMING WAS EVERYTHING when a person was planning their unapproved escape.

Okay, escape was maybe an exaggeration. Cecilia wasn't being held *prisoner*. She was just trying to avoid her family's arguments.

So, that morning, Cecilia waited until Duke and Sarah were out with the cattle. Cody, Nina and Brianna had stayed at the Knight ranch last night to put up some extra security measures, but Nina and Brianna had gone over to the Wyatts' this morning so Gigi and Brianna could have their homeschool lessons. Cody was currently installing something on the entrance gate. All Cecilia had to do was wait to hear Rachel turn on the water to the shower, and she could slip out.

They'd decided it safest if Mak stayed at the Wyatt ranch, since they already had a crib and a few baby supplies that Brady had brought in with his backpack. There wasn't anything at the Knights', so it would have required bringing baby things in and out—which could have been detected by anyone who might be watching.

Cecilia could have spent the night at the Wyatts', but she'd decided to say her goodbyes last night. That way she could get a handle on her emotions for today. Today required strength of spirit, not doubts born of the selfish need to be with Mak.

A quick note, a careful route across the property to the back exit—avoiding the pastures Duke and Sarah were in today—and she was home free.

Her gut twisted at the idea of causing her family worry, but worry was better than harm. No amount of words or arguments would allow them to accept Elijah's prime target was *her*, which meant she needed to be far away.

So, as she'd learned to do as a teenager, instead of fighting the brick wall of a united Wyatt-Knight front, she'd sneak away and do the thing she knew was right.

She *knew* it was right. If only she was in danger, maybe she'd agree with her family. Teamwork was better than going off on your own.

But it wasn't about her. It was about Mak.

So, Cecilia wrote her letter. She decided not to leave it in the kitchen, just because it would set the alarm too quickly. She needed a head start so they didn't think they could come after her.

Mailbox. Perfect. She'd slip it in on her way out. Duke or Sarah didn't usually head out that way until the end of the day. Plenty of time.

Satisfied with her plan, she slung her bag over her shoulder and slid the letter into her pocket. If she happened to get caught, she'd just pretend she was taking some stuff for Mak over to the Wyatt ranch. Then she'd try again tomorrow.

She heard the groan of pipes as Rachel started the shower. She took a deep breath and reminded herself she knew she was right. This was the right thing for Mak and that was all that mattered.

She slid out the door as quietly as she could. Keeping her eyes on the horizon on the off chance Sarah or Duke would unexpectedly come back to the house before lunch. Or one of Dev's dogs—he'd insisted Sarah start keeping them with her—might start barking.

Nothing. She moved quickly and stealthily to the

other side of the house where her truck was parked—purposefully away from views of the doors or windows.

But she stopped short when she turned the corner and spotted Brady leaning negligently against the hood of her truck.

He tipped down his sunglasses, clearly made a mental note of her bag, and then smiled. "Going somewhere?"

For a few full seconds all Cecilia could do was gape. Surely…this was a coincidence. He wasn't sitting there because he knew what she was up to.

She kept walking toward her truck, trying to keep the suspicion out of her tone. "Just gotta run some errands. I left in kind of a hurry yesterday," she said, trying to sound casual.

Brady gestured to the tinted out truck Liza had driven to the ranch. He'd parked it behind hers so she couldn't back out. "I'll drive you."

She frowned, clutching the strap of her bag. "Why would you do that?"

"You can't get very far on that doughnut tire, and I'm assuming you want to go a little farther than the rez."

He laid that accusation so casually, she almost agreed. She caught herself in time, harnessing her indignation that he'd clearly seen through her. "I don't know what you're talking about."

"Sure," he agreed easily. "But I'll drive you all the same."

"I don't need a chauffeur, Brady. Go back to the ranch and rest up that bum shoulder of yours."

He rolled the shoulder in question, then shrugged. "Feels plenty rested to me. Think I kicked that infection this time around. Isn't that handy?" He gestured at her. "Might be kind of hard to see around that swollen eye. Probably be better if I drive."

She didn't know what to do with…whatever he was doing. The way he was acting. "Did you and Gage switch bodies or something? Is that why Felicity jumped ship so quick?"

"Careful," he warned, and his tone had an edge to it that reminded her of last night when he'd been so *angry*.

His expression was calm, though. And she felt two inches tall for making a comment about Felicity's old crush on Brady, when it was clear to anyone who paid half a second of attention she genuinely loved Gage.

"Go away, Brady," Cecilia said, her control slipping. This was hard enough without having to fight him. "I've got stuff to do, and it's got nothing to do with you."

"That'd be easy, wouldn't it? But we both know it isn't true."

"Whatever," she muttered. She wasn't going to argue with him. She was going to get in her truck and leave.

She stalked toward the door. Brady stepped in front of it. Her temper snapped and she gave him a shove.

He didn't budge.

"I'm not afraid to hurt you, Brady," she seethed through gritted teeth.

"Try me."

The arrogance in his tone had her lashing out without thinking the move through. He dodged the elbow she almost landed on his gut, then grabbed her arm and moved it behind her back like he was getting ready to cuff her.

Her temper didn't just snap now, it ignited. She kicked out, landed a blow to his shin, which weakened his grip. She wrenched her arm away and swung.

He blocked the blow, feinted left well enough she fell

for it. Then he had both her wrists in his grasp and held them against the truck behind her so she was trapped.

They both breathed heavily and Cecilia didn't fight the hold. She could get out of it, but as much as she didn't have any qualms about sparring with Brady, she didn't feel right about actually hurting him—which she would have to do to escape his grip.

She took a deep breath, tried to turn the fire of fury inside of her into ice. She angled her chin toward his wounded shoulder. "I could get out of this in five seconds flat if I fought dirty." Even if he was finally healing, one well-placed strike to his wound would have him on his knees.

He didn't even blink or wince. "Not if I fought dirty right back."

"You?" She snorted, even though his hands were curled around her wrists and his body was way, way, *way* too close to hers. She could feel his body heat, and he didn't have to be touching her anywhere but her wrists to get the sense of just how big and strong he was.

And this was really not to the time to wonder what it would feel like if he *was* touching her anywhere else.

Except, then that's exactly what he did. Inch by inch, he pinned his body to hers—her back against the metal door of her truck, her front against…him. And she wasn't sure which was a harder, less giving surface.

It was meant to be threatening, maybe. A show of power, and that he was bigger and stronger than she was. But she didn't think it had any of the desired effects, because what she really wanted to do was press right back. Even with his hands tight around her wrists.

Brady's face was too close, and he had that fierceness from last night that, God help her, it really did something for her. She liked he had some secret edge. That he wasn't perfect or so easily contained.

Which was not at all what she should be thinking about. She should be fighting dirty. Getting out of his hold, even if it meant hurting him. But she couldn't bring herself to.

"He knows you took Mak," Brady said, his voice a razor's edge against the quiet morning. "I get it. He's not going to stop until he figures out what you did with him. But his men also followed me and Liza. Maybe they gave up, but Elijah has some unknown beef with me too. We're in the same boat. Stay, we lead him to Mak. It can't happen. But if we leave? We lead Elijah away."

Cecilia had to swallow to speak, to focus on his words instead of the heat spreading through her. The throbbing deep inside of her. "Just what are you suggesting?" she managed to demand. Or squeak. She wasn't sure which sound actually came out of her mouth.

"That we do this together, Cecilia. Lead Elijah away, and take him on. While having each other's back."

Chapter Eight

There was a faint buzzing in Brady's head, and he was having a hard time not letting it take over. If it won, this wouldn't be about Elijah or danger or anything else. It would be about *them*.

But today wasn't about the surprisingly soft woman he was currently pressing against a truck. Today was about keeping Mak safe. Keeping Cecilia safe.

Seriously, *why* had he pushed her against the truck? To prove some point that he was physically stronger? He was well aware Cecilia could hold her own if she was giving it a full 100 percent. She had gone easy on him in their little tussle because of his shoulder, just like he'd gone easy on her because neither of them wanted to actually *hurt* each other.

So, why was he crowding her against the truck as his body rioted with…reaction? A heat that *should* have warned him of danger. He shouldn't want to lean into it, explore it.

Relish it.

He realized belatedly he was leaning in, getting closer. He could smell her, feel her. What would it matter if he—

That just could not happen. He was *not* this person.

He released her abruptly. Which wasn't his best move. It showed her way more than he wanted to admit. He stopped himself from scraping his hands over his face. Stopped himself from gulping for air like he wanted to. He tried to picture himself encased in ice so any and all further reactions were frozen deep inside of him.

What was wrong with him? He felt like there was some rogue part of himself sprouting up and refusing to be caged away like it usually was.

He wasn't attracted to Cecilia. She irritated him. She challenged him. That *infuriated* him—it didn't make him want her. This was simply an aberration. A…hallucination.

Something real and enticing for the first time in a long time.

Which didn't matter. Not now. What mattered was outwitting Elijah.

"Get in the truck, Cecilia," he managed to say, without sounding like he felt. Raked over coals. Shaken until his brain was mush. "Or we'll be found out before we leave the ranch."

Cecilia stood there, still pressed to the truck like she was afraid to move. Which was ridiculous. Cecilia was never afraid. Certainly not of him. She'd fought right back when he'd tried to stop her from getting in her truck.

But he could see her pulse rioting in her neck. She breathed unevenly, lips slightly parted. And she didn't move.

Everything inside of him *ached* with something he refused to acknowledge or name.

"No one else knows?" she finally asked, her voice

more or less a whisper. Infused with suspicion, but a whisper nonetheless.

Brady forced his body to level out. When he spoke, it was controlled. Even. "Grandma Pauline. She's the one who convinced me to go with you, not stop you." And not go on his own. But Cecilia didn't need to know he'd had the same plan as she did. "She said we should leave Mak."

Cecilia visibly swallowed as if that hurt, but she nodded. "He'll be safer here. Away from me."

He could *see* the way that pained her, just like he could feel an echoing of that same pain inside of him. There was something about taking care of Mak that had crawled inside of him, lodged somewhere near his heart.

"He'll be safer away from us," Brady corrected, because he needed the verbal reminder himself. "It might not connect, but I'm Elijah's target too."

Cecilia nodded, as if agreeing. Then she pushed herself off the truck and went to the one with tinted windows that he'd been driving. They both climbed inside in silence, buckled in that same heavy absence of noise.

Brady spared Cecilia a glance as he turned the key. She had her hands clasped in her lap and she looked straight ahead. Long strands of black hair that had slipped out of her braid framed her face. He'd known her since he'd come to Grandma Pauline's. She was as familiar to him as his brothers, more or less.

But he found himself staring, when he had no business staring. When he had no business being...affected by said staring.

"It'd earn him respect," Cecilia said abruptly. "Elijah. For him to screw with one of those Wyatt brothers who left, who went into law enforcement and thumbed their nose at their father, at the Sons—"

Brady jumped on this thread he could follow without getting as lost as he felt when he was staring at her. "Who got Ace thrown in jail. There are plenty of men in that place who like Ace. Hell, worship Ace. He's the best leader they've ever had. If Elijah takes a chunk out of us, my bet is he gets the respect of those who follow Ace even now." Brady nudged the truck forward, watching the surroundings to make sure they weren't spotted.

"But us leaving together... Doesn't that prove Mak is here? That we left him here?"

"Depends. I think we can make it look like anything, if he doesn't know where Mak is right now. We can make it look like we have him. We can make it look like we've taken him somewhere else. We can even make it look like we split up, so he won't know which thread to follow. He'll have to split resources thinking we're apart, but we'll be together the whole time."

"We," Cecilia echoed. She squeezed her hands together. If it were someone else, he might have attributed that gesture to fear.

"We," Brady said firmly, because at least in that he was sure. "Whatever his reasons, Elijah's targeting us both right now. He followed us both. So it's a we. I want to keep Mak safe as much as you do."

"Is it that bad?" She squeezed her eyes shut and shook her head. "I don't know why I even asked that. Of course growing up in a gang is *that bad*."

"I wouldn't know it was that bad if I hadn't gotten out. I knew it was... Wrong isn't the right word, because when you have nothing else it's not wrong. It didn't fit, though. It didn't seem right. And Jamison, well, he could remember living with Mom at Grandma Pauline's. He'd had that glimpse of different. He made us all believe in it. Believe we deserved it. Mak wouldn't have that."

Cecilia inhaled sharply. "Would it have been different? If you didn't have Jamison?"

She'd never know how often he'd asked himself that. How often he'd wondered if Jamison was the reason he'd followed the straight and narrow against the bad that must be inside him. How often he'd hoped it was something deeper, something good inside of *him*.

But he could never be sure. "I'll never know," he said, pulling out onto the gravel road on the back of the Knight property. It would lead them to the highway. And then...

"Where are we going?" She sounded more like herself again. In control and ready to fight whatever came their way.

"That's an excellent question. Got any ideas?"

CECILIA GAPED AT BRADY. "I'm sorry...you don't have a plan?"

He gestured her way, though he kept his gaze on the road. "This is the plan."

"This isn't a plan. It's not even half a plan. It's the teeny tiny beginning of a plan." She forced herself to take a breath so she didn't start sounding panicked, even though that was the exact feeling gripping her throat. "*I* had a plan. You come in and ruin my plan and then... I can't believe you of all people would do something without thinking it through."

"I've thought it through. We find someplace to hunker down. We contact Elijah and see if he'll come after us. Then we work together to arrest him."

"*Someplace* is not a plan. *See if* is not a plan!"

Brady rolled his eyes. "We'll work it out. Do you think my apartment is far enough away?"

"No. Besides, too many innocent bystanders in an apartment building. Same with my place. Too close to neighbors he could use."

"And where were *you* going to go?" Brady asked loftily.

"Motels. Crisscross around. Make it look like I'm running, trying to lose him." She threw Brady a condescending glance that he didn't see since his eyes were on the road. "You can't contact him. That's too obvious."

Brady shrugged negligently. "I think Elijah runs toward the obvious."

"Maybe. But he doesn't think *we* will. He reacts to fear." Cecilia looked out of the windshield at the highway flying by, the rolling hills, patches of brown from the fading summer heat against the green, slowly morphing into the landscape of the Badlands. Rock outcroppings in the distance that would take over the whole horizon. She thought of the dead prairie dog, the dead raccoon, the simple notes. "He wants me afraid. If we act like we're running, he'll take the bait. Though I wouldn't mind leaving a few dead animals for *him* to find, I think acting like we're on the losing side is what we should do."

"He left you dead animals?" Brady asked, and for a second she was fooled by the deadly calm in his voice, so she simply shrugged.

"That's serial killer behavior."

She turned at the cold edge of fury in his voice. It was mesmerizing, seeing anger on Brady. She knew he'd been angry before. It wasn't that she'd ever been truly fooled by the careful armor he placed over himself. It was just she couldn't understand why it had broken down *now*. The Wyatts had been through some bad things the past few months.

Maybe it was the gunshot wound, and the infections. Just frustration bubbling over. Maybe it had nothing to do with this.

With you.

Uncomfortable with that thought, she pushed it away and focused on what he'd said rather than how he'd said it. "Like you pointed out last night, he's a sociopath. Though I don't fully understand how so many sociopaths can congregate in one group, follow one leader. How do people like Elijah and Ace get whole swaths of men following them? Willing to kill for them?"

"They normalize each other's behavior and lack of feelings. That's how groups like the Sons form. People with all sorts of mental problems normalized by each other, exacerbated by each other. They're told the outside is the enemy. If they're miserable, if they're poor, if they've been hurt—the outside is the reason for it. The outside is the reason they're miserable, and if they strike out enough they'll finally be safe and happy."

It made a sad kind of sense.

"But make no mistake, Cecilia, people like Ace and Elijah are worse. They know what they're doing. They know how to manipulate people. Maybe they have their own warped view that the world has harmed them, so they have to harm the world, but there's nothing to feel sorry for."

"Did you mistake me for someone with sympathy?"

He flicked a glance her way. "You aren't without sympathy."

"You know how it is. You're a cop long enough, it starts to eat away at you. Hard to watch people make bad decisions over and over for no good reason and not develop a certain kind of cynicism." She wasn't sure why she said that. She wasn't in a habit of admitting her cynicism—though she knew Brady would understand, would have to. He'd been a cop a few years longer than she had, and he didn't have the same connection to the people he served as she did.

"I think everything you did for your friend, and for Mak, proves that whatever you might feel on a bad day isn't who you actually are. That's not a criticism. If you lose all your humanity, badge or no, you're no different than Ace or Elijah."

The way he said it had her stomach twisting painfully. "Do you worry about that?"

He stared hard at the road, his grip on the steering wheel tightening before she watched him carefully relax it. "Sometimes."

"You shouldn't. I don't know a better man than you, Brady."

"Duke," he replied automatically, trying to defer the attention to someone else, it was clear.

"Duke's a great man," Cecilia agreed. She didn't like feeling soft, didn't like this need to soothe. But Brady brought it out in her, because she knew a lot of men and Brady *was* the best. Whether he wanted to believe that or not. "He's a wonderful father or father figure. But he's a crusty cowboy with a chip on his shoulder who still hasn't quite accepted his daughters are grown women. Jamison is like that too—he looks at all of you, and all of us like we're still kids. It doesn't make them bad people, it just... Well, you don't do that."

He shifted uncomfortably, like he didn't know what to do with the praise. She doubted any of the Wyatt men were particularly used to having nice things being said to their faces. Grandma Pauline was amazing—but she wasn't *complimentary*.

"I guess that's just being the middle child. One foot in each door. Understanding the oldest side and the younger sides." He slid her a look. "Or maybe not, since technically you're in the middle and you still treat Rachel and Sarah like babies who need protecting."

Cecilia frowned. "I do not."

"Okay."

She stared at him in shock. He was *patronizing* her. "Don't *okay* me. I do not treat them like babies!" She was being *nice*, and he was turning on her. The jerk.

"You're right," he added, with almost enough contrition to mollify her. "You treat them, and Felicity, come to think of it, more like toddlers than babies."

Her mouth dropped in outrage. She couldn't believe Brady was criticizing her. And over how she treated her sisters. Which was not any of his business, and certainly not an area he was an expert on. "I was being *nice* to you."

"Yeah, and I'm telling you the truth," he replied, still so casual as if they weren't arguing at all. "Which you know is the truth or you wouldn't be pissed off." He nodded toward the road sign for the next three towns. "You have a motel in mind?"

Cecilia crossed her arms over her chest, tried not to feel petulant. She did *not* treat her sisters like toddlers. She was just protective of them, because she knew all the awful that was out in the world. Who cared if Brady understood that or not? They had far bigger problems at hand. "The Mockingbird in Dyner."

Brady winced, but nodded. "All right. Hope you brought your hazmat suit."

Chapter Nine

Brady drove toward the scummy motel Cecilia had named. It wouldn't have been his choice, but he understood Cecilia's thinking. They had to look like they were trying to evade notice. A cash-only, by-the-hour motel room would be just the place. He'd have to put his comfort aside.

The trick was going to be to get Elijah himself to come after them. He likely had a never-ending supply of men who'd take orders under the right incentives or threats. Brady figured they could fight off attacks, as long as Elijah didn't know where Mak was, but that would be the constant, overwhelming worry.

Brady slowed the truck about a block away from the Mockingbird. He turned to Cecilia, who was still pouting by his estimation. He didn't know why that *amused* him. It should be irritating or frustrating or *nothing*, but something about tough, extreme Cecilia pouting over being called overprotective made him want to laugh.

This was very much not the time or place for that, so he focused on the task at hand. "I think you should go in there alone. We should try to make it look like you're running away by yourself. We're more likely to lure him out that way."

Cecilia blinked at him. "That's what *I* was going to say."

"Then we're on the same page."

She turned in her seat to face him, to study him as though she were somehow confused by their agreement. "You're not going to pull the macho you-need-a-man-to-protect-you card?"

"No, in part because you don't need a man—you just need a partner. But also in part because, if Elijah is anything like Ace, he thinks less of women. Which means you being on your own is going to be impossible for him to resist. It won't occur to him he could be beaten by a woman. He's more likely to go after you, most especially if he thinks you're alone."

She nodded grimly. "True enough. So, I'll walk the last block, and you'll stay here. Can you do that?"

He nodded, though the idea of her walking that last block on her own made him edgy. "You'll have to watch for anyone who might be following you. Have your phone and your gun and—"

She rolled her eyes. "*Duh*, Brady."

"Duh. Really?"

She shook her head, digging through her backpack to pull out a holster. She slid her gun inside. "I'll walk over and check in. I'm thinking you should stay here till dark so no one at the hotel sees you."

Brady glanced at the clock. No, that'd be too much time. "You'll text me the room number and leave the rest up to me."

"We want everyone to think I'm alone so no hotel employees can give us away if Elijah or his men come sniffing around. You're hardly inconspicuous."

"What does that mean?"

"You're—" she waved a hand at him, from his head to his foot on the brake "—big."

He raised an eyebrow.

"Come on. You're all Wyatt. Tall and broad and it isn't going to take a genius to put it together. There's no mistaking a Wyatt."

He didn't like it, but she was probably right. Much as he'd rather not admit it, he and his brothers all looked like Ace. Whoever Elijah sent would be able to put it together pretty easily even if they'd never seen Brady.

"He's after both of us. Maybe we both—"

"Don't start second-guessing just because you want to protect me, Brady. You were right the first time. If he thinks I'm alone we're more likely to get Elijah."

"It's not about wanting to protect." He wasn't sure what it *was* about, but surely he was more evolved than that.

"My butt." She slid out of the truck. "Wait until dark," Cecilia insisted before quietly closing the door.

He did not like being told what to do, and liked even less the high-handed way she'd ended any more discussion on the matter. They were supposed to be partners, working together.

Even if he'd all but forced her into that. Still, she'd *agreed*. Which meant they had to agree on the next courses of action. Teams *agreed* on what they were doing.

He could have gotten out of the truck and followed her. He could have driven over to the parking lot. There were a great many things he *could* do—she wasn't in charge of him.

But they'd come up with this plan, and he knew it was the best one. Even if it bothered him, on a deep, cellular, not-intellectual level that she was walking by herself, getting a room by herself. He wouldn't even know if she'd been intercepted.

He tightened his grip on the steering wheel and tried to talk himself out of all the worst-case scenarios. But worst-case scenarios existed because sometimes the worst case did.

He didn't have to blow their plan to bits to try and mitigate some potential worst cases. He'd parked on the curb of a pretty deserted street. Empty storefronts, a few with broken windows on the higher stories. There were two cars parked on the street—one in front of him, and one behind. Both were rusted severely, and one had a flat tire, so they likely hadn't moved in a while.

If he backtracked, there was a narrow alley. He could fit the truck back there, and as long as he made sure the buildings on either side were empty, and it looked like the alley was unused, he could park there without being noticed.

Then he could sneak up to the motel behind the building. Check things out and see if Cecilia had anyone watching her. He hadn't spotted a tail on the drive over, so he was pretty sure they hadn't been found yet.

Satisfied with his plan, he took a circular route to the alley—still no tail, and there weren't many places for one to hide in this deserted part of Dyner. He parked the truck, searched the alley for signs of use, and when he found none, settled his bag on his shoulder and started walking toward the motel.

It was easy to go around back and avoid the parking lot. The motel was a small, old, bedraggled building. It was squat but long, and separated into two sides of rooms with the main office at the end. The back of the buildings abutted a small copse of scraggly-looking trees.

Brady used the trees as cover as he moved toward the motel. From the back it was just a slab of concrete with the tiniest of squares in each unit that were bleary windows that didn't look like they'd been cleaned in decades.

The two sections of rooms were split by a breezeway in the middle. Brady stopped and watched the narrow space. It would have taken Cecilia some time to not just walk up to the motel office, but also check in. If Brady stayed put and watched the breezeway and Cecilia passed, he'd know her room was on the east side. If she didn't pass after a certain amount of time, she was likely on the west side.

Unless she'd already gone to her room. But just as he was considering that possibility, Cecilia walked briskly past the breezeway.

He moved out of the woods, careful and alert to the potential of being watched. He moved through the breezeway, looked out just in time to see Cecilia step into the last unit.

He retraced his steps to the back of the building, moved down the length of the east side until he reached the end. He sent her a text telling her to unlock the door.

Her response was about what he expected.

I told you to stay put.

So he repeated his previous text: Unlock the door.

She didn't reply to that one. He moved around the corner, watching the entire area around him for someone who might be watching the door Cecilia had gone into. She hadn't just left it unlocked, she'd left it ajar.

He slid inside.

She closed and locked the door behind him, and while her stance was calm, her eyes were fury personified.

"I told you to wait."

"It was too long to wait. I could have just as easily been spotted in that truck. I haven't seen any tails or any signs of being watched. Have you?"

She frowned. "No."

"They haven't figured us out yet."

"That only means they're hanging around the ranches. I don't like that."

"Neither do I, but you yourself said we can't contact Elijah and lure him out. He has to think we're on the run." Brady looked around the room. It smelled like stale cigarette smoke and mildew. He was sure the bedding hadn't been updated since 1990, at best. Everything had a vague layer of grime over it.

"I gave a fake name at the desk," Cecilia said, pacing the small patch of threadbare carpet. "They didn't ask for my ID."

"He'll be looking for someone with your description, not your name."

"I know." She hugged her arms around herself. "I just hate that while we wait for him to find us, he's going to be harassing our families."

"Cody will have that covered."

She didn't say anything to that, but he could read her doubts. There was no way to assuage them. He had doubts of his own. No matter that Cody had trained with the CIA and been part of a secret group who's purpose was to take down the Sons, no amount of security could protect everyone 100 percent. Not long-term.

So, they had to focus on the short term. "Tomorrow, we'll head east. I'll check in at the next motel and you'll hang out in the truck till the coast is clear. We'll switch off like that—in different directions, buying two or three days in the motels and only staying one. I think he'll follow you, but if he sends some men after me, it'll split his resources."

"You're not in charge here, Brady. You can't just stomp in and order me around."

"I wasn't ordering, and I most definitely wasn't stomping."

She crossed her arms over her chest and lifted her chin. "Weren't you?"

"Is there a problem with my plan?"

She made a face—pursed lips, wrinkled nose, frustration personified. "No," she ground out, clearly irritated.

"Well, then."

"You're infuriating," she said disgustedly.

"I don't see how."

"You're a Wyatt. You wouldn't." She plopped herself on the edge of the bed. She sat there like that, looking irritable and pouty. After a few moments it changed. She looked around the room, then narrowed her eyes at him.

After a few more seconds, she smiled, and boy did he not trust that smile.

THERE WAS NO way to fight Brady when he was right. No one was onto them yet, so it made sense he'd come into the room. Moving to another motel tomorrow and doing the same thing, only with Brady being the one to check in made sense too.

It would work better if they split up, but that would leave them both in danger. It made more sense to be partners in this.

But if he was going to irritate her, she had the right to irritate him right back. So, she smiled. "Guess we're gonna share a bed tonight." Because if there was one way to *really* make Brady uncomfortable it was to acknowledge that little spark of heat between them.

"No."

"Afraid I'm going to take advantage of you?" she asked sweetly.

His eyes darkened, and it was probably warped, but she shivered a little. She could picture it just a little too easily. Especially now that he'd pinned her to the truck and she'd felt his body against hers.

What she knew now, that she hadn't known or fully believed back on New Year's Eve, was that he felt it too. That undercurrent of attraction. She wasn't sure she'd ever felt a buzz quite that potent. She'd always assumed she was immune to that—something about being a cop, being tougher and harder than most of her past boyfriends. They'd all liked the *idea* of her, but in practice it had never worked.

No man wanted a superior. At best they wanted an equal.

Brady is definitely equal.

"We shouldn't both sleep at the same time, Cecilia. That's just common sense."

Oh, she hated that *reasonable, condescending* tone. More annoying, the fact he was right when she was just trying to get under his skin. There really *was* something wrong with her thinking he was so attractive when he was equally as obnoxious.

There was something really pathetic about the urge to needle him when she should let it go. So, he hadn't listened and stayed in the truck. She had no doubt he'd evaded any kind of detection. Everything was as fine as it could be under the circumstances.

But she wanted to poke at him until he exploded—until she saw some of that reaction she'd seen last night when he'd been angry and incapable of controlling it.

Apparently he was having the same kind of thoughts.

"Would calling the ranch and checking in make you feel better? Check in on your babies—I mean sisters?"

He asked it so blandly she might have missed the direct dig. She might have even let it go if it didn't make her think she was having the same effect on him that he was having on her. That edginess that left each other incapable of acting reasonably.

When they *had* to act reasonably. They had to focus on the danger they were in, and first and foremost, keeping Mak safe. "I do not treat them like they're babies, but maybe I should treat you like you're one. Or just a cranky five-year-old in need of a nap."

"It was just a joke, Cecilia," he said in a bored tone. "Let it go."

Which of course meant she couldn't. "I will not let it go. I do not treat them that way. If I'm a little protective, it's because *I'm* a cop."

He rolled his eyes. *Rolled. His. Eyes.* "Okay."

She jumped up. "You don't understand because you Wyatts are all cops. So you don't have to worry about any of you being naive." She winced a little. "Or were cops." A reference to Dev whose injuries had ended his police career after just a few months on the job.

"What does it matter if I think you treat your sisters like toddlers?"

It didn't. Not at all. But he was purposefully goading her. And she had to be the bigger person. She had to let it go. "It doesn't matter. At all, in fact."

"There you go." Then he reached out and patted her on the head.

Patted her. On the head.

She poked him square in the chest, which was quite the feat when what she really wanted to do was deck him. "Don't *pat* me on the head, you pompous jerk."

"Don't *poke* me," he returned, taking her wrist and pulling her hand away from his chest. But each finger that wrapped around her narrow wrist was like fire.

It was ridiculous and so over-the-top potent, this thing between them. And it was just going to keep happening. Trying to lure Elijah toward them while working together—spending nights in the same room together—the fights would get old, and they would all end in this. Attraction was going to keep leaping up until they dealt with it head-on. One way or another.

She met his gaze. "We can't pretend this away, Brady."

He dropped her wrist, his armor clicking into place clear as day. "Watch me."

Chapter Ten

Pretend. Brady didn't have to pretend anything away, because this…thing between them was nothing more than weird timing and circumstance. It was just an illusion made up of frustration and fear and danger.

If there was some teeny tiny ember of attraction, it could be easily stomped out.

Once she stopped poking at him.

Why he'd expect her to do that was beyond him. Cecilia was not someone who stepped back from any kind of challenge. She met them head-on. She said things like *we can't pretend this away*.

But clearly she had no clue who she was talking to, because there were a great many things he could pretend away. This included. *This* was at the top of the list.

He pulled his phone out of his pocket and dialed Cody. "Need to check in," he muttered to Cecilia without looking her way.

He didn't watch for her response, so if she had one, it wasn't verbal. When Cody answered, Brady kept his greeting short.

"What's the status?"

"You can't be serious."

"Why not?"

Cody sighed. "You just took off. You and Cecilia. We agreed—"

"We didn't agree on anything. Have you had any incidents?"

Cody muttered something Brady couldn't make out, which was probably for the best. "We've definitely had some people poking around, but it's all been pretty weak. I think they know you guys aren't here, and don't suspect you left Mak. Unless they're biding their time."

"Any word on Elijah himself?"

"No. He's laying low as far as we've been able to figure—without digging too deeply so he might realize we're looking into him. Where are you?"

"Best if you don't know."

"I've been in this exact position," Cody said, his tone serious and grave. "Working together, all of us, was—"

"Something that worked for *your* situation, and it might in the future work for this one. But right now, we have to keep Elijah away from Mak any way we can. This is the best way."

Before Cody could respond, the phone was plucked out of his grasp. He turned to scowl at Cecilia.

She had his phone to her ear and a *screw you* expression on her face. "Cody? Yeah. Listen. Stay away from Elijah. Your priority is Mak. All of you out there—your priority is Mak. You let me and Brady deal with Elijah."

Whatever Cody said in response must not have met with her approval because she clicked the end button and then tossed his cell on the disgusting bed.

"Mature, Cecilia."

"I don't need to be mature, and I don't need your baby brother's approval." She crossed her arms over her chest. "We need Elijah to follow us. That's it."

"Did it occur to you I wasn't seeking approval so much as diplomatically trying to get everyone on the same side without barking out orders?"

She waved a dismissive hand. "We do not have time for every Wyatt and every Knight to get on board. Not right now."

"And if they go after Elijah themselves? You're not the only one who does something just because someone tells them not to."

"They won't," she said, as if she actually believed it. "Not only is it not in anyone's best interest—if they start reaching out to Elijah, it puts us in more danger. He'll build his forces for a Wyatt showdown. If he thinks we're working on our own, we have a better chance. Every one of your brothers will come to that conclusion before they try to take something upon themselves, especially with Mak there to remind them."

She wasn't wrong. His brothers might not approve of the plan, but they wouldn't try to interrupt it unless they could guarantee it didn't put more danger on him and Cecilia. Knowing the Wyatts were involved would no doubt increase the danger, so no matter how they complained about it, they wouldn't interfere unless they had a safe way of doing it.

"You can admit I'm right at any time." She smiled at him, all smug satisfaction. Then she moved closer, a saunter if he had to characterize it. With that same look in her eyes she'd had on New Year's Eve.

She did the same thing too. Moved right up to him and placed her hands on his shoulders like they belonged there.

This time though, he knew. She wasn't drunk. She wasn't joking. She was…probably projecting. Better to irritate him, to come on to him and make him angry, than think about the reality of her life.

Which almost made him feel sorry for her. Almost.

If her hands felt good there, if his system screamed in anticipation, he didn't have to—and in fact wouldn't—react.

But she didn't just leave her hands on his shoulders, she slid them up his neck, locking her fingers behind it. She molded her body to his, and it was that same blazing heat as when he'd backed her up against the truck.

Why did all this make his body tighten when he knew better. *Knew* better. "It's just attraction." He had to say it out loud. He had to hear the words himself. Because there was only one tiny little thread of reason holding him back.

She widened her eyes, all fake innocence. "Gee. I thought it was chaste, attraction-less, pure-hearted happily-ever-after."

He puffed out a breath and reached behind him to pull her arms from around his neck.

She didn't let herself be pulled. In fact, she sort of rolled against him and for a second he was frozen, holding her arms, pressed to her, blood roaring in his head.

What would be the harm?

"It doesn't have to mean anything, Brady," she said, her voice soft. "Consider it a distraction under stress. You're not exactly *unmoved*."

That at least poked holes in the haze of attraction and want, because it was a lie. Because he heard a hint of desperation she was trying so hard to hide. "You think it'd be that easy?" He laughed, though it wasn't a particularly nice laugh. "How naive are you?"

She looked a bit like he'd slapped her, and while that

gave him a stab of pain, she had to understand what she was saying. And he had to be kind of a jerk so she'd stop...doing this. "Did you forget about that kiss at New Year's Eve, Cecilia?"

"No."

"It didn't mean anything, so it never occurred to you to think about it again?"

"Brady, I—"

"You kissed me and any attraction that prompted it evaporated. You didn't want to anymore." He gestured to the small space between them. Derisively. "Clearly. It all went away."

She blinked at him, some of that sexy certainty slipping off her face. "That was just a kiss."

"And what you're suggesting is just sex." He unwound her arms from around his neck and she finally released him. "If a kiss lingered, what would sex do?"

"It doesn't have to be like that," she said stubbornly.

"Doesn't it? You've actually slept with someone and all feelings and attraction immediately disappeared?"

Her eyebrows drew together like she was trying to make sense of a foreign language. "Of course."

"Of course? Cecilia, you must have had some spectacularly bad sex." Which was not an easy thing to think when she was still so close. Clearly...missing out.

She bristled. "You have no idea what kind of sex life I've had."

"No. And I don't want to." Not in a million years did he want to imagine what kind of morons she'd been with. "But sex changes things. It's nakedness and intimacy, and that's fine if you're casual friends or you pick someone up at a bar. It's fine if you think you're going to date and see if you're compatible. It's not fine if you're practically family."

"Because you decreed the laws and rules of what's fine and what's not?"

She was the most frustrating woman in the world. He had no idea why that made him want to put his hands on her face, to show her—long, slow, and thoroughly— what a real kiss would do.

Luckily he was distracted from the impulse by the alarm going off on his phone. "I need to change my bandage," he said stiffly, and grabbed his bag and walked into the bathroom, hoping he could leave all *that* behind him.

CECILIA DIDN'T PARTICULARLY enjoy being chastised, or other people being right, but there was something about the way Brady had handled her that made her feel both— chastised and very, very wrong.

She wanted to pout over it, but the predominant feeling—nearly eclipsing the ever-present worry that she couldn't keep Mak safe—was a heavy sadness.

She sat down on the bed and rested her chin in her hands. He wasn't wrong exactly. It was nice to throw herself at him, argue with him, because it didn't leave much room for worry. She could turn that off, and *God* she was desperate to turn that constant, exhausting anxiety off.

There were other ways to argue with Brady. Not such easy ones, but she didn't have to throw herself at him. Especially when he so easily countered all her moves.

You must have had some spectacularly bad sex.

She scowled. What did Brady know? He was uptight and repressed. Sure, he was hot. And that brief moment he'd returned the New Year's Eve kiss had been something like electric, but there was no way Brady wasn't just stern vanilla.

Then I think you're attracted to stern vanilla.

She heard a muttered swear from the bathroom and leaned sideways to see through the crack in the door.

Brady was clearly struggling with removing and bandaging his wound himself. Stubborn mule.

She got to her feet and marched for the tiny bathroom. She inched the door the rest of the way open. "Oh, for heaven's sake. Let me help you."

He scowled at her in the mirror over the sink. "I can do it on my own."

"Not well." She stalked over to him and tugged the alcohol wipe out of his hand. She set to tending the wound, ignoring the fact he was shirtless. She was mad at him, and she wasn't going to soak in the sight of pure *muscle* on display. She was above that. "It looks better." She coughed. "Your wound."

"Antibiotics must have worked this time," he said in that robotic Brady voice that made her want to scream.

Instead she finished disinfecting the area. "That's good."

"It is."

She rolled her eyes at the inane conversation. She pulled the new bandages out of the box on the rusty sink, then pointed to the bed. "Oh, go sit down."

He grunted, but did as he was told. She followed, noting that the beautifully muscled torso and arms both had their share of scars. "Where'd you get all those?" she asked, positioning herself in between his legs so she could get close enough to adhere the bandage on both the front of his shoulder and the back.

He didn't answer her, merely shrugged as she

smoothed the bandage over the slow-to-heal gunshot wound. His skin was surprisingly soft there, her hand looking particularly dark against the expanse of pale skin that rarely saw the sun.

Brady wasn't a shirtless guy, so his shoulder was all white marble, aside from the bandage she'd adhered herself.

She was standing between his legs and something... took over. It wasn't wanting to poke at him; it wasn't even that flare of attraction. This was something softer and different than she was used to and she didn't know how to fight off the urge to run her fingers through his hair.

He looked up at her, something flickering in his stoic gaze. It wasn't anger like usual. Or even annoyance at her. There was something deeper there. Her heart twisted and she suddenly wanted...

She wasn't sure. Not to throw herself at him or annoy him or try to start a fight. She didn't even want to act on that flare of attraction. She wanted...she didn't know. Just that it was deeper. Like he'd be some kind of salve to a wound.

"I get it. This is scary. You're scared for Mak," he said, his voice grave. Weighted, like he really did understand. "You're worried about your friend. It'd be nice to just chuck it all out the window for an hour or so. But it would change things. Things we can't afford to let change. It *would* mean something, whether either of us wanted it to."

She stared at him. He was right. It was terrible and true, and so completely right. And there was this part of her she didn't recognize that, for one second, wanted that change.

"Cecilia."

"Shh."

She cupped his face with her hands, and she ignored…everything she usually listened to. She did something without purpose, without certainty. She pressed her mouth to his, and it was almost timid. Not like she had on New Year's Eve—bold and a little drunk and mostly just *determined*. This was born of something else altogether. Seeking out that solace, or an understanding, that had always evaded her.

No one understood her. Not really. Not her family, not her friends, certainly not any ex-boyfriends. They thought she was tough and fearless.

But Brady had said she was scared for Mak, and she'd be damned if that wasn't the truth.

So, she kissed him with a softness she'd never found inside of herself.

He kissed her back. Not in that second of shock and reaction, but actual response. As if it was her gentleness that unlocked all his concerns and denials. And though she was standing, holding his face, there was no doubt that he took control of the kiss.

Kept it soft, kept it warm. Kept it like a connection, like a comfort.

She felt vulnerable, like her heart was soft. Like he wasn't just right, but had only scratched the surface when he'd said things would change.

It was fine enough to be attracted to Brady, to think sleeping with him would just solve that. It was something else for her to feel…*this* big thing.

She dropped her hands from his face and took two big steps back and away. "You're right. This is a bad idea.

I'll stop." She had to gulp in some air to calm her shaky limbs, her even shakier heart.

He looked at her and the gaze was inscrutable. His words had no inflection whatsoever. "Well. Good, then."

The stoic way he delivered those words stung, even if they shouldn't. She was reeling—turned inside out, and he was a robot. "Fantastic."

And it was. She wasn't going to get *involved* with Brady Wyatt. After that kiss…she was willing to finally admit that if they acted on anything, involved was just what they'd be.

There was no way that was ever going to work. Not knowing that she'd sacrifice everything to keep Mak away from Elijah.

No, she had to listen to Brady for once and let this whole thing go. Because sliding in headfirst was a disaster waiting to happen.

Chapter Eleven

Even when it was his turn to sleep, Brady didn't do a very good job of it. Between the musty smell of the bed, the slightly sticky feel of the sheets, and the whirr of the pitiful air conditioner, there just wasn't much in the way of comfort.

Then there was his own…state. After Cecilia had kissed him on New Year's Eve, and even after yesterday morning with the truck, he'd been able to redirect the pang of attraction into indignant anger. A righteous certainty that she was wrong and he was in the right.

After last night's kiss, full of gentleness and something bigger than even he'd imagined, he didn't have that anger. Didn't have much of anything except confusion. And a baffling sense of loss.

Which didn't make any sense whatsoever, so he pushed the feeling and the nagging ache away and focused on the task at hand. It was always how he got through life. Why should this be any different?

They moved to the next motel on the west side of the county with limited conversation and absolutely no interference. Another night in another crappy motel with no one finding them passed in the same uncomfortable, grimy way. Another check-in with the Wyatt and Knight ranches to find nothing had really happened.

"I don't like it," Cecilia muttered, driving the truck north to another seedy motel in the neighboring county. They'd agreed she would drive when it was her turn to check into the motel and vice versa. "It shouldn't take this long to peg one of us. And the fact they're not going after the ranches... Something isn't right."

"If he's really been watching Ace, taking hints from Ace, he knows patience is Ace's greatest strength. Regardless, if they're not poking at the ranch, Mak is safe."

Cecilia slid him a look before returning her gaze to the road. "What do you know about Elijah that you haven't told me?"

"Nothing." If only because *know* was a tricky word when it came to Elijah Jones. He kept his expression carefully blank, ignored the need to shift in discomfort.

"I don't think that's true."

Brady shrugged and didn't elaborate. Cecilia kept driving.

The tension between them wasn't gone, but it had certainly shifted. Before it had been almost antagonistic and definitely argumentative. This was flat and...almost timid. Like they were suddenly tiptoeing around a bomb that might detonate.

He supposed, in a way, they were.

When Cecilia reached Frisco, a tiny town north of Valiant County, she did what they'd been doing this whole time. Found a deserted place to park the truck a block or so from the motel. In this case it was a roadside park surrounded by trees.

But she didn't immediately slide out of the truck to

start her trek to the motel. She turned in the seat to face him, her expression grave.

"I need you to tell me whatever you know or think you might know. You keeping secrets about Elijah doesn't do anyone any good."

"I don't know anything, Cecilia. Anything I could say would be…supposition. Inference. Not fact."

Her eyebrows drew together. "I want those things from you. I think we need it all out in the open. I've told you everything I know about his relationship with Layla. Every time I've had an interaction with him on the rez or heard someone else relate one. You know my side. You're here, and I don't know your side. Just that you arrested him a long time ago and he's 'poked' at you ever since."

She wasn't wrong, much as he hated to admit it. Fact of the matter was, when Elijah was poking at him but never bothering his brothers, it didn't matter. But that wasn't going to last, and if he'd kept this secret…

He didn't want it out in the open. Was always waiting for his worst fears to be disproven. But maybe he had played into Ace's hands the whole time.

He could ease into it. Lead Cecilia to her own conclusions, but because it was Cecilia, he knew he could just…blurt it out. She'd take it, work through it, and make her own opinion. He didn't have to lead her anywhere.

Still, the words stuck in his throat. He'd never vocalized his worst thoughts. Never wanted to. But he needed to do it—to keep Mak, and Cecilia, safe as he could.

She reached forward, rested her hand on his knee. Everything about her was earnest and almost…pleading. Which wasn't Cecilia at all.

The words tumbled out. "I think Ace might be Elijah's father."

"What?" Cecilia screeched. "How? Why? When? What?"

"Which of those questions do you actually want me to answer?" he replied dryly.

"Brady. Holy… Oh my God. Why do you think that?"

"I don't know," he returned, frustrated with things he couldn't fully name. "There's something about…" She was right, he reminded himself again. Knowing everything gave them ammunition. It gave them armor. Ace had made a habit of keeping secrets and using them against people.

Brady wouldn't be like his father. Wouldn't let this potential secret, no matter how far-fetched, be the thing that felled him or Cecilia.

That didn't make it easy to explain the gut feeling he had. "Maybe he's not. But there's more to their relationship than a random Sons member taking a shine to our psycho in chief. Elijah would say things, when he'd goad me into arresting him. 'We're more alike than you think.' Lots of pointed remarks about my brothers. It just started to make me think…there's more there. Maybe it's not a father-son relationship, but there's more there. I can't imagine a man like Ace was faithful to my mother, especially toward the end when she was just getting pregnant to keep him from killing her."

"Did he kill her?" Cecilia asked, and her tone was simple. Straightforward. There wasn't that layer of pity he was so used to.

Which made it impossible to avoid, even if he hated this line of conversation. "Can't prove it."

"But you think he did," she insisted in that same even tone.

Brady shrugged jerkily. "Thinking it doesn't matter. Not when it comes to Ace and the Sons. Elijah being one of Ace's. We need fact."

Cecilia was quiet for a few humming moments. "I don't know about that," she said after a while. "If Elijah was Ace's son, don't you think we'd know?"

"Why would we?"

"Elijah wouldn't keep that a secret. He'd want everyone to know he was the president's son. He would have already taken over, I'd think."

"Unless Ace wanted him to keep it a secret." Brady shifted in his seat, wishing he'd kept his big mouth shut. "Like I said, Ace's best weapon is his ability to be patient. If he wanted to use Elijah when it would do the most damage… I'm just saying, there's a reason to keep it quiet. And it makes sense why he only ever hinted at the truth with me—why he focused on me. If he'd messed with all my brothers, wouldn't we put it together? But just one of us he could goad without the clues lining up."

"He's lived on the rez as long as I can remember."

It was suddenly too much. This was why he'd never brought it up with his brothers. It didn't matter when there was no way to know for sure. When it probably *wasn't* true. "I don't want to argue the validity, Cecilia. I'm just saying, that's my theory. One I don't even fully believe but you convinced me to tell you."

"You don't have to get touchy." She frowned out the windshield in front of them. "I'm trying to work it out. He's always lived on the rez, but he bounces from house to house. I don't know who his parents are. Not even his mother. I always figured they were both dead."

"And they very well might be."

"But your theory is based on eight years of watching this guy, right? Eight years of him toying with you. Eight years of you not telling anybody someone was harassing you." She blinked, looking up at him. "That's why you didn't tell your brothers."

He refused to meet her gaze. "I didn't tell them for lots of reasons."

"You didn't want them to have to think there were more Wyatts out in the world. Ones who didn't get out."

"Look. We're here." He pointed in the direction of where the motel would be. "Go check in and—"

"You could never be like them, Brady," she said quietly, but with a vehemence that had him looking over at her. "Jamison or no," she said, dark eyes straightforward and fierce. "Grandma Pauline or no. You could never be like them."

Something inside of him cracked, because it was the lie he'd always wanted to believe. But how could he? "We don't know that. I don't need to know that. Because I'm *not* like Ace or Elijah. But Ace and Elijah are the constant threats in my life, and I'm tired. I want this over. So, why don't you go check in, huh?"

She pursed her lips, but nodded eventually. "All right," she said, and slid out of the driver's side, leaving him in the truck alone with his thoughts.

Not a place he really wanted to be.

CECILIA'S MIND REELED as she walked toward the motel. Elijah as Ace's secret son. It made a creepy kind of sense. An awful kind of sense.

No matter how she tried to reason and rationalize it away, she kept coming back to the simple fact it was *possible*. Maybe even *probable*.

It put Mak in even more danger, especially with the Wyatts. Hell, it made Mak part Wyatt.

If it were true. She understood Brady's hesitation to believe it. There wasn't evidence and it didn't make sense why Ace would have kept it a secret. It also opened the horrible Pandora's box that Ace might have more children. Children who hadn't been saved like the Wyatt brothers had been.

And if Ace had kept them all a hidden secret—or even just Elijah—the reasons could only be bad. Really, really bad.

Cecilia stepped into the motel's cramped front office.

"Got a room available?" she asked the woman behind the counter, remembering belatedly to smile casually rather than frown over the problem in her head.

The woman looked her up and down.

"You a cop?"

Cecilia managed a laugh even as she inwardly chastised herself for walking in here with her cop face on. "No. I really look like one of those nosy bastards?"

The woman wasn't amused. "Got any ID?" she demanded with narrowed eyes.

"Oh, sure," Cecilia said casually even though her heartbeat was starting to pick up. The woman's careful inspection might just be the sign of a conscientious business owner.

But Cecilia doubted it.

She patted down her pockets. "Must have forgotten it in my car."

"Then I suggest you go get it, if you're really wanting to stay here."

Cecilia rolled her eyes. "My money ain't good enough for you, that's fine." She tried to sound flippant rather than irritated.

The woman behind the counter didn't say anything, just crossed her arms over her chest. Which Cecilia took as a clear sign that she would *not* be handing over any keys, regardless of money, without ID.

A little prickle of unease moved up the back of Cecilia's neck. She couldn't help but wonder if Elijah, or his men, had already been here and warned the woman off letting Cecilia get a room. She hadn't run into any motel owner this discerning yet.

Or maybe they'd been asking questions and that had simply made the woman nervous enough to take precautions.

The woman hadn't seemed afraid, though. Suspicious, distrusting and a little rude, yeah. But not afraid.

Cecilia moved back out of the office into the early-afternoon sun. She immediately picked out two men pretending to be otherwise occupied, but she knew they weren't. She didn't recognize them on a personal level, but she'd bet money they were Elijah's messengers.

She could take two. Unfortunately she had the sneaking suspicion there were more. Surely Elijah realized that she had no problem fighting off two of his peabrained followers.

Still, she walked through the parking lot as if she didn't have a care in the world. She didn't have to look behind her to know the two were following her. Carefully and at a distance, but the farther she got from the hotel, the closer they got—to each other, and to her.

She'd made it maybe half a block, the park still not in view, when a man stepped out from behind a building in front of her.

Two behind. One in front. Not great odds, but if these three were as dim-witted as the two who'd knocked her off the road with Rachel, she could do it. Probably get a little banged up in the process, but she could do it.

She reached into her pocket and palmed her phone. She'd made a deal with Brady that if she didn't text within twenty minutes, he could come barreling after her. It hadn't been more than ten. Maybe she could get off a quick text and—

"Wouldn't do that if I were you." A fourth one popped out right next to her. Unlike the other three, who were likely armed but had their guns hidden, this one had his out and pointed at her. She froze with her hand still in her pocket.

As a police officer, Cecilia had learned how to defuse situations. How to talk men out of doing stupid things. Her goal, always, was to remain calm and use her words first.

As a woman in the world, she knew the opposite to be true. So, she didn't use her words, or wait.

She fought. Her immediate goal was disarming the man closest to her. She managed to get the gun out of his hand, but the others were quickly circling her.

She couldn't pay much attention to them when the one she'd disarmed was coming at her with a big, solid fist, but the fact no gunshots rang out meant they were supposed to keep her alive.

She had to hope.

She dodged the fist, landed a knee and her attacker dropped. She whirled to the ones she could feel closing in on her. They stood in a triangle around her. One had rope, one had a knife, and the other was just big as a Mack truck.

Crap.

Chapter Twelve

Brady surveyed the White River in the distance. It was narrow, the banks a grassy green where most of the landscape around him had gone brown under the heat of late summer. But here, near the river with a constant supply of life-giving water, things were green.

He tried to focus on that, on the landscape of his home state, on anything except the ticking seconds.

He'd promised Cecilia he wouldn't come barreling in like he had last time, though he did not characterize his previous actions as *barreling*. Still, there was no need today. They had their routine down pat and they'd found a compromise with her texting an okay after twenty minutes.

Still, the seconds seemed to tick especially slowly as he waited for a text message.

Brady got out of the truck. Not to *barrel* after her. Simply to stretch his legs. To walk off a little of his anxiety over the situation. Just in the little park.

He checked his watch. Twelve minutes down.

Now, *technically*, if it was twenty minutes from when they'd *stopped*, there'd only be three minutes left. And it would take him those three minutes to walk to the motel, so really he could head that way and not be break-ing their deal.

She'd argue, but he had a…thin, shaky argument. Still, it *was* an argument.

She'd probably call it sexist, but he considered it just two different temperaments. She apparently couldn't fathom every possible worst-case scenario while she'd waited for him yesterday.

It was *all* Brady could think about while waiting for her. It wasn't a gender thing. It was a personality thing.

He'd start walking, but he'd do it slowly. Eke out the minutes but at least get the motel in his sights. Scout out a back way to get to the room without being detected.

Nothing wrong with that.

He locked the truck and started out. He stopped and frowned at a strange, faint noise. Something like a shout. Probably his imagination.

But maybe it wasn't, and he was a cop, trained to in-vestigate that which didn't add up.

He moved stealthily up the street, hand already rest-ing on his weapon with the holster unsnapped. He heard the noise again, closer this time, in the direct path be-tween the park and the motel.

He forced away all those worst-case scenarios and focused on the task at hand. He approached the cor-ner where he'd have to turn to continue the route to the motel. He took one calming breath, readied his body and his nerves, and then moved carefully to get a view of what was happening.

Immediately he could tell there was a fight. Four men—one on the ground crawling away from three men who seemed huddled around something. Maybe another person, it was hard to tell from this vantage point.

Brady inched forward, gun pointed in the direction of the scuffle. If he announced himself, they'd no doubt scatter and he wanted to get an idea of what was going on and descriptions of who he was dealing with before he decided which one to target.

The crawler wasn't going to be hard to pin down, but Brady noticed he was moving toward a small pistol. If he ran, he could beat the injured man to it, but judging by the fact he was hurt, the guy might just as well be a victim in the whole thing.

Brady glanced back at the trio. One let out a howl of pain and bent over, giving Brady a glimpse of what the three were huddled around.

He froze for less than a second, then immediately pointed his gun at the man crawling. No one had seen him yet, and shooting would put all four men on alert, but Brady couldn't let the crawling man get the gun. Not with Cecilia in the middle of that pack of jackals.

Brady shot, aiming for the arm that was reaching for the gun. The crawling man rolled onto his back, grabbing at his arm as he screamed. The three men around Cecilia jumped. They looked toward the crawling man, then wildly around until they found Brady.

Cecilia struggled to her feet, a piece of rope dangling from one arm, blood trickling down her face in a disturbing number of places.

Despite the fact she was clearly severely hurt, she didn't even pause. She kicked out, landing a blow to one's back. He stumbled forward, then whirled on Cecilia.

Brady charged forward as one man brandished a knife. Brady found it odd none of these three seemed to have guns, but he didn't have time to question it.

He ducked the first jab, pivoted and landed an upper-cut so the man went pitching backward. Someone behind him landed a nasty kidney punch, but Brady only sucked in a breath and flung a fist backward. He connected with something that let out a sickening crunch followed by a wail of pain.

The knife flashed into his vision, and an ungainly leap backward allowed him to duck away from the sharp blade's descent with only a centimeter to spare. As the knife missed and momentum brought the assailant downward, Brady used his elbow as hard as he could.

A loud, echoing crack and the sound of a gurgling scream as the man stumbled onto his hands and knees. Brady kicked him with enough force to have the man falling onto his back. Brady stepped on his wrist—eliciting another gurgling scream from the man, but he let go of the knife.

Brady kicked it away and turned to find Cecilia. She'd taken one of the other men out, but the third man was trying to drag her by a rope he'd apparently tied around one of her arms.

"No, I don't think so," Brady said, reaching out and grabbing the taut rope. He ripped it out of the other man's grip with one forceful tug. He aimed his gun at the man's chest. "You want me to kill you, or you want me to let Elijah do it, nice and painful?"

The man sneered. "One of these days, every last high-and-mighty Wyatt's going to be wiped off this earth."

"I wouldn't count on it." Brady decided not to shoot—with the men unarmed he could call up the sheriff's department and have these four rounded up once he got Cecilia to safety. So, instead, Brady leapt forward and used the butt of the weapon to deliver a punishing blow to the head.

The man crumpled immediately and fell to the ground.

Brady whirled to Cecilia. She was kneeling next to the two men on the ground and had used the rope that had been tied around her wrist to tie them together.

"Want to add him?" she asked, her voice raspy. She was shaking, but she'd managed decent knots.

"He'll be unconscious for a while."

She struggled to get to her feet. There was blood just…everywhere. Parts of her shirt were torn and her hair had come completely undone so it was a wild tangle of midnight around her face.

"Almost had 'em," she managed to say before she swayed a little.

Brady scooped her up before she fell over. He didn't think he could stand to listen to her tell a bad joke in that ragged voice.

She wriggled slightly in his grasp as he started walking purposefully back to the truck. They weren't staying here. Not in this town or at that motel. He needed somewhere clean and sanitary to check out her wounds.

"I can walk."

"I can't say I care what you *can* do right now, Cecilia." He walked toward the crawling man who'd apparently gotten over the initial shock of his gunshot wound and was dragging himself toward the gun again.

"Don't know when to stop, do you?" Brady adjusted Cecilia's weight in his arms and then kicked the gun as hard as he could into the grassy field. If the injured man found the gun before Brady managed to call for backup, Brady'd consider him a magician.

He walked briskly back to the truck. With care, he placed Cecilia on her feet, though he kept one arm around her and supported almost all her weight.

"I'm fine," she muttered as he dug his keys out of his pocket. He ignored her and unlocked the truck, opened the door, then lifted her into her seat over her protestations. He even buckled the seat belt for her, though she weakly tried to bat his hands away. Then he looked her right in the eyes. "Don't you dare move," he ordered.

He was more than a little concerned that she listened.

CECILIA ONLY HALF listened as Brady drove and made a phone call. First she knew he was talking to the police. He was giving descriptions and accounts and locations of the fight that had transpired.

Cecilia closed her eyes against a wave of nausea. Four against one wasn't such great odds and as much as she'd held her own she was pretty banged up. She'd never admit it to Brady because he'd fuss, but she wasn't sure when she'd ever had such a bad beating.

But all four men would wind up in jail, and she would heal. So. There was that.

Brady made another call, driving too fast down deserted highways. She couldn't watch or she'd throw up. At first she'd figured he was calling his brothers, or worse, a hospital. But then he'd said something about cabins and fishing and her brain was a little fuzzy.

It was hard to focus and think over the bright fire of pain in various parts of her body. Harder still not to whimper every time the truck hit a bump. But if she showed any outward signs of pain Brady was going to baby her even worse than carrying her around.

It had been kind of nice to be carried but it was certainly not behavior she wanted to encourage. Maybe it was the worst beating she'd ever gotten, but she'd been in her share of fights. Breaking them up, having big men take swings at her. She wasn't some helpless stranger to a few punches.

Of course, she'd never been stabbed before, and she wasn't quite sure how she was going to hide that from Brady. Surely she could find some Band-Aids and take care of it.

She winced a little, knowing it was probably too deep to be handled by a Band-Aid. It was fine, though. She'd figure it out. Brady would whisk her away to a hospital if he knew and that just couldn't happen. Not now when they'd delivered a blow to Elijah.

God, he'd be pissed she'd taken on *four* of his men. It almost made her smile to think of.

She wasn't sure if she'd fallen asleep or lost consciousness or what, but suddenly the truck was stopped and Brady was already standing outside. She tried to push herself up a little in her seat, but it nearly caused her to moan in pain.

She bit it back last minute as Brady was opening the passenger door.

"Where are we?" she demanded. She looked around, but nothing was familiar. They were on a little gravel lot and there was a scrubby little yard in front of a tiny, *tiny* cabin on a small swell of land.

Beyond the cabin was pure beauty. A sparkling lake stretching out far and wide, bracketed in by rolling rock. If she had to guess, they were closer to the Badlands than they'd been out in Valiant County.

It distracted her enough that Brady had her unbuckled and back in his arms before she had a chance to protest.

"I can walk, Brady."

"But you're not going to. Not until I check you out." He started walking, as if she weighed next to nothing and his shoulder hadn't been hurt for months. He took the little stone stairs up to the cabin without even an extra huff of breath.

"Buddy of mine's," he offered conversationally, even though his expression was completely... She didn't have a word for it. Tense, determined, fierce. "Well, more Gage's buddy. Pretended like I was Gage. Haven't done that since middle school, and it was never me. Gage was always the one pretending."

"He couldn't have fooled anyone who actually knew you two."

"You'd be surprised." He set her down, with the kind of gentle care one might use with a one-hundred-year-old woman. Then he futzed around with a planter in the shape of a bass. Something wilted and brown was growing out of the fish's mouth, but Brady pulled a key out from underneath.

He unlocked the door, pushed it open, then turned to her.

She held up her hands to ward him off. "If you pick me up again, I'm going to deck you."

With quick efficiency, he moved her hands away and swept her into his arms again. Why did her stomach have to do flips every time he did that? And why couldn't she muster up the energy to actually punch him?

"Guess you're going to have to deck me."

She was so outraged she couldn't do anything but squeak as he marched her to the back of the cabin in maybe ten strides. He went straight into the bathroom and gently placed her on the floor again.

"Take off your clothes."

For a full ten seconds she could only stare at him. "I most certainly will *not*."

"You're bleeding God knows where. We need to get you cleaned up and patched up. Now. Shirt and pants off. You can leave your underwear on if you want to be weird about it, but I've got to see what kind of injuries we're dealing with."

"Weird ab—" She could feel fury and frustration somewhere deep underneath the pulsating pain of her body, but she couldn't seem to change any of that irritation into action. She leaned against the wall, trying to make it look like she was being casual, not needing something to prop her up. "Not the time to try to talk me into bed, Brady."

"Don't mess with me right now. Take off the clothes. I'm an EMT. I've seen plenty of naked women and manage to control myself each and every time. I have to see what kind of injuries you have so I know how to patch you up. Lose the clothes, Mills."

"How about you listen to the woman with the injuries. I'm fine. Just a bit banged up. I'll take a shower—alone, thank you very much. If I need a bandage, I'll ask for your expert services."

It didn't have the desired effect—which was to get him to back off. She figured it might at least hurt his pride a little if she took a shot at the EMT side of his profession. She knew Brady took the paramedic stuff very seriously, that he'd once wanted to be a doctor. Acting like all he did was slap on bandages should offend him.

But he merely narrowed his eyes at her. "What are you trying to hide?"

She bristled, her tone going up an octave. "Nothing."

"Bull," he returned. "You want to be difficult? Fine. I'll do it myself."

He moved toward her, and if she'd been 100 percent she would have fought him off. She would have done whatever it took to keep his hands off her.

But she was beaten up pretty good. There wasn't any fight left in her, there was only fear, and she was very afraid she'd cry if she let him take her shirt off her.

So, she whipped it off herself. It wasn't about being shirtless in front of him. Her sports bra was hardly different than a swimsuit or what she'd wear to the gym. But she knew his reaction to her wounds was going to... hurt somehow.

He swore, already leaping for the little cabinet under the sink. In possibly five seconds flat he had a washcloth pressed to the stab wound. She hadn't dared look at it herself, but maybe she should have, judging by the utter fury in his gaze.

"What the hell were you thinking?"

"It's not that bad," she said weakly. Maybe it was bad enough to have mentioned it. She'd only wanted to handle it herself. She didn't need him manhandling her and...

She blinked, desperately holding on to the tears that threatened. She didn't want to break down in front of him ever again. That one time in his apartment over Mak was bad enough. This would be worse.

Because she wasn't sad or upset. It was the adrenaline of the fight wearing off. It was the need for release. She didn't want to be petted or taken care of.

She wanted to be alone. To handle it herself. To build all her defenses back without someone here...taking care of her. Because if he took care of her, he'd see all the marks of how she'd failed to take care of herself.

What kind of cop was she, then?

She looked up at the ceiling, didn't answer his questions and definitely didn't dare look at him. She blinked and blinked and focused on staving off the tide of tears.

But then he did the damnedest thing. He rested his forehead on her shoulder and let out a shuddering breath. Something deep inside of her softened, warmed, fluttered. Without fully thinking through the move, she lifted her arm that didn't hurt too much and rested her hand on his head.

"I'm okay. Really," she managed to say without sounding as shaky as she felt. "Just a little flesh wound."

The sound he made was some mix of a groan of frustration and a laugh.

"You've fixed worse on people," she reminded him. "Your own brothers in fact."

He shook his head, but lifted it from her shoulder. He didn't look at her, his gaze was on the washcloth he was pressing to the wound. "All right." He blew out another shaky breath, but the inhale was steadier. He seemed to shrug off the moment. When his eyes finally met hers, they were clear, steady and calm. "Let's get you really cleaned up, and I'll see what I can do for the stab wound."

Chapter Thirteen

Brady instructed Cecilia to hold the towel firm against her wound. Even the brief glimpse he'd gotten told him she needed stitches. He was no stranger to stitching up his brothers, but mostly as a paramedic that skill was left to doctors at the hospital.

He started the shower and tried to focus on the practicalities. She didn't just have the stab wound. She had bruises and he'd need to make sure she hadn't broken anything. He'd also need to check for a head wound because she'd dozed off in the truck—whether exhaustion as the adrenaline wore off or loss of consciousness he couldn't be sure until he examined her.

But first and foremost she had to get the grime and blood off of her. She could stand and she was lucid, so a quick shower was the best option.

The fact she hadn't even acted like she was in that much pain just about did him in. Why had she hidden it? To what purpose?

He couldn't focus on that. He'd nearly fallen apart when she'd finally taken off her shirt and he'd seen that deep, bloody gash.

It hadn't even occurred to him she was *that* hurt. She'd been acting so...flippant. At least when he'd worked on his brothers it had always been pretty visible how bad off they were up front. And when he dealt with them he'd have privacy after to rebuild his defenses.

There wasn't going to be any privacy here until the Elijah threat was taken care of.

Still, he was a trained EMT. He should have a better handle on his reactions and he would. He would.

"Do you think you can handle a shower?"

"No. Why don't you sponge bathe me, Brady? Of course I can handle a *shower*. You know, if you give me some privacy."

"Sorry. I'm not going anywhere until we know you didn't suffer a head injury."

"I didn't."

"How do you know?"

"Wouldn't I know if I got knocked in the head?"

He didn't look at her, even to give her a raised-eyebrow look. "Does your head hurt?"

She was stubbornly silent, which was as clear a *yes* as an immediate denial would have been.

"I'll keep my eyes closed." He moved away from the shower that was going, nice and hot, enough to make the room a little hazy.

"You don't have to be *that* much of a gentleman. I don't think a glimpse of nipple is going to send you into a crazed sex haze."

Still, Brady kept his back to her and the shower. "Use soap," he instructed, trying to pretend like she was a child who needed to be told what to do. Not someone some warped part of his brain wanted to see naked.

Which could *not* be considered, so he focused on the next. He had a first aid kit in his pack. It had the appropriate disinfectant. He didn't have anything strong enough to numb the area where she'd need to get stitches. That was going to be a problem, because while he was in no doubt she'd handle it, he wasn't so sure *he* could handle giving her that much pain.

"Probably gonna need a little help with the sports bra," she said after a few seconds. "It clasps in the back, but…"

She didn't come out and say one of her arms hurt, but that was clearly the implication. She couldn't get them both behind her back, which was a bad sign. "You have to be in a lot of pain," he said flatly, turning to face her.

She still held the cloth to the gash on her side. "I'm alive, Brady. Managed to hold off four guys, one with a knife and one with a gun. I'll take the pain, thanks." She frowned. "What pack of four morons only brings one gun to kidnap someone?"

"The kind that aren't allowed to kill you," Brady said wryly, motioning for her to turn around so he could unclasp her bra for her. "Elijah will want to hurt you himself. Trust me. It's why my brothers and I are still alive." He focused on that, not the smooth expanse of her back.

She shivered—he was sure because of what he was saying, not because his fingers brushed her bare back to unclasp the bra.

"So, why doesn't he come after us?"

Brady forced himself to drop his hands and turn around again. "That I haven't quite figured out. Do you need help with anything else?"

"No. I think I can manage."

Brady focused on finding a towel rather than the sound of her taking off her pants or stepping into the shower. He breathed in the heavy, steamy air and refused to think about showers or nakedness, because the naked woman was hurt and bleeding with a potential head in-jury. He wouldn't even be able to determine if she had breaks or fractures. He wasn't a doctor. He didn't have the right equipment.

He should take her to a hospital. It left them with less control of the situation, but she'd get checked out. Fully checked out. It had to be worth the risk.

The water stopped and Brady heard the clang of the curtain rings moving against the shower curtain rod.

He held out the towel, keeping his gaze and body an-gled away from her.

The towel was tugged from his hands. "God, do you have to be so noble?" she demanded irritably as if it were some flaw.

"I don't know how to respond to that."

"Of course not. I managed to stay upright in the shower. Are you going to let me walk on my own or do I get the princess treatment again?"

"Put pressure on that gash," he instructed, rather than answer her question. "We should—"

"If you mention the word *hospital* I won't be respon-sible for my reaction, Brady. You're a trained, licensed EMT. You can check me out."

"You need stitches."

"I'm fine."

"You're not. I can tell without even a full examina-tion that it's deep, long and in a bad spot. We bend and move our sides far more than we know. If you don't get stitches, not only is it going to scar, but we're going to have to watch out for too much blood loss. Infection is a near certainty, and just plain not healing is an even bigger one."

"He says, from experience," she replied sarcastically.

She didn't know the half of it. "I know my way around a knife wound personally and medically, Cecilia."

"Get in a lot of knife fights?"

He ignored the question. Just closed that whole part of him off, encased it in ice. Had to or he'd never get through this.

"Oh, turn around for Pete's sake," she muttered. "I've got the towel on."

"A hospital would be a better bet," he insisted. Though he did turn around and face her, he kept his gaze on her eyes. Refused to dip to even her nose. Didn't check the towel placement or if she was putting pressure on her side where the gash was.

"Surely it's not that bad."

He tried not to let his irritation, and all the other feelings clawing inside his chest, get the best of him. "It's not that good."

"Right, but you've patched up worse," she insisted.

"Yeah. Usually with help or better supplies. I had an actual medical doctor talk me through fixing up Cody after his car accident, and that was only until he could get to the hospital. I don't have what I'd need to stitch you up, and you need more than a temporary solution."

"I'll be fine with a temporary solution." She waved a careless hand. "Just do what you can."

It was that carelessness, the utter refusal to listen to him that had his temper snapping. Every time his brothers came to him and said the same thing. Years of that, the past few months especially. Everyone was so sure they were *invincible* simply because he knew some basic emergency medical treatment.

He sucked it up and did his best, knowing it might not be good enough. What else was there to do?

But she didn't seem to get it. She was *seriously* hurt, and he wasn't a damn magician. "Did it occur to you—any of you ever—that you might not be fine? That I'm *not* a doctor. That I can't just magically *fix* you all when you come to me bloody and broken because of Ace Wyatt."

She stood very still, regarding him with a kind of blankness in her expression he recognized because it was the same face he put on when dealing with someone not quite stable.

"This doesn't have to do with Ace," she said, softly, almost sympathetically.

Which pissed him off even more. "It all has to do with Ace. Always. And forever. Now I need to find someplace to examine you, so stay put."

CECILIA WAS ALMOST tempted to do as Brady ordered as he stormed out of the small bathroom. There'd been something painful about his little outburst. A little too much truth in his frustration. If she stayed put, he'd compartmentalize it away and they could focus on the real problems in front of them.

But the fact he had all of that... Insecurity wasn't the right word. She was certain Brady understood his abilities, and knew he was an excellent EMT. The thing none of them had ever really thought about was the fact that doctors and EMTs weren't supposed to work on their families. That's when emotions came into play, and that put undue stress on the people doing the work.

The past few months, Brady had been tasked with working on some of the people he loved most in the world. They'd all asked it of him without a second thought—because it had been necessary. But no one seemed to think about the emotional toll it might put on the one cleaning up everyone else's injuries.

Especially while he was still trying to heal from his own complicated injury.

Cecilia inhaled. She didn't need to feel sorry for Brady. She was the one standing here wet, naked under a towel, bleeding and bruised. *She* was the one people should feel sorry for.

Trying to keep that in mind, she finally forced herself to move out of the bathroom and into the rest of the cabin. There was a kitchen/dining/living room all in the center, but right next door to the bathroom was another door.

It was open, and Brady was inside the bedroom fussing with the bedding. He'd already set out a line of first-aid stuff on one side of the bed. He didn't even look up, though clearly he knew she was standing there.

"Lay down. Once I've made sure everything aside from the stab wound is fine, you can get dressed and we'll decide what to do from there."

"No broken bones, Brady. No head wound. I've had both, I'd know what they'd feel like. I've got one nasty cut there, and a much less nasty one on my back. The rest are scratches that don't need any attention and bruises that could use some ibuprofen or some ice or a heating pad."

"Lay down, please."

She groaned at his overly solicitous tone, but she slid into the bed, still holding the towel around her. Once she was settled, Brady pulled the blanket up to her waist, then carefully rolled the towel up to reveal her abdomen without showing off anything interesting. Didn't even try.

Seriously, would it kill the guy to try to cop a feel or something?

He'd put on rubber gloves and immediately began inspecting the stab wound on her side. He sighed and shook his head as he inspected it. "I know what happens to a wound this deep that doesn't get stitches, Cecilia. We need to get to a hospital."

"Let's say we don't—"

"Ce—"

"Hear me out. Let's say we give it another couple days. You wash it out, bandage it up, and we try to get a few answers on Elijah's whereabouts or plan. *Then* I go to the hospital and get it stitched up. What's the risk of a few days?"

"Infection," he said, so seriously as if that was going to scare her off.

"Last time I checked, they have meds for that. Which you should be well acquainted with."

"I'm also well acquainted with what happens when you try to let a wound like this heal on its own but don't actually take it easy."

"How?"

"How what?" he muttered irritably. He grabbed some disinfectant from his lineup of first aid and Cecilia immediately tensed, waiting for the pain.

"How are you well acquainted with what happens when you don't care of a wound like this?" she asked through gritted teeth, waiting for the sting.

He stared at her for a full five seconds like she'd spoken in tongues, holding the cotton swab in one hand. "I…have a dangerous job." He focused back on her wound. "This is going to hurt."

She snorted. "Look, I'm a cop too. I know we get into

dangerous situations and we get hurt. I'm sure we've both got a few scars from *work*. But getting stabbed isn't exactly a day at the office." She hissed the last word out as the disinfectant stung like fire. "I think I would have heard about your stab wounds."

After a few humming breaths as she tried not to outwardly react to the sting, Brady spoke. His words were quiet and measured, but there was something lingering inside of him that was neither. "What do you think happens when you're a kid in a gang, Cecilia? Someone bakes you brownies?"

She blinked. *Oh.* Well, of course. Being hurt and not getting medical attention was probably life in the Sons of the Badlands. She just so often forgot he'd actually... spent years there. Innocent, vulnerable years. He was so good. So strong. She couldn't even picture it knowing what he'd looked like as a boy—reserved and gangly. It *hurt* trying to imagine. "Who stabbed you? Other kids?"

He was silent, but he was unwrapping butterfly bandages from their plastic wrapper, which meant she was getting out of a mandatory hospital visit for now.

"Brady."

He paid very careful attention to the wound on her side as he attached the bandages, one by one, along the line of sliced skin. "Ace had a game, is all. A nice little game just for me. Usually he missed."

Cecilia's blood went cold, but she knew if she let that seep into her voice he'd shut down and shut her out. She breathed, steadied her voice. "Usually?"

He shrugged, attached another bandage.

Then it dawned on her. She'd seen him with his shirt off that first night. She'd been somewhat surprised he'd been so marked up, but it hadn't occurred to her to wonder *why*. "All those scars. They're from not-misses. He stabbed you."

"He threw knives," Brady corrected, as if that were better instead of somehow worse. "Gotta learn to expect the unexpected. Though he was always pulling them out to toss my way, so I'm not sure how it was unexpected, but here I am trying to rationalize a madman's thinking."

"He threw knives at you," Cecilia said, because she *couldn't* picture that. Not just because it caused her pain, because it was nonsensical. It was *insane*.

Brady lifted his gaze to hers over the bandages. She realized she'd let emotion, horror mostly, seep into her tone.

"I'm alive, Cecilia. I survived. But I'd rather not take a trip down memory lane if you don't mind. Can you sit up?"

She blinked. It was her turn to feel like a foreign language was being spoken. After a few seconds she managed to sit up. He put a pad of gauze over the butterfly bandages, then used a wrap bandage around her waist to keep it in place.

"This is stupid. You need stitches. The chance of infection, of losing too much blood, of this not healing, are extraordinarily large."

She heard the exhaustion in his tone. The worry. And maybe even the ghost of a little boy whose father had thrown knives at him. She hadn't had that rough of a childhood. She'd thought it had been the worst, but it really hadn't been. Being poor and neglected and then moved into a loving house at the age of six had nothing on Brady's experience.

But she thought they needed the same thing in the face of those old ghosts. The only thing that had ever helped her had been to face down the current ones. And win. "Elijah's not coming for us, Brady. We have to go to him."

She thought he might pretend to misunderstand her, but his words were stark. "We don't know where he is."

"I know where he'll be. I know you do too."

Brady inhaled. "I promised myself a long time ago that I'd never go back there, Cecilia." He met her gaze. "Never."

She was closer to crying than she'd even been in the bathroom, but she didn't look away. "We need to."

Chapter Fourteen

Brady didn't precisely agree with Cecilia, but in the end he didn't argue with her. He'd patched her up best that he could, got her some clothes from her pack, ibuprofen for the pain, and ice for the particularly nasty bump under her eye—because apparently she'd gotten hit in the same exact spot as a few nights ago.

He ignored his own aches and pains as he ran through a shower. They'd agreed to spend the night at the cabin and get a fresh start in the morning. A fresh start doing *what* was still up in the air.

Go to the Sons camp? He'd promised himself he'd never do that, with one simple caveat: only if his brothers ever needed him to.

Cecilia wasn't his brother. Mak wasn't his brother. But wasn't it all the same? You went back if you had to protect the people you...cared about.

Brady dried off from the shower, examined his own injuries. His gunshot wound continued to heal, and that was something to be thankful for. He had a riot of bruises rising across his chest and arms, but that was to be expected after the fight they'd had. He was in a lot better shape than Cecilia.

He'd brought in a change of clothes but forgotten to

grab his own stash of bandages. They were going to run out at the rate they were going.

He took a moment to look at himself in the foggy mirror. He wasn't sure what he'd expected when he'd started down this path. He hadn't really *planned*—he'd only wanted to protect.

He'd been somewhat…disapproving of his brothers rushing in to face what they'd all left behind. He'd understood Jamison's need to help Liza save her young half sister from the human trafficking ring the Sons had been starting. A person, especially Jamison, couldn't turn his back on that. And yes, Cody obviously had to save his ex and his secret daughter from Ace's threats. And when Gage helped investigate the murder Felicity had been framed for, of course it ended up connecting to the Sons.

Everything did.

He'd known going in Elijah had ties to the Sons and his father, so going back to Sons territory seemed inevitable.

Still, he recoiled from it.

He scrubbed his hands over his face. A good night's sleep and surely he'd have a better handle on everything roiling around inside of him. He'd be able to compartmentalize and function as he normally did.

But there was something about *this* situation that made it harder. He'd patched up Cody's horrendous injuries. He'd helped Gage after he'd been basically tortured by Ace. Granted, those were after-the-fact situations. Mopping up a mess, not wading into one while worrying about the woman wading into it with him.

He didn't understand it, though. He trusted Cecilia, as much as any one of his brothers, to take care of herself. He didn't understand why this felt harder. Maybe it was his own weakness. A mental softening from all his time off.

He stepped out of the bathroom, determined to shove it all away again.

She was sitting up in the bed, though he'd told her to be as still as possible. Her hair was damp and leaving spots of wet on her T-shirt. She had an impressive bruise forming on her cheek.

She was not a weak woman, or even a soft one. She was all angles and muscle with a smart mouth and a sharp mind, who could take care of herself and save herself, no questions asked. He did not understand his desperate desire to wrap her up and keep her far from harm.

He wanted to protect his brothers, no doubt, and same for the Knight girls. He'd quickly and easily thrown himself in the way of harm to protect them, save them.

But this was different. This *thing* he felt toward Cecilia was different, and not liking it and pushing it away didn't seem to change anything.

When she glanced his way, she threw the covers off and started to move. "Oh my God, Brady. Look at you."

"Don't you dare get out of that bed. You are supposed to keep that cut immobile." He looked down at himself and frowned. "What?"

"You're *covered* in bruises," she said, outrage tingeing her words, though she had stopped herself from getting out of bed. "You didn't say you'd been hurt."

"I'm not hurt. Like you said, I know what serious injuries feel like. Just a little bruising."

"These aren't little. And there are quite a few."

"You really want to have this argument when I can still load you up in that truck and take you to a hospital?"

He stalked over to his pack and pulled out the bandage and disinfectant he needed for his shoulder.

"You really *don't* want to have this argument when you gave me hell for not telling you right away I'd been stabbed?"

"Stabbed. A stab wound that needs stitches and I—"

"You're insufferable." She held out a hand toward him when he sat down on the opposite side of the bed. "Give it to me."

"You need to be still."

"Give me the damn bandage, and scoot over here if you don't want me to move."

He grumbled and did as he was told. She smoothed the bandage on the back side, then he turned so she could do the front as well.

She touched his most pronounced scar, which was in a similar spot as her wound. The injuries were in fact quite similar, though he'd been ten when he'd gotten his. She sighed. "I don't know how you survived this and still became you, Brady. I really don't."

He shrugged, trying to ignore the effect her touch had on him. "You just do." He reached for his shirt, but something about her touching his scar kept him from his full range of motion.

"*You* do. You did. I know you don't want to go back there." She looked up at him, though her fingers lingered on his scar. "I don't want you to have to go back there."

"If you're about to suggest you go alone, you can—"

"No. No, I know better than that, believe it or not. We have to do this together. Have each other's backs. At some point that might mean splitting up, but not yet."

"Not ever."

She studied his face, as if looking for something. An

answer. A clue. A truth. She reached out and cupped his cheek with her hand, the other hand still pressed to his scar.

He held himself very still, trying to think back to all the arguments he'd had against this when she'd been throwing herself at him to irritate him.

But this wasn't that. Even he knew this wasn't that.

"Brady, I really thought I was going to die. Maybe not out there, but if they'd gotten me, taken me to Elijah, I knew it was over."

Fury spurted through him. "He won't—"

"Shh," she said lightly, her thumb brushing against his cheekbone. "I'd do it. I don't *want* to, but if it would keep Mak safe, I'd die for him. I think we all feel that about our families, but I've never actually been put in a position where I had to specifically accept it would be at someone's hands. Elijah's hands."

Maybe she wouldn't let him say it, but he'd do everything in *his* power to make sure that never, *ever* happened.

"I don't want him to take anything from me. I will fight tooth and nail to make sure you and Mak *and* I come out of this in one piece. I'm not being fatalistic here, I'm just telling you…"

She cupped his other cheek, moved so they were knee to knee. He would have admonished her for moving, but her body brushed his—lightning and need.

"I know it would change everything, but maybe everything needs to change. Maybe it's already changed."

He had to clear his throat to speak. "It wouldn't just change us. Our families. Duke isn't exactly thrilled with my brothers for similar happenings."

Her smile was soft, her touch on his face even softer.

"Duke doesn't approve of anything I've done. Becoming a cop. Living on the rez. Et cetera. He loves me anyway." She trailed her fingers over his cheeks. "You didn't have to do any of this. I brought you into this. I plopped Mak in your arms and—"

"Elijah already—"

"Shut up and *listen*, Brady. I came to you and convinced myself it was because you were the one who had the time, but it was because you were the one I trusted. I could have gone to Jamison or Cody—they have experience keeping children away from the Sons' reach. I could have gone to Tucker, he's a detective for heaven's sake. They all would have helped me. I came to you."

He didn't know how to react to that, or how to sift through the assault of emotions. Hope too big among them.

But then he didn't have to, because she kissed him. It was soft and gentle. He didn't think either of them had much of that in their lives. Maybe it was why they needed to show it to each other.

Maybe all this time he'd avoided her and that New Year's Eve kiss because he hadn't wanted to allow himself that. It certainly didn't feel right to take it now, except she needed it too.

And how could he resist giving her what she needed?

CECILIA WASN'T SURE what had changed inside of her. Only that something had opened up or eased. Something had shifted to make room for this, and once it had, she couldn't hide it away again.

She'd kissed Brady on New Year's Eve because he made her feel something she couldn't name, and for a long time she hadn't wanted to. Still, it hadn't gone away so she'd convinced herself it was merely attraction and backed off when Brady made her understand it couldn't be only that.

Now, just a little while later, she was the one kissing him. Saying things had already changed.

His hands were gentle, his kiss was *dreamy*, and it was as if those tiny pieces inside of her that had still felt so out of place clicked together and made sense.

If it hadn't been for this afternoon, fear of change would have continued to win—continued to keep her hands off when it came to Brady. But fear of death— and the possibility of that death being very much right in her face—made the fear of change weaker. Change was hard, but regret was too steep a price to pay.

What would be the point of this life she'd been given if she didn't accept all the emotions inside of her? She wasn't perfect. She wasn't even good half the time, but the things she felt for Brady were real. They were here.

Why had she been avoiding that? To not be embarrassed? To not be hurt? It seemed so *silly* in the face of what could have been her last day on earth. Maybe that was dramatic, but it had led her here.

No one had ever kissed her like she was both fragile and elemental all at the same time. But it was more than just the kiss.

No man, including Duke—the only man in her life she'd let herself truly love as both uncle and father figure—had ever made her feel understood. No one in her whole life had made it seem like the strong parts of her and the weaker parts of her were one complex package…one that someone could still want and care for. She was either fully strong or fully weak to others, but inside she was both.

She didn't want to be protected, but sometimes she wanted to be soothed. She didn't need anyone to fight her fights, but sometimes she needed someone to dress her wounds. Literally. Figuratively.

Brady was that. Just…by being him.

His fingers tightened in her hair, and the kiss that had begun as soft and lazy heated, sharpened. Something ignited deep inside of her, a hunger she hadn't really thought *could* exist inside of her. It had certainly never leapt to life before.

But now…now she wanted to sink into that heat and that unfurling desperation. It was new and it was heady and it was better than all that had come before.

But she could feel Brady pulling back. "You're hurt," Brady murmured against her mouth, as if he wanted to break the kiss but couldn't quite bring himself to.

She was vaguely aware of her sore body, but mostly those aches and pains were buried underneath the sparkling warmth of lust. She didn't just want a kiss, she wanted Brady's body on hers. She wanted to get lost for a few minutes in something other than pain and fear.

Some part of her she didn't fully understand wanted the hope of more with Brady when this was all over. Change seemed better than standing in the same place feeling alone. Feeling as though no one understood her or loved her as a whole, complex human being.

She sank into another kiss, desperate for him to forget her injuries. Forget where they were and what they had to do and finish *this*.

"I'll live," she insisted. "I want this, Brady. I want you."

He undressed her, and she *knew* he was being mindful of her injuries, but she didn't *feel* it. She felt worshipped and surrounded by something bigger than she could describe. A light, a warmth, a renewal of who she was.

Made somehow more awe-inspiring by the fact the man currently kissing her scrapes and caressing her many bruises was…gorgeous. He was all muscle and control. In another world he might have been a movie star, if he wasn't so raw and real. So… Brady. Good and noble and making her body hum with a desperate need she was sure, so *sure*, he could take care of.

And he did, entering her, moving with her, a gentle, heated tangle of all those things she'd been afraid of: change, need, hope.

Why had those been fears? When they were this *good*. This comforting and *right*.

He said her name and it echoed inside of her. It felt like a hushed *finally*. Like they'd been waiting all their years to do this, when she didn't think they had. Certainly not consciously.

But it was here now, and she knew this was just… it. Him. Them.

She slid her fingers through his hair, focused on pleasure over the pain of her injuries, and gave herself over in a way she'd never done before. Because she trusted Brady. Wholeheartedly. He was the person she went to when she was in the most trouble, and he was the person she wanted to be with in this dangerous, desperate situation.

Always.

The crest of release washed over her, a slow roll of pleasure and hope and relaxation. A *finally* whispered through her body as Brady followed her into oblivion.

She sighed into his neck, snuggled in when he carefully tucked her against his body, and slept.

Chapter Fifteen

When Brady's phone trilled, waking him from a deep, restful sleep, he jerked, then immediately relaxed his body so he didn't jostle Cecilia, still curled up against him. Naked.

He hadn't meant to fall asleep. Then again he hadn't meant to sleep with Cecilia. But both had happened and left him feeling…settled. Instead of the scatterbrained panic, hopping from one problem to another, he felt clearheaded.

Guilt could seep in if he let it. That this was the wrong time and the wrong place and it was not precisely…*right*.

But it had felt right. Righter than most of the choices he'd made in the past year or so.

He had spent a lot of years in his life convincing himself that no one could understand him like his brothers did. They'd shared a kind of tragedy, something other people couldn't imagine. Based on the way Cecilia had reacted to his explanation of his scars, she couldn't imagine it either.

But she treated him like something other than the boy who'd spent his formative years in that gang. More than a piece of the Wyatt whole.

He yawned when his phone trilled again. He'd almost forgotten that's what had woken him up in the first place. A repeated phone call when the world was still dark could mean nothing good. He grabbed his phone and saw Cody's name on the screen.

He only got half of his brother's name out before Cody was talking over him. "There's been a fire at Duke's. Everyone's safe and fine, but it was set purposefully and in the middle of the night like this. It was meant to scare us."

Any good feelings or relaxation seeped out of him. He tensed and disentangled himself from Cecilia, pushing into a seated position on the bed. "You're sure everyone's all right?"

"Thank God for Dev making the dogs stay with us at the Knights'. Cash was barking before I think the thing was even lit. I thought for sure it was a ploy to get us out, but nothing else happened. We're all over at Grandma's and we haven't been able to find anyone on the property."

"What is it?" Cecilia hissed from behind him.

He waved her off. "It's got to be Elijah, though."

"Seems the only option. Everyone is fine, so I'm not sure what his purpose was. They got around my security measures, but didn't actually hurt anyone or take Mak? All these near misses seem...unlikely."

"Yeah. Yeah, they do. Listen, I've got to explain it to Cecilia. Then we'll go from there. Keep watch, though. Be careful. Anything else happens, keep us updated."

"Same," Cody said before Brady ended the call.

"What is it?" Cecilia demanded, before he'd fully pressed End. "Mak? Is it—"

He took her hands in his, trying to find his own calm and reason before he attempted to give her any. "Mak is fine. Everyone is fine. There's been a fire at Duke's house. Luckily, Dev had been making Sarah take care of his dogs and they—"

She immediately threw the sheets off and began to pick up her clothes. He could tell she regretted the sudden movements by the hiss of her breath, but she kept going. "We have to go. We have to go to them."

"No. No, I don't think so." He got out of bed himself, slid his own boxers and shorts back on before crossing to her side of the bed where she was now fully dressed and looking at him furiously. "Sit down. Don't hurt yourself. Listen."

"Listen? Listen!" She waved her arms wildly, then winced. "They burn down Duke's house—his *house*—at night which means even if they're okay Duke and Sarah and oh, God, Brianna and Nina were staying there and Rachel, she—"

Brady stood in front of her and took her hands in his again. It was the only thing to keep her still, and when she tugged he squeezed hard enough to have her taking a sharp breath. "Another one," he ordered. "Deep breath in, and then out."

He didn't expect her to listen, but she did. Still, when her gaze met his it was determined. Haunted. "We have to go. Now."

"Cecilia, no. We can't do that. This is what he wants from you. From us. Think."

She wrenched her hands out of his, groaning out loud this time. "I don't give a flying leap what he wants from me. He burns down my family's home and thinks I'm going to what? What would you have me do, Brady? Sit here? No. I refuse. I don't care what Elijah's plans are."

"You need to," he said sharply. He didn't like being sharp with her, not right now, so he softened his words by cupping her face with his hands. "*We* need to. Remember you're not alone. Mak's not alone. So, we have to work through that fear and not let it lead us. That's what he wants. It's what they always want. When fear wins, so do they." He couldn't let Elijah win *ever*, but now it seemed even more imperative to find an end. For all of them. So Cecilia could heal, so Duke could rebuild, so they could live…normally, if that was ever possible.

She rested her hands over his on her face. "But I *am* afraid, Brady," she said in little more than a whisper.

He knew that was a great big hard admission for her, so he made his own. "I know. So am I. Fear is normal. We just can't let it make the decisions. When you got Mak, you didn't panic. You didn't run right to me. You made plans. You were careful, and so far Mak is safe and sound. So that's what we have to do."

She sucked in a breath and nodded with it. "Okay, okay. Maybe you're right. I knew… I knew I couldn't just run with him or he'd be hurt. I had to think. I had to plan. So, yeah. That's what we have to do. So… He set a fire—"

"That didn't hurt anyone. It's important to remember that. Everyone is fine. He set a fire to lure us home. To *scare* us home. I believe that. Don't you?"

She didn't answer right away. He could tell she gave herself the time and space to really think it over. "Yeah. He's tired of sending his goons after us and failing. He's setting a trap."

"We can't fall for it. We need to do the opposite of what he'll expect. I think…" He sighed heavily. This changed things. There was no escaping what he'd hoped to avoid. "You were right. We need to go into Sons territory. He doesn't think we will, which means we'll have the element of surprise. We need to take him off guard. It's the only way we win."

She searched his face, as if looking for doubt or that earlier reticence. She didn't find it. He wouldn't let her.

She nodded once. "All right. Let's pack."

BRADY EXPLAINED TO her where the fishing cabin was located, and that it wasn't that far from the Sons' current camp on the east side of the Badlands. They were going to have to be strategic about where and how they entered the area, but getting there wouldn't be too long of a haul.

They'd both gotten a couple hours sleep, and that would have to tide them over for a while. She wanted to be in Sons territory by sunrise, but they'd have to hurry.

She didn't let herself think about Mak, or her childhood home being on fire. She didn't think of poor Nina and Cody having to get Brianna out, or what the confusion might have done to Rachel in worse circumstances. She couldn't even begin to let herself think about what would have happened if the dogs hadn't been there.

Her brain wanted to go in *all* those directions, but she couldn't let it. She had to focus on Elijah. How to take him off guard. How to take him down before he did another thing to hurt or scare her family.

"I found a backpack," Cecilia offered, coming into the bedroom where Brady was carefully counting first aid items and foodstuffs and the few camping supplies Grandma Pauline had thought to pack them. "We can both carry a pack now," Cecilia said.

"You better fill yours with bandages and anything that can be used as bandages," Brady muttered.

"I think we've got a lot bigger fish to fry than fussing over a few..." She trailed off at the look he gave her. It was a warning and a censure and yeah, a little hot. Since they didn't have time for a repeat earlier performance she held up her hand. "Okay, the injuries are dangerous and we have to take them seriously."

"You shouldn't be hiking, camping or fighting off biker gang members at all. Nothing is going to heal. *Something* will get infected, and I promise you it's not the picnic you seem to think."

"I suppose not, but once we do all those things, and get Elijah arrested, you can lock me up and nurse me back to health in whatever ways you see fit."

He snorted. "You wouldn't agree to that in a million years." He surveyed the items he'd spread out. "Your pack needs to be lighter. I don't want you arguing over that. It's because of the extent of your injuries, not because you *can't*. Got it?"

She wanted to argue, just out of spite or pride, but both had to be left behind. Elijah had started a fire at Duke's house, and even if he hadn't hurt people, he'd made it clear he could.

That couldn't continue.

She put the pack she'd found on the bed next to Brady's, then let him divvy up the supplies as he saw fit. She didn't let herself watch, because she would have argued.

"We'll get as close as we can to Flynn in the truck. It'll be a hike to get to the main camp."

"Yeah, but I don't think he'll expect us here. Even if we never show up at the ranches, he won't think we've come for him. He'll think we've only run farther away. He won't expect a direct attack. I don't think he could."

"No, I don't think he could," Brady agreed. "But, we have to be prepared if he does." Brady stood back and examined both packs, now full. He scratched a hand through his hair. "This could easily be a suicide mission. Even if the Sons are weaker than they were, the fact they're still inhabiting Flynn and not moving on to a new, smaller camp means they're not falling apart, or even factioning off from what we can tell."

"The camp wasn't at Flynn when you were a kid."

"No. Flynn is Ace's origin story. It's where he was abandoned. It's his mecca, and it's where he tried to make us all into Wyatt men." Brady rolled his shoulders as if to physically move past those old, awful memories. "He built camp there this year to make his final stand... or something. Didn't quite go as planned for him."

"And if Elijah is Ace's son, he might be the cohesive reason they're not splitting off."

Brady nodded grimly. "Exactly."

He was being stoic. Planning and trying to figure the situation out, but the weight of what he would be facing hung over him. "I know this is hard for you."

Brady shrugged that away. "Jamison did it. To save Gigi. I can do it."

"The ability to do something and the toll it takes to do something aren't the same."

His gaze met hers over the bed. "If you're trying to talk me out of something, you don't know me very well."

"Situation reversed, you'd do the same thing, only you'd tell me you were trying to protect me."

"Is that what you're trying to do?"

She shrugged much like he had. "Maybe." It felt a little uncomfortable. After all, Brady was bigger, stronger and more versed in what the Sons could do than she was. It seemed kind of ludicrous, even with her law enforcement background, that she *could* protect him.

But the more she learned about his horrifying childhood, the more she wanted to at least shelter him from that.

"It won't affect my ability to get this done."

Cecilia frowned. Were all men this dense or only Wyatt men? "Maybe I was worried about something else."

"Like what?"

"Like your *feelings*, Brady."

His eyebrows drew together like he didn't understand how that could possibly be a concern.

Which irritated her enough to say something she'd planned to keep to herself. "When you care about someone, you care a little if they have to relive their childhood trauma."

He stared at her for a minute before skirting the bed. She wanted to run away. To forget they'd ever had a conversation about anything. There were far bigger problems than *feelings*.

But he came right up to her and touched her cheek. "I'd relive a hundred childhood traumas for that innocent baby. For my brothers. For the Knights. For a lot of people."

Outrage and hurt chased around inside of her chest, leaving her unable to speak or move. He'd do it for *anyone*. Fine and dandy.

"It would be my duty, no question. But I'm doing this not just as a duty, Cecilia. Not just because you'd do it without me or because God knows you need someone making sure you take as much care of those injuries as possible."

His fingers traced her jaw, causing a shiver to snake through her even as she tried to stand tall and unmoved.

He had just told her he'd do this for *anyone*, as if that wasn't some kind of warped slap in the face.

"I love my brothers with everything I am, but because of how we grew up there...we have to protect each other. Have to. I'm sure we've all felt a certain level of protectiveness for you girls, but it's not the same. Early on I had to accept I can't save or protect everyone."

"What is your *point*, Brady?" she muttered, wishing she had the wherewithal to pull away from his hand gently caressing her cheek.

"The point is there's no obligation here. Not really. I could convince myself I don't need to help you but that would be denial. Because in the end, for whatever reason, I want to be by your side for your fights, and I want you by my side for mine. Not blood, not obligation, not shared crappy history, but because you're the person I need. Because there's something here. I wouldn't say I would have chosen that, but there's no turning back now."

Cecilia didn't often find herself speechless, but that just about did it. Words were not her forte, more so, she didn't think they were particularly Brady's forte. But he'd laid it all out. Honesty complete with uncertainty of how or why, but a certainty it existed.

And he was still touching her face, watching her like there was anything she *could* say.

She cleared her throat. "When this is over..." She didn't know what she was trying to say. Or maybe she did and just didn't want to admit it to herself. The words stuck in her scratchy throat anyway.

Brady pressed a kiss to her forehead, briefly rested his cheek on the top of her head. "Let's get it over, first."

Which somehow wasn't the answer she wanted. Or

the reassurance. "Just know, if you take it all back, I'll kick your butt to Antarctica *and* tell your family you're a turd."

A smile tugged at his lips despite the pressing, dangerous circumstances. "Deal."

Chapter Sixteen

Brady did best with a specific goal in mind. The goal was to get to Elijah before they were expected. If he focused on that goal, he didn't think about how close he was to stepping into his own personal hellscape, or that Cecilia was seriously compromised by her injuries.

It was still dark when they reached as close to the Sons camp as he dared go by truck. The sky to the east hinted at the faint glow of dawn, but the stars still shone brilliantly above the inky dark of the shadowy Badlands.

It was beautiful and stark and it had Brady's chest tightening in a vise. His father had believed this land had anointed him some kind of god, and so Brady had never had any deep, abiding love for it.

But he remained, didn't he? He could have moved. He could have left South Dakota altogether, but he still lived just a quick drive from the place where all his nightmares had been born.

He wasn't sure what that said about him, and knew he didn't have time to figure it out now.

"Jamison and Liza did their best to give me an idea of the different areas of camp. Liza wasn't familiar with Elijah—not as a member, or a high-ranking official."

"What about as Ace's potential son?" Cecilia asked.

Brady shook his head. "I didn't bring it up, but she would have told Jamison if she'd heard anything like that."

"And you think Jamison would tell you?"

"Maybe not before, but knowing Elijah is after Mak and we're after Elijah? Yeah. He would. He'd have to."

"So, we have an idea of how the camp is laid out. Any idea where we find Elijah in it?"

"Depends. What Liza described to me isn't all that different than the camps when I was a kid. Different location, but same basic tenants. There were a few more permanent residences than the Sons are used to, but those were blown up a few months ago by North Star."

Cody had been part of North Star, a secretive group working to take down the Sons of the Badlands, and had delivered the first devastating blow to the Sons by taking out some of their higher-ranking members and arresting Ace, but still the Sons continued to exist, and cause harm.

Brady considered what he knew about the gang both from growing up within its confines, his work as a police officer, and what Liza had told him during their phone call.

"My guess is they constricted. Got closer together. That'll help. But I don't know where Elijah fits in the hierarchy. Ace was still in charge when Liza was there."

"He has men he can send after us. Doesn't that put him high up?"

"I think so. The guy with the gun yesterday—I recognized him. Not by name, but I remember that face. He's not just Elijah's man, he's been a Sons member for a while. Elijah has to be some kind of leader to have veteran members doing his bidding."

"Unless it's a coup. Maybe he's trying to overthrow Ace? He's recruited men in the Sons like he recruited some kids from the rez?"

"Could be. One thing we know is that with Ace in jail, the foundations of the Sons have been shaky. Cody overheard them talking about power vacuums a few months ago."

"Maybe Elijah filled it."

"Maybe." Brady took a deep breath. "It's the hypothesis I'm going to work off of, and it just so happens I know where the powerful men of the Sons congregate."

She shifted in the seat. They were sitting in the dark so he couldn't see her face, but he didn't really want to. He didn't like to be reminded of his father's former standing in the Sons. He didn't imagine other people found it very comfortable either.

"You know, I don't know anything about my father. He could be the leader of some gang somewhere. He could be a murderer. He could be a million terrible things."

"The difference is I do know. I appreciate you trying to comfort me, but I know exactly what my father is and what he's done." Probably not everything, but certainly enough to be haunted by it.

"And I know exactly who you are and what you'll do." Her hand found his in the dark of the truck.

He squeezed it. They needed to get going, put some distance in before the sun rose. He kept her hand in his. "I need you to promise me that you'll be honest with me about the state of your injuries. If things hurt. If there's bleeding—or bleeding through bandages. You have to let me know when we need to stop and take care of those issues. I need you to promise."

She was quiet for a few humming seconds, and he waited for the lie or the argument.

"All right," she said gravely, with enough weight and time between his words and hers for him to believe her. "I promise."

He gave her hand a squeeze. "Then let's get going."

They both got out of the truck, loaded their packs on their backs, and set out into the rocky landscape before them.

Brady had his cell phone on silent, though the service out here would be patchy at best. He had a mental idea of the area that hadn't changed all that much since he'd been tasked with survival out here as a child. He had the pack on his back and he had an injured Cecilia hiking beside him in the dark.

Not exactly where he'd planned to be a few weeks ago, or months ago, or certainly after New Year's Eve.

He'd had some disdain for the way Gage and Felicity had gotten together. Brady could admit it now, in the privacy of his own thoughts. He'd understood Liza and Jamison, Nina and Cody—they'd had a history before going through their ordeals. But Felicity had been harboring a crush on Brady for he wasn't sure how long. Brady hadn't understood how dangerous situations gave way to honest, deep feelings.

No matter that he could see Gage and Felicity now and knew they were happy, he'd been skeptical.

But now he understood that danger and running stripped away the walls and the safety exits you built for yourself without fully realizing it. He'd been able to lecture Cecilia about kissing him on New Year's Eve because his life had been intact and he'd been able to use that as an excuse to wedge between them.

But danger—life or death danger. Worry—keeping a baby safe worry. These were the things that stripped you to nothing but who and what you were.

It was a lot harder to fight feelings here.

Brady took a deep breath of the canyon air. He didn't love the Badlands, and he didn't love the act of hiking—both brought back ugly memories of an unpleasant childhood. He preferred the rolling hills of the ranch or the sturdy, square grids of town.

Because in the dark, in the unusual shapes of the Badlands built by rivers and wind, Brady knew the only thing they were really going to find was danger.

DAWN BROKE, PINK and pearly. A gentle easing of sun over dark. It felt like some kind of promise. Peace.

Cecilia knew Brady was keeping the hiking pace slow for her. Normally she would have chastised him for it, but everything hurt. Her feet, her body, her injuries—especially the stab wound. Her head pounded and even though he made her stop every so often and drink water, her mouth was miserably dry.

She was both hungry and nauseous and utterly, completely miserable. She walked on anyway, because Elijah or his men had set a fire at her childhood home with the people she loved most in the world inside.

She glanced at the man in front of her, bathed in the golden light of sunrise.

Love was a very strange, complicated word. She adjusted her pack, happy to focus on how heavy the light load felt rather than anything like *love*.

"Need a break?"

"No. No. Rather get this over with than break."

"I think we're close enough if we can get high enough,

we can see the camp. I want to climb up here and try," Brady said, pointing to a large, steep rock outcropping. "You can stay put, be the lookout."

Cecilia shaded her eyes with her hand. The climb looked difficult even if she were in perfect health. Still, she didn't want to be down here caught off guard if someone came upon her, or vice versa. "Let's see what I can do."

"Favor that side," he instructed. Clearly he didn't want her to make the climb, but didn't want to leave her alone either. They started the climb, and Brady basically hovered over her trying to mitigate any effort to her side.

She wanted to be irritated, but she wouldn't have made it without his help. Even *with* his help, she felt more than a little battered when they reached the top. But she could almost put that aside when she looked out below.

This wasn't strictly national park land, but the Badlands still stretched out, all canyons and valleys with only the occasional patch of flat and grass. In the lowest valley, some distance off, there was clearly a camp of some kind

And while they were alone in *this* moment, it was clear people used the flat area of this rock outcropping. There was a lockbox dug into the ground, rocks pushed together to form a kind of bench. Signs of footprints.

"Lookouts," Cecilia muttered, toeing the locked box.

"Might have caught them during the dawn changing of the guard," Brady said, looking out over the valley below. "But they don't keep lookouts all the time. With their diminishing numbers they probably only do it when there's a threat."

"What would be considered a threat?"

"Cops or federal agents mostly. A few months before Jamison got Cody out, there was a big ATF investigation. Nerves were high. Always a lookout then."

She couldn't help but watch him when he offered little pieces of his childhood like that. It was purposeful. He'd never once spoken about his time in the Sons to her before, and so doing it now had to be because…

Well, because he'd decided to trust her. Or care about her. Or something.

He pointed to the camp below. "If Elijah has an actual position of importance, and I'm thinking he does, that's his compound right there to the north. He might not have the main tent, but he'd have a tent in that area."

"So we climb back down and hike around to the north side?"

"Not to the north, no. The main compound is more guarded than the rest. They'll have guards positioned all along the north perimeter to make sure no one tries anything. I think especially with all the factions and power issues, you're going to have a lot of presence there."

"We can't exactly cut through the camp."

"No. I'm too recognizable, and you may be too at this point. It's going out on a limb, but I don't think he'd be here right now. He's either at the rez, or close to the ranches. He's going to be somewhere he thinks we're going. So, our goal is to cut him off before he gets to the camp when he realizes we're not rushing home."

Brady pointed again, this time to the southern portion of the camp. "That's the main entrance. See how they've got it set up? You've got tire tracks coming in right there—and I don't see any other vehicle points of access. So, that's the road in."

"He's not going to be alone."

"No. And we can't just ambush him. All that does is land us in another fight, and it doesn't give us any grounds to arrest him."

"So, what are you proposing then?"

Brady finally took his gaze off the camp below. "Do you know how Jamison created a big enough distraction for me and Gage to escape?"

Cecilia wasn't sure she wanted to know. Every time he told her some awful story about his childhood she wanted to wrap him in a hug. Which wasn't exactly a comfortable reaction for her, even if she was coming around to the idea of...well, whatever she felt for Brady.

"He'd gotten Cody out almost two years before us. A few months before us, he'd gotten Tuck out. Obviously, the suspicion was that Jamison had orchestrated it, but no matter how Ace tried, he couldn't figure out how. He beat Jamison, he beat Gage, he beat Dev. He threatened, raged, demanded answers from the people around us, but he never could find actual evidence that Jamison was behind the escapes."

"Why didn't he beat you?" Cecilia asked.

Brady blinked. Then he turned away from the camp, made a move to climb down.

"Brady. I asked you a question."

"He believed me when I said I didn't know since he said I couldn't lie to save my life. It wasn't worth the energy to beat me." He held out his hand to help her down the first steep descent. She knew she should just take his hand, not react to that...horror.

But it was so *complex* in its horror, and the more she got a glimpse into what he'd endured the more in awe of him she was. No *wonder* he could be a little stuffy and standoffish. No *wonder* the rules meant so much to him.

Why on earth had he slept with *her*?

Which wasn't a question they had any time for.

"The point of the story is that Jamison created a distraction," Brady continued, waiting for her to take his hand. "He ambushed someone he knew had been working with the cops, called a Sons meeting and told Ace this was the man he'd been looking for."

Cecilia nearly stumbled as Brady helped her down. "Jamison threw someone under the bus?" She couldn't begin to imagine. He'd be right to. He and his brothers stuck in hell, she wouldn't blame Jamison a bit. Still, it surprised her.

"Not exactly. The guy *had* been working with the cops, but he'd gotten pissed off and killed one of them. So, while Jamison had set this meeting in motion, he'd also managed to send evidence to the local police department that this man was the culprit. So, the distraction was twofold—finally finding the perpetrator, and the cops coming to the compound."

"That sounds complicated."

"It was. I don't know how many weeks he spent working it all out, getting the timing right. And he did it all on his own. Well, I think Liza helped him. We still almost got caught. All that and we still almost got caught." Brady shook his head as if he could shake away old, bad memories with it. "Anyway, point is we need that kind of distraction. Something to keep Elijah focused and busy on one hand, while we're working to arrest him on the other."

Cecilia looked around the vast landscape. The camp was now hidden behind the rocks to their backs. "How on earth are we going to do that?"

Brady paused. "Well, he wants both of us for different reasons. If he had one of us…"

Brady trailed off.

"You don't honestly think one of us could be a distraction?"

"It makes sense. One to distract, and one to observe the arrestable offense. And then move forward with the arresting."

"And let me guess—you think *you* should be the distraction?"

"Actually, no. I think it should be you."

Chapter Seventeen

Cecilia stared at him, mouth actually hanging open. She'd stopped her forward progress down the steep incline, but she still held on to his hand.

Brady couldn't say he *liked* his idea, but unfortunately it was the most sensible. He thought she would have seen that herself, but apparently not.

"Unfortunately it makes sense. You're hurt, which means it's going to be harder for you to be stealthy. It'd make more sense for you to pretend to be caught. I can move around easier, observe with more ease and care, *and* arrest with more force. Plus, your jurisdiction is limited to the rez. While we're outside Valiant County lines, I've got more of a legal standing than you. In a court of law."

She blinked, mouth still hanging open. When she finally spoke, it was only to echo his own words. "Court of law."

"It has to be legal, Cecilia."

She blinked again, multiple times, as if that would somehow change anything. "You're going to let me be a sacrificial human diversion. You said we'd never split up and you want to do just that."

"Let's not use the word *sacrificial*. All the elements

have to come together right. Including making sure we've isolated Elijah before we allow you to be any kind of diversion. Then, it has to be absolutely certain I'll be able to follow, observe and arrest. Not split up, give the illusion of splitting up."

She finally started moving forward again, letting him take some of her weight on the way down. When they reached more even ground and a tuft of grass amidst the rocky terrain around them, he started leading her toward the best positioning for their purposes.

"We'll want to keep ourselves by the road, a ways away from camp. The biggest challenge right now is to figure out a way to block Elijah from getting to camp— and keeping him separate from camp if we do let him catch you."

"Let him catch me. You're going to *let* Elijah catch me."

"No, *I'm* not going to let him, Cecilia. You're going to either make the decision to be the diversion or not. If you don't want to do it, we'll devise a new plan." And part of him really wanted her to refuse, even though he knew she wouldn't. Even though this was the only way.

"We can't do this alone. It's just not possible with only the two of us. Not this close to literally *hundreds* of people who'd help him."

"What about three of us?"

At the sound of a third voice, Brady whirled, gun in hand. He hadn't heard a sound, even a potential for someone sneaking up on them. He was ready to shoot first and ask questions later, but the voice was too familiar.

Brady stared at his brother for a full twenty seconds,

gun still pointed at him. "Tucker. How... Wh... What on earth are you doing here?"

Tucker's smile was easy, but it hid something that made Brady fully uneasy. "I'm a detective. I'm detectiving."

That didn't make any sense. Brady could only frown at Tucker. "This isn't your jurisdiction."

Tuck shrugged. "I needed to do some looking myself and get a grasp on what I'll need local law enforcement to do when we're ready to move. It's a pretty complicated case. Lots of departments and moving parts."

None of that made any sense, least of all Tucker having some case that tied to the Sons that none of them knew about.

"And you just *happened* to come across us here in the middle of nowhere?" Cecilia demanded, not even trying to hide her suspicion.

Brady didn't know how to be suspicious of his own brother, even when none of this felt right.

"It's not exactly the middle of nowhere," Tucker replied, unoffended. "It's the Sons lookout that gives the whole camp's layout." Tucker waved an arm as if to encompass the camp behind the large outcropping they'd just climbed down. "And now I can help you guys."

"How did you find us?" Brady returned.

"I'm not here for you, Brady. I mean, I can help. I want to. But it isn't why I was here. I was here for my job. I heard you guys and came closer. By the way, I listened to your plan and it kind of sucks without backup."

"I wouldn't call one more person backup," Cecilia replied, her demeanor still suspicious.

Brady could only feel conflicted. His gut was telling him that something was off, but this was Tucker. Tucker was… Probably the most well-adjusted out of all of them. He was good like Jamison, without Jamison's penchant for taking on too much responsibility. He worked hard like Brady without letting it make him too uptight. He had Gage's good humor without using it as a shield.

But none of this made sense, and Brady didn't like the fact Tucker was clearly lying to them. To *him*. When had Tucker ever lied?

"Elijah was camped out near the ranches. Had a small group with him. Only two other men that we could tell. The group or person who started the fire is gone, so he's traveling light. So if we can somehow take out his communication, three against three isn't such bad odds."

Brady opened his mouth to tell Tucker Cecilia was hurt and didn't count as a full person, but he found something so off-putting about all of this, he just closed it right back up. He couldn't put Cecilia at risk until this felt less…wrong.

"You can't be serious," Cecilia said. "You can't honestly think we buy any of this."

Some of the forced cheerfulness melted off Tucker's face. "But if you buy it, I can help." He turned his attention from Cecilia to Brady. "Surely you trust me to help."

Brady had never once questioned his brother's honesty or loyalty. Even as kids. Tucker was honest to a fault. On more than one occasion the Wyatt brothers had ganged up on Tuck for telling Grandma Pauline something she would have been better off not knowing.

Nothing about this felt right or honest, but it was *Tucker*. "Of course we do."

"Speak for yourself," Cecilia interjected. "You're acting fishy as hell. I don't trust that for a minute."

"Cecilia," Brady muttered.

"No, it's all right. She doesn't have to trust me." Tuck smiled. "But you trust me, Brady. Right?"

Never in his life had he hesitated to trust one of his brothers. It was alarming to hesitate now. But something wasn't right—and he didn't know how to figure out what.

CECILIA FELT A little bit like crying. Tucker Wyatt wasn't some Sons spy. She knew that in her gut, in her heart.

But her mind was telling her he was sure acting like one.

It didn't take anyone with some great understanding of Brady to see that the hesitation cost him. Hurt him. Hence the tears, because the idea of Brady being laid low by his brother's potential betrayal just ate her up inside.

But how could they trust Tucker with their lives when he very clearly wasn't telling the truth?

"I trust you, Tuck. How could I not?" Brady said, very gravely, very carefully as if every word was picked for greatest effect. "You've never given me a reason not to."

Cecilia kept her mouth shut, even though *shady appearance out of nowhere* was at the top of her list for not trusting him.

"My theory is they'll head back to camp this afternoon. They won't wait around at the ranches *too* long for you to show up, because if you're not going to rush back, you're probably not coming, right?"

"Were you there when Cody called me to tell me about the fire?" Brady asked, frown still in place.

"In the room? No. Dev and I were out searching for signs of Elijah's men."

"But you were home at the ranch when the fire started?"

"Well, yeah, we've all been taking turns keeping

close. If we're all there it looks suspicious, so Jamison and Liza were back in Bonesteel with Gigi. Cody is having some guys work on his house so it looks like he and Nina and Brianna are staying with the Knights during renovations. And I come and go like I usually do, though I try to stick around a little extra time without being too conspicuous. That's what we planned from the beginning, isn't it?"

It all sounded good, and Tucker seemed at ease with the questioning and with his answers. Cecilia shouldn't have that gut feeling that something was all wrong.

But she did.

"We've got a few hours to set up some kind of… booby trap, for lack of a better word. Something that will stop Elijah from getting close to the Sons camp. Of course, our main problem is he could easily message for backup—and backup would come ASAP."

Brady helped her over a particularly unsteady part of the rock where she was struggling to get her footing. He didn't say anything, so she did the same. Tucker followed, as if happy to walk in utter silence with no feedback on his plan.

"We put out a few things that take his tires out. Then a little ways down the road we do some kind of…ambush? Trap? Something they can't get past. The only problem we're up against is their phones."

"Won't they immediately call for help if they blow out a tire? Before they even get out of the car?" Brady returned.

Tucker shrugged, continuing to follow them down closer to that makeshift road. "Depends on how in a hurry they are. Out here blowing a tire wouldn't be that uncommon. Probably used to it. No reason to get extra people when they'll have the ability to make a quick change themselves."

Cecilia studied Brady. He seemed to be considering Tucker's ludicrous argument. Brotherly love or not, Cecilia would not walk them into an ambush like that.

"That's ridiculous," Cecilia said forcefully. "Elijah wouldn't sit around waiting for the tire to be changed. Especially if he's trying to figure out why we didn't come chasing after him like he hoped. He'd call for another ride, or he'd walk it. He's not going to sit around and change a tire or wait for his men to."

Tucker didn't argue, but he didn't pipe up to agree with her assessment either. So, she kept talking. "It can't be something they need to be rescued from or can be helped out. It has to be their idea to get out of the car, without raising any red flags that might make them call ahead to the camp."

Tucker and Brady mulled this as they walked. When she hissed out a breath from landing too hard on her already aching leg, that sent a jolt of pain through her stab wounds, Brady held out a hand to help her again.

She noticed Tucker watched the exchange carefully, and it dawned on her that Brady hadn't mentioned her injuries to Tucker. It was pertinent information, especially as they made plans. But he'd avoided the topic.

Maybe he didn't fully trust Tucker either. Her heart twisted because she knew that had to be eating him up alive. To question one of his brothers. And if Cecilia was right in her gut feeling? If Tucker was up to something wrong?

The whole Wyatt clan would be...wrecked. There was no other word for it.

They walked farther in silence. Cecilia kept her eye

on Tucker. Something was up with him. She didn't want to think it was nefarious, but what else could it be? If it was anything *good*, he'd tell them.

They were coming up on the path that worked as entrance into the camp now. "If I'm going to be the prisoner anyway, why not use me as a diversion here?" Cecilia pointed to the road a ways off.

"He might think something's fishy about stumbling upon you," Brady returned.

They all stopped and Brady passed her a water bottle, which earned another careful look from Tucker. Cecilia met his considering gaze and raised an eyebrow. Tucker only turned away.

Something was *really* not right here.

"We'd have to set it up. Make it look like I'm trying to get to camp, trying to not be seen, only we have to make sure he sees me. And doesn't see either of you."

Brady studied the area around them. "It's too open. Why would you be hiking through here when you could be in the rock formations?"

Cecilia considered Tucker. Her best idea was to milk her injuries, pretend like she was struggling to hike and needed the even ground. But Brady hadn't mentioned her injuries, and that had to be purposeful. So she flashed a fake smile at Tucker. "You mind giving us a few minutes?"

Tucker's eyebrows drew together. "Huh?"

"I want to talk to your brother in private. Without you listening. Can you go over there?" She pointed to some rocks in the distance.

"You can't be serious," Tucker replied, and his outrage didn't seem fake. That felt very real. The first real reaction he'd given since they'd "bumped" into him up on the lookout point.

It was good to see *something* could elicit a real response out of him. "I'm very serious. What I have to say to Brady is private. So..." She made a shooing motion.

Tucker turned his indignant gaze to Brady.

Brady sighed. "Just give us a few, Tuck. This isn't about you anyway."

Tucker's mouth firmed, but he walked toward the pile of rocks Cecilia had motioned to. And boy, did he not seem pleased about it.

Which, in fairness, could be his reaction whether he was trying to help or sabotage. The younger Wyatt brothers were never very good at being dismissed. Which was why she'd always gone out of her way to find ways to dismiss them.

She glanced up at the Wyatt brother still with her. He'd always handled it the best. With just enough disdain to irritate her right back. None of the carrying-on or male bluster, just a calm nonchalance that always had her losing her temper first.

That warm feeling was spreading through her chest again, but she had to shove it away and focus on the problem at hand. "I didn't want to say it in front of him, but if I overact my injuries, it might be a plausible enough reason for Elijah to believe I was taking the easy route in."

"Maybe, but only if it was dark. I don't think he'd believe you doing it midday. There'd be no reason."

Cecilia frowned. True enough, but if Elijah was coming back this afternoon, they didn't have time for that.

"Why'd you send him over there for that?" Brady asked.

"Why didn't you tell him I'm hurt?"

Brady scrubbed a hand over his face. "I...don't know."

"I know why, Brady. You didn't tell him because we can't actually trust him. Something isn't right about all this."

Brady's forehead lined and he stared at Tucker bent over the rock. "Maybe it's not right, but… I can't let myself not trust my own brother. Not Tuck. He wouldn't… He just wouldn't. Whatever is off is something he can't tell us, but that doesn't mean it's wrong or bad."

Cecilia frowned at him even as her heart pinched. She understood his loyalty, the need for it.

But she absolutely could not be caught in the cross fire of his misplaced loyalty.

Chapter Eighteen

Brady felt as though he was being pulled in two very correct directions. This was not black-and-white. There was no one clear, right answer.

He had to trust his brother. His younger *brother*. Tuck, who had always been good and dedicated to his law enforcement career, to taking down Ace and the Sons. Brady absolutely had to trust Tucker—it was the right thing to do.

Brady had also made a successful law enforcement career through listening to his gut, and the facts. Both the facts and his gut pointed to this being all wrong. Those things told him not to trust Tucker.

Then there was Cecilia. He'd made her sit down because she looked too pale. She was all but staring daggers at Tucker who was moving back over to join them.

"I have an idea," Tucker said grimly. "You probably won't like it."

"You're finally catching on," Cecilia muttered.

Tuck pretended not to notice. "The thing is, he expected you both to run back to the Knights after the fire. He expects you to be mad, right? Probably doesn't expect you to run to the Sons camp, but it wouldn't be out of the question for either of you to come after him directly. He wouldn't necessarily find it out of character if one of you were waiting here for a standoff."

"That'd be suicide," Brady replied.

"Would it though? I don't have any evidence Elijah has ever killed anyone. Do you?"

"We could say the same about Ace," Brady replied, resisting the need to rub his chest where that truth always lodged like a weight.

Tucker shook his head. "We know better. And sure, Elijah could use his goons as mercenaries to keep his hands clean. Ace did enough of that. But Elijah isn't Ace. He's not the leader of the Sons. He's trying, sure. Maybe he's even getting there. But he's lived his life outside the camp. No matter how involved he's gotten."

"He thinks we're dumb, Brady," Cecilia offered. "He thinks he's smarter than us. And I think he'd want to have a face-off. He'd want to talk. He wouldn't shoot first."

"But he could," Brady insisted. "We could let Cecilia stand out there in the middle of the road, ready for a showdown, and he could just flat-out kill her in two seconds. Not happening."

"*I* took Mak. *I* know where Mak is, and his goons didn't try to kill me. They tried to take me."

"Which is exactly why you wouldn't be stupid enough to go after him. He might underestimate us, but I don't think he's going to be fooled by a standoff with you."

"Not her," Tucker agreed. "Mak or no, I think the potential for Elijah killing her is certainly higher than not. He'd want to torture her a bit, but if she was antagonizing him, he'd be fine with just taking her out. You, on the other hand, are a Wyatt. Ace Wyatt's son. Ace might be in jail, but we both know he still has some power here.

You're worth more alive than dead as a power move. Even if you were threatening him, if he could bring you into camp, make some kind of example out of you in front of the group members—"

"Yeah, no," Cecilia said firmly, pushing up from the rock with a wince. "We picked me to be the distraction for a reason."

"But it's not just you two anymore," Tucker said evenly. "You have me."

"If I'm not standing there facing Elijah, neither is he. End of story."

"You two seem really worried about each other."

"So what if we are, Tuck? Got a problem with wanting people to stay alive?" Cecilia returned, and clearly wasn't thinking of her injuries when she stepped toward Tucker threateningly, like she was ready to fight him.

Tucker didn't react except to move his gaze from Cecilia to Brady. "Would you do it?"

Cecilia whirled, her eyes all flashing fury. "Think very carefully about how you answer that question, Wyatt."

Which gave him some pause. He didn't care for being ordered about in that high-handed tone, but the reason behind it was, well, care. She cared about him. Didn't want to see him taking unnecessary chances any more than he wanted to see her taking them.

The more they talked about variables, adjusted plans, the more he realized...he couldn't let any of them get caught by Elijah. It was too much risk.

"He'd expect some kind of ambush if we were the aggressors," Brady said, carefully avoiding Tucker's direct question. "No matter how stupid or emotional he thinks we are, he'll suspect there are more of us waiting."

Tucker's expression was inscrutable, and the awful *don't trust this guy* feeling burrowed deeper. Tucker was never inscrutable, except at work. He had said this was work. But it was also life.

All three of them turned toward the sound of an engine. It was far off, carrying over the wide-open landscape around them.

"We don't have enough time for a plan. Just hide."

Tucker swore. "Where?" he muttered, whirling around. "You two, there," he said, pointing to the small pile of rocks. "Three of us can't fit, but I can run over to those."

Tucker didn't wait to see if Brady would agree. He started to run and Brady couldn't argue with him. They didn't have time. He grabbed Cecilia's hand and they ran for the pile of rocks.

"If we're here they shouldn't see us unless they look back, which they'd have no reason to. You get situated in the most comfortable position. I'll get in around you."

"Just get out of sight, moron," she returned, settling herself behind the rock. He sat beside her. He'd need to sink lower.

"You need to be in a comfortable position that isn't putting too much pressure on that stab wound."

She muttered irritably under her breath, readjusted her position lying behind the rock, then he pretzeled his body to fit around her so they were hidden by the rock. Someone would really have to be looking for them to see them.

God, he hoped.

The engine was getting closer, though it was hard to tell how close the way noise moved and echoed in the vast valley. He could only keep his body as still as possible, focus on keeping his breathing even, and not crushing Cecilia.

Seconds ticked by, stretching long and taut, but he had been trained to deal with these kinds of situations. He couldn't think of what-ifs. He couldn't let his brain zoom ahead. He had to breathe. Steady himself and believe the car would pass. Everything would be fine.

He could tell the engine was getting closer, but how close was impossible to discern. He wouldn't be able to believe it was past them until he didn't hear it at all. So he focused on the even whir of the engine carrying on the air. Once it was gone, it would be safe.

A car door slammed above the low buzz of the engine. Both he and Cecilia jerked, almost imperceptibly. Training could keep them tamping down normal reactions, but it couldn't eradicate reflexes completely.

Cecilia's hand found his arm and she squeezed. Their breathing had increased its pace, but he could feel them both working together to slow it. In then out. Slow. Easy.

He couldn't hear over the pounding in his ears, or maybe there was nothing happening. Maybe the car door was miles away. Maybe they were overreacting.

"I saw something."

The voice was clear, close, and most definitely Elijah.

Brady listened as footsteps thudded. It sounded like the men Elijah was speaking to split up and went in different directions, but he couldn't be sure. He was tempted to risk a look, but Cecilia was still squeezing his arm as if to say *don't*.

Silence was intermittently interrupted by footsteps, the faint murmur of voices, or a scuttling sound that Brady eventually figured was rocks being kicked.

Then suddenly the sounds of a scuffle, maybe even a punch and a grunt. Then a voice Brady didn't recognize.

"Found a Wyatt."

More footsteps—farther away from Brady. The sounds seemed to fade away, but he could just make out Elijah's words. "Well. This is an interesting development."

Cecilia's nails dug into his arm, as if she could keep him here. And it should. Brady should stay put. So, he held on to the fact that Tucker could take care of himself. He was smart. A detective. And a Wyatt, so like he'd said—more valuable alive than dead.

Elijah seemed surprised to have found him. Which meant whatever odd reason Tucker had for being here, chalking it up to coincidence, didn't have to do with the Sons.

Or does it just not have to do with Elijah?

"Not the Wyatt I expected, I have to say," Elijah's voice echoed through the midday heat. "Of course, where there's one, there's usually more."

"Yeah. Probably," Tucker replied, sounding almost cheerful. "Home sweet home, you know?"

Cecilia's intake of breath was sharp and audible. Brady shook his head just a bit, even though he doubted she'd see or feel it.

Tucker wasn't ratting them out. He was bluffing to Elijah so Elijah didn't go looking for them.

"Hurt him till he talks," Elijah ordered crisply. The order was immediately followed by a thud and a whoosh of breath.

Brady had to close his eyes, even though he couldn't see from behind the rock anyway. Tucker could take it. He could handle it.

Brady needed to stay put. Protect Cecilia. Tucker could take care of himself. This wasn't all that far off from what they'd been planning. Let him be taken, carefully follow. Arrest.

Tucker could handle it. Brady repeated that fact to himself as he heard the thud of blows, the grunts of pain. This was still better than sending an injured Cecilia to do the job.

He opened his eyes as the sound of fighting increased.

Brady couldn't stand it. He simply couldn't listen as Tucker got beaten by three men. Even if they kept him alive, they could do anything to Tucker, and Brady couldn't live with himself if he just…stayed put. He tried to move, but Cecilia's fingernails dug into his arm.

"Let him get captured, Brady," she hissed as quietly as possible. "It's half our plan anyway. We'll save him after. We'll—"

Brady shook his head, taking her hand off his arm. He quietly got to his feet and quickly shook off his pack. Gently and as silently as possible, he knelt and set it next to her. He looked her in the eye. "I can't. I'm sorry. I just can't do it." He pressed a quick kiss to her mouth. "If it were you like we planned, I wouldn't have been able to do it either. I'm sorry."

Then he left her. She had weapons and a cell phone and the chance to escape. Tucker didn't, and Brady couldn't let him go down alone.

CECILIA WAS SHOCKED into stillness for probably more than a minute. All their talk and debating about plans, and it had just gone up in smoke. Brady walked away, all grim determination.

I wouldn't have been able to do it either.

That echoed inside of her. He'd planned to let her get caught, but he would have never been able to go through with that plan. She wanted to be angry, furious. She wanted to march after him and drag him back behind this rock and their little bubble of pretend safety.

But she understood too well what he'd meant. She was half-convinced Tucker was on the wrong side of things, even now, and it was still hard to listen to someone she'd grown up with and cared about get beaten up.

If it was one of her sisters? She wouldn't have lasted even as long as Brady. Still, this was…suicide. Surely. Maybe Brady and Tucker could *fight* three men off, but Elijah's men had to have weapons. Maybe Brady and Tucker were somewhat protected by their Wyatt name, but if they fought back hard enough, would Elijah really care to keep them around to use them as examples to the other Sons.

And what could she do? There was no cell service out here. She could shoot, but that made her a target too, and if she was a target, how would they get out of this mess? Someone needed to be safe to find the option to *get* help.

She heard the sounds of fighting and closed her eyes, taking a steadying breath. She had to think clearly, without emotion clouding her judgment. Emotion would get all three of them killed. And probably only after Elijah tortured them.

Torture. Would Brady give under torture? Tell Elijah exactly where Mak was? She didn't think so. She thought he'd die first.

But Tucker? Once she would have put her utter faith into him, but not today. Not with his weirdness.

She couldn't let them get captured, or at least not for very long. But in order to figure out what she was going to do, she had to look. She had to know what was going on to make an informed decision.

Maybe it'd be easy to get a shot off, to pick all three men off and end this here and now. It was possible, but she wouldn't know it unless she risked being seen.

She unholstered her weapon, and took another slow breath, calming her heart rate, trying to keep her limbs from shaking. Slowly, she peeked over the rock.

Tucker and Brady were holding their own in the fight. Brady was a little worse for the wear, probably since he'd already been beaten up the day before. But he and Tucker worked together like a team to take on the other two men, who fought like individuals. Elijah's men landed blows on Brady and Tucker, but they didn't make any headway on actually taking Brady or Tucker down.

Both of Elijah's men had guns strapped to their legs, but they didn't use them. Why not even use them as a threat? Brady was living proof you could shoot a man and have him survive. Why wouldn't they use the strongest weapons they had at their disposal?

"Why does none of this make sense?" Cecilia muttered to herself. She lifted her gun, trying to test if she could make two successive shots and take down both men before they returned fire.

There was too much struggle, though. She'd be just as likely to hit Brady or Tucker with the way they were all moving and stumbling and swinging at each other. And she wasn't guaranteed to make a glancing blow either. What if she missed altogether?

Wait. Two against two. Why were there only two men? Where was Elijah?

She looked toward the car Elijah and his men had left in the middle of the path to camp. It was still running, but she didn't see anyone. Had Elijah walked on to camp, leaving his lackeys to handle the Wyatt brothers? No. He wouldn't have done that.

There was a crack of sound behind her, like a gun being cocked, then the cold press of metal against the back of her head. She froze.

"Well hello, Cecilia," Elijah's voice said softly in her ear. "Didn't see this coming, did you?"

He peeled the gun out of her hand, and she had to let him. Because she had no doubt Elijah would pull that trigger if she provoked him.

"Now. On your feet. We have so much to talk about."

Chapter Nineteen

Brady took another ham-fisted punch to the kidney and nearly lost his balance, but Tucker was there, backing him up, blocking the next blow and landing one of his own.

All of them were breathing heavily, not doing much more than landing punches that hurt but didn't take anyone out or down. Brady's gun had been knocked out of his hand before he'd been able to get a clear shot, and Tucker had lost his long before Brady had come to help.

It felt...pointless, Brady realized, ducking another punch with enough ease dread skittered up his spine. "Something isn't right," he muttered to his brother.

Tucker dodged a blow, landed a decent fist to one of the men attacking them.

One of the *two* guys. There were only two.

"Where'd Elijah go?"

Tucker swore, and not half a second later landed an elbow to one guy's temple that had him crumpling. In a fluid, easy move and with absolutely no help from Brady, he managed to get the other in a choke hold.

Had Tucker been...holding back?

No time to think about that. He let Tucker deal with

handcuffing the two debilitated aggressors and searched the area around them for Elijah. Nothing.

He looked over to the rocks where Cecilia should be out of sight. Instead, past the rocks, he saw two figures. They were far away so he couldn't make them out well enough to be certain it was Elijah and Cecilia, but who else would it be?

"Go ahead," Tucker said. "Follow. I'll be right behind you. We can't have these guys coming behind us, and we have to see where he takes her. Go."

"No, Tuck. You don't follow me. You go get help. We can't do this alone. We need backup. You have to go get backup." His brother hadn't been acting normal. His actions didn't make sense, but Brady had to be able to trust Tucker. "Promise me."

Tucker was kneeling, tying the men's feet together with rope Brady had no idea how he'd gotten. "You could both get killed in the time it'll take me to get help. You don't even have a gun," he returned, not meeting Brady's gaze.

"We'll take our chances." Brady was already walking away from Tucker, toward Cecilia. He didn't have time to search for the one that had been knocked out of his hand or he'd lose sight of Cecilia. "We don't have *any* if we both go in there. But we do if you get help. We can arrest him. He's taken Cecilia against her will. We have arrestable grounds. All we need is enough law enforcement to make it happen."

He was running by the time he was done talking. Cecilia and Elijah had disappeared behind a large rock formation. Brady headed for the rock first, thinking to grab the pack quickly on his way.

But there was a fire. Small and it wouldn't spread

thanks to the rocky landscape, but both his and Cecilia's packs were in the middle of the blaze. There was no chance of saving anything or finding a weapon.

Brady didn't stop to think about the implications, and while he considered the fact that Elijah could just shoot him dead in the middle of the Badlands, it didn't really matter.

If he'd wanted him dead, Brady could have been dead multiple times. He had to bank on the fact that either Ace's shadow, or potential family loyalty, or *something* was keeping Elijah from taking him out.

Maybe that wouldn't extend past an attack, or an attempt to get Cecilia back, but it was a risk Brady was willing to take.

And if Tucker doesn't get help?

Brady slowed his pace. It was an irrational fear. His brother had taken down those two men, fought beside him. Tucker would go get help.

He could have ended that fight a lot quicker.

Whatever it meant, whatever weird thing was going on with Tuck, it didn't mean he was helping Elijah or the Sons. Brady had to stop letting stupid doubts plague him.

Even with Cecilia's life at stake?

It was too difficult a choice. Trust his brother over all else? Risk Cecilia over it? There was too much at stake to make an error.

He could only focus on himself. On what he could do.

He'd laid out a plan where Cecilia was captured, and even though he wouldn't have been able to *let* it happen, it was currently happening. And he was following, just like he'd planned. With or without backup, he could arrest Elijah. He had grounds.

All he had to do was catch up, somehow get Elijah

away from Cecilia without her getting hurt and arrest him...with no weapon, no handcuffs and no help whatsoever.

He'd eased into a brisk walk instead of an all-out run. With the dust and rocky debris, there was a decent enough trail to follow as long as the wind didn't pick up and Elijah didn't realize Cecilia was digging her heels in and making enough of a track for him to follow.

Occasionally, he paused to listen to try and figure out how close he was, but he never got close enough to hear actual footsteps or the struggle Cecilia must be putting up.

She wouldn't go easily. Even if Elijah had a weapon. She wouldn't just docilely be marched along. Which meant, surely, Elijah had no plans to kill her either.

Brady wasn't sure how long he'd walked, following a trail, and not getting close enough to hear a scuffle before the landscape started to feel...more familiar. Too familiar. Bad familiar.

Brady stopped short. He knew this area too well. Old memories tried to surface, but he couldn't give them space. Couldn't give them power.

Couldn't allow himself to picture Ace on that rock above, throwing knives. Leaving him out here, seven years old and all alone.

Brady looked at the towering rock around him, preparing his body for that searing pain out of nowhere, as if he expected Ace to jump out and do what he'd always done. Brady wouldn't put it past Ace to share with Elijah how he'd tortured his children.

Ace had tortured them each in different ways, and they'd each kept that a secret from each other, thinking it was an individual personal shame. After Gage's ordeal, he'd told Brady about the ways Ace had tortured him.

Gage's admission had prompted them all to share their secrets. Which Ace wouldn't know. He'd think those secrets were ammunition, and wouldn't it make sense for Elijah to have been given all the ammunition to hurt Brady and his brothers?

Maybe Ace was in jail, but that didn't mean Elijah couldn't put men up there, armed with knives and Brady's nightmares.

The trail led right through the narrow chasm of rocks where Ace had often left Brady, only to torture him later. Where Brady had been forced away from his brothers to survive. On his own. As a child.

When he had nightmares, they all took place here, no matter how incomprehensible his dreams might be. Following that trail would be walking into his own personal hell.

I'll never go back there. Not for any reason. That's a promise I'm making to myself and I won't ever break it. No matter what.

He could hear his own words, spoken to his brothers, to his grandmother, to anyone who'd listen during that first year they'd all been out and with Grandma and *living* a real life.

Brady could stop here. He could go back. He could wait for help. He didn't have to brave his own personal hell.

Except Cecilia was at the end of this trail, and no matter what that twelve-year-old had told himself, there were reasons you broke promises to yourself. Reasons you did the things that scared you the most.

And that reason boiled down to one thing, always.

A thing Ace didn't understand, and Elijah probably didn't either.

Love.

EVERYTHING IN CECILIA'S body hurt. Which wasn't new, it was just worse when there was a gun to her head and she knew Brady would come after her and they could both end up dead.

She tried not to let herself think like that. Fatalism *could* be fatal in her current situation. She needed to believe in Brady, and Tucker and even herself, that they could find a way to survive this.

No matter what hurt, no matter how impossible it seemed, she had to believe or she'd never find a way to survive this.

"Ah, here we are," Elijah said as if he were a waiter showing someone to their reserved table. Instead it was a tower of rock interrupted by a small crevice.

Without warning, he shoved her into that opening hard enough she stumbled and fell to her hands and knees. Which would have been his mistake if her body was cooperating. She would have immediately jumped up and disarmed him.

But her arms gave out on her so she fell onto her side, unfortunately her bad one, which hurt so badly she had to fight back tears and an encroaching blackness that wanted to take her away.

But she fought both away, breathing through the pain and the frustration. At first she'd thought he'd pushed her into a cave, but above her was bright blue sky. The air was hotter here, like the rocks were trapping it between them or radiating heat. She desperately wished she had her pack and could drink some water.

Though if she were wishing things, she supposed she should be wishing she wasn't here at all. Or that she'd shot Elijah before he'd snuck up on her.

"On your feet now."

Cecilia grimaced, but did as she was told. If it came down to it, she'd fight and run, but for now it seemed in her best interest to listen to him.

"You're bleeding," Elijah offered, with a slight frown. He almost sounded concerned, but that tone was belied by the fact he was aiming a gun point-blank at her forehead as he moved closer to her, studying the red stain that had seeped through her gray T-shirt.

He stepped closer, reaching out. Cecilia braced herself for pain, for *something*. But all Elijah did was carefully lift her shirt and look at the stab wound.

Cecilia tried to control her breathing, tried to keep a handle on her revulsion. She failed. Miserably. No matter that it was preferable to say, being shot, it was creepy. It made her skin crawl as he kept her shirt lifted and studied the wound.

"You really should have gotten some medical attention for that. No stitches?" He tsked, lifting his gaze to meet hers. "What *were* you thinking."

She didn't answer him. Why would she? Still, she kept his gaze rather than stare at the gun that was so close to her forehead she could hardly think about anything else.

"You know, Layla quite liked being hurt," he said mildly. "Maybe you two have that in common."

"And maybe I puke all over your shoes."

Elijah lifted a shoulder as if it were of no concern of his. "I don't mind a little force, a little hurt, but you would invariably do something stupid, and as much as you fancy yourself the center of this, I'm not here for you."

She tried not to show her confusion, but Elijah's smile told her she'd failed.

"Don't worry. Brady will appear soon enough, ready to swoop in and save the day." He tapped his wrist. "I'm surprised it's taken two Wyatts this long, though. I wonder why it *did* take so long. Seems odd. Two strong, perfectly able-bodied men working together. Almost as if they, or one of them, wasn't trying to take the men out."

Cecilia's blood went cold. She refused to take anything Elijah said at face value, but could that mean Tucker was working for Elijah?

Please God, no.

She didn't speak until she knew she could do it and sound steady. Strong. "Brady will come with backup, and then where will you be?"

"He won't come with backup." Elijah let out a snort. "He'll run after you immediately. Especially since you're hurt. Wyatts and their noble pride are endlessly predictable."

"And yet alive. All six of them. And not incarcerated, unlike a certain Wyatt." Still, Elijah's words created some doubt. Surely Brady wouldn't come after her without backup... Except, wasn't that what he'd done with Tucker? Taken off to help without thinking about how he'd get himself out of it.

No. He'd expected *her* to get them out of it. So, she had to. Somehow.

"You know, Cecilia, you're making a grave mistake if you think I'm like Ace or your average thug. Killing leads to jail time. You don't always need to *kill* someone to get what you want."

She eyed the gun. If he wasn't going to kill her...

His smile was slow and self-satisfied. "Now, don't get too excited. Killing is often an excellent plan when it certainly can't be traced back to you. Which is why we'll wait for Brady's grand entrance."

"We know you're Ace's son." It was a gamble. Maybe it would make him more inclined to kill her. But maybe it would set him off-balance enough to give her a chance to best him.

Instead, Elijah laughed. If they were in a different situation, she would have believed it an honest, cheerful, good-humored laugh. "You know I'm Ace's son. You *know* that, huh?"

"Yes, I do."

He leaned in close, so their noses almost touched and the steel of the gun touched her forehead.

"You know *nothing*, Cecilia. And you're smart enough to know that, deep down. You're in over your head. Completely lost and completely expendable. You think I care about a *baby* when I'm building an *empire*?"

Cecilia didn't know how to parse that. He wasn't after Mak? Then what was the point of the fire? Of threatening her at the rez? Why on Earth were they *here* if not for Mak?

Whatever the reason, he wasn't lying when he said she was expendable. Which meant she had to tread very, very carefully.

Brady would have gone to get backup. He wouldn't have followed her half-cocked. Tucker wouldn't let him. He'd been impulsive when Tucker was getting beaten up so he'd waded in, but he would think before coming to her rescue. Or Tucker would.

If Tucker wasn't on the wrong side of things.

She had to close her eyes against the wave of debilitating fear, because God knew none of what she told herself was true.

Chapter Twenty

The heat was excruciating. Dehydration was likely, if not a foregone conclusion. Brady was surrounded by his own personal nightmare and he had lost Cecilia and Elijah's trail.

Brady stood in the middle of the vast Badlands and wondered where the hell he'd gone so wrong in his life. He'd tried to be good and do the right thing. He'd been *shot* helping Gage save Felicity. He was a good man.

Why did he have to be a failure?

Failure or no, he couldn't give up. Not while there was a chance Cecilia was still alive. He couldn't have fully lost the trail. He'd made a wrong turn was all.

He backtracked, wiping the sweat off his face with his shoulder. He went back to the last place he saw the trail. It didn't end abruptly so much as got fainter and fainter. Perhaps a breeze had blown through and made the track lighter.

He stopped where he absolutely couldn't be certain it went on, then stood still and studied the land around him. All rock. All gradients of brown, red and tan broken up by the occasional tuft of grass. But there was a familiarity here, like there'd been in that corridor of rock earlier.

He was somewhere near…something he recognized. He couldn't place it yet, but he would.

Then he heard a thud. The lowest, quietest murmur of voices. It would be hard to tell where it was coming from the way sound moved in the Badlands, but he used the direction of the trail and his own instincts to propel him forward.

Then, as landmarks became clearer, he realized he didn't need to use either. He knew this place again. He knew where Elijah would have taken her.

There was no way Elijah wasn't Ace's son if he knew all Ace's spots. All Ace's ways of torture. They had to be linked *somehow.*

Brady took a moment to pause, to send up a silent prayer that Tuck would get backup and manage to find them in time, then moved quietly toward the entrance of the circle of rock.

But Elijah poked his head out of the small entrance between the rocks. "Welcome," he greeted sunnily. "Come on inside. Have a chat." Elijah cocked his head. "Unless you want her brain matter splattered across the rocks. Can't say *I* do, but I'll oblige if necessary."

Brady stepped into the wall of rocks. It was where he and Gage had hidden during their escape. It was where Andy Jay, a random member of the Sons, had taken pity on them and lied to their father, allowing them to continue on to Grandma Pauline's.

Brady had no doubt it was where Andy Jay had died at his father's hand, as punishment for letting them go. Andy's son hadn't forgiven the Wyatt brothers for their role in his father's death. He'd tried to take down Cody not that long ago and failed.

Brady couldn't think about that. His sole purpose was not letting Cecilia die here too.

He didn't do more than give a quick glance to make sure she was all right before he turned his attention to Elijah. Brady positioned his body between the gun Elijah was pointing and Cecilia.

Elijah rolled his eyes. "Do you really have to be so noble? It's boring and predictable. I can shoot her regardless of what you do, so take a seat next to her like a good little soldier and we'll keep her brain intact."

Brady considered rushing him. They were in a small enclosed space, and Cecilia would back him up, even injured.

But if he could keep Elijah talking, he might get more information to use against Ace. To keep Elijah in jail longer, and to bide time until Tuck got back with reinforcements.

If Tuck comes back with reinforcements.

Brady took a careful seat next to Cecilia on the rock. She looked pale. He noted the splotch of blood on her shirt. She was bleeding through her bandages, surely dehydrated, and nothing about the situation they were in was good for that.

"If you don't think I've figured out you're Ace's son, you're not as smart as you think you are."

Elijah laughed, enough to make Brady...uncomfortable. He was certain it was true, but Elijah's laugh was... off.

"I'm not Ace's son," Elijah replied, keeping the gun trained on Cecilia's head.

"Is that what he makes you say? I wonder why it's gotta be such a secret."

Elijah shook his head. "See, I was chosen, Brady. I

wasn't just born. Ace picked me. He saw something in me. He didn't knock up some dim-witted gang groupie and have some warped sense of loyalty because of *blood*. I was chosen because I'm better. Smarter. I can see things people like you never will."

"You mean you were his brand of crazy and you listened to what he said?"

Elijah's humor was quickly sliding away. His eyes went icy, his grip on the gun tightened, and his smile turned into a sneer.

"You're his weakness. The lot of you. You aren't the reason he's in jail. His delusion that one of his blood-born children would take over the Sons is what got him there. Blood. As if that matters. I will take over the Sons." Elijah tapped his chest. "I'll leave Ace behind if I need to. I'm the next in line because he saw something in me, and I'm the best prospect to take over."

"I'm not part of the Sons. What do I care if you're better? It'll always be my job to take down the illegal activity in my jurisdiction."

"You're a part of Ace, which means that you're currency, Brady. Not important, but usable. Taking you out was an option, but it doesn't send the message I want. I don't want blood and destruction like Ace. No, I want the Sons to be a real machine. Murder leads to anger and revenge and all that nonsense with Andy Jay and his son coming after you. I don't want that. I want consensus. I want loyalty."

"What about Mak?" Brady asked, to draw out the conversation but also because he didn't understand what any of this had to do with Cecilia.

"I don't care about that kid. I don't care about *blood*. Being chosen is what matters." Elijah took a deep breath as if to calm himself. "But I don't appreciate being *stolen* from. Sometimes you have to make a statement. Besides, I've studied you. I know your weakness." The gun pointed at Cecilia. "Damsels in distress. Long as I have a gun to her head, you'll do what I say."

"But I won't," Cecilia returned.

"You will. Because he wants you to."

"This is a really terrible plan, even for you," Brady muttered. Cecilia gave him a look as if to say *back off*, but Brady knew this kind of delusional behavior. He'd grown up under its highs and lows.

Anger would create an unstable environment, and Elijah might lash out, but he'd also lose sight of his plan.

"We've got two against one here. I've got more help on the way. You'll never win." Brady shifted, trying to get his feet beneath him in a better position so he could lunge at Elijah.

He could take him out before he could shoot Cecilia. If he got a shot off, he'd hit Brady. Surely it could give her enough time to finish the job. He glanced at Cecilia. She was still too pale, and looked a little shaky, but she gave him a nod as if she knew what he was thinking.

Elijah lifted the gun and pointed it at Brady. His hand shook, color was rising in his face. "You're very lucky killing you isn't part of my plan."

Brady was pushing too far. He should stop, but his own anger was swelling up inside of him. That this continued to be his life. Tormented by power-hungry men, invested in being smarter and more important than everyone else.

Even when Ace was in maximum-security prison, Brady was fighting back the things Ace wrought, and he was tired of it.

"Face it, Elijah. You're a crappy leader. Your son will grow up knowing you were right about one thing, though. Blood doesn't matter."

"Crappy leader? I will rule the Sons, and they will reach more glory than they've ever known. He *chose* me."

Brady shrugged, ready to strike. "Ace chose wrong."

Brady leapt, but in that same second, Elijah's gun went off.

THE SOUND OF the gun echoed in the chasm they were in, followed by a howl of pain. Both men were on the ground, grappling, but Cecilia wasn't sure which was moaning in pain, or if they both were.

She couldn't see the gun either. Just a tangle of limbs rolling across the rocky ground.

The rocks. Cecilia lunged for the biggest one she could hold. She'd just need one clear second and she could bash Elijah over the head.

But there was no opportunity. There were only grunts and groans of pain. She saw blood, but couldn't tell who it came from. Her stomach turned, but she had to focus on getting Elijah's gun.

Screw the rock and her own injuries. She had to get in there and do what she could. When Elijah was on top, she grabbed his hair and pulled. He reached back with the hand holding the gun, and she grabbed it by the barrel, trying to point it anywhere but at her and Brady.

Out of the corner of her eye she saw Brady scoot out from under Elijah. Elijah had one hand still wrapped around Brady's leg, but Brady kicked it until he shook off Elijah's grasp.

The blood was Brady's. It was already soaking

through his pants leg, but Cecilia couldn't focus on that when she was grappling over the one gun in this godforsaken place.

She tried to rip the gun out of Elijah's grasp, but he held firm. With his other hand free, he swung up and landed a blow right on her stab wound.

The pain knocked her to her knees, but she kept her grip locked on the gun. She couldn't give in. She wouldn't give in.

Elijah was trying to scramble to his feet, pulling the gun with him, but she held fast. She used her whole body weight to keep the barrel pointed down rather than at her.

"You're going to die," Elijah said as he huffed and puffed and wrestled over the gun. "I'm going to make sure of it."

Pain screamed through her, but this was life or death. She had to try to shut out the pain and focus on getting the gun away from the man who would most definitely kill her, and then probably Brady too. If he hadn't already.

She couldn't let it happen. There had to be a way to survive.

She saw out of the corner of her eye Brady try to get to his feet, only to fall to his knees. She couldn't let the fear he'd been irreparably hurt weaken her limbs or her resolve. She needed to get the gun so she could get help for Brady.

It's a lot of blood.

She adjusted her footing, still pulling down on the barrel of the gun, as Elijah readjusted his grip. She kicked out, managing to land a decent blow. Elijah didn't go down quite the way she'd hoped, but she got a better handle on the gun. With one more yank she could—

Brady grabbed her, pulling her off Elijah, which wrenched the gun from her grasp. She wanted to protest, but it was lost as he pushed her out of the opening at the same time something exploded.

Reflexively, she ducked and covered her ears. Rock rained down on them and Brady tried to cover her body with his. She shoved ineffectively at him. *He'd* been shot. She should be covering him.

From…an explosion? She finally managed to dislodge Brady from on top of her and looked at where she'd been not a minute ago.

The rocks had exploded. There was little more than rubble on two sides.

How… How?

She looked around the rest of the area, stopping short at the figure standing a few yards opposite the explosion site.

Tucker.

She blinked at him. Was she hallucinating?

"What on earth just happened?" Her ears rang, so her words sounded muted and far away. She looked at Brady. He was sitting on the ground, leaning against a wall of rock, injured leg out in front of him.

There was so much blood. So much…

Tucker handed her a strip of fabric. He must have torn it off his own shirt. She took it and wrapped it around Brady's leg.

"Let me guess, you need a hospital," Tucker said grimly, looking down at Brady's seated form and bloody leg with a certain amount of detachment. The rubble behind them seemed to be of no consequence to him.

The words were still heard through a muffled filter, but Cecilia *could* make them out.

"Wouldn't hurt," Brady returned, his voice strained as Cecilia pressed the cloth Tucker had handed her to his wound.

"Ambulance is getting as close as it can. Paramedics will take the rest by foot and will be here any minute." Tucker's gaze moved from Brady to Cecilia. "You'll both be transported. Depending on Elijah's status, he might need to go first. And I'm not putting the three of you in the same ambulance."

"Shouldn't you…" Cecilia trailed off because she realized there were two people moving the rubble. Where had they come from?

Cecilia looked at Brady. His complexion was gray, but his eyes were open and alert.

"Elijah didn't think you'd get backup."

His mouth tugged upward ever so slightly. "I'm stupid, but not that stupid. Sent Tuck."

Cecilia looked back up at Tucker. She really thought he'd been against them, but here he was with backup.

Apparently the kind of backup who could explode rocks. She frowned. "How did you…"

Tucker shook his head. "Keep the pressure on that. You seem in better shape. I'm going to go help the paramedics find us."

He walked off and Cecilia looked at Brady. He was so gray and so still. "I hope you're not entertaining any grand plans of dying, because that's not going to work for me."

His mouth tugged up at one corner. "Nah. Surviving close range gunshot wounds is my specialty. You know what they say. Getting shot twice in a year is lucky."

"No one says that, Brady."

"Well, unlucky would be dead, and I am not that."

The word *dead* gave her a full body shudder, so she rested her forehead against his, still keeping the pressure on his wound. She let out a shuddered breath, and said what she never thought she'd say to a man. A near-death experience changed a girl, though. "I love you."

He let out his own shaky breath, and she just couldn't stand it. This. His hurt. Her hurt. God knew what had happened to Elijah, but here they were. Alive. Bleeding, but alive.

"So. You know, you better feel the same way or I'm going to kick your butt."

He chuckled, winced, made a half-hearted attempt to raise an arm that just fell by his side.

"And you can't die."

"Not going to die," he said, though he seemed incredibly weak. "Gage is never going to let me live this down after the hard time I gave him about Felicity." This time he seemed to focus all his energy and lifted his hand to briefly touch her cheek. "If I'm a little out of it here for a few minutes, it's just the shock. I'm not going to die. Got it?"

She swallowed down the lump in her throat and nodded.

"But you can be sure that I love you too. Because God knows I'd be a lot more pissed about getting shot again if it wasn't with you."

"That doesn't make any sense," she muttered, losing her battle with tears as one slipped over.

Brady opened his mouth to say something else, but one of the men by the rubble spoke first.

"He's alive."

Chapter Twenty-One

Brady had been shot before, and not that long ago. There was less fear this time. More irritable acceptance.

Cecilia was sitting next to him. A paramedic had done a quick patch job, but they were currently working on getting Elijah out of the rubble and onto a stretcher.

Brady had heard them mutter that if there was any hope of saving Elijah, he'd have to be transported ASAP. Brady's and Cecilia's injuries were serious, but they'd have to wait for a second transport.

"Why are they prioritizing saving him? He would have killed us," Cecilia muttered in Tucker's direction.

"Elijah might have some information that would... help my investigation."

Brady frowned at his brother. It was news to him he had any current investigation that connected to Elijah.

But there was something about this whole thing that made him keep his questions to himself.

The paramedics strapped Elijah to the stretcher, which would stabilize his body and keep him from being able to fight any of the paramedics, nurses or doctors who would deal with him on the way to the hospital.

His head was turned toward them as the paramedics walked by.

"There's so much worse coming for you Wyatts. So much worse," Elijah rasped. His face was bloody and torn up, but the hate in his eyes was clear and fierce.

"I think we'll handle it," Cecilia returned.

"Just like we've handled the rest," Brady added. If Ace kept coming, in whatever form, they'd keep fighting. Because they'd built real lives—with love and loss and right and wrong and hope. Real, life-changing hope.

Everything Elijah and Ace had was a delusion. It made them dangerous, sure, but it didn't have to rule their lives. If every time Wyatts and Knights came together they fought for right and good, well, that was life.

As long as they built one.

"Do you think…" Cecilia leaned close to his ear, eyeing the men who were still going through the rubble. "Do you think Tucker's part of Cody's old group and that's why he's being so weird?"

"It seems possible. We can't say anything, though. They kicked Cody out once other people knew he was part of the group. If Tucker is working with them, we have to keep quiet."

Cecilia nodded once, then rested her head against his shoulder. "We're okay," she murmured, as if she had to say it out loud to believe it.

It was odd. He was in an unreasonable amount of pain, bleeding profusely, and she wasn't doing much better. Bloody and banged up, sitting in the middle of the Badlands with the afternoon sun beating down.

But he felt…right. Like the things that had been all wrong for the past few months, all that gray and frustration and anxiety had lifted.

The Sons still existed, Ace and Elijah were both alive—if in jail. But even in the face of that, Jamison and Cody had reunited with their first loves. Cody had a daughter, Jamison had Liza's young half sister looking up to him like a father figure, and Gage and Felicity were getting married and starting a family.

And Brady Wyatt had at some point fallen in love with Cecilia. Who didn't care so much about right or wrong, but did what she had to do. Who fought, tooth and nail, for the people she loved.

What wasn't to love about that? "I love you," he murmured into her dusty hair.

"Sure you're not dying?" she joked. Or half joked. He could feel the anxiety radiating off her.

But he was going to be just fine.

Epilogue

Two weeks later

Cecilia sat in Grandma Pauline's kitchen. It was a full house these days. Sarah and Rachel were staying here while the Knight house was repaired from the fire. Duke had insisted on staying on the property, and no one could get through to Duke when he had an idea in his head.

Cecilia had been forced to stay at Grandma Pauline's once she'd been released from the hospital, and so had Brady. Everyone had been surprised when Cecilia insisted they share a room, but people seemed to be getting used to their new normal.

Well, not Brady, who was back to being surly as he recovered. The gunshot wound to his leg had been serious, and though it hadn't shattered any bone it had done some damage that would take considerable time to heal.

Having to accept help to get around did *not* make for a happy Wyatt, but he was the one who'd come up with their current plan. If she hadn't already been in love with him, she would have fallen for him when he'd suggested it.

The door opened, and Jamison stepped inside, gesturing Layla to follow him. She looked nervous, but better than she'd been in the hospital.

Cecilia immediately got up and went to gather Layla into a hug. Layla squeezed back, sniffling into Cecilia's shoulder. "I wasn't sure I wanted to come, but I knew you'd come get me if I didn't. And you need your rest." Layla pulled away. "Where is he?"

Cecilia nodded thanks at Jamison who slipped away. "I can't hold him yet because of my injuries, so he's upstairs being spoiled. Jamison will go get him, but I wanted to talk to you about something first."

"I know. I can't have him back. I… I feel better, but I can't—"

Cecilia kept her hands on her friend's arms. "I think you can. But you don't have to, Layla. You've got to do what's right for you, first and foremost."

"The state can't take him, Cecilia. And when Elijah gets out of jail—"

Cecilia led Layla to the table and made her sit down. "We're going to protect you and Mak from Elijah. Always. Never worry about that."

"I lost my job. My therapist said I'm doing better, but—"

"But it's hard. You've been through *a lot*." Cecilia took her friend's hands in hers. "You should be around your son. You should have work that allows you to do that. And you should feel safe."

"I don't—"

"I'm going to offer something, and I want you to understand it was the Wyatts' idea. I didn't have anything to do with it, so don't feel like you have to take it because you owe me."

"I owe you my life. I owe everyone…"

"Layla."

She sucked in a deep breath and nodded. "I know. You're my best friend and I would have done the same for you. I'm just…fragile, Cecilia. I don't feel strong enough for anything." She winced. "My therapist says it's good to tell people that, but it feels awful."

"Which is why we want you to move in here. We've got two people recovering from major injuries. The Wyatt brothers come and go with their families in tow. Grandma Pauline is…well, let's just say everything she has to do for this big house and ranch is a lot for a woman her age." Cecilia prayed to God Pauline didn't hear that one. "She could use help. Live-in help. You'd work for her, be part of taking care of your son, and those of us hobbling around until we're better. It can be temporary until you feel well enough to look for a new job, and live on your own. Or it can be permanent."

"But…" Layla blinked, tears filling her eyes. "That's too good to be true."

Cecilia smiled, squeezing Layla's hands. "The Wyatts are a little too good to be true sometimes. It's easier if you just accept it, not question if you deserve it. So, what do you think?"

Layla hesitated. "What about when you and Brady are better and go back to your real lives? Will Pauline really need my help? Will Mak have…stability, you know?"

Cecilia blinked. She hadn't been thinking about when she and Brady were better. At all. She cleared her throat, trying to hide her uncertainty from Layla. "Well, Pauline will still need help. And Brady and I come out here all the time. We wouldn't just abandon Mak."

Layla's eyebrows drew together. "His own mother did."

"No. His own mother got sick, and now she's doing better. And she has a whole village who wants to take care of her and her son. Mak's very lucky."

"I…" She sucked in a deep breath. "I can't say no, can I? It would be…it'd be stupid to say no." Layla abruptly got to her feet. Cecilia turned in her chair. Pauline had brought in Mak and Layla was crying over him.

Cecilia smiled at Grandma Pauline, but Layla's words were rattling around in her head. *What about when you and Brady are better?*

"Why don't you take him into the living room, sweetheart. Let me show you," Grandma Pauline said, ushering a crying Layla holding a babbling Mak into the living room. "We'll give you a few minutes of privacy, huh?"

Layla sniffled and nodded and disappeared into the room. Cecilia stood alone in the kitchen.

What about when you and Brady are better?

No, she wouldn't sit around worrying over that question. She went to her and Brady's makeshift room and found him lying on the bed, reading a book.

"What about when we're better?" she demanded with no preamble. She didn't know why she felt so…angry. So shaky. But they hadn't discussed this. Why hadn't it even come up?

Brady looked up from his book. "Huh?"

"What's going to happen when we're better?"

He blinked then, shifted in the bed. "Well…" He cleared his throat. "I'm not sure what you're asking me, Cecilia."

"Where are we going to go? Are you going back to your apartment and I'm going back to the rez? Does this continue?" She gestured between them. "What are we *doing*?"

He set the book aside. "I'm not going to have this conversation with you standing there, acting like you're accusing me of something. Come sit down."

"Oh, don't use that high-handed tone to boss me around."

He raised an eyebrow. He had a tendency to do that and make her feel like an idiot for wanting to stomp her foot and yell.

She plopped herself on the bed next to him because she *was* reasonable, even if it felt like one simple sentence had sent her a little off the deep end. Then he wrapped his arm around her, pulling her close until she rested her head on his shoulder.

"Once you're back to work, you'll want to stay on the rez," he said rationally.

"I guess so."

"I don't have to live in the county, and it's not like it's too far to drive every day."

She sat up straight, something like panic beating through her. "Are you suggesting you move in with me?"

"Isn't that what *you're* getting at?"

"No... Well, sort of. I mean, we're basically living together now. Just with a grandma hovering around."

"Exactly."

"I..."

"Alternatively, we could stay here and both commute when we're reinstated. Or I could just stay here, and you could live on the rez. Commute will suck, but I'm not going to be able to deal with those stairs at my apartment for a long while yet. Hell, I'm half convinced to just give up my badge."

She pulled out of his grasp, outraged. "You can't do that."

"Why not? I've been out for months. I'll be out for longer now. Why go back?"

She shook her head. She knew he was tired of being hurt. Tired of not working, but he couldn't honestly be thinking about quitting. "Because you love it."

He was quiet for a while. "I guess I do." He squeezed her close. "I think the point, Cecilia, is that we'll work out whatever we do next together."

She tipped her head up to look at him. Life was funny. She'd always looked up to Brady. Always been in a certain amount of awe of him, even when he was irritating her to death. She wouldn't have admitted it. Even at New Year's Eve, kissing him, she hadn't admitted she had *this* inside of her.

It had taken fear. Struggle. Now, she wouldn't stop admitting it. Her pride wasn't as important as being honest with him.

"You're a pretty good guy, Wyatt."

"Yeah, yeah. What did Layla say?"

"She's going to do it."

"Good. You know, it wouldn't be so bad. Staying here. Helping Grandma and Dev out. Keeping close to Mak. I wouldn't mind it so much."

Cecilia settled back against his chest. "No, I wouldn't mind it either."

This was not ever what she'd planned for her life. A guy like Brady. Living this close to home. Having her best friend and her best friend's baby under one roof. It wasn't a normal family by any stretch, but she'd never had *normal*.

What she'd had was love, and now she had more of it.

She settled into Brady and sighed. "I love you," she murmured. Because no matter what happened, love was always the reason you gutted through, fought for what you had to, and most of all, survived.

* * * * *

HARD CORE LAW

ANGI MORGAN

There is never a book without my pals Jan, Robin, Jen, Lizbeth and Janie. Lena Diaz, thanks for the brilliant ideas and personal information you shared about raising a child with diabetes.

Tim…I love you, man!

Prologue

"It was great to meet you. Night." The last of the birth-day guests waved from their cars.

Tracey Cassidy stood at the front door waving good-bye to another couple she barely knew. Two sets of little arms stretched around her thighs, squeezing with an appropriate four-and-a-half-year-old grunt.

"What are you two doing up? I tucked you in three hours ago."

"Happy birthday," they said in unison.

Jackson and Sage giggled until the sound of a dish breaking in the kitchen jerked them from their mer-riment. Their faces, so similar but different, held the same surprise and knowledge that their daddy was in super big trouble.

"Daddy's going to get it now." Sage nodded until her auburn curls bounced.

"Hurry." Tracey patted them on the backsides and pointed them in the right direction. "Back upstairs be-fore the Major has to scoop you up there himself. You know you'll have extra chores if he catches you down here."

The twins took each stair with a giant tiptoeing mo-tion. It would have been hilarious to watch them, but

their dad was getting a bit louder and might come looking for her to help.

"Scoot, and there's sprinkles on Friday's ice-cream
cone."

Bribery worked. They ran as fast as their short legs
could carry them up the carpeted staircase. Tracey
was sure their dad heard the bedroom door close. Then
again, he was making enough noise to wake the barn
cats.

"Tracey!" he finally yelled, seeking help. "Where's
the dustpan?"

Hurrying to the back of the house, she found Major
Josh Parker holding several pieces of broken glass in
one hand and the broom in the other. A juggler holding his act. Yep, that's what he looked like. He was still
completely out of his element in the kitchen. Or the
laundry. Good thing he had a maid.

"It should have been in the closet with the broom.
Here, let me take these." She reached for the pieces of
crystal covered in the remnants of spinach artichoke
dip.

"I'm good." He raised the mess out of her reach.
"Sorry about the bowl. I thought I was actually helping for once. Damn thing slipped right out of my hand."

"Here, just put it in this." She pulled the covered
trash can over to the mess and popped the lid open.

"Hell, Tracey, you don't have your shoes on. This
thing splintered into a thousand pieces."

Two forbidden words in one conversation? She'd
never seen Josh even the little tiniest bit tipsy. But the
group had toasted a lot tonight. First her birthday, then
an engagement, then to another couple who'd looked at
each other like lovebirds. Then to her birthday again.

"Are you a little drunk?" She ignored his warning

and crossed the kitchen to look for the dustpan, which was hanging on the wall of the pantry exactly where it should have been. She turned to tell Josh and walked straight into his chest.

"Well, would you look at that." He cocked his head to the side emphasizing his boyish dimple. "If it had been a snake it would have bitten me."

"Bitten a big chunk right out of your shoulder." She tapped him with the corner for emphasis, but he still didn't back up out of the doorway.

Josh leaned his forehead against the wood and exhaled a long "whew" sound. The smell of whiskey was strong. He had definitely drunk a little more than she'd ever witnessed. Maybe a little more than he should have. But he'd also been enjoying the company of his friends. Something long overdue. Most of his free time was spent with the twins.

"We need a cardboard box or something. This stuff—" He brought the glass from his side to his chest. "It'll bust through plastic."

His head dropped to the door frame and he closed his eyes. This time he relinquished the broken glass to her and backed up with some guidance. She helped him to the table, set a cold bottle of water in front of him and went about cleaning the floor.

Technically, it wasn't her job. She was officially off duty because Josh was home. But she couldn't leave him with his head on the kitchen table and glass all over the place. The kids would get up at their normal time, even if it was a Saturday. And the maid service wouldn't stop back around until Tuesday.

"The way you look right now, this mess might still be here after school Monday."

She moved around the edge of the tiled kitchen

avoiding as much of the mess as she could. He was right about one thing, glass was everywhere. She retrieved her sandals from the living room next to the couch. She'd kicked them off while watching the men in Josh's company interact with one another.

The wives hadn't meant to exclude her, but she wasn't one of them. She was the hired help. The nanny. She detested that word and told those who needed to know that she was the child care provider. In between a few bits of conversation, she silently celebrated in the corner. Not just her birthday, but also the achievement of receiving her PhD.

I need to tell him.

She pulled her sandals from where they'd crept under the couch and slipped them on her feet.

"They weren't very…approachable tonight, were they." A statement. Josh didn't seem to need an answer. One hand scrubbed at his face, while the other held a depleted water bottle. "Sorry 'bout this."

"Hey, nothing to be sorry for. The cake was out of this world."

"Vivian ordered it."

"Yeah, I was sorry she couldn't stay." Josh's receptionist had done her best to keep Tracey involved in the conversations. "Would you sit down before you fall down?"

"I'm not drunk. Just real tired. We've been working a lot, you know."

"I do. I've been spending way too many nights here. The neighbors are going to start talking."

"Let 'em." He grinned and let his head drop to the back of the couch cushions. "They can whinny all they want. And moo. Or just howl at the moon. I might even join 'em."

"I think you need a dog to howl."

Josh's closest neighbor was about three miles away. He did have several horses, three barn cats and let Jim-Bob Watts run cattle on their adjoining field. No one was really going to know if she was there all night or not.

No one but them.

They'd become lax about it recently. Whatever case the Texas Rangers were working on had been keeping him at Company F Headquarters in Waco. The case would soon be over—at least their part in it. She'd gathered that info from one or two of those whiskey toasts.

Tracey looked around the room. Plastic cups, paper plates with icing, napkins, forks. How could ten people make such a mess? A couple of the women had tried to offer their help, but everyone had seemed to leave at the same time.

Of course, the man now asleep on the couch, might have mentioned it was late. And if she worked in his office, she might misinterpret that as an order to get out. Tracey sighed and picked up a trash bag. What did one more late night matter?

Not like she had any reason to rush back to her campus apartment. She dropped two plastic cups into the bag and continued making her way around the room. She might as well clean up a little. It was mostly throwaway stuff and it wasn't fair to make the twins help their dad.

After all, it had been *her* birthday party.

Josh had his hands full just keeping up with the twins. The floor would be horrible by Tuesday if she didn't pass a mop across it. So she cleaned the floors and stored the cake—not to mention put the whiskey bottle above the refrigerator. On the second pass

through the living room, she took a throw from the storage ottoman and covered her boss.

It might be triple-digit weather outside, but Josh kept
the downstairs like a freezer. She draped the light blanket across him and his hand latched on to hers.

JOSH SHOULD BE ashamed of himself for letting Tracey
clean up while he faked sleep. *Should be*. He wasn't
drunk. Far from it. He was hyperaware of every one of
Tracey's movements.

"Tonight didn't go exactly like I planned."

"Oh shoot. I don't know why you scared me, but I
thought you were asleep. It was fun. A total surprise."
She placed her hand on top of his, patting it as if she was
ready to be let loose. She also didn't have a mean bone
in her body. She'd never intentionally hurt his feelings.

But Josh had to hold on. If he let her go, he might
not ever get the courage again. "You're lying. You were
miserable. I should have invited your friends."

"It was great. Really." She patted his hand again. "I
better head out."

"No." He stood, letting her hand go but trapping her
shoulders under his grip. He lightened up. "I mean.
Can you stay a couple of minutes? I didn't give you
your present."

"But you threw the party and everything."

Was it his hopeful imagination that her words were
a little breathier when he touched her? Touching was a
rare occurrence now that the twins walked themselves
up to bed and didn't need to be carried. Not his imagination. Her chest under the sleeveless summer shirt was
rising and falling faster.

One wayward strand of dark red hair that she tried
so hard to keep in place was curled in the middle of her

forehead. Most of the time she shoved it back in with the rest, but he practically had her hands pinned at her sides. This time, he followed through on a simple pleasure. He took the curl between his fingers and gently tucked it away.

Josh allowed the side of his hand to caress the soft skin of Tracey's cheek. His fingertips whispered across her lips and her eyes closed. It was time. Now. A conscious decision. No spur-of-the-moment accident.

He leaned down as he tilted her chin up. Their lips connected and his hands wrapped around her, smashing her body into his. They molded together and all the dormant parts of his soul ignited.

Four years since he'd really held a woman in his arms. The last lips he'd tasted had been a sweet goodbye. It had been a long time since he'd thought about passion.

Tracey's eyes opened when he hesitated for a split second. He didn't see fear or surprise—only passion waiting for him. He kissed her again, not allowing them time to think or reconsider.

Her lips tasted like the coconut-flavored lip balm she recently began using. But her mouth tasted of the butter-flavored icing from her birthday cake. Lips soft and rich. Her body was toned, yet pliant against him.

Yes, he analyzed it all. Every part of her. He wanted to remember just in case he never got another chance.

Intimacy hadn't been his since… Since… He couldn't allow himself to go in that direction. Tracey was in his arms. Tracey's body was responding to his caresses.

Their lips parted. He wanted to race forward, but they needed a beginning first. He'd worked it all out a hundred times in his head. This was logical. Start with a kiss, let her know he wanted more.

"Okay, that was…surprising for a birthday present."

No doubt about it, her voice was shaking with breathlessness.

"Sorry, that wasn't it. I kept the box at the office so the kids couldn't say anything. It's in the truck." He slipped his hands into his jeans pockets to stop them from pointing to one more thing. One step away from her and he wondered if she was breathless or so surprised she didn't know how to react.

"Josh?"

No.

"It'll just take a sec."

Tracey caught up with him and followed him onto the porch. "Maybe I should go home?" She smiled and rubbed his arm like a pal.

"Right." He slipped his thumbs inside his front pockets. He lifted his chin when he realized it was tucked to his chest.

"It's just… Well, you've been drinking and I don't want…" Her voice trailed off the same way it did when she was sharing something negative about the twins' behavior. She didn't want to disappoint him. Ever.

"Got it." He marched to her car and forced himself not to yank the door off the hinges.

"Don't be mad. It's not that I didn't—"

"Tracey. I got it."

And he did. All he knew about Tracey was that she'd been there for him and the kids. Assuming she felt the same when— Dammit, he didn't know anything about her life outside their small world here.

"I'm going to head out." Purse over her shoulder, she waved from the front door of her car. "Night." She waved and gently shut the door behind her.

Change is a mistake. Nah, he'd had this debate with

himself for weeks. It was time to move on. He couldn't be afraid of what might or might not happen.

Tracey's tires spun a little in the gravel as she pulled away. He hoped like hell that he hadn't scared her away. From him, maybe. But she wouldn't leave the twins, right? She was the only mother they'd ever had in their lives.

For a while, he'd thought he admired her for that. But this wasn't all about the kids. He needed her to say that she felt something for him. Because four years was long enough.

He was ready to love again.

Chapter One

Nothing. Two weeks since Josh Parker had kissed her, and then avoided her like the plague. Two weeks and she'd barely seen him. Adding insult to injury, he'd even hired a teenager to watch the kids a couple of nights.

Tracey tilted the rearview mirror to get a better view of Jackson and Sage. They were too quiet. Smiling at each other in twin language. It was ice cream Friday and they'd behaved at school, so that had meant sprinkles. And they'd enjoyed every single colored speck.

The intersection was busier than usual. The car in front of her turned and Tracey finally saw the holdup. The hood was up on a small moving van at the stop sign. She was making her way around, pulling to the side, when another car parked next to the van.

"Tracey, we're hungry," Sage said.

"I know, sweetheart. I'm doing my best." She put her Mazda in Reverse trying to turn around in the street. "Can you reach your crackers, Jackson?"

"Yep, yep, yep," he answered like the dinosaur on the old DVDs he'd been watching. She watched him tug his little backpack between the car seats and snag a cracker, then share a second with Sage.

"Just one, little man. You just had ice cream."

Two men left the moving van and waved at her to

back up. She was awfully close to the other van, but she trusted their directions. Right up until she felt her car hit. She hadn't been going fast enough for damage, but the guy seemed to get pretty steamed and stomped toward her door.

Great what a way to begin her weekend.

The men split to either side of her car, where one gave her the signal to roll down her window. She lowered it enough to allow him to hear her, then she unbuckled and leaned to the glove compartment for her insurance card.

"Sorry about that, but your friend—" Tracey looked up and froze.

Now in a ski mask, the man next to her window shouted, pulling on the door handle, tapping on the window with the butt of a handgun before pushing the barrel inside. "Open the door!"

She hit the horn repeatedly and put the car back into gear, willing to smash it to bits in order to get away. But it was wedged in tight. Once she'd backed up, they'd quickly used two vehicles to block her, parking in front and behind, pinning her car between the three.

Would they really shoot her to carjack an old junker of a Mazda?

"You can have the car. If you want money, it'll take a little while, but I can get that, too. You don't have to do this." She kept careful control of her voice. "Just let me unsnap the twins and take them with me."

"Get out! Now!" A second gunman shouted through the glass at the passenger door.

Where were all the cars now? Why had she lowered the window an inch to answer this man's question? What if they didn't let her get the kids out? Her mind was racing with questions.

They shouted at her, banging on the windows. The twins knew something was wrong and began to cry. Tracey gripped the steering wheel with one hand and blared the horn with the other. Someone had to hear them. Someone would come by and see what was happening.

"Lady, you get out of the car or I'll blow you away through the window." Gunman One pointed the gun at her head.

"You don't want these kids. Their dad's the head of the Texas Rangers in this area."

With a gun stuck in her face, Tracey didn't know how she was speaking—especially with any intelligence. Her hands were locked, determined to stay where they were. That's when she had the horrible feeling it wasn't a random carjacking.

"You're wrong, sweetheart. That's exactly why we want them," Gunman Two said.

"Shut up, Mack!" Gunman One screamed, hitting the top of the car. "You!" he yelled at her again. "Stop blabbing and get your butt out here before I blow your brains all over those kids."

One of the drivers got out of his box truck with a bent pole. Not a pole. It looked like it had a climbing spike on the end.

"No!" She leaned toward the middle, attempting to block what she knew was coming.

The new guy swung, hitting the window, and it shattered into pebble-size glass rocks. The kids screamed louder. She tried to climbing into the backseat. The locks popped open and three doors flew wide.

Gunman One latched on to her ankles and yanked. Her chin bounced against the top of the seat. Jarring pain jolted across her face. Before she could grab anything or brace herself, her body tumbled out of the car. Twisted, her side and shoulder took most of the fall to the street.

She prayed someone would drive by and see what was happening. She looked everywhere for help. Wasn't there anyone who could intervene or call the police? Her small purse was still strapped across her chest, hidden at her hip. Her cell phone was still inside so maybe she could—

Gunman One flipped open a knife and sliced the strap, nicking her neck in the process. "We wouldn't want you to call Daddy too soon. You got that tape, Mack?" He jerked her to her feet, hitting the side of her head with his elbow. "You just had to play the hero."

"Here ya go, Mack." Gunman Two, already in the car, tossed him duct tape.

Gunman One smashed her face into the backseat window, winding the tape around her wrists. Both of the children were screaming her name. They knew something wasn't right. Both were trapped in their car seats, clawing at the straps then stretching their arms toward her.

"It's okay, guys. No one's going to hurt you." She tried to calm them through the glass. "Please don't do this. Jackson has diabetes. He's on a restricted diet and his insulin level has to be closely—"

Gunman One rolled her to her back and shoved her along the metal edge of the Mazda to the trunk.

Oh my God. They knew. She could tell by his reactions. She was right. It wasn't a carjacking. This was a planned kidnapping of Josh Parker's twins. Gunman One knocked her to the ground. The other men cut the seat belts holding the kids, took them from the car in their car seats, grabbing their tiny backpacks at the last minute.

How could men in ski masks be assaulting her in broad daylight and no one else see them?

"Please take me. I won't give you any trouble. I swear I won't. I…I can look after Jackson. Make sure he doesn't go into shock."

Gunman One pulled her hands. "You won't do, sister. It's gotta be somebody he loves."

"Let him have crackers. Okay? He has to eat every three or four hours. Something," she pleaded. "Sage, watch your brother!"

When this had all started, Tracey hadn't paid attention to what the man coming to her window had looked like. An average guy that she couldn't swear was youngish or even in his thirties. They were all decked out in college gear. She searched this man's eyes that were bright and excited behind the green ski mask, memorizing everything about their brown darkness.

The tiny scar woven into his right eyebrow would be his downfall. He raised the butt of the gun in the air. She closed her eyes, anticipating the blow. The impact hurt, stunning her. Vision blurred, she watched them carry the twins, running to the back of the moving van. Her legs collapsed from the pain, and she hit the concrete without warning.

I'm so sorry, Josh.

Chapter Two

How were you supposed to tell someone you'd allowed their kids to be kidnapped? Tracey would have a doctorate in nutrition soon, but none of the courses she'd taken prepared her to face Josh. Or the future.

When someone found Tracey unconscious on the sidewalk and the paramedics revived her, she'd cried out his name. She could never articulate why she was calling to him. Once fully awake and by the time anyone would listen, the twins had been missing for almost an hour. Tracey hadn't been able to explain to Josh what had happened. The police did that.

"He's going to hate me," she mumbled.

"I don't think he will. I've dealt with a lot of kidnappings. This isn't your fault. Major Parker will realize that faster than most." Special Agent George Lanning had answered her with an intelligent response.

The problem was...

"Intelligence has nothing to do with emotional, gut-wrenching pain. I lost his kids. He'll never trust me again and I don't blame him."

After she awoke in the hospital, she'd only been allowed to talk with one police officer, her nurse and a doctor. The door had been left open a couple of inches. She'd recognized rangers passing by, even heard them asking about her. But the officer had refused her any visitors. At least until this FBI agent showed up.

Two hours later she was sitting in a car on her way to the Parker home to face Josh for the first time. Where else was she supposed to go? She'd refused to return to her apartment as they'd suggested. "How bad is my face?"

"As in? What context do you mean?"

She flipped down the passenger mirror to see for herself. "Well, I don't think makeup—even if I had any—would help this." She gently touched her cheekbone that felt ten times bigger than it should. "I don't want to look like…"

"Tracey. Four men yanked you from a car and hit you so hard they gave you a concussion. They kidnapped Jackson and Sage. No matter what you think you could have done differently, those men would still have the Parker twins."

She wiped another tear falling down her cheek. Agent Lanning might be correct. But nothing anyone said would ever make her feel okay about what had happened.

Nothing.

The road to the house was lined with extra cars and the yard—where they needed to park—filled with men standing around. The police escort in front of them flipped on the squad car lights with a siren burst to get people out of the way. Tracey covered her ears.

Everything hurt. Her head pounded in spite of the pain medication the doctor had given her. But she was prepared to jump out of the car as soon as it slowed down. First she needed to beg for Josh's forgiveness. And then find out what the authorities had discovered.

"You really took a wallop," he said. "You should probably get some rest as soon as possible."

She had rested at the hospital, where so much had been thrown at her. Part of the argument for her going home was to sleep and meet with a forensic artist as soon as one arrived. She'd refused, telling Agent Lanning it was useless to draw a face hidden with a ski mask. Then they'd finally agreed to take her directly to Josh.

The sea of people parted and the agent parked next to cars nearer to the front porch. She didn't wait for the engine to stop running. She jumped out, needing to explain while she still had the courage.

Moving quickly across the fading grass of the lawn, she slowed as friends stared at her running inside. She completely froze in the entryway, looking for the straight dark hair that should have towered over most of the heads in the living room. But Josh wasn't towering anywhere. She pushed forward and someone grabbed her arm. A ranger waved him off.

Everyone directly involved in Josh's life knew who she was. The ranger who had spotted her was Bryce Johnson. He put his hand at her back and pushed the crowd of men out of her way.

"You doing okay?" he asked, guiding her through probably every ranger who worked in or near Waco. "Need anything? Maybe some water?"

She nodded. There was already a knot in her throat preventing her from speaking. She'd assumed a lot of people would be here, but why so many? "Why aren't you guys out looking for the twins?"

Everyone turned their attention to a man near the window seat. But she focused on the twins' dad. Josh looked the way he did the day Gwen had died. From

day one, neither of Josh or Gwen had felt like employers. They were her friends. She wanted to be there for
him again, but didn't know if he'd let her. He glanced
at her, and then covered his eyes as though he were
afraid to look at her.

The guy in the suit near the window jerked his head
to the side and they left. All of them. Except for a
woman and Josh, both seated at the opposite end of the
breakfast table. They were joined by Agent Lanning,
who pulled out a chair and gestured for Tracey to sit.

It was a typical waiting-on-a-ransom-demand scene
from a movie. The three professionals looked the parts
of FBI agents. The woman sat at something electronic
that looked as if it monitored phone calls. Agent Lanning moved to the back door and turned politely to face
the window. The other man, who they both seemed
to defer to, uncrossed his arms and tapped Josh on
the shoulder.

Josh's head was bent, almost protected between his
arms resting on the table. He hadn't acknowledged the
fact that nearly everyone had left. He hadn't acknowledged anything.

"I don't know what to say. I'm sorry doesn't seem
like enough," she began.

Josh's head jerked up along with the rest of him as
he stood, tipping the chair backward to the floor. She
winced at the noise. She assumed he'd be disappointed
and furious and might even scream at her to get out.
But feeling it, seeing it, experiencing the paralyzing
fear that they might not get the kids back...

"This might sound stupid, but we need to verify that
Jackson was wearing his insulin pump," he whispered
without a note of anger.

"Yes. I checked it when I picked him up."

"Thank God. I knew you would. You always do."

The woman opened her mouth but the agent at the window raised a finger. She immediately smashed her lips together instead. Josh covered his face with his hands again. What had she expected? That he'd be— *oh, everything's going to be okay, Tracey. Don't worry about it Tracey. We'll find them together, Tracey.*

"Has anyone seen anything? Said anything?" she asked no one in particular.

"Let's step into the bedroom, Miss Cassidy." The agent by the window took a step toward her.

"She stays," Josh ordered, holding up a hand to halt him. "I want to hear everything firsthand. Same for anything you have to say to me. She can hear it, so she stays."

"All right. I'm Special Agent in Charge Leo McCaffrey and this is Agent Kendall Barlow. No, the kidnappers haven't called. There's been no ransom demand." He pointed to the woman at the table and crossed his arms. "Have you remembered anything else that might help?"

"Not really. A van was broken down. Two men came to my car to help me back up. It seems like one purposely let me reverse into the rental van. Then one came to the passenger window and tapped. I thought they needed my insurance or license or something. They looked like college students until they pulled the masks over their faces. I have to admit that I didn't pay any attention to their faces when they were uncovered." Tracey latched her fingers around the edge of the kitchen chair, hoping she wouldn't fall off as the world spun a little on its side.

"You didn't think that was unusual?" the woman asked.

"Not really. Students walk a lot around here. That part of Waco isn't far from downtown."

It was weird what she noticed about Agent McCaffrey. Average height, but nice looking. His short hair had a dent around the middle like Josh's did when he wore his Stetson. Or after an afternoon with his ball cap on. She glanced at his feet. Sure enough, he wore a pair of nice dress boots. And then she remembered the men abducting her had worn work boots.

"Wait. The men who got out of the moving truck. They both wore an older Baylor shirt from about five years ago. And they all wore the same type of work boots. I could almost swear that they were new and the same brand. The man who...who pulled me from the car..." Everyone looked at her, waiting. "He had dark brown eyes and thick eyebrows. Not thick enough to hide a scar across the right one."

"That's good, Miss Cassidy. Anytime something comes to you, just make sure to tell Agent Lanning. Anything special about the others?"

"I wasn't close to the other two. It all happened so fast that I didn't know what to do." She choked on the last word. She hadn't known. Still didn't.

"When you were questioned at the hospital, you had a hard time remembering the small details, but they'll probably come back." The woman spoke again, pushing a pad toward the center of the table. "You should keep a notebook handy."

"I...uh...couldn't get to the hospital," Josh said loudly. He swallowed hard and shook his head, looking a little lost.

Tracey had never seen that look on his face before. "I didn't expect you to."

"It's just... I haven't been there since Gwen..." Josh

looked at her asking her to understand without making him say the words. "I guess I had to have been there once with Jackson." He pushed his hand through his short hair. "But I can't remember when for some reason."

"I know. It's okay," she whispered, wanting to reach out and grab his hand. "You needed to be here."

Major Parker was her employer, but she couldn't stand it. Someone needed to help him. To be on his side like no other person would be. This time she shoved back from the table and her chair was the one that hit the floor. She pushed past Agent McCaffrey and covered Josh with her arms. He buried his face against her, wrapping his arms around her waist as if she were the only thing keeping him from falling off a cliff.

Until two weeks ago, they hadn't hugged since Gwen had died. Had rarely touched each other except for an accidental brush when handing the kids to each other. Then there'd been that kiss.

An unexpected kiss after an impromptu surprise birthday party with several of his friends. A kiss that had thrown her into so many loop-de-loops, she'd been dizzy for days. But it must have thrown Josh for a loop he didn't want. He hadn't spoken to her except in passing. Which was the reason she'd accepted the out-of-state position.

She held him, feeling the rapid beating of his heart through the hospital scrubs they'd given her. They had so much to face and right now he needed to be comforted as much as she did.

Someone at the hospital had said she was just the nanny. She didn't feel like *just* the hired help. She'd avoided that particular title and thought it demeaning when Josh's friends referred to her that way. Months

when the rent was hard to come by, her friends asked
her why she didn't move in to take care of the twins.

At first it had been because she thought it was a temporary job. Eventually Josh would hire a real nanny.
Then she'd been certain Josh would eventually date and
remarry, so she hadn't wanted to complicate the situation. And this past year it had been because she was
falling in love with him.

Now the word *nanny* didn't seem complex enough
for their situation. She'd been a part of the twins' lives
from infancy. She'd been told to go home and stay there
with a protection detail so she could be easily reached
if needed. She was *just* the nanny.

Just the person who provided day care—and any
other time of the day care when Josh was on a case. But
his lost look was the reason she hadn't obeyed the order.

Technically, Tracey knew she *was* just the nanny.
Yet, her heart had been ripped from her body—twice.
Once for each child.

She held Josh tight until Agent McCaffrey cleared his
throat. She sat in the chair next to Josh. Bryce brought
the bottle of water he'd offered when she first arrived
and dropped back to the living room doorway.

"Is this a vendetta or revenge for one of the men
you've put away?" Tracey asked Josh, who finally
looked her in the eyes. "I tried to convince them to
take me instead. They said it needed to be someone
you loved."

Chapter Three

Someone you loved...

Did she know? Josh searched her face, seeing nothing but concern for his kids. It was on the tip of his tongue to tell her they would have gotten it right if she'd been taken.

That sounds ridiculous.

He didn't want her abducted any more than he wanted the twins to be gone. He reached out, touching her swollen cheek.

"They hurt you." Stupid statement. It was obvious, but he didn't know what else to say. "Of course they did. They took you to the hospital."

He noticed what she was wearing, the streak of blood still on her neck, the bandage at her hairline. Hospital scrubs because her clothes had been ruined.

Time to shed the shaking figure of a lost father. Tenoreno had hit his family—the only place he considered himself vulnerable. But he was stronger than this. He needed to show everyone—including himself. Gathering some courage, he straightened his backbone and placed both palms flat on the table to keep himself there.

He knew what McCaffrey was thinking. The agent had repeated his questions about Tracey's possible motives more than once. Agent Kendall Barlow had been ordered to run a thorough background check on "the nanny." If Tracey heard them call her that she'd let them know she was a child care provider and personal nutritionist.

Definitely not the nanny.

The FBI might have doubts about Tracey—he didn't. First and foremost, she had no motive. They might need to rule her out as a suspect. No one in the room had mentioned Tenoreno by name. But Josh knew who was responsible.

Drawing air deep into his lungs, he readied himself to get started. Ready to fight Tenoreno or whoever he'd hired to take his kids.

"The agents need to know how long Jackson's insulin will be okay. Can you give them more details?" All the extra chatter around him died. He took Tracey's hand in his. "I took a guess, but you know a lot more about it than I do. These guys need an accurate estimate. I couldn't think straight earlier."

"It depends." She drew in a deep breath and blew it out, puffing her cheeks. "There are stress factors I can't estimate. A lot will be determined by what they give the twins to eat, of course. The cartridge can last three days, but he might be in trouble for numerous reasons. They could give him the wrong food or the tube might get clogged. The battery should be fine."

"Hear that everybody? My son has forty-eight hours that we can count on. Seventy-two before he slips into a diabetic coma. Why are you still here?" He used his I'm-the-ranger-in-charge voice.

It worked. All the rangers, cops and friends left the house.

"I'm more worried that Sage might try to imitate

what I do with the bolus when he eats. She knows not to touch it. But she also knows that when Jackson eats, I calculate how much extra insulin to give him. She's a little mother hen and might try since I'm not there."

"What's a bolus?" George Lanning asked.

"An extra shot of insulin from his pump. You calculate, it injects." The female agent shrugged. "I read and prepare for my cases."

Josh hated diabetes.

Bryce stayed by the kitchen door. He'd driven Josh and wouldn't leave until he had confirmation of orders that the two of them had already discussed. Unofficial orders when no one had been listening. Ranger headquarters had someone on the way to relieve him as Company F commander. Whoever was now in charge would make certain every rule was followed to the letter and that personnel kept their actions impeccable.

"Everyone is working off the assumption that the Tenoreno family is behind this. Right?" he asked McCaffrey, finally stating what everyone thought.

The FBI agents' reactions were about what he expected. No one would confirm. They zipped their lips tight and avoided eye contact. But their actions were all the confirmation he needed.

The Mafia family connection was the reason the FBI had been called as soon as Josh had received the news. He'd rather have his Company in charge, but the conflict of interest was too great.

Bryce stood in the doorway and shook his head, warning him not to push the issue. They'd talked through the short list of pros and cons about confronting anyone called in to handle the kidnapping.

The more they forced the issue, the less likely the FBI would be inclined to share information. It could all blow up in his face. But it was like a big bright red button with a flashing neon sign that said Do Not Push.

The longer the agents avoided answering, the brighter the button blinked, tempting him to hit it.

"The Tenoreno family?"

Tracey was the only one left who didn't know who they were. She needed to know what faced them because she was certain to be used by the Mafia-like family. No one wanted to explain so it was up to him to bring her up to speed.

Two hours and thirty-eight minutes after Tracey was found unconscious on a sidewalk, his phone rang. Brooks & Dunn's "Put a Girl in It" blasted through the kitchen.

"That's my ringtone for Tracey. They're using her phone. It's the kidnappers."

EVERYONE STARED AT the phone. Only one person moved. Agent Barlow pulled a headset onto her ears, clicked or pushed buttons, then pointed to Agent McCaffrey. It really was like being a part of a scripted movie. Tracey could only watch.

"You know what to do, Josh. Try to keep them on the line as long as possible," Agent McCaffrey said.

Tracey cupped her hands over her mouth to stop the words she wanted to scream. They would only antagonize the kidnappers and would probably get her dragged from the room. She needed to hear what those masked men were about to say.

Agent Barlow clicked on Josh's cell.

"This is Parker." Josh's fingers curled into fists.

"You won't hear from us again as long as you're working with the FBI." The line went dead.

"No. Wait!" Josh hammered his hand against the

wood tabletop. But his face told her he knew it was no use.

"What just happened? Shouldn't they let us know how to get in touch with them?" Tracey looked around the room, wanting answers. What did this mean? "You do have a plan, right?"

Agent McCaffrey clasped Josh's shoulder, then patted it—while staring into Tracey's eyes. "That's what we expected."

Everyone's stare turned to Agent Barlow, who shook her head. "Nothing. We've been monitoring for Miss Cassidy's phone, they fired it up, made the call and probably pulled the battery again."

"So we're back to square one." Agent Lanning tapped on the window, silently bringing attention to the suits monitoring the outside of the house.

"We have instructions." Josh stared at the only other ranger left in the house—Bryce.

Tracey was confused. It was as if they were speaking in some sort of code. Or maybe they were stating something obvious and the concussion was keeping her from recognizing it. The others shook their heads.

"You don't want to do that, Josh." Agent McCaffrey kept his cool. He clearly didn't want whatever Josh had just silently communicated to Bryce. "This case is going to be difficult—"

"It's not a case. They're my kids." Josh hit his chest with his fist. "Mine."

"You need our resources." Barlow dropped the headphones on the table.

"I *need* you to leave. I've told you that from the beginning." Josh stood. Calmly this time, without tipping the chair to the floor. "I've played along for the past couple of hours hoping it's not what we thought, but it is. These guys aren't going to play games. They either get what they want or they kill—"

"You can't do this," Barlow said.

The agent seemed a little dramatic, but what did Tracey know?

"Yes, I can. It's my right to refuse your help." Josh gestured for Tracey to lead the way to the back staircase.

"Look…" Agent McCaffrey lowered his voice. "We'll admit that the kidnapping involves Tenoreno. We assume these men are going to ask you to do something illegal. You're better off if we stay."

"I haven't done anything illegal. You need to go." Josh took the Texas Ranger Star he was so proud of and dropped it in the agent's open palm. "Bryce. You know what to do."

Josh caught Tracey under her elbow and led her up the staircase. They went to the kids' bedroom, where he shut the door.

"What is Bryce going to do?"

"First thing is to get my badge back. I shouldn't have given it to McCaffrey. But the agent wanted it for show in case the kidnappers are watching. I'll surrender it to the new Company commander if they ask me to resign, not before. Then he'll get everyone out of the house. Before the FBI arrived, we assumed we knew who was behind the kidnapping. There's really no other motive. It's not like I have a ton of money to pay a ransom."

Tracey winced, but Josh was looking out the window and couldn't have seen. The twins' kidnapping didn't have anything to do with her. The man said it has to be someone he loves. *He meant someone Josh loves. Right?*

"What if…" She hesitated to ask, to broach the subject that this entire incident might be her fault. She cleared her throat. "What are you going to do without the FBI's help?"

"Get things done. Bryce has already arranged for friends in the Waco PD to watch the agents who will be watching us." He quirked a brow at his cleverness, sitting on the footstool between the twin beds.

His wife's parents had chosen that stool to match a rocker Gwen had never gotten to hold her children in. She'd been too weak. It's where Josh refused to sit. The stool was as close as he'd get. The chair was where Tracey had rocked the babies to sleep.

"Have you told Gwen's parents?"

"There's nothing they could do. McCaffrey thinks it's better to wait."

"The FBI will be following us when we leave the house." He stood again, wiping his palms on his jeans. "They'll wait for me to issue an order to my men. I'd be breaking the law since I've been asked to step away from my command. Then they'll swoop back in like vultures and take control of things."

"Will you?"

"What? Leave? Don't worry." He straightened books on the shelf. "When I do, I'll make sure someone's here with you. Bryce will be close. I won't leave you alone."

"No. That's not what I'm talking about. Will you break the law?"

He gawked at her with a blank look of incredulousness. Either surprised that she'd asked, insulting his ranger integrity. Or surprised that she questioned...

"What are you willing to do to save Jackson and Sage?" She tried not to move the rocker. She was serious and needed to know how far he'd go. "For the record, I'm willing to do anything. And I mean anything, including breaking the law."

Did he look a little insulted as he bent and picked up Jackson's pj's from the floor? Well, she didn't care. It was something she needed to hear him say out loud.

"Don't look so surprised. I've heard about the integrity of the Texas Rangers since the first day I met you. How could I not after listening to the countless kitchen table conversations on the subject? Not to mention this past year when three of your company men might have been straddling the integrity fence, but managed to come out squeaky clean heroes."

"You act like having integrity is a bad thing." He clutched the pajamas and moved to the window instead of placing them back in the dresser.

"Not at all." She stood and joined him, wishing she could blink and make this all go away.

All she could do was wrap her palms around his upper arm, offering the comfort of a friend. Even though they'd been raising his children together for four years, she couldn't make the decisions he'd soon be faced with.

"Are you going to tell me about the Tenoreno family? At least more than what I've heard about them in the news? Are you in charge of the case?"

Josh didn't shrug her away. They stood shoulder to shoulder at the pastel curtains sprinkled with baby farm animals. He stared at something in the far distance past the lake. Tracey just stared at him.

"In charge of the case? No. Company F has prepared Paul Tenoreno's transportation route from Huntsville to Austin. I finalized the details this morning. Now that this…the kidnapping, your injuries…" He paused and took a couple of shallow breaths. "Tenoreno's transport to trial has to be what this is all about. Thing is, state authorities are sure to change everything. It's why they brought the FBI onto the case so quickly."

"Is Tenoreno mixed up in the Mafia like the news insinuates?"

"Tenoreno *is* the Mafia in Texas."

A chill scurried up her spine. The words seemed final somehow. As if Josh had accepted something was about to happen and there was no going back. He hadn't answered her question about how far he'd go. But he wouldn't let the Mafia take his kids. He just wouldn't.

"You need to make me a promise, Tracey."

"Anything."

He removed her hands and crossed his arms over his chest, tilting his head to stare at the top of hers because he was frightened to meet her hazel eyes. Frightened of the desperation she might see in his face.

"Hear me out before you give me what for. I made you the guardian of the twins last year."

"Without asking me?"

"Yeah. I was afraid you'd say no." Josh shrugged and lifted the corner of his mouth in a little smile.

It was Tracey's turn to look incredulous. "Seriously? When have I ever told you that I wouldn't do something for those kids?"

He nodded, agreeing. "I need you to promise that no matter what happens to me…"

"I promise, but nothing's going to happen to you."

Of course, she didn't know that. This afternoon when she'd headed to the day care to pick up the twins, she wouldn't have believed anything could have happened to any of them. It has been an ordinary day. She'd finally made up her mind to talk with Josh about finding a permanent nanny to take her place.

"You asked what I was willing to do. They're my

kids, Tracey. I'll do anything for them, including prison time." Josh still had the pj's wrapped in his hand. "Believe me, that's not my intention, but you have to know it's a possibility."

Was he aware that she was willing to join him? She meant what she'd said about doing anything for Jackson and Sage. And if that meant *she* was the one who went to jail—so be it. And if it came down to it, she'd do anything to keep them with their father.

"Just tell me what to do, Josh."

"Nothing. If Tenoreno's people contact you, tell me. You can't be involved in this. It has to be me." He gripped her shoulders and then framed her cheeks. One of his thumbs skated across the bruised area and settled at her temple. "You got that? *I'm* the one who's going to rescue my kids and pay the consequences."

She believed him. She had to. But she couldn't promise to stay out of his way. She might have the answer. What if money could solve their problem? Even if it wouldn't, now wasn't the time to tell him she'd never let him be separated from the twins.

Chapter Four

Josh pulled Tracey to his chest, wrapping his arms around her, keeping someone he cared about safe. He stared at the green pajamas decorated with pictures of yellow trucks—dump trucks, earthmovers, cranes and he didn't know what else. He used to know.

How long had it been since he'd played in the sandbox with the kids? Since he'd been there for dinner and their bath time?

Mixed feelings fired through his brain. He couldn't start down the regret road. He needed to concentrate on the twins' safety. The overpowering urge to protect Tracey wasn't just because she was an unofficial member of the family.

Tenoreno had hired someone to assault her and steal his children. Her cuts and bruises—dammit, he should have been there to protect her. To protect all of them.

"There has to be something we can do to make this go faster." She pressed her face against his chest and cried.

It was the first time to cry since she'd entered the house today. He fought the urge to join her, but once a day was his limit. If he broke down again, he wouldn't be able to function. Or act like the guy who might know what he was doing.

A knock at the door broke them apart. Tracey went to the corner table and pulled a couple of Kleenex from the box.

"Yeah?" It could only be one of two people on the other side. Bryce or Agent McCaffrey.

"You fill her in yet?" McCaffrey stepped inside, closing the door behind him.

Tracey looked up after politely blowing her nose; a questioning look crinkled her forehead.

"We were just getting there."

"Here's the phone you can use to contact us. We won't be far away."

"But far enough no one's going to notice." Josh took the phone and slid it into his back pocket.

"Anyone following you will see the obvious cars. They'll lose you after a couple of miles, but George and I will be there."

"Josh?" Tracey said his name with all the confusion she should be experiencing. After all, he'd just demanded the FBI and police leave him alone, get out of his house and off the case.

"It's okay, Tracey. All part of the plan. We need the kidnappers to think I'm in this on my own. No help from anyone. Hopefully that'll limit what they ask me to do."

When he left the house he'd have a line of cars following and hoped it didn't look like a convoy. A bad feeling smothered any comfort he had that law enforcement would be close by.

"So everything you just said—"

"Was the truth. Every word." He shot her a look asking her to keep that info to herself.

He knew that stubborn look, the compressed lips, the crossed arms. It would soon be followed by a long exhale after holding her breath. Sometimes he wanted to squeeze the air from her lungs because she held on to it so long. Each time he knew she wasn't just controlling her breathing. She was also controlling her tongue because she disagreed with what he was saying or doing.

Mainly about the kids.

Lately, it had been about how often he worked late or how he had avoided necessary conversations. Like the one congratulating her on finishing her thesis. Yeah, he'd avoided that because it would open the door to her resignation. What they needed to talk about was serious. She'd most likely accepted a position somewhere—other than Waco. If he could, he'd also like to avoid a conversation about what happened two weeks ago when they'd kissed.

This time, he could see that she didn't believe the lines he was spouting to the FBI. He just hoped that Special Agent McCaffrey couldn't read her like a book, too. Then he might suspect Josh had his own agenda.

"I don't think they'll wait very long to make contact after I leave." The agent unbuttoned his jacket and stuck his hands in his pockets. "My belief is that they knew about Jackson's diabetes and believe it will scare you into following their orders faster. If they didn't, they've seen the pump by now and are scared something might happen to him. Either way, I don't think they're really out to hurt the kids."

Agent McCaffrey stood straight—without emotion—in his official suit and tie. Just how official—they'd find out if he kept their deal to let Josh work the case from the inside.

"But you can't be sure of that," Tracey said. "How can anyone predict what will happen."

Tracey was right about part of Josh's inner core. He

was a Texas Ranger through and through. He'd try it the legal way. But if that didn't work, they'd see a part of him he rarely drew upon.

"George said you held up at the hospital exceptionally well, Miss Cassidy."

McCaffrey had a complimentary approach, where George looked like a laid-back lanky cowboy leaning on a fence post. Josh had met George several times on cases. He trusted him. George had given his word that McCaffrey would be on board. But Tracey didn't know any of that history. She had no reason to trust any of them.

"Don't I get a phone for you to keep track of my location?" Tracey asked.

"Actually, yes." McCaffrey handed her an identical cheap phone to what they'd given him. "By accepting this, you're allowing us to monitor it."

The man just didn't have the most winning personality. Josh saw the indignation building within Tracey and couldn't stop her.

"Were you really going to wait for my permission? That seems rather silly to ask. Just do it." Her words seemed more like a dare. She was ready to go toe to toe with someone.

"Tracey. That's not the way things are." Standing up for the FBI wasn't his best choice at this precise moment. Tracey looked like she needed to vent.

"Have you ruled me out as a suspect?" she asked.

Why was she holding her breath this time? Did she have something to hide? Josh opened his mouth to reason with her, but McCaffrey waved him off.

"I have a lot of experience with kidnappings, Tracey. I imagine you're familiar with the statistics that most children are abducted by someone in their immediate family or life. My people ran our standard background check on you first thing. We would have been reckless not to." He leaned against the doorjamb not seeming rushed for time or bothered by her hostility. "A reference phone call cleared you."

Tracey stiffened. She drew her arms close across her chest, hugging herself, rubbing her biceps like she was cold. Her hand slipped higher, one finger covering her lips, then her eyes darted toward the window. She was hiding something and McCaffrey had just threatened to expose whatever it was.

"Tracey, what's going on?"

"We're good, Josh." The agent looked at Tracey.

She nodded her head. "I don't know why I said anything. I was never going to keep you from tracking this phone." Tracey sank to the footstool. "I already told you I'd cooperate and do anything for Jackson and Sage."

The special agent in charge crossed the room and patted Tracey's shoulder. He'd done the same thing to Josh earlier, but it didn't seem to ease Tracey. There was nothing insincere in his gesture. But it seemed a more calculated action, as though McCaffrey knew it was effective. Not because it was real comfort.

Josh wanted to throw the agent out of his kids' room and be done with the FBI. "Do you need anything else?" he asked instead.

"I can't help you if you keep me out of the loop, Josh." McCaffrey quirked an eyebrow at Josh's lack of a reaction. "You've got to work with my people to get the children back. We stick with the plan."

"That's all nice and reasonable, but we both know that there's nothing logical about a kidnapping. You can never predict what's going to happen."

"The quicker you pick up that phone and let us know what they want the better."

"The quicker you clear out of here, the faster they'll contact us." Josh's hands were tied. He had to work with the FBI, use their resources, find the kidnappers. Or at least act like he was being cooperative. He sighed in relief when the agent left and softly closed the door behind him.

What the hell was wrong with him?

His twins had been kidnapped. It was natural to want to bash some heads together. But for a split second there, he'd wanted to just do whatever Tenoreno's men wanted and hold his kids again.

Tracey was visibly shaken by whatever McCaffrey's team had uncovered. His background check five years ago when he'd hired her hadn't uncovered it. And in the time that she'd been around his family, she'd never shared it. He had his own five years of character reference. No one else's mattered.

"I don't know what that was about." He jerked his thumb toward the closed door. *Should he ask?* "Right now I don't care."

"I swear I was never… It's just something I keep private. But I can fill you in. I mean, unless it's going to distract you. This shouldn't be about me."

"Will it make a difference to what's going to happen?" Sure, he was curious, but what if she was right and it did distract him? The FBI didn't think it was relevant. He could wait until his family was back where they belonged. "You know, we have more important things to worry about, so save it."

"Okay." Tracey sat straight, ready to get started. "So how is this going to work? Do you think the kidnappers will use my phone to call yours again? Wait!" She popped to her feet. "We don't have your phone. It's downstairs."

Josh blocked her with an outstretched arm. "If it rings, Bryce will let us know. He'll come up here before he leaves and that won't be until everyone else is out of the house."

They stared a second or two at each other. He wanted to know what she was hiding from him. She bit her lip, held her breath, and then couldn't look him in the eyes.

"Tracey, we have to trust each other. If you don't want to go through with this..."

"Of course I want to help. It's my fault they're missing. I don't know how you're being kind to me at all or even staying alone in the same room. I'm not sure I could do it."

"I don't blame you for what's happened. How can I?" He kept a hand on her shoulder. She didn't fight to get away. "I'm beating myself up that I didn't put a security detail on all of you. If anyone's to blame, it's me. Tenoreno has come after three of my men and their families. Why did I think you or the kids weren't vulnerable?"

"We have to stop blaming ourselves," she said softly. "If you have a plan, now might be the time to share it with me."

"It's not so much a plan as backup. What I said before McCaffrey came in, I meant it. But if I can keep the FBI on my side...we're all better off."

A gentle knock stopped the conversation again. "They've cleared out, Major. I've secured all the windows and doors. Here's your phone." Ranger Johnson said through the door.

Josh turned the knob and stuck out his hand. "Thanks, Bryce. You guys know what to do. My temporary replacement's going to have a tough time. The other men are going to resent that he's there. They're also going to want to help with the kidnapping. You've got to make the men understand that none of you can get involved and that those orders come from me."

"Good luck. And sir—" Bryce shook his hand, clasping his left on top of it "—let's make sure it's just a temporary replacement. You know we're all here when you need us."

"We appreciate that."

"I think this is one time that One Riot, One Ranger shouldn't apply. I'll take care of things." Bryce walked downstairs.

Tracey gently pushed past Josh, nudging herself into the hall. "I can't stay in their room any longer. And I really think I need a drink."

Josh followed her. "But you don't drink. And probably shouldn't, with a concussion."

"Don't you have some Wild Turkey or Jim Beam? Something's on top of the refrigerator, right? It's the perfect time to start."

"Yeah, but you might not want to start with that." How did she know where he kept his only bottle of whiskey?

"Actually, Josh, I went to college. Just because you've never seen me drink doesn't mean it's never happened. A shot of whiskey isn't going to impair my judgment."

She was in the kitchen, pulling a chair over to reach the high cabinet before he could think twice about helping or stopping. He sort of stared while she pulled two highball glasses reserved for poker night that had been collecting dust awhile. A finger's width—his, not her tiny fingers—was in the glass and she frowned before sliding it toward him across the breakfast bar.

"Drink up. You need it worse than I do."

He stared at it. And at her.

She suddenly didn't look like a college student. He noticed the little laugh lines at the corner of her eyes and how deep a green they were. It took him all this time to realize she was wearing a Waco Fire Department T-shirt under the baggy scrub top. Something he'd never seen her wear before.

She threw the whiskey back and poured herself another. "Am I drinking alone?"

He swirled the liquid, took a whiff. That was enough for him. Clearheaded. Ready to get on the road. That's what he needed more than the sting and momentary warmth the shot would provide.

Tracey threw the second shot back, closing her eyes and letting the glass tip on its side. Her eyes popped open as if she'd been startled. Then they dropped to the phone that was resting next to his hand, vibrating.

Her hand covered the cell.

His hand covered hers.

"Wait. Three rings. It'll allow the FBI time to get their game face on."

Ring three he uncovered her hand and slid through the password, then pushed Speaker.

"Time for round one, Ranger Parker. You get a new phone from a store in Richland Mall. We'll contact you there in half an hour. Bring the woman."

The line disconnected.

"Do they really think that no one is listening to those instructions he just gave us?" Tracey asked.

"We follow everything he says. He'll try to get us clear of everyone. We get the phone, but the next time he makes contact—before we do anything else—we get proof of life." Josh dropped the phone in his shirt pocket realizing that the kidnappers had just made Tracey a vital part of their plan. "I hoped they'd leave you out of this. We just need to know both kids are okay before I argue to take you out of the equation."

"Of course." She hurried around the end of the breakfast bar, grabbing the counter as she passed.

"You look a little wobbly. You up for this?"

"You probably should have stopped me from drinking alcohol when I have a head injury and they gave me pain meds." Tracey touched her swollen cheek and the side of her head, then winced.

Josh held up a finger, delaying their departure. He walked around her and pulled an ice pack from the freezer, tossing her an emergency compress. "This should help a little." Then he pulled insulin cartridges from the fridge, stuffing them inside Jackson's travel and emergency supplies bag.

Instead of her cheekbone, Tracey dropped the cold compress on her forehead and slid it over her eyes. "You're right." She took off to the front door. "You should definitely drive."

Proof of life. That's what they needed. He looked around his home. Different from the madhouse an hour ago. Different because the housekeeper had come by this morning. Different because Gwen was no longer a part of it.

Different because Tracey was.

Chapter Five

Josh wandered through Richland Mall with the fingers of one hand interlocked with Tracey's. With the other he held the new phone securely in its sack. No one had the number so the kidnappers couldn't use it for a conversation. He expected someone to bump into him. Or drop a note. Maybe catch their line of sight, giving them an envelope.

"Hell, I don't know what they plan on doing. The dang thing isn't even charged."

"You've said that a couple of times now," Tracey acknowledged. "My head is absolutely killing me and I'm starting to see two of everything. Can we get a bottle of water?"

"Sure."

He kept his eyes open and wouldn't let go of Tracey as he paid for the water at a candy store. She looked like a hospital volunteer in the navy blue scrub top.

"Josh, you are making my hand hurt as much as my head." She tugged a little at his thumb.

"Sorry. I just can't—"

"I know. You're afraid they'll grab me. I get it. But my hand needs circulation. Come on. Let's park it on that bench."

He looked in every direction for something suspicious or a charging station for the phone. Whatever or whoever was coming for them could be any of the people resting on another bench or walking by.

"Here, I'm done. Drink the rest." She capped the bottle and tried to hand it to him.

"No thanks."

"If I drink it, I'll have to leave your side for a few and head into the restroom all alone. I know you don't want that."

"Then throw it away. No one's telling you to drink it." He watched the young man with the baby stroller until he moved in the opposite direction.

"Lighten up, Mack," a voice said directly behind them. "Don't turn around."

Tracey stiffened next to him, the bottle of water hitting the floor. A clear indication that she recognized the voice. The guy behind him tapped on Josh's shoulder with a phone.

"Pass me the one you just bought."

Josh forced himself not to look at the man. No mirrored surfaces were nearby. The guy even covered the phone before it got close enough to see his face in the black reflection of the screen.

"That's good, Major. You're doing good. Now, I know you're concerned about your kids. You can see them when you play the video in about twenty seconds. Just let me get through this service hallway. Yeah, you've got a choice—let me go or follow and lose any chance of ever seeing your brats." The kidnapper tapped the top of Josh's head. "Count to twenty. Talk to ya soon."

Josh had his hands ready to push up from the bench and tackle the guy to the ground.

"No." Tracey pulled him back to the bench. "You

heard him. He means it. We have to stay here and let him walk away. You promised to do whatever it took. Remember? So please just turn the phone on and get their instructions."

He listened to Tracey and stayed put. The phone had been handed to them with gloves. Most likely no prints, so he turned it on. He clicked through the menu, finding the gallery.

There were several pictures of the twins playing in a room—sort of like a day care crowded with toys. The video shattered his already-broken heart. Sage was crying. Jackson was "vroom vrooming" a car across his leg and through the air.

A voice off camera—the same as behind them—told them to say hi to their daddy.

"I want to go home." Sage threw a plush toy toward the person holding the phone. "Is Trace Trace picking us up?"

Tracey covered her mouth, holding her breath again.

"Can you remember what you're supposed to say? You can go home after you tell your daddy," the kidnapper lied.

The twins nodded their heads, tucking their chins to their chests and sticking out their bottom lips. They might be fraternal, but they did almost everything together.

"Daddy, Mack says to go to...I don't remember." Jackson turned to his sister, scratching his head with the truck. "Do you remember?"

"Why can't you tell him?" Sage pouted.

"Come on, it has a giant bull." Another voice piped in.

"We've been there, Jacks. It's got that big bridge, 'member?" Sage poked him.

"Can you come there and pick us up, Daddy?" Jackson cried.

"Maybe Trace Trace can?" Sage's tears ran full stream down her cheeks.

"You have twenty minutes to be waiting in the middle of the bridge. Both of you. No cops," a voice said on top of the twins cries.

The video ended. All Josh wanted was to rush to the Chisholm Trail Bridge and pick them up. But they wouldn't be there. Instructions would be there. The guy who'd dropped the phone off would be watching them to make certain they weren't followed.

"Let's go." He wrapped his hand around Tracey's. It killed him to hear his kids like that.

"Are they going to keep us running from one spot to another? What's the point of that? And why have us buy a new phone only to replace it with this one?"

While they were leaving the mall in a hurry would be the ideal time for a kidnapper to try to grab one or both of them. He locked their fingers and tugged Tracey closer to his side.

"Before we get to the car…" He lowered his voice and stopped them behind a pillar at the candy store. He leaned in close to her ear, not wanting to be overheard. "We need to look closely where he touched us. He might have planted a microphone."

He dipped his head and turned around to let Tracey check. She smoothed the cloth of his shirt across his shoulders.

"I don't see anything, Josh." She shook her head and turned for him to do the same.

He pushed his fingers through his short hair. Found nothing. Then ran them through Tracey's short wavy strands and over her tense shoulders.

"If I were them, I'd use this time to plant a listening device. I'd want to know if we were really cooperating or playing along with the Feds."

"Who *are you* playing along with?" She looked and sounded exasperated.

"I'm on team Jackson and Sage. Whoever I have to play along with to get them back home. That's the only thing that's important to me."

"All right. So you think they're planting something in the car?"

"Got to be. Or this phone is already rigged for them to listen. Stand at the back of this store and keep an eye out while I call McCaffrey on his phone." Josh took a last look around the open mall area to see if they were in sight of security cameras or if anyone watched them from the sidelines.

Tracey smothered the kidnapper's phone with the bottom of her shirt. "I hope you know what you're doing."

"So do I." He waited for her to get ten feet away from him then took the FBI-issued phone and dialed the only number logged.

As soon as he was connected he blurted, "They have a new phone listed in my name. Bought it prepaid at a kiosk. No idea what the number is. Handed us another and told us to head to the Brazos Suspension Bridge."

"You can cross that on foot. Right?" McCaffrey was asking someone on his staff. "You know they'll be waiting on the other side."

Tracey kept watch, walking back and forth along the wall. She'd look out the storefront window, then make the horseshoe along the outside walls again to look out the other side.

Josh kept his head and his voice down. "I can't contact you on this again. It'll be in the car."

"We'll have men on the north side of the bridge waiting," McCaffrey stated. "Trust me, Josh."

"For as long as possible." He pocketed the phone, waved to Tracey.

"Josh, the kidnapper called you Mack. I remember that they all called each other Mack."

"It kept them from using their real names. Helped hide their identities." He didn't speak his next thought—hoping that they kept their masks on in front of his kids.

They both walked quickly from the mall toward the car.

"We just used five of our twenty minutes. Aren't you going to call Bryce and let him know where we're headed?"

"No need. If the Rangers are doing their job, they'll already know."

Josh pointed to a moving van that matched the description Tracey had regarding the vehicle blocking the intersection. If law enforcement spotted it, they'd be instructed to watch and not detain.

The truck pulled away from the end of the aisle as soon as they reached the car. He was tempted to use the phone, but he'd just proved to himself that they were being watched. He couldn't risk it.

Josh didn't wait around to spot any other vehicles keeping an eye on them. He didn't care if any of them kept up. "Flip down the visor, Tracey." He turned on the flashing lights and let traffic get out of his way. "We're not going to be late."

Tracey braced herself with a foot on the dashboard. "I'm rich. That's my secret."

He slowed for an intersection and looked at her while

checking for vehicles. She cleared her throat, waiting. Josh drove. If that was all the FBI could dig up on her, how could that be leverage?

The flashing lights on his car made it easy to get to the bridge and park. He left them on when they got out. Tracey reached under the seat and retrieved a second Jackson emergency kit. He snagged the one he'd brought from the house.

Armed with only a phone and his son's emergency kit, they walked quickly across the bridge to wait in the middle of the river.

"Not many people here on a Friday night." Tracey walked to the steel beams and looked through. "I hope they don't make us jump."

"That could be a possibility." One that he hadn't considered.

"I don't swim well. So just push me over the edge."

"You don't have to go." Josh stayed in the middle, his senses heightened from the awareness of how vulnerable they were in this spot. "How's your head?"

"Spinning. You grabbed extra insulin cartridges and needles. That's what I saw, right? I think I should take a couple, too."

It made sense. He opened the kit. She reached for a cartridge and needle. If the kidnappers took only one of them, they'd each have a way to keep Jackson healthy.

TRACEY WAS SCARED. Out-of-her-mind scared. If today hadn't happened, she would have felt safe standing on a suspension bridge above the Brazos River in the early moonlight with Josh.

But today *had* happened and she was scared for them all.

"What kind of a secret is being rich?" Josh walked

a few feet one direction and then back again. "I don't get it. Why is being rich a secret McCaffrey would threaten you with?"

"You really want me to explain right now?"

"You're the one who brought it up." He shrugged, but kept walking. "It'll pass the time."

"My last name isn't Cassidy. I mean, it wasn't. I changed it."

That stopped him. There was a lot of light on the bridge and she could see Josh's confused expression pretty well. He was in jeans and a long-sleeve brick-red shirt that had three buttons at the collar. She'd given it to him on his birthday because she wanted to brighten up his wardrobe. The hat he normally wore was still at home. They'd left without it or it would have been on his head.

"I ran a background check on you. Tracey Cassidy exists."

"It's amazing what you can do when you have money. In fact, I could hire men to help you. My uncle would know the best in the business."

"Let's go back to the part that you aren't who you say you are." The phone in his palm rang. He answered and held it to his ear. "We're here."

Josh looked around the area. His eyes landed on the far side of the bridge, opposite where they'd left the car. Tracey joined him.

"Whatever you want me to do, you don't need my babysitter."

"No, you need me. I can take care of the twins, change Jackson's cartridge." She held up the emergency pack.

"I don't need any extra motivation. Leave her out of—" He pocketed the phone.

"I'm sorry for getting you into this mess." He hugged her to him before they continued across the bridge then on the river walk under the trees. The sidewalk curved and Josh paused, looking for something.

Another couple passed. Josh tugged on Tracey's arm and got her running across the grass toward the road. If the couple were cops, he didn't acknowledge them. Their shoes hit the sidewalk again and a white van pulled up illegally onto the sidewalk next to Martin Luther King Jr. Boulevard.

The door slid open. That's where they needed to go.

The blackness inside the van seemed final. But she could do this. She'd do whatever it took. Whatever they wanted.

Out of the corner of her eye she saw a man approaching. Then another. The more the two men tried to look as if they weren't heading toward them, the more apparent it was that their paths would. Maybe they were the cops that Bryce had arranged to follow them. If they got any closer, the men inside the van would see them, too.

"What are those guys doing?"

Josh looked in their direction, but yelled at her. "Run. I think they're trying to stop us."

"But—"

"Just run."

It wasn't far. Maybe fifty or sixty feet. The men split apart. Josh dropped her hand. She ran. The van slowly moved forward—away from her. One of the men shot at the van. Then she was grabbed from behind and tripped over a tangle of feet. The man latched on to her waist, keeping her next to him.

"Let me go. I have to get— You don't understand what you're doing."

Another shot was fired. This time from the van. The

man's partner fell to the grass. The guy holding her covered her with his body. These men weren't police. The real police raced after the van in an unmarked car, sirens echoing off the buildings across the water.

The man on top of her didn't move and wasn't concerned about his injured partner. She was pounding with her fists on a Kevlar vest trying to get the man off her when a loud crash momentarily replaced the police sirens.

"Oh my God! What have you done?"

Chapter Six

Fire trucks. An ambulance. At least three police cars—maybe more—with strobe lights dancing around in circles. College students edging their way closer in a growing crowd. An angry FBI agent in her face. And a bodyguard who kept insisting that she was too open as she sat on a park bench.

The lights, the voices, the desperation—all made her head swim. Of course it might have been a little remnant of the whiskey. Or possibly the head injury from the kidnappers this afternoon. Maybe both.

Whatever it was, she didn't like it. It was the reason she rarely drank at any point in her life. She simply didn't like being under the influence of anything. Including her uncle Carl, who had taken it upon himself to dispatch bodyguards to protect her. They'd destroyed any chance of getting insulin to Jackson.

The van lay on its side. The driver had escaped before anyone could reach the crash site. Both the guard and Josh had run to the scene, but he was gone. Vanished.

"Miss Cassidy, if you're ready to go. Your uncle instructed us to bring you back to Fort Worth as soon as possible. We've cleared it with the police to pull out." The guard spoke to her with no remorse for what he and his partner had caused. As if she was the most important person in the entire group.

She hated that. She always had.

"How can you stand there and talk as if nothing's happened? Your partner may have shot someone in that van. The driver's disappeared along with the instructions to rescue the twins. What if the kids had been inside? If anything happens to Josh's son—"

"We were just doing our job." He stood in front of her with his hands crossed over each other, no emotion, no whining—and apparently no regrets. His partner had his breath back—which had been knocked out of him by the bullets hitting him in the chest or him hitting the ground.

Jackson and Sage were missing and now the kidnappers would be angry. What would happen now? She needed these men gone. There was only one way to do that. One man. One man could make it happen.

"Let me have your phone."

"Ma'am?"

"I don't have a phone. I need to borrow yours."

He reached inside his jacket pocket, turned on his phone and handed it to her. She searched the call history and found the number she'd almost forgotten. The phone rang and rang some more, going to voice mail, which surprised her. Unless he was with someone—then nothing would disturb him. Not even the fact that he thought her life was at risk.

Hadn't he sent the guards because he was worried?

A more likely story was that he thought the kidnappers would find out who she was and try to extort money from him. Just the possibility of the family being out any cash would send him into a frenzy to get her safely back inside a gilded cage.

Should she leave a message? She hung up before the beep. What she had to say didn't need to be recorded.

"Where's Josh?" The men standing close to her shrugged in answer. "You do know which man I was with when all this began? The father of the children you just placed in more danger."

The big bulky bodyguard looked like he didn't have a clue. He didn't search the crowd. She followed his gaze to the edge of the people, then across the river where another line of people formed, then back to just behind her where the emergency vehicles were parked.

"Hey. Don't play dumb. I ask. You answer," she instructed, using the power that came with her family name. "And don't think I can't stop your paycheck."

"They moved him to a more secure facility," he finally answered.

"You mean we're trying," Agent McCaffrey corrected as he approached. "I was just coming for you, Tracey. We're heading back to Josh's house. He insists on driving himself but would like to speak with you first."

The agent and bodyguard parted like doors when Josh barreled through them.

"My car's been brought to this side of the river. I'm heading back to my place. You ready?" He extended a hand and she took it.

What would she say to him this time? "Sorry. I should have told you about my powerfully rich uncle who might send bodyguards." Those words didn't roll off her tongue and she'd had no idea he'd send anyone to protect her. Actually, it seemed surreal that he'd found her so quickly.

Josh put his hand on her lower back and guided her through the crowds. Her silent guard followed. The one who hadn't been hit by two bullets in his chest ran toward the road, presumably to get their vehicle.

Josh stopped and did an about-face. "I need to talk with Tracey. Then she's all yours."

"What?" *What did he mean? He was turning her over to her uncle?* She'd been right. Josh wouldn't forgive her this time, but she had something to say about where she went and with whom.

"I can't let her out of my sight, sir." The bodyguard stood more at attention, looking ready to attack. Had he just issued a challenge to a Texas Ranger?

"I don't have time for this. I need to know how you found her." Josh responded by placing his hands on his hips and looping his thumbs through his belt loops. Either to keep from dragging her the rest of the way to his car, or to keep himself from throwing a punch at the bodyguard. She would prefer that he not restrain himself from the latter.

"We tracked her phone. We're assuming it was in the van."

"How did you get the number?" she asked. "I didn't give it to my uncle."

"I have a job to do. And I don't work for either of you."

Josh's hands were pulling the guard's collar together before the man could nod at them both. The guard's hands latched on to Josh's wrists to keep from being choked. Agents who had been watching them closely as they approached the car began running.

If any of them were afraid of what Josh might do, they didn't shout for him to stop. Tracey couldn't bring herself to call out to him, either. After all, it was this man's actions that caused them to lose their main lead to the twins. It was this guy—she didn't even know his name—who had flubbed everything up.

"If you lift one finger…" she said to the guard. But she couldn't blame him or let Josh take out his frustration on the hired help. She'd lost the kids on her watch. She should have been more careful. She laid her hand on Josh's arm, trying to gain his attention. "It's not his fault."

Josh's strong jaw ticked as he ground his teeth. His wide eyes shifted to hers in a crazy gaze, but his muscles relaxed under her fingers.

"Earlier I asked how being rich could be an awful secret." He released the guard shoving him away when two FBI agents were within reaching distance. "I think I have my answer."

"You don't, but I'd rather talk about it in private."

Josh turned and stomped toward his car—the agents close behind.

"Whatever my uncle is paying you, I'll give you the same to stop following me," she said to the bodyguard.

Tracey fell into step next to Agent Barlow, who held up her hand for the guard to stop and not follow. It didn't work. Josh spun around so fast Agent Lanning nearly collided with him.

"No! I need to be alone. That means all of you." He waved everyone away from him. He shook his head, chin hanging to his chest. Then he looked only at her. "They might need you around, but I can't do it. And I don't have to."

"He doesn't mean that," the agent said.

Tracey stopped. Exhausted from everything but really rocked by Josh's words. Her words had been similar when she'd walked away from her uncle when she was twenty-one. She'd left him, the man designated by her parents and grandparents as her guardian, about the same way Josh had disappeared in his car.

Tracey hadn't only meant every word back then, she'd changed her name and began working for the Parkers. Oh yeah, some hurts just couldn't be fixed with "I'm sorry."

JOSH DROVE, HEADING for the long way home. Flashing lights to warn the cars ahead of him that he was going fast. He was angry. More than angry—he was back to being scared that he'd never see his kids again.

Different than Gwen's last days. That was something he'd prepared for, something he'd known was possible even though he couldn't control it. If those men hadn't shown up, the kidnappers would have given him more instructions. He'd know what he needed to do. Or at least his son would have another insulin cartridge.

There was a blood sugar time bomb ticking away for Jackson, and at the moment Josh had no way to defuse it.

He sped under Lake Shore Drive and realized where his subconscious was taking him—the Rescue Center. He slowed the car to a nonlethal speed and switched off the lights. The phone he'd been given from the kidnappers was still in his back pocket. McCaffrey knew it was there but hadn't obtained the number yet. A true burner that wouldn't lead anyone to his location.

Josh could wait for the kidnapper's next call and instructions. They wanted him to take care of their problem. Right? They had to call back.

Whatever they demanded, he'd do. Alone. No more plans behind the plans or counterespionage. He was on his own and would stay here so no one would find him.

With that decided, Josh parked close to the back door

and rang the buzzer. At this time of night there would only be a couple of people on duty. The door opened to a familiar face.

"Hey, Josh. You haven't been around in a while. What's it been, about six or seven months?" Bernie Dawes stepped to the side, holding the door open and inviting him inside.

Six or seven months ago he'd been thinking about asking Tracey on a date. He'd chickened out. Funny how he could be the tough Texas Ranger ninety percent of the time, making decisions instantly that saved lives. But the possibility of asking a girl on a date caused his brain to malfunction.

"Got any dogs that need to be walked?"

"One of those kinds of nights?" Bernie asked.

"Yeah. I'm waiting on a phone call." Josh stuck his hands in his back pockets, willing the phone to ring. Nothing happened.

"Well, I just took 'em all out about half an hour ago. How about I set you up with an abandoned litter of pups? They've had a pretty rough start."

"That'll do the trick."

Bernie led the way to the kennels and pulled a chair into a small room with a box of four or five black fur bundles. Five. They were all cuddled on top of each other.

"What's on their heads? Are those dots of paint?"

"We've got a Lab that just whelped, so we rotate these dudes in. But they're black, too." Bernie laughed and scooped up one of the pups. "We have a chart with their different colors. It's the only way to tell if they've all been fed. These guys are all full. They just need a little TLC."

"I shouldn't stay long. I might not have much time."

"Whatever you give them is more than they have."
He leaned against the wall.

Loving on the puppies was easy. Seeing the other
animals—the strays, the injured, the unwanted... The
tough guy he appeared to be suddenly needed to know
how this man survived day after day. "How do you do
this, Bernie?"

He shrugged. "I like animals."

Bernie turned to go, but hesitated. He might have
realized that Josh was back because there was a problem. It was like he was the bartender, wiping down the
counter a little more often in front of the man sipping
his third whiskey.

"I got in trouble today," Bernie said, picking up a
puppy. "I didn't mention my wife's hair. She told me
to find my own dinner because I didn't notice she had
highlights. She's always doing something. I didn't think
I had to say anything about it. Sometimes it's the little
things that cause you all sorts of big problems. Catch
what I'm throwin' at ya?"

Josh nodded. He could still see Tracey as she walked
into the kitchen. He'd wanted to look into her eyes and
reassure her that everything would be okay, but she'd
been staring at the floor. He could only see her thick
red hair, messed up as if someone had placed angry
hands on her. Seeing her hair like that, he knew she'd
been hurt and it killed him.

"Tracey doesn't think I notice that she dyes her hair
red." He picked up the first puppy and stroked the entire length of its body. He wasn't completely sure why
Tracey's hair color was important, but he could breathe
again. "She started about three years ago, getting a little
redder every couple of months. Further away from the
brown it used to be."

The room was quiet. No barking or whining. Bernie kept wiping down that metaphorical bar's counter. Josh felt...relief. There weren't too many people Josh could just talk to. He was the commander of the Company. Being a single dad, he didn't go for a drink with the guys after a case very often. It had been a long time since he'd had friends.

"I should have told her I liked it," he admitted.

"Probably," Bernie agreed. "You get that phone call, just make sure the door closes behind you. You come around anytime, man. We understand. Hey, aren't your kiddos old enough to choose a dog? Maybe one of these will do?" He handed the pup with a green dot to Josh. He brushed his hands and gave up waiting on an answer. "Well, I've got a cat who had surgery today and it's having a hard time so I'm going to leave ya to it."

Bernie left in a hurry. Josh figured he must have scowled at the mention of the twins. Poor Bernie thought his visit was about work. Getting a dog? He brought the pup to his face. It was about time. There hadn't been a dog at the house since before he got married.

A whirlwind relationship, elopement and pregnancy that led to Gwen's diagnosis. There hadn't been time to add a dog to the family. Maybe it was part of the reason these types of visits helped. He didn't know who got more out of them—him or the dogs he comforted.

Admit it. The comfort was for him. The idea had come from Company F's receptionist, Vivian. She volunteered for the shelter, trying to place animals and fostering.

The gut-wrenching pain hit him again like it was yesterday. It had been at least a year since he'd felt the loss of his wife so strongly. He put the puppy down and bent forward knowing the pain wasn't physical, but trying to relieve it like a cramp.

When Gwen had been diagnosed with leukemia, every minute of his time had gone to either the job or research or treatment. There had come a time when he'd protected himself so much that he could barely feel.

After the third or fourth late-night trip out here, he'd realized that his unofficial therapy was working. Petting and walking the dogs made him reconnect. He switched puppies and gently stroked, letting the motion replace the fright. It freed his mind. A couple of minutes later he switched again and realized that's why he'd come to the shelter.

It was also a reason he kept the visits to himself. Vivian was the only person in his life that knew he came here to get his head on straight. And he sure needed a minute to think calmly tonight.

The last two pups were smaller than the others. Each had one white paw—one right and one left. He concentrated on those paws and cuddled both of them together. They both almost fit into his palm.

Jackson and Sage had been small. But when they were born they were strong and hadn't needed machines. Trips here to sit with dogs had been fewer when the doctors attacked Gwen's cancer full force. Some days, just taking the time to hold his kids was an effort that made him sleepless with guilt.

The twins were four months old when Gwen realized she was losing the battle. Somehow that had made her stronger. She'd gotten everything in order—with Tracey's help. Gwen fought hard, but in the end, she was at peace that her family would be taken care of.

Removing the phone from his pocket, he replayed the video of his kids. "Ring," he commanded.

He got on his knees next to the box and arranged the blanket where the pups would be secure as they piled on top of each other seeking sleep.

"It can't be over for them. You've got to give me another chance. This can't be the end. She fought so hard to bring these kids into the world," he told the puppies or God or anyone else who might be listening.

The phone rang and he didn't hesitate. "This is Parker."

"You're a very lucky man, Ranger."

"I'm not sure I share your definition of lucky. Does this mean you haven't hurt my kids?"

The insulin cartridges and needles were on the front seat. *Meet me tonight. Ask me to do something right now. I need to make sure my kids are safe.*

"The deal's still moving forward, no matter where you're hiding out."

He heard the uneasiness in the man's voice. Whoever they were, they had no idea that he was at the animal shelter. That might work to his advantage.

"What do you need me to do?"

"You know what we want. Get it. Keep the phone close and wait for instructions."

"Can I talk to Jackson? Is he okay? He has—"

"Diabetes, yeah, we know. We're dealing with it."

"I need to see him, talk to him. His pump and needle will need to be changed. He has to be monitored closely." There wasn't any way he could talk anyone through all the different possibilities that might happen if something went wrong.

"I said we were taking care of it!" the voice yelled. "Don't forget to bring the woman."

"That's not possible."

"Make it possible. Or they'll die."

Chapter Seven

Josh drove to his second home—Company F headquarters. The lights were on and he recognized the vehicles in the parking lot. They were all there. All of his men.

Bryce met him at the door. "We didn't expect to see you, Major. At least not tonight."

"My replacement here?" Josh waited while the ranger secured things, so he could be escorted through the building like a visitor. "I need a minute of his time."

"How you holding up?"

"Can't take time to think about it."

"Captain Oaks is in your office." Bryce led the way through the men.

All of them stood and offered support. They were the best of the best and working the case with or without him as their leader. He entered his office. Nothing had changed. The lifetime he'd been away was actually less than twenty-four hours.

"Aiden." Josh closed the door and dropped the blinds. He didn't want witnesses to the conversation. Nothing that could hinder the case or put his men at risk of something to testify about later.

Aiden left the chair behind the desk and sat next to Josh. The Captain was much older, but barely looked it. Josh only knew because the "old man," as he was referred to, had been eligible for retirement a couple of years ago. He'd proved his mettle earlier that year when he'd been shot defending the witness of the Isabella Tenoreno murder.

Captain Aiden Oaks had been after the Tenoreno and Rosco Mafia families longer than a decade. It was fitting that he'd take Josh's place as head of Company F.

Even if it was temporary.

"I could ask how you're holding up, but it's obvious. What can I do for you?" Aiden kept his voice low. No chance anyone would overhear them. He also leaned forward, seeming anxious to know what was needed.

There was a chance that Aiden Oaks was the only man in a position of authority who would keep his word. Josh needed to make certain that the captain wasn't going to turn him over to the authorities—state or federal. Or call them as soon as he pulled out of the parking lot.

"They want Tenoreno's transportation route."

"Everyone assumed that's where this was headed." Aiden pressed his lips together into a flat line. "Your men filled me in and headquarters gave me a rough outline before booting me this direction."

"I shouldn't be here." Josh started to rise from the chair, but Aiden coaxed him to sit again. "Just talking to me could get you written up, but I don't have any options."

In his years as a Texas Ranger, Josh had never doubted whether he could count on his partner or the men in his company. If this case was just about him, there'd be no doubt about what he'd do. But his kids' lives had never been dependent on that trust.

Until now.

"I guess the strategy to follow and catch these guys

when they weren't looking fell apart when your baby-sitter's bodyguards showed up." Aiden nodded. "Yeah, I'm staying on top of things. But you're here. You obviously have a plan. How can I help put it in action?"

Could he trust this man so intent on helping save his kids?

"I need the route or Jackson dies." Josh watched Aiden's eyes. They never wavered. Never looked away like someone hiding something. "I heard the panic in the kidnapper's voice—both about my son and whatever his original plan was. This character is smart enough to know that he had a short window before everything changed. He's playing it by ear now, just like us."

Aiden nodded again, acting like he understood. "Even if you deliver the route there's no guarantee. Say we give 'em a bit of rope, hoping they might hang themselves, it won't guarantee that your kids will be safely released. Won't mean they'll release you either for that matter."

"But I'll be with them." Josh choked on the words, took a second, then stood. "My kids aren't going to be the victims in this. I know the limits of the Rangers, of the FBI, of the state prosecutors. They're hoping for an easy fix. We both know there isn't one."

Josh stared at the frame hanging above the door. Gwen stitched the Ranger motto when she'd first been confined to bed rest with the twins. It was a reminder every day of what he'd lost, but he kept it there. Over the last year, it had also become a reminder of what he'd gained—the twins. *And Tracey.*

"One Riot, One Ranger," Aiden said.

Strength and truth were in his voice. Josh had to trust him. His plan could only work if he did.

Aiden gripped his shoulder with a firm, steady hand.

"I yanked your company into this mess when I sent Garrison Travis to a dinner party and they witnessed Tenoreno's assassin. I owe you, Josh. So what's the plan?"

Eager to help or eager to learn how to stop him? Aiden might be giving him a long piece of rope to hang himself. It was a risk Josh had to take.

"I need a feasible route, you supply a decoy, we bring these guys down like the rest of the Tenoreno family."

"It's a good start. Are you going to exchange yourself for your kids?"

"That's what I was planning, but I'm not sure it'll work. They're insisting that I bring Tracey."

Aiden rubbed his chin and leaned back in the chair he'd reoccupied. "That does throw a kink in the works. Could possibly mean that they'll keep all three as hostages until you do whatever they want."

"Yeah, that's the most likely scenario."

"It seems that the only way to get your kids back is to tell the kidnappers the truth. We'll need to inform them how and where Tenoreno is really being moved from Huntsville to Austin. Company F will just have to be prepared."

"Are you going to run this through state headquarters?"

"They won't approve it—not even as a hypothetical." He winked. "Just like they wouldn't have approved the last-minute operation that brought Tenoreno down to begin with. Might be one of those situations where it's better to ask forgiveness than permission. Of course, there's nothing at all to stop us from talking hypothetical situations. Your experience would be valuable and much appreciated."

"My experience. Right." Josh's gut told him to go for it. *Trust him.*

His friend pointed to the motto. "This is one time, more than one of us might be required."

No more stalling. This fight was bigger than just one man. He had to trust that Aiden wouldn't turn him in.

"If I were still in charge of Tenoreno's transport, I'd arrange for air travel. It would be limited ground vulnerability. At this point the state prosecutor is probably scrambling to even make that a private jet."

"I'm not disagreeing with you," Aiden said. "Hypothetically."

In other words, Josh was right. They planned to move Tenoreno from the state prison via plane to Austin for the trial.

"Since we're just talking here, you know what's bothered me? Why did the kidnappers go to so much trouble to put your situation in the public eye? I mean, they could have kept the kidnapping quiet, but they drew you to a popular, normally crowded place."

"If I were Tenoreno's son, a plane is the fastest route out of the country. Huntsville's just a hop into the Gulf and then international waters. All he has to do is hijack the plane."

"That's a fairly sound guess of what they're likely to do." Aiden tapped his fingertips together, thinking.

"Dammit. Is that what all of this is about? Make the kidnapping public so the transfer is by plane instead of car? I thought it was just about gaining access to my credentials so the kidnaper could get close enough to free Tenoreno."

"They manipulated the kidnapping to force you to hijack a plane?" Aiden nodded his head, agreeing, not really asking a question.

"It would make it harder to recapture Tenoreno.

Harder for the FBI or Rangers or any law enforcement not to comply since the twins are at risk."

The kidnapping made sense.

"Did you find out why Tracey's uncle sent the guards? Who notified them?"

Josh shook his head, shrugging.

"Too upset? I understand." The older man stood, joining Josh by sitting on the opposite corner of the desk. "We'll be ready. I guarantee that. And if you just happen to let me see the number you're using on that new phone, then I might have a misdial in my future letting you know what plane and airfield."

Josh turned on the cell and Aiden nodded his head.

"Here's something to ponder while we wait." He jotted down the number. "How did Miss Cassidy's entourage get here? On one hand maybe the kidnappers really want her to take care of the kids. Maybe they just made a mistake not abducting her at the same time. On the other, Xander Tenoreno might have alerted her uncle. That means he knows she's from money. Maybe the kidnappers know too and want a piece of that cash cow."

"How rich is rich?" Josh asked.

"Probably need to have a conversation with the source about that."

Aiden was a wise man. Josh stuck out his hand, grabbing the older man's like a lifeline. It was the first hope he'd had since the van had crashed.

"I can't thank you enough, Aiden."

"I haven't done anything yet. A lot of this depends on you."

Josh looked at Gwen's artwork. "I'll do whatever it takes."

"Just remember, you're not alone."

PULLING A LIGHT throw up to her chin, Tracey curled up as small on the couch as she could get. She closed her eyes, pretending to be asleep, wanting everyone in the house to leave her alone. The FBI agent who'd picked her up at the hospital encouraged her to take the up-stairs bedroom.

Josh's room?

George Lanning had no way of knowing she hadn't been in that room since Gwen had gotten very, very ill. It was better to be bothered by people in the living room than to be alone in Josh's bed.

"Miss Cassidy?"

"What?" she answered the bodyguard, who hadn't left her side since coming into her life.

"It's your uncle."

Part of her wanted to tell him to call off these guard dogs and part of her wanted to ignore him—as he'd obviously ignored her for the past several hours. The best thing was to confront the situation and attempt to discover his true motives.

She sat up, tugged her shirt straight and was ready to get to the heart of things. It had been a while since she'd thought of her grandmother's advice when fac-ing a problem. But the words were never truer than at that moment.

Taking the phone, she drew in a deep breath placing the phone next to her ear, ready for an attack.

"Tracey, darling, are you okay?"

"Who is this?" The female voice was a little familiar, but it had been a long time since she'd had contact with her family. She couldn't be sure who it was.

"It's your auntie Vickie, dear. Are you on your way home yet?"

"I don't have an aunt Vickie." At least she hadn't

when she'd gone to court to change her name. There hadn't even been a Vickie in her uncle's life. Then again, there'd always been someone *like* a Vickie.

"I know I've met you, dear. I'll admit—only to you— that it's been much too long."

"Where is my uncle? I was told he was calling." She didn't have time to speak with a secretary or even a new wife. She wanted the confrontation over and the guys in the black suits off her elbow.

"Well," the woman's voice squeaked, "he's not really available, but I thought you needed to know that it's important for you to come home."

"Wait, my uncle didn't tell you to call?"

Vickie began a long, in-depth explanation why she'd taken it upon herself to contact her and explain the complexity of the situation in her childhood home. Tracey tuned her out.

Home? The room surrounding her, keeping her warm and safe, was more of a home than any room had ever been in Fort Worth. That place had been more like a museum or mausoleum. Beautiful, but definitely a do-not-touch world.

As a little girl, she'd had the best interior designers. Everything had been pink. She couldn't stand pink for the longest time. Now she had to bite her tongue whenever Sage wanted a dress in the color.

Realizing the phone was in her lap instead of her hand, she clicked the big red disconnect button and put an end to a stranger's attempt to coax her home. Her new constant companion reached to retrieve it, when it rang again.

Tracey answered herself, more prepared, less surprised. "Yes?"

"Listen to me, you spoiled little brat." Vickie didn't

try to disguise the venom. "Carl wants you back here pronto. Niceties aside, you should do what you're told."

"Vickie...dearest—" she could make the honey drip from her voice, too "—I walked away a long time ago. There is absolutely no road for me that leads back there."

The red button loomed. Tracey clicked. It wasn't hard. Not now.

The phone vibrated in her hand. She tossed it to the opposite end of the couch. Totally content with her decision. Her uncle wasn't calling her back and, whoever Vickie was, she couldn't do anything to help save the children.

"I only have two things for you to do," she said to the guard. "My first is that you both get in that car of yours and leave. Without me. The second is not to interrupt me again unless it's really my uncle calling. Period. No secretaries. No Auntie *Vickies* that haven't celebrated as many birthdays as I have. No one except him. And don't say that you don't work for me."

"Yes, ma'am." He nodded and backed up to the door.

What he was acknowledging, she didn't care. Just as long as he stayed next to the door and let her wonder where Josh had gone or whether he was coming back. If she were him she wondered what she'd be thinking.

Before she could lean back into the cushions, the man answered his phone and held it in her direction.

"Speaker, please."

He mumbled into the phone, pressed a button and...

"Tracey? You there?"

She raised her hand, using her fingers to indicate she'd take the call. She popped it off Speaker and paused long enough to fill her lungs again.

"Hi, Uncle Carl."

"You okay, Tracey?" Her uncle didn't sound upset. He might even sound concerned. "I heard there was an accident and a car fire."

"I'm good. My head hurts from earlier, but I'm sure you already have the hospital records."

"It's been a while. I have to apologize for Vickie. She sometimes gets...overly enthusiastic."

"She sounded like it." He hadn't called to talk about his girlfriend, which was the category she could safely put the woman in. He hadn't said anything about getting married. The man was in his fifties and had avoided a matrimonial state his entire life.

"I assume you don't want to come home."

"I am home. My place is here and the men you sent— You did send them, didn't you?"

"As soon as I heard you were assaulted."

"You should have asked me first." As if that step had ever been part of his trickeries.

"You would have said no."

"Of course I would have said no. I work for a Texas Ranger who has a lot of law enforcement access. Why in the world would I need two bodyguards to muck things up?"

"Muck?"

"Yes, Uncle Carl, muck. They arrived and everything became a big mess. Josh is gone, the kids are still in danger, Jackson doesn't have anyone there that understands diabetes. Yes, everything's pretty *mucked* up."

"Mr. Parker's children are in danger?"

"They were kidnapped. That's the reason the FBI called you."

"The FBI? Did they tell you they spoke with me?"

"No. I just assumed that's how you found me." Wasn't that what Agent McCaffrey had insinuated?

"That's ridiculous. I've never *not* known where you are. Just because you changed your name doesn't stop you from being my niece and my responsibility. I'm your guardian, but more importantly, we're family."

It sounded good. The speech wasn't unlike the words that she'd heard most of her life. It did surprise her that he'd known exactly where she was. Well, then again, it didn't. She hadn't gone far.

Same city, same school—she only lived four blocks from the place he'd been paying for. That all made sense. What didn't was his statement that he hadn't heard from the FBI.

"Concern for me was never a problem."

"Ah, yes, you wanted your freedom. Well, anonymously donating to your university down there, did keep me informed."

Same old, same old. Carl was very good at saying a lot of nothing.

"Can we stop this? Just tell me what it's going to take to call off your bodyguard brigade."

"I think you need to sit the rest of this out. Come back here where I can keep an eye on you. Better yet, you've finished your presentation, so why not take a long overdue vacay to someplace breezy. You always liked the beach."

"You're wrong, and this time you have no control over my life." She caught the upward tilt of lips— mostly smirk—of the man at the door. Right. Her uncle's money would always have influence over her life. Money always did. "Just call off your goons."

"That won't be happening. They're there for your safety. You need them." Carl's voice was more than a little smug. As usual, it was full of confidence that his choice was the only choice.

"That couldn't be farther from the truth."

Her uncle never did anything without proper motivation. So what was motivating him this time?

"No need to argue the point any longer, Tracey. I returned your call, answered your questions and have informed you what your option is. Yes, I'm aware you only have one. I must say good night."

"You aren't going to win." It embarrassed her to feel her face contract with a cringe. She knew the words were a fool's hope as soon as she said them.

"My dear, I already have. Those men are not about to leave your side. They'd never work anywhere again. Ever. And they know it."

The phone disconnected and she was no closer to discovering the truth of why her uncle sent the bodyguards. Man, did that sound conceited. Josh would want to know the entire story and specifically that answer when he returned. *If* he returned.

Part of the discussion in the past couple of hours was that Josh had a new phone and it was taking much too long to discover the number. Something to do with finding the kiosk owner, then a person who actually had keys to obtain the sales records. Followed by getting permission to enter the mall.

In other words, they had no clue where Josh was. No one could find him on the road. Some of their conversation had been that the kidnappers may have already contacted him. If so, then at least he had the Jackson emergency kit with him. Josh could monitor his son, save both of his kids.

The bodyguard silently retrieved his phone. He stepped on the other side of the door to take a phone call, but she mostly heard manly grunts of affirmation.

Tracey wanted to run and lock the door. Of course,

there wasn't a lock, but it didn't stop her from wanting to be completely alone. She could sulk as good as the rest of them. But it felt ridiculous feeling sorry for herself.

What problem did she have? It was Josh's twins who were missing. Josh would have to do whatever it took to get them back. She could sit here and offer support. Be the loyal day care provider. Her role in the family had been made quite clear when Josh had left her behind.

"Your uncle wants you back in Fort Worth in the morning. We'll leave here at eight sharp, giving you time for some rest." He stood with his back to the door as if he were a guard in front of the Tower of London. Eyes front, not influenced by any stimuli around him.

"I'm not a child and you can't force me to get in a vehicle, especially with the FBI here. I'm not going anywhere. I'm waiting here for Josh." At least she hoped he'd return. "And I'm going to help find his kids. Get with this agenda or leave."

The guard didn't answer. He was a good reflection of her uncle, not listening to her. She curled into the corner of the couch again, pulling the blanket over her shoulder. He was right about one thing—she did need some rest. Because when Josh came back, he would need her help.

And she would be here to give it to him.

Chapter Eight

"Where the hell have you been?" McCaffrey burst through the front door, storming across the porch before Josh had the car in Park.

"Not my problem if your guys can't keep up." He didn't care if the agent thought he was a smart-ass. He had barely been thinking when he'd left the river.

During the twenty-minute car ride from Ranger headquarters, he hadn't come up with a way to get him and Tracey out of the house. It didn't help that he lived in the middle of nowhere and there wouldn't be any sneaking off without guards noticing. Men were everywhere again. One of the bodyguards who had stopped Josh from reaching the van sat in a dark sedan parked in front of the barn.

Bodyguards complicated the equation.

What the hell was he going to do?

"Oh thank God! You're all right," Tracey said when his feet hit the porch. "Can we talk? Let me explain?"

Did he want to go there? Then again, when had it mattered what he *wanted*? Life had proven his wants didn't matter. He had to confront Tracey and talk things out. But when? That was the question he decided was relevant. And who else needed to be confronted—the FBI, local PD or Tracey's bodyguards?

Notably absent was the only organization that held the answer he needed. He had to trust Aiden Oaks, but knew the men in Company F had his back. He'd find out the specifics of moving Tenoreno.

He hadn't been able to speak with Bryce. Maybe find out where their tail had been during the bridge incident and why the rangers had been unable to follow the kidnapper from the van.

If they had, Josh would know. First things first. He had to deal with the people back in his house. McCaffrey was standing on the front sidewalk. Looked like he was first, then Tracey.

"You aren't supposed to be here. Pack it up, Agent."

"Did they make contact with you? Is that the reason you returned?"

"I don't know who's out there watching this conversation. Leave." Josh pointed to the empty dark sedans. Then he turned to the cop on his front lawn. "They have two minutes to clear out or arrest them for trespassing."

"I'm not sure I have that authority," he replied.

"Dammit." Josh glared at McCaffrey. "I probably don't have a choice, but I'm begging you for my kids' lives…leave."

"I have my orders."

Josh was dazed to a point that he couldn't speak. No words would form. His mind went to a neon sign that flashed. "Jackson might die."

"Josh, come on inside. You can't do this."

Tracey tugged on his hands. Hands that were twisted in the shirt collar circling McCaffrey's neck. How? When? The blackness. It all ran together until everything sort of blurred.

He released the FBI agent and let Tracey lead him inside. He thought she pointed at a man who took care of emptying the room. "How do we get rid of him and his partner?" he asked once he realized it was the second bodyguard.

"Are you okay?"

"Sure. No. I just… I don't know what happened back there." Josh shook his head in disbelief. "I can't remember going for McCaffrey."

"You're upset, exhausted. The stress that you're under is—"

"Things like this don't happen to me. I don't let them." He shrugged away from the comfort Tracey might offer. He wasn't a pacing man.

When he needed to think he lifted his feet up on the corner of his desk and flipped a pencil between his fingers. He paced so Tracey wouldn't be near him. What if he lost it again?

The television in the far corner of the room was muted. No news bulletins. He hadn't expected any since the FBI was keeping a tight lid on things. There hadn't been any Amber Alerts for his kids. Special circumstances, he'd been told.

That part he agreed with. They all knew who had hired the kidnappers. Now they just had to find them.

"I owe you an explanation," Tracey said softly.

"Not sure I can process anything." He scrubbed his face with his palms, desperately attempting to lift the haze. His mind screamed at him not to. If it did, he'd have to find a way to save his kids.

Too late. He was thinking again.

He dropped onto the cushions, breathing fully and under control. For the moment.

"I don't know how to apologize for what happened." She nervously rubbed her palms up and down her thighs. Gone were the scrubs, replaced by regular clothes.

"Forget that for now. Before the van showed up, I asked why being rich needed to be a secret. Have your family problems put my kids in danger?" He shook his head as if he needed to answer that himself and start over. He didn't want to blame Tracey, but the words slipped across his tongue before he could shut himself up. "If I wasn't certain that Tenoreno's people were behind this... Go ahead—explain to me why I should trust you again."

Tracey snapped to attention, cleared her throat, then shrugged. "I was raised like every normal millionaire's kid."

Josh was too tired to be amused until it hit him that Tracey was serious. She sat on the sofa next to him, knee almost touching his leg, hands twisting the corner of a throw pillow, bodyguard at the door.

"You're serious."

"My family's been wealthy for a couple of generations. West Texas oil fields."

"Let me guess. You wanted to see how the other half lived so you went to work as a nanny?"

"I understand why you're mad, but—"

"I'm not sure you do." Josh burst up from the couch with energy he didn't realize he had. *Pace. Get back under control.* "I looked into your bank accounts, Tracey. There wasn't money there. You drive a crappy car. You've lived in the same off-campus apartment for four years. Why? If you have enough money to buy the state of Texas, why are you slumming it?"

"I didn't lie and *I* don't have all the money. My family does. At first, I thought you knew about all this. I told Gwen when she interviewed me who my uncle was.

I gave you permission to run a background check. Later, when it was obvious you had no idea about the money, it was nice that you didn't want a favor or something from my uncle."

She thought that he'd want something from her family? Second curve... Gwen had kept this from him. He closed his eyes again. The blackness returned along with the thought he had to get moving. He was ready to move past this, leave and find his children. But he had to understand what he was dealing with regarding the bodyguards and Tracey's family.

"Is Tracey Cassidy your real name?"

"Yes. I legally changed it when I was twenty-one. I just dropped the Bass. Not that anyone actually associated me with the Bass family in Fort Worth."

He stared at her after she'd thrown two curveballs at him. She was a Bass? As in Bass Hall and the endowments and three of the wealthiest men in Texas?

"Why now? Why have bodyguards come into your life after you've lived in Waco for this long without them? I know they haven't always been hanging around. I think I would have noticed them."

"My parents divorced when I was six. I went to live with my grandparents. They said it was for my own good. Everyone threw the word *stability* around a lot back then. It might have been better. I'll never know. Both my parents remarried, started new families. By then, I was too old and filled with teenage angst."

He paced until he landed in front of the television screen and the dancing bubbles in the commercial. "Were you hiding from your family?"

"No. My uncle controls the trust fund left to me by my grandfather. With that, he thought it gave him complete control of my life. I decided not to let him dictate who was trailing after me in a bulletproof car, or what I did or when. So I left. I walked away from that life."

He couldn't let the bodyguards or Bass family screw things up the next time he received instructions. "Why didn't Gwen tell me about any of this?"

"I honestly thought she had. Look, Josh, my life changed after I walked away from my uncle. I sold my expensive car and lived on the money for almost a year. I had to keep things simple. I had to find a job. I did that through Gwen. She helped before and after I came to work here."

"I wanted her to hire a nurse. In fact, we argued about it a lot." He swallowed hard, pushing the emotion down. "She was right, of course. It was better to have someone she could be... She needed a friend."

"I told her that—the part about a nurse. But she was insistent that you needed a friend, too. She was a very determined woman."

"Yeah, she was."

"I first came here because a secretary in the department wanted to help me make ends meet. I stayed because Gwen asked for my help."

"Why are you still here? I know about the job offer in Minnesota."

She stared at him. Her lips parted, a little huff escaping before she pulled herself straight. Back on the edge of the couch she shook her head as if she couldn't believe what she'd just heard.

"I've spoken to the men who work for my uncle. They said they work for him and he's the only one who can give them new orders." She ignored his question.

The proverbial elephant was sitting in the middle of the room. Neither of them wanted to talk about her leaving. That's why he hadn't discussed the possibility or their accidental kiss.

He had made it a point to work late to avoid talking to her. "I don't have any control of your life, Tracey."

"Of course you don't. I never thought you did."

"You deserve more."

"I seriously don't believe you. After everything we've been through—are going through." She jumped up from the couch. Her sudden movement caught the attention of her guard at the door. He took a look and didn't react. "More of what, Josh? This is *so* not the time to be thinking about my future. We have to get the twins back before Jackson crashes or worse."

"The kidnappers called me."

"What? Why are we talking about me? Do they want money? I can force my uncle—"

"No. It's not about you." He scraped his fingers through his short hair. "It involves you. I mean, I need your help."

"Anything. I already told you."

"I think they want you to come and take care of Jackson. If they'd known about your family, they would have taken you this afternoon."

"I begged them to."

"It's dangerous. This is possibly one of the hardest things I've ever said, but I don't think you should." *Damn!*

"Why would you even think that? You want me to run to safety while Jackson may be…he might be…"

Control. He needed control. But he wasn't going to get it by ignoring that Tracey needed comfort. Or by pretending she wasn't a part of the situation.

She straightened to the beautiful regal posture he'd

noticed more than once. "I'll do it. I'm not hiding. I'd never be able to live with myself."

He stood, wanting to go to her. To hold her. Take as much comfort as he could, possibly more than he was able to offer her.

"If you said that back at the bridge to hurt me..." she sniffed "...maybe to get me back in some way for messing up the exchange at the bridge...well, it worked. I get it. As soon as Sage and Jackson are okay, I'm leaving for Minnesota."

"Yeah." The resignation in his voice was apparent—at least to him. But he hadn't meant it and didn't want her to go. He needed her.

She walked to the window that opened to the back of the house. Sometime in the hour that he was away, she'd gone by her place and picked up clothes. Now she was in jeans, a long-sleeved gold summer sweater over a black lace top.

The boots Gwen had given her for Christmas years ago were on her feet. He recognized the silver toes. She wore them a lot and every time he thought back to that last gift exchange...

So much about her reminded him of his wife. But the strange thing was he'd actually had a longer relationship with Tracey. God, he was confused. Mixed-up didn't sit well. He wasn't a soft or weak guy.

Not being able to concentrate was killing him or would get him killed. What he wouldn't give for the dependability of his men and a solid plan of action. Give him an hour to be in charge and he should be able to resolve this. But he wasn't going to be in charge. He had to accept that.

Thinking like this wasn't helping. Besides, no one

could have predicted that Tracey's uncle would send bodyguards. Or that they'd arrive at exactly that moment.

Whoever was in charge—he stared at the phone still in his possession—a bastard on the other end was dictating the fates of every person he loved.

All he could do was wait.

Tracey sniffed. Her shoulders jerked a little. She was trying to conceal that she was crying. He'd hurt her and been a... Hell, he didn't want to be a jerk.

"I didn't mean it," he said without making a move toward her. "It's just...everything."

"I know. Everything has to work out somehow."

"I need to be doing something."

"Leave."

Josh looked up from his pity party about to ask her where she wanted him to go. But she'd directed her command at the bodyguard still at the slightly open door.

"If you don't leave, I'm going to encourage this... this Texas Ranger to take your head off. Are we clear?" Tracey wrapped her fingers into fists and snapped them to her hips.

With her short hair whipped up like it had just been blown by a big gust of North Texas wind, she almost looked like Peter Pan. Her shapely bottom would never pass for a boy who'd never grown up. But she did look like she was about to do battle.

The bodyguard backed through the door. Tracey took a step forward and slammed it in his face.

"What was that for?"

She spun around and marched across the room. Her battle stance had been switched to face Josh. "No more tears. You think you need action? So do I. What can we do?"

He sputtered a little. The change in her threw him even more off-kilter than he had been. If he'd had any doubts about her, they flew out the window along with the fictional character he'd been envisioning. Tracey was real and very determined.

"When did they contact you?" she asked, hands still on her hips, unwavering.

"How did you—?"

She came in close, taking his hands. "Let's clear the air and get down to business," she whispered. "I understand that whatever might have been developing between us is gone."

Josh wasn't as certain as her upturned face staring at him seemed to be.

"There's only one reason you would have come back here," she continued. "Me."

He deliberately lifted an eyebrow while he glanced at the closed door and searched for the men who'd been passing in front of the windows.

"The only person I've ever worked for is you, Josh Parker. I want to help." She squeezed his hands.

Clarity returned. Her reassurance seemed genuine when he looked into her eyes. As her strength flowed through her grip, sanity returned.

"Whatever it takes. I mean that." The catch in her voice made him want to draw her into his arms again.

Yet, there was something else hanging there, left unsaid. "But?"

She dropped his hands. "We get through this without doubting each other again. But afterward, I'm really leaving. You need to know that."

"I understand." He didn't. Then again, he did.

After knowing her for five years. After trusting her with his children. Yeah, he'd turned on her with a pittance of circumstantial evidence. She was hurt, but there was no going back. He'd lost her trust and maybe even her respect.

Tracey squeezed his left hand—the one where he'd recently removed his wedding ring. Had she noticed? No one in his life had said anything if they had. Another slight tug encouraged him to look at her.

"Now tell me, what do those bastards want us to do?"

Chapter Nine

Tracey had free run of the house. She'd publicly insisted that Josh shower and change, claiming he smelled like dogs. Fingers crossed it made the men watching him less aware of her. She had her fingers on the back door...

"Where are you heading, Miss Cassidy?" Agent Lanning strolled to the breakfast bar, looking as cold as the granite he leaned on.

"I just realized that no one fed the horses yesterday evening." She pointed toward the barn even though it couldn't be seen from the kitchen.

"I'll go with you. It's been a while since I've set foot in a barn." He continued his laid-back attitude and sauntered to the door as if there were no other explanation for her sneaking outside.

He stepped onto the already-dew-soaked grass, paused, lifted the corner of his slacks and tucked them into his boots. "Like I said, it's been a while, but I've done this once or twice."

Great. Just her luck. He really was going to help her. The bottoms of her jeans would be wet by the time they crossed the yard and opened the gate. The agent who'd sat with her at the hospital stretched his arms wide and waved off the bodyguards who would have followed.

The very men she wanted to follow.

"Did Josh leave in the car or his old truck?"

"I beg your pardon?" She tried to look innocent and knew she'd overacted when George Lanning laughed.

"I may not have kids of my own, but I know what I'd do if they were abducted. And that's anything. I've been through this before with my first partner. Josh came back here for a reason. Has to be that the kidnappers decided they need you to take care of Jackson. So is he leaving using the car or the truck?"

She couldn't look directly at him, but saw that his shoulders sort of shrugged. Right that minute, she could see the tall lanky cowboy who seemed to be her friend. But she wasn't easily fooled. Nor was she going to admit she and Josh had planned an escape.

"We've told all of you several times now. That's what the bridge exchange was all about. Or that's what we assumed. And for the record, Josh completely blames me that it got messed up." She tilted her head toward one of her uncle's bodyguards, who followed them across the yard. "I'm not exactly Major Parker's best friend at the moment."

"So it would appear." He waved a gentlemanly hand indicating for her to precede him down the worn path to the barn.

Feeding the horses was a ruse that he'd seen through immediately. She'd had no intention of feeding them at two in the morning, but now she was stuck. At least an extra scoop wouldn't hurt them. And she wouldn't be there when Mark Tuttle came in the morning to clean up and take care of them before school.

George only thought he'd caught her trying to get free. He'd know for certain in a couple of hours—along with everyone else.

They walked through the barn door and right on cue, the bodyguard followed. Josh had come up with several ways for them to leave. That is, once he'd focused and told her what the kidnappers wanted.

Something had changed for the men who had abducted the children. It might have been the fiasco at the bridge, but their fear was that Jackson's condition had worsened. The faster she got to him, the better.

One thing stood in her way—being confined here at the house. She dipped the scoop into the feed, filling the buckets to carry to each stall. Her hand shook so much that some pieces scattered onto the ground.

"You must be pretty scared." George leaned against the post near the first horse, closely watching her actions.

"Any normal, caring human being would be."

"That's right. So I guess you had to explain your background—or should I call it previous life—to Josh." He rubbed his stubbled chin.

"Is my life as a rich girl pertinent to getting the children back?"

"Isn't it?"

"I don't know what you mean."

He nodded toward the bucket. "The horses only missed one meal, right?"

She'd been intently watching his every move instead of paying attention to what she was doing. The bucket now was overflowing onto the floor, making more cleanup for her. The bodyguard snickered a little at her mistake before he clamped his lips together tight and returned to his stoic expression.

"Let me."

George picked up the bucket, held his hand out for the scoop, then finished putting the right amount into each bucket and then each stall. She let him while she wrapped her hand around the handle of a wooden tail brush. This wasn't the original plan, but it was one of its versions.

Josh had argued against it because they didn't know if the bodyguards would fall in line. She had to risk it. When George bent in front of her to scoop up the spilled feed, she raised her hand and let it fall across the back of his head.

She hadn't rendered him unconscious and hadn't expected to. It wasn't a movie, after all. But he did fall face-first into the dirt. She had seconds. "You! Tie him up. We're leaving."

George grabbed the back of his neck and rolled to his shoulder. The man at the door ran quickly forward, for a man of his size. He stuck a knee in the agent's back, practically flattening one of his hands under him.

"Tracey, stop! You don't want to do this," George called.

She looked around for something, anything to stuff inside his mouth to keep him quiet. The bodyguard yanked George's hands around to his back, looped the lead rope and tied it off. Then he jerked George to a sitting position and tied him to the closest post.

"I don't see anything to keep him quiet."

The guard loosened the tie around George's neck, pulled it up around the man's ears and tightened it enough to quiet any yelling. Then he removed the cell and handgun from under George's jacket.

"Call your partner and tell him to bring the car closer to the gate." She set the cell inside the bucket and stuffed the gun down the back of her pants. That was what everyone always did, right? It didn't seem to want to stay. "Damn." She couldn't run worrying about where the gun would end up and decided to leave it. She grabbed it again and handed it to the guard. "Unload this. Leave the gun, take the magazine."

He followed her instructions. George didn't struggle. In fact, he hadn't put up much of a fight at all. She locked gazes with him and he quirked an eyebrow, then lifted his chin toward the door. "Be careful," was what she could decipher through his muffled speech.

She flipped the barn lights out and waited at the door for her uncle's hired help to make his call. She could see the outline of the car move toward the fence line without its lights. One more look at the agent left behind and she tried not to debate whether George had set her up or helped.

"You know we can take you to a hotel or to your uncle's, but nowhere else." Her guard placed his hand in the small of her back and gently nudged her forward.

Tracey didn't answer him. They silently moved across the paddock to the far fence. Up and over, then a short distance to where the car waited. Part of her wanted to back out and let him take her to the protection waiting in Fort Worth. Just a small part.

The section of her heart seeking to be fixed needed to find those two kids. It was the half of her that won. She ran to the car and stopped at the driver's door.

"Don't say a word," Josh said, getting out of the car holding a gun on the guard who'd been so helpful. "Your partner's in the trunk. You and I are going to ride in the back. Any trouble, Tracey?"

"George Lanning is tied up in the barn."

Even in the starlight, she could see that Josh was surprised. "Turn around." He cuffed the guard, held the gun until the man got into the car and slid in the back, too.

They didn't need to say anything. She drove to the place off Highway 6 where they'd decided to abandon the guards. It was a long walk back to Waco. She doubted her uncle's men would be picked up by a friendly driver after they'd been forced to strip to their underwear.

"Your clothes will be about a mile down the road." Josh merged onto the road and raised the window.

Less than an hour ago she'd been feeling sorry for herself. "I thought you'd left me behind."

"To be honest, Tracey, I would have. I told you coming back wasn't my choice." Josh shifted in his seat. "I don't want to put you in more danger or ask you to do anything illegal."

"Right. Where to now? They didn't call while I was in the barn. Did they?"

"No."

"So do we need to come up with a plan?"

Josh slowed down on the deserted highway. She dropped the clothes that were in her lap to the edge of the gravel shoulder. The bodyguards would be able to find them easily, and they were far enough off the road not to draw attention.

Josh turned in the seat, facing her.

"Shouldn't we be in a hurry to get away from here?" she asked cautiously.

He tossed the phone they'd bought earlier into the seat between them. "They said they'd call."

"So we wait." She slapped her thighs and rubbed. Nervous tension. She looked around, wondering what he really wanted to say.

The car was still in Drive and his foot was on the brake. No reason to ask if they were going to wait on the guards to catch up with them. Josh kept looking at her and she kept looking everywhere but at him.

"I lied."

"About what?"

"I would have come back. I didn't want to bring you with me to the kidnappers, but I would have come back."

Her mouth was in the shape of an O. She said the words silently and rubbed her palms against her jeans again. *He would have come back.* Despite everything happening to them, her heart took off a little. She needed hope.

He let off the brake, steered the car onto the road and placed his palm up on the seat covering the phone. It was an invitation, confirmed by the wiggle of his fingers. She accepted, slipping her hand over his and letting it be wrapped within his warmth.

"I think I know what they want me to do, Tracey. There are some good men out there on our side. The ones at the house can't help. George Lanning realized that. I owe him a debt. In fact, I'm going to owe a lot of people when this is over."

"Not me. I'm the one who lost the kids."

He squeezed her hand. "I should have anticipated a move like this from the Tenoreno organization. They've been threatening Company F all year. I never thought... Hell, I just never thought about it. I'm sorry."

"Do you have any place in mind for us to wait? Or are you just driving?" Her stomach growled loud enough to be heard, jerking Josh's stare to her belly. "Have you eaten anything since breakfast?"

"Sounds like you're the one who hasn't." He chuckled. Things were too serious to really laugh. "I don't feel like eating."

"But you need to eat, right?"

"We need to switch cars first." He pulled into a visitor's parking garage at Baylor and followed the signs to park almost on the top floor. Grabbing a bag she hadn't noticed before from the backseat, he pushed the lock and tossed the keys inside before shutting the door.

"You know...it would lower my anxiety level if you'd let me in on whatever plan you've already formed. And don't tell me you don't have one," she finished. He unlocked an older-looking truck. "Aren't you worried about campus security finding the car? Then Agent McCaffrey will be able to figure out what you're driving."

"I'm only worried about Vivian getting in trouble for leaving it. Of course, it'll take them a little while to discover the connection to me. I have high hopes that this is over by then."

"Whose truck is this?" She grabbed an empty fast-food sack and gathered the trash at her feet.

"Vivian's son's best friend. I'm...uh...renting it."

"Not for much, I hope." The half-eaten taco that emerged from under the seat's edge made her gag. "I don't think I'm hungry anymore."

"We should get something anyway. No telling how long it'll be before we can eat again. Looks like we're on empty. Might be good to get Jackson snacks and juice." Josh exited and swung into a convenience store and handed her three twenties without finishing his sentence. "Better pay cash for the gas."

Even with all the media coverage, neither of their pictures had been flashed on the screen—at least from what she'd seen. If she'd had long hair, she would have dropped her head and let it swing in front of her face. Her hair was the exact opposite. Thick and short and very red, but not very noteworthy.

For Jackson and Sage, she picked up some bottled juice, two very ripe bananas, crackers and animal cookies. Not knowing how much gas Josh was purchasing, she didn't know if she had enough money for a full bottle of honey. She looked in the condiments, but could only pick up grape jelly. That would have to do if—if his blood sugar was too low. She'd have to evaluate him and see.

For them—unfortunately—two overpriced and over-cooked hot dogs were in their future. She pointed toward the truck and the teenager behind the counter scanned her items. Josh finished pumping the gas and there was enough cash left for a supersized soft drink for them to share.

The clerk popped her gum and sacked everything. "Want your receipt?"

"No thanks."

Tracey lifted the sack from the counter while the girl continued thumbing through a magazine. It hit her that she'd never experienced that kind of work. Normal young adult work. The only job she'd ever had was helping Gwen and taking care of the kids. It was almost as if she got married her senior year of college, but without all the benefits.

Her life, her classes, her study time were all centered around the Parkers' schedules. That's the reason Josh hadn't known who to invite to her birthday. There wasn't anyone really.

It wasn't his fault. She'd made the choices that had led her to this moment. Josh waved at her to hurry back.

She'd had a very fortunate life. This event didn't seem like it. But they would get the kids back. Josh and the twins would be together again. She took comfort from the way he'd waited to hold her hand. Hopefully that meant there was a place for her in his life, too.

Chapter Ten

"So you have a plan. The Rangers are helping you even though they're not supposed to." Tracey's voice was soft and whispery once the truck engine was off. Josh parked in front of Lake Waco and opened his window.

"The Company isn't involved like you think. I don't have contact with any of them. I won't be sure Aiden is on our side until I get the text with details about the flight. If there is a flight. They might transport Tenoreno some other way."

She rubbed her hands up and down her arms as if she was trying to get warm. Thing was, it had to be ninety degrees outside and he'd cut off the engine quite a while ago. Was she as frightened as he was? Maybe.

He kept his arm across the top of the seat instead of draped over her shoulders where he wanted to put it. Then he extended his hand in an invitation to sit next to him. She took it.

In spite of the trauma and fright, it was a night of firsts. He wanted to hold her because she gave him strength, made him able to face what was coming next. But he couldn't explain that yet. Not while the kids were missing.

He laced her fingers through hers. The tops of her

hands against his palms. His larger hands covered her shaking limbs and she drew them closer around her.

"Want to talk about…anything?" she asked.

"My experience is sort of taking me to the deep end."

"Is that why you're so quiet?"

"I'm quiet?" He never said much. People called him a deep thinker. The Company knew not to interrupt when his feet were up on the corner of his desk. "There's a lot I could tell you. Rain check? It's not the time to think about distractions."

"I look forward to listening and I agree. We need to prepare." She moved their arms as if throwing a punch with each hand.

"Probably. Dammit, Tracey. Do you have any idea how I feel?"

"If your emotions are half as mixed up as mine… Then yes." She squeezed his fingers.

"There's a lot we need to talk about."

"Past, future and present. I know. We've avoided it for quite a while. I understand. I sort of feel disloyal. Then again, I can't help the way I feel."

"You feel disloyal?" he asked, finally looking at Tracey.

"Of course I do, Josh. Gwen was my friend."

He nodded, knowing what she meant. But he also knew that Gwen would want them to be happy…not guilty. When they had the kids back, they'd talk. They'd work it out.

"Do you have any idea what's in store? I know you've worked a couple of missing children cases." She spoke in his direction, but he could only see her in profile.

"Those were more parent abductions. Nothing on this scale."

"But you think they're all right. They wouldn't need

me to take care of Jackson if something had happened." She sat straighter, talking to the front windshield. "Wait. You're not sure why they want me, too. Are you?"

"There's a possibility that they've discovered your family has money. They could want that on top of what they want from me. I don't think that's the reason, though."

Tracey relaxed against him, pulling his arms around her like a safety blanket. They shared comfort and intimacy, and the knowledge that they were both scared without having to admit it.

"So everything's just a big mess. I can never tell you how sorry I am about my uncle's interference."

"It wasn't your fault. No need to think about it." In spite of the August heat, she shivered, so Josh hugged her tighter. "I wish there was time to give you some training to protect yourself. It's probably better to get some rest—while you can."

"You think I need self-defense?"

"More like, if you know you're about to be hit—" He had to clear his throat to say the rest. The thought of her being hit was tearing him apart. "Yeah, if that happens, then turn with the...um...the punch. You'll take less of an impact. But the best-case scenario is to keep your head down and don't talk back."

"In other words, don't give them a reason to hit me. I can do that."

"Right." As much as he loved holding her in his arms, they turned until they could face each other again. "Dammit, Tracey. You can't do this. It's too dangerous. When they call I'm going to tell them you refused."

"No. What if it *is* about the money and not just about Jackson's diabetes? What then? We'll be right back where we are now." She scooted back to the passenger seat. "I totally get why you don't think I can handle this."

"What? That's not it. I have more confidence in your ability to take care of Jackson than I do in mine. It's dangerous, that's all."

"I haven't forgotten how dangerous it is." She rubbed the side of her face that had been hit during the kidnapping.

Josh took her hand in his again. He wasn't going to let tripping over his own words create a misunderstanding. There was a chance that when they faced the kidnappers they may never have another moment—anxious or tender.

"It's not a lack of confidence. I'm just—"

"Shh. Don't say it out loud. It's okay. I am, too."

Afraid. They were both afraid of what was going to happen to them, to the kids, to their world. Changes were coming.

Dawn was still an hour away as Josh watched Tracey sleep. Her head was balanced on her arm, resting on the door frame, window down with every mosquito at Reynolds Creek Park buzzing its way into the cab.

He swatted them to their deaths in between the catnaps he caught. He hadn't tried to fall asleep. Maybe if he had, he would have been wide-awake. He'd drifted to the sounds of crickets and lake waves splashing against tree stumps.

The lakeside park was quiet during the early morning. On any usual morning, he would get up, feed the horses, make breakfast, dress the twins and drop them off at their day care before heading into the office. Normal for a single dad.

He wanted to believe that their life was just as normal as the next family's. He heard the whining buzz of another mosquito and fanned the paper sack from the convenience store to create a breeze. The everyday stuff might not be that much different for the kids.

Who could say what normal really was in the twenty-first century? Not him. If he got his family back, who was to say it would ever be normal for them again? Tracey waved her hand next to her ear.

"Ring, dammit."

"What's wrong?" Tracey whispered.

"I'm willing the phone to ring."

"Is it working?" she asked with her mouth in the crook of her elbow.

"Nope."

Normal? Since it was Saturday, he should be waking his kids up three or four hours from now, searching their room for shin guards and taking them to a super peewee soccer game. He should be standing on the sidelines, biting his lip to stop himself from yelling at the twins to stay in their positions and not just chase the ball.

She stretched. "I know how to make it ring. Take me to the restrooms and it's sure to buzz while I'm inside. You know, that whole Murphy's law thing."

"You have a point." He moved the truck up the road and around a corner, keeping the headlights off so as not to wake the campers.

Tracey jumped out. He watched a possum by the park's trash area. It had frozen when the truck had approached. Would his kids be afraid after this? Afraid of strangers? Cars? Afraid of being alone? Were they being kept in the dark? Possibly buried alive?

"Anything?" She'd been gone less than five minutes.

He shook his head and took his turn in the restroom. His movements were slowing and his thoughts progressing at the horrors his kids could be facing right at that moment. The hand dryer finished and he heard Tracey yell his name.

"Should I answer it?" She was out of the truck running toward him.

"Do it."

"Hello?" she said, on Speaker.

"That's good. Glad you could join the party, Tracey."

It was the kidnapper. If his ears hadn't confirmed it, then Tracey's look of fright would have. Her hand shook so much that he took both it and the phone between his.

"Put Jackson and Sage on the phone." He sounded a lot more forceful than he felt. Inside he prayed that they'd both be able to talk to him.

"The brats aren't awake yet and you don't want me to send one of the boys in their room to wake them up."

"I need to know—"

"Nothing! You need nothing. You're going to do whatever I want you to do, whenever I want you to do it."

He was right.

Tracey stared at him, nodded. He couldn't say it was okay. He couldn't admit that this man threatening to harm his children could ask him to do anything…and he would do it.

"What do you want us to do?" she asked.

His heart stopped just like it had the day the doctor told him there was no hope for Gwen. He couldn't move. Tracey's free hand joined his, pulling her closer to the phone. Whose hand was shaking now?

"Wherever you're hiding from the cops, you have fifteen minutes to get to Lovers Leap. Don't be late." *Click*.

"Do you know where Lovers Leap is, Josh?" Tracey shook his arm. "Isn't it over by Cameron Park?"

"Yeah. Sure. I know where it's at."

"Then let's get moving." She tugged on his arm.

"I can't seem to move."

"What's wrong?" Even in the low golden light from the public restroom he could see her concern. She moved to his side, tugged his arm around her shoulders. "Come on. Just lean on me and I'll get you to the truck."

It was slow going, but she managed it. It felt like they used all fifteen minutes of their time, but a glance at his watch told him they still had ten.

"Shock. I think you're in shock and I'm not sure what I can do." She turned the engine over.

"Drive. I'll... I'll be okay when we get there."

He needed to see his kids. Needed to get Tracey there to take care of them. Needed to do whatever these crazy bastards wanted him to, so they'd be free.

Whatever the price. Whatever it took.

"ARE YOU HAVING a heart attack?" She split her focus from the dark road to Josh's pale face.

"I'm okay. Just drive. You have to get to the opposite side of Lake Waco." Josh braced himself in the truck. He rubbed his upper arm, kept it across his chest.

And he was scaring her more than the phone call.

"I think I know where I'm going. You really don't look okay."

"I will be by the time you get there. Quit driving like an old lady."

"Quit trying to change the subject. Do you hurt anywhere? Is your arm numb?"

"I told you I'm not having a heart attack." His voice was stronger and he pushed his hand against the ceiling as she took a corner a little too sharply. "Whatever it was it's gone. Your driving has scared the life back into my limbs."

Panic attack. Thinking it was okay. Saying it aloud might just make it begin again. She'd never tell. Josh's men didn't need to know that the major of Company F was human.

"Is there any of that soda left? Maybe you need sugar or something?" They were nearing Cameron Park and she had to change her thoughts to what was going to happen. "What if they take me and the kids?"

"Your first priority is the twins. In fact, that's your only priority. Your only responsibility. No matter what they do to me, say about me, or threaten me." Josh shook his head and swallowed hard.

"The same goes for me, Josh. You do whatever it takes to keep Jackson and Sage alive."

"Remember, they seemed a little scared about dealing with Jackson. If you can convince them to drop him off at a hospital, then do it."

"I will." She gave the keys to Josh. He didn't look as pale as when they were at the last parking lot.

"Why did they all call each other Mack? It's confusing."

"Or smart. They call everyone Mack so no real names are used. They wear masks so we can't identify their faces. Hopefully that gives them the security they need not to kill us. So refer to them by body type or what they do. Like the one that gives the orders. He can be In-Charge Mack."

"Is that what you do with the Rangers?" She nervously looked around the park and raced on before he could answer. "No one's here. I wonder if we should get out."

"They're here. There's no vehicle close by. That means they didn't bring the kids. One's on the back side of the restroom building. Another has a rifle behind the north pillar of the pavilion."

The phone was in the seat between them. It buzzed with a text message for her to get out of the car and go with Mack. The second message told Josh to stay.

She tried to brush it off, but admitted, "Josh I'm... I'm scared."

"So am I. I want you to remember this. I'll insist on a video chat when we make contact. They might force you to say whatever they want. I need to know that you and the kids are really okay. So if it's true, then tell me..."

"Something just we know. It'll have to be short."

"Right."

Tracey was nervous. For her, it would be unusual to say I love you. It was on the tip of her tongue to admit that. Thinking like a criminal wasn't her forte, but she understood that they might force her to say those words.

"Let's keep it as simple as possible. Tell me you think you left the whiskey bottle on the counter if you're okay and still in Waco. If you're not okay, play with your ring. If you don't think you're in Waco, then put the whiskey in a friend's house. Can you remember that? Totally off the wall for them, memorable for us."

"What do I say if you can't see me playing with my ring?"

"Say that you wish we hadn't ditched your bodyguards." He smiled and took her hand in his and tugged her across the seat. "Come on over here to get out. I can always get back inside if they order me to."

He defied their instructions when his feet hit the ground. Turning to help her from the truck, he pulled her into his arms. Their lips meshed and melted together from the heat of the unknown to come. It was a kiss of desperation, representing all the confusion she'd been feeling for months.

Shoes were hitting pavement behind her. Men were running toward them. She'd already experienced how brutal these men could be.

"You need to be in one piece if you're going to rescue us," she whispered to the man she was falling in love with. Before any of the kidnappers could grab her she got her hands on Jackson's emergency kit, juice and snacks inside.

Josh cupped her face with his hands. "You're the bravest woman I've ever known. There's no way to thank you." He gently kissed her again.

This kiss felt like goodbye. Sweet, gentle, not rushed in desperation or as fast as her heart that was pounding like it would explode.

The men pulled them apart, taking Jackson's bag from her. "Stop. Jackson needs that."

"But you don't. We'll give you what you need when you need it." Tracey fell back a step trying to get out of his way. It was the man who'd hit her. The man who'd been talking to them over the phone...In-Charge Mack.

His cruel eyes peeked through the green ski mask. But they weren't looking at her. No, they watched Josh. They scanned him from head to toe, sizing him up just before shoving him into the side of the truck. Hard.

"When I give an order you better follow it. Don't push me, Major Parker," In-Charge Mack screamed. "Take her to the van."

Birds flew overhead as the world began to brighten. She couldn't see the sun yet, but it was that golden moment where you knew the world was about to be brilliant. She also knew—before his hand raised—that

In-Charge Mack intended to hit Josh. It was part of the man's makeup.

The gloved hand moved.

"Stop!" Her hand moved, too. Directly in the path of In-Charge Mack's arm, catching part of the force and slowing him down. "You put me in the hospital. Don't you need Josh without a concussion?"

In-Charge Mack's hand struck as quickly as a snake taking out its prey. The force sent Tracey stumbling into Mack with the rifle. She couldn't see, but she heard the scuffle, the curses, the "don't hurt her" before Josh was restrained by two other men.

"I'm okay. It's okay," she said as quickly as she could force her jaw to move. She looked back at Josh straining at his captors, then at the man who'd hit her. "You need both of us, remember?"

"What I don't need is you talking at all." He gestured with a nod and thrust his chin toward the bike path.

The man who'd grabbed her, slung the rifle over his shoulder and latched on to her arm again. Jerking her toward the park area, she stumbled often from watching Josh instead of the path. When she could no longer see him, she looked in front of her just in time to miss a tree.

The sun was up. Light was forcing the darkness to the shadows. Fairly symbolic for their journey today. She needed good to triumph. She needed hope because they were on their own. Somehow she'd get the twins out of this mire and keep them safe until their dad came home.

THE INSTINCT TO be free was tremendous. The two men holding Josh weren't weaklings by any definition, but he didn't try. He saw the cloth. Then they poured liquid over it. He jerked to the side avoiding their effort to bring him forward.

Chloroform?

Maybe his hunch about the plane wasn't so far off after all. If they felt like they needed him to be out cold for a while, then whatever he was doing wasn't nearby. One of the extras joining the party was digging around the emergency supplies they'd brought. Tracey must have dropped them when she'd been hit.

"Hey! Jackson needs the stuff in that bag."

"Don't worry about your kid. That's why the baby-sitter's here."

"Shut up, Mack," instructed the ringleader. "Put the juice back in the bag and take it to the other Mack."

The guy giving all the orders approached him with the cloth and bottle.

"Look, tell me Jackson's still okay. Is he alert? Talking? How's Sage? Just tell me and I'll behave. No problem. There's no reason to knock me out."

"Your kid is fine."

The guy running the show nodded to the men holding Josh. They planted their feet and tightened their grips. It might be inevitable, but he wouldn't just stand there and inhale peaceably.

Chapter Eleven

Blindfolded. Tracey swore the man driving her to wherever the twins were being held was lost. They had to be close by. It felt like he literally drove in circles. No one had mentioned Jackson or Sage. She thought they'd been joined in the van by a second person back at the park, but the one who'd escorted her could have been mumbling to himself.

You're the bravest woman I've ever known.

A lie. Gwen had been that woman. Strong and fearless in the face of death. But Tracey wasn't going to take Josh's words lightly. She couldn't forget that he'd said them, any more than she could ignore that he was saying goodbye.

The van stopped and so did her thoughts about Josh. Now it was about Jackson. Every piece of knowledge she'd learned and could remember about diabetes would be important.

They'd kept such a close eye on Jackson before yesterday, that he hadn't had any close calls since his initial diagnosis. They even monitored Sage regularly to make certain juvenile diabetes wasn't in her future. There was no guarantee, but they wouldn't be unprepared.

"Get out."

"Can I take off the—"

"Just scoot to the edge and I'll take you inside."

She did what they said. She didn't hear anything unusual. It was still very early in the morning, but there were few natural sounds. She thought she heard the faint—sort of blurry—noise of cars on I-35. The low hum could be heard from multiple spots—and miles throughout Waco. At least she'd be able to find her way to safety.

The twins...your only priority. Your only responsibility.

The men each held one elbow and led her through a series of hallways. She assumed they were hallways. She heard keys in locks, dead bolts turning, doors opening and shutting. Three to be exact.

Inside there wasn't any noise. It was like the world had turned off. Then the blindfold was removed and she blinked in the bright sun reflecting into a mirror. She was still blinking when the fourth door was opened and she was pushed inside. Jackson's emergency bag was tossed in after her.

Thank goodness.

She expected a dark, dingy place. Maybe full of cobwebs or a couple of mice running around. She'd completely forgotten about the video that showed the kids playing with a room full of toys.

They were everywhere. Plastic kitchens complete with pots and pans. Lawn mowers that blew bubbles. A table where they could build a LEGO kingdom on top. Stuffed animals piled in a corner.

Where were the kids?

Who would buy all these toys for a kidnapping? What would be the purpose? She looked closer at them and noticed they were all clean, but very well-used. They were probably from garage sales or thrift shops.

Wherever they'd been purchased, no one would remember the person.

But where were the kids?

She picked up one of the many stuffed animals and sat in a chair made for children. Two mostly eaten sandwiches were on the table. Two bottles of water, barely touched, sat next to them. She spotted Sage's backpack under a giant bear. Next to it, her gold glitter slipper.

Tracey crossed the room and bent to pick it up. There, huddled under the pile of used stuffed toys, with their eyes squeezed tightly shut, were the twins. Relief washed over her, but she had to remain calm. Even a little excitement might overtax Jackson's blood sugar at this point.

"Hey kidlets, it's Trace Trace," she whispered, afraid to scare them.

Stuffed giraffes, dinosaurs, bears and alligators flew in all directions as the kids scrambled to their feet. Their backpacks were looped around their shoulders, ready to walk through the door. Shoes on the wrong feet meant they'd been off at least once.

Grape jelly was at the corner of Sage's mouth. But the most important thing was that Jackson looked alert and safe.

"Are you okay?"

She opened her arms and they flew into a hug. The relief she felt that they were both alive and okay… She couldn't think of words to describe the emotion.

"Can we go now, Trace Trace?" Jackson asked. "Where's Daddy?"

"I want to go, too," Sage said. "Why didn't Daddy come get us?"

"Have you had breakfast? Are you really okay?" She turned to Jackson again, gauging his eyes, looking for any indicators that his blood sugar was too low. "Do you have a headache or feel nauseous?"

"Nope."

"He's been good." Sage lifted her hand to her mouth, trying to whisper to Tracey—it didn't work. "I hid the candy they gave us in the oven."

"Oh, I knew where you put it. But I didn't want to get sick if there wasn't anybody here to take care of me."

"Sage, hon, run and get that bag with Jackson's medicine stuff."

The little girl skipped over and skipped back. Both children seemed okay on the outside.

"Do we have to stay?" Sage whined, deservingly so.

"For a little while longer." Tracey pulled the materials she needed to test Jackson's blood sugar from the bag.

The little darling was so used to the routine that he sat with his finger extended, ready for the testing. She put a fresh needle into the lancing device, and took a test strip from the container.

Sage tore the alcohol wipe package open and handed it to her. They all lived with this disease. They'd had their share of ups and downs, but they stayed on top of it.

"I love you guys. Do you know that?" She wiped off the extended finger, punched the button, dropped the droplet of blood on the strip and placed it in the meter.

Two little heads bobbed up and down. She hid her anxiousness waiting on the results. He was in the safe zone, ready to eat his breakfast and start his day.

Thank God.

"Have you two been alone all this time?"

"Nu-uh."

"Some guy sits with a mask all over his face. Says

he's hot." Sage was the talker, the observant one, the storyteller. "Then he leaves and comes back sometimes."

"Sometimes he tries to play," Jackson added. "That guy came in with his phone one time. 'Member?"

"Yeah, but he wasn't fun. He was angry and mean."

They sat in the chairs next to her at the table. She put a banana on each little plastic plate. Wiped out the glasses as best as she could and poured a little bit of juice in them. She noticed that one of the juice bottles was missing so she kept a third of the bottle, placing it back in the bag.

"So, eat and I'll get some crackers."

"For breakfast?" they said together.

"There's nothing wrong with bananas and crackers."

"Aren't you eating?" Jackson asked, peeling one section and turning the banana sideways for a bite. He left it there, like a giant smile, then posed until she acknowledged him.

He swallowed his bite and laughed, showing the mashed banana on his tongue. Sage said "yuck," and then they all three laughed, making Tracey want to cry. How could any of this be funny? But if she didn't laugh and act as if it was, then they'd get anxious and stressed.

Stress was bad for blood sugar.

Very bad.

Laughing, playing and maybe casually looking for a way out of this room. That's what their day would be. Maybe the man who was scary and mean would stay away.

Maybe if they were really lucky, Josh would haul all the mean Macks to jail. Then the Parker family could all live happily ever after.

"I want to go home, Trace Trace."

"I know, Jackson. And we will. But while we're here, what do you want to play?"

"Princesses. I thought of something first, so we play my game." Sage darted around looking through the toy pile for princess gear.

"I don't feel like playing." Jackson crawled into her lap and rested his head on her shoulder.

She wasn't going to panic. His level was within normal range. He was outside his routine and would be tired even if he didn't have diabetes. "Okay. Sage, would it be okay if I just told you a story?"

"I can't find any princess hats anyway."

"You know, Sage, you don't have to have a princess hat to be a princess."

"You don't? But isn't it more fun if you do?" She smiled and twirled. "What story are you going to tell?"

"Let's go sit on the mattress so Jackson can take a nap. I mean rest 'cause Prince Jackson doesn't take naps." Then she tickled Sage. "Neither does Princess Sage. Right?"

"Right."

They sat down and Tracey created a story about a prince and a princess who lived with their father, the king. When they asked the king's name she told them King Parker. Sadly, the queen didn't live with them anymore. The story went on and of course the kids recognized that it was about them.

"Then one day a horrible evil dragon swooped down and stole the beautiful princess and handsome prince. The dragon…" The kids held on to her hands tightly and snuggled a little closer. "What should we name the awful dragon?"

"Mack," they said in unison.

"Okay. Mack the dragon was tired of flying around

burning up all the bridges. So he went back to the cave where he held the princess and prince. 'What do you want with us?' said the beautiful princess."

Tracey changed voices for each character in the story. The kids were nodding off. Both rested their heads in her lap when one of the Macks came through the door, bolted it behind him and sat on the bench.

She stopped referring to the dragon as Mack. There was no reason to antagonize one of them. And no reason to continue the story since both of the kids were asleep.

Tracey left them curled where they were and propped another blanket behind her head. She pretended to rest and assessed the room through half-closed lids. There didn't seem to be any other way out. The next time they left her alone, she'd be bold and just look.

All those years growing up a rich kid, she'd been warned to be careful. Super careful. She was never allowed to go anywhere alone. Not until her second semester at Baylor.

She remembered the guy who looked like a college student and had followed her around campus. He even had season tickets to football games. Probably not the section he wanted, but her uncle's money had bought him access to a lot.

It took begging her grandfather and whining that she had no friends to get him to call off the hounds. Promising that she'd be overly careful, she was finally on her own. That's when she realized she didn't really know how to make friends.

Then a bad date had shot her overprotective uncle into warlord status. He declared she didn't have any rights and as long as he was paying the bills—blah blah blah. Poor little rich girl, right?

Who would have thought that the first time she'd be

placed into real danger would be because she worked for a Texas Ranger? What a laugh her grandfather would have had about this mess.

So there she was, thinking about her grandfather, sitting awkwardly with two precious children asleep on her lap, praying that they'd grow up without being frightened of the world. And then more simply, she just prayed that they'd be able to grow up.

"Trace Trace?" Sage said sleepily. "What happened to the king? Did he get his kids back?" She yawned. "Did he get to be happy?"

"Sure, sweetie. He used his strong sword and killed the dragon. And all the Parkers lived happily ever after."

"Trace...is your name Parker, too?"

"No, kidlet. It's not."

Sage drifted back to sleepy land giving Tracey more time to think about it. She wouldn't be a part of the Parker happy-ever-after. It was time for her to ride into the sunset alone.

Chapter Twelve

Josh lost track of how many times they'd covered his face with the sweet-smelling gauze. Enough for him to have a Texas-size headache. Long enough that his body recognized he'd been in one position too long, lying across the metal flooring of a panel van. And long enough that his stomach thought his neck had been cut off.

The skyline through the van window showed only trees and stars. Definitely not the skyscrapers that would indicate a city. They could still be in Waco, but he had a feeling they'd driven closer to the state prison where Tenoreno was being held.

The men surrounding him were unmasked, but it was too dark to make out any of their faces. Now wearing garb like a strike force—military boots, pants, bullet-proof vests, gun holsters strapped to their thighs. Tracey was right. The idea of calling each other Mack tended to be confusing. He had to admit that it was effective. But they didn't act like a cohesive team.

Josh's hands were taped behind him. Tightly. The hairs on his wrists pulled with each tug he tried to hide. There must be several layers because it wasn't budging. He wouldn't be getting free unless he had a knife.

For the Macks, it had been a good idea to knock

him out cold while they traveled. His brain was still fuzzy while he attempted to soak up everything about his situation and process it for a way out. If he'd been awake, the problem would be resolved or at least he'd have a working theory.

Someone kicked the back of his thigh. He held himself in check, but a grunt of pain escaped. He tried not to move. He needed time for the cobwebs to clear. But there wasn't any use trying to hide that he was awake. Even if he wasn't alert.

"Masks on. He's awake."

The thought at the forefront of his mind was Jackson's health and his family's safety. He could only estimate how long his captors had been driving. It might still be early afternoon.

One step at a time.

"I need to talk to Tracey."

If only he could get In-Charge Mack and his men to confirm what they had in store for him. As in why did they need him personally? Whatever it was, they felt like they needed hostages to keep him in line. Once they confirmed, he'd know how to proceed.

Or where to proceed.

"It's time to earn your keep, lawman." The guy who'd kicked him laughed.

They had his phone. Aiden must have texted the location information. Good, they also had his bag from the house. He had a few tricks in there that would help get his family back.

"We're talking to the men that are with her in ten minutes. Behave and you might get an update." The In-Charge Mack didn't even glance back from the front seat.

Laughing Mack looked around, saw where they

were, and then pulled a gun to point at Josh's head. "Behave." The gun went under a loose sweatshirt—still aimed at him.

They pulled even with another vehicle, the drivers nodded at each other and separated. He could see the other car lights in the rearview mirror as it did a three-point turn in the road and followed closely behind.

"Where are we?"

"Thanks to you, daddy dearest is scheduled for a private plane ride to get to trial. You're our passport," In-Charge Mack said from up front.

"Daddy? Aren't you a little short to be Xander Tenoreno?"

Laughing Mack kicked out, connecting with Josh's knee.

He'd actually confronted the son of Paul Tenoreno several times. At each encounter he'd looked him straight in the eye. The guy giving the orders here was only about five foot ten. Average height for an above-average criminal.

But he couldn't reject the hunch that these men were regular employees of the Mafia ring in Texas. They were definitely well funded and prepared. The animosity that was associated with their talk about Tenoreno was a bit intense. Why free a man you hated so that he could run the operation again?

"If you'd told me your plans a little earlier, I could have saved you the trouble. They pulled all my authority yesterday when you kidnapped my kids." He wanted to see their reaction. What was their ulterior motive? "I can't get you on that plane."

"Don't be so modest, Major. We have every confidence in your abilities." The one calling the shots turned to show him a picture of Tracey with the kids. "We also have very little confidence that Mack in toy land will keep his cool if you don't get the job done. He's itchy to pull the trigger, don't ya know."

"Isn't it time to stop talking in riddles and tell me what you really want?"

"You haven't figured it out? But you're so good at this. Your Texas Ranger buddies got poor old Mr. Tenoreno moved to the Holliday Transfer Facility. He's waiting to be flown to Austin. We're going to pay him a visit."

"I can't get you inside there, either." Josh attempted to push himself up to a sitting position. His ankles were also taped tightly together. He pushed on a hard-sided case.

"Are you being dense on purpose?" Laughing Mack lashed out with his boot, catching the back of Josh's leg.

"Your kid here is going to make walking anywhere a problem. Call him off. I need my knees." Josh made note of how many guns were in the van.

"Mack, mind your manners." He spoke to the guy still pointing the gun in Josh's direction, but he pointed twice like he was giving directions to the driver.

Josh used the bumps in the road to help shift his position. He was finally upright and could see more of the view. A field, lots of trees, nothing special out the front. But when he glanced out the back, just behind the second vehicle were soccer and baseball fields.

He knew exactly where they were—Huntsville Municipal Airport. He'd assumed that they'd attack here. He'd just expected a little more time to figure out how to throw a kink in their plan.

"Whatever you're planning, I'm not doing a damn thing until I talk to Tracey. And I mean talk, not just see her picture."

"I figured as much. Almost time."

The van started up, speeding down the dirt road, then pulled under a canopy of trees. The second vehicle pulled in next to them.

"They've left the prison. We have six minutes," the Mack next to him said.

"No Tracey. No cooperation."

"Dial the phone. Remember it's face-to-face and you watch," he told Laughing Mack. "Make it quick."

One thing about this outfit, everyone in it obeyed In-Charge Mack without hesitation. Tracey's face was on the phone screen. She reached out toward the phone at her end, looked sharply away and then back at him.

"They won't let me hold the kids so you can see them but they're doing okay. Sage has been watching over her brother, as usual.'"

"And how is Jackson?"

"He's doing okay. I'm sure he's going to bounce right back after this."

"Have they hurt you?"

"Nothing that a shot of whiskey wouldn't cure. Did I leave it in the middle of the house?"

"What was that?" In-Charge Mack asked.

"She said she wanted some whiskey," Laughing Mack relayed to him.

"That's enough. Disconnect."

"Josh? I wanted to tell you that I—"

Laughing Mack got a big kick out of cutting her off. *Tell me what?*

He didn't have time to process. They opened the van doors and Josh could see the airfield.

"Out."

He lifted his bound ankles and the Mack nearest the door sliced them free with a knife Josh hadn't seen. He really did need to clear his head and become aware of his surroundings. Think this thing through.

The Macks moved the hard-sided case that had been near his feet to outside and flipped the lid open. Machine pistols.

"You really think those are necessary?"

"Glad you asked, Major. Obviously, this is the backup. If you fail, we're bringing down that plane."

"What exactly do you want me to do? I thought you were here to free Tenoreno." Josh kept his eyes moving. Trying to remember how each of them stood. If they showed any signs of weakness or additional personal weapons.

"Wrong, Major. You're here to kill him."

Chapter Thirteen

Tracey was taking a huge risk. What if they weren't rescued before Jackson needed this cartridge? And what if she *didn't* use the insulin on the sleeping guard? It might be her only opportunity to try to escape. What if Josh didn't—

No! Josh was coming back. He'd never give up and neither would she. She put the kids to sleep on the mattress, leaving their shoes on their feet so they'd be ready. Jackets and bags were by the door. They wouldn't leave without them. It was their routine and no reason to argue.

Taking this risk was necessary, not just a shot in the dark. It would work. She knew what the side effects of too much insulin were. In a healthy person, he'd probably vomit, but he'd eventually pass out. She didn't know how many men were on the other side of the door.

The young man watching them had already complained about how warm it was while wearing the ski mask. The room had its own thermostat. It looked like an old office space. She switched the cool to heat and cranked the temperature up. It was going to be unbearable in a couple of hours. Their guard would get hotter, faster—of course, so would they.

The last thing to do while he was gone from the room

was to prep the needle with insulin and hide it. They'd take the emergency kit back and return it to the other room as soon as a Mack came to keep an eye on them. Their ultimate weapon to keep her in line was taking away the emergency kit for Jackson.

"I bet your boss wouldn't like knowing that you don't stay in here while I check Jackson's blood sugar. Nope. None of this would be possible if you did," she said to herself, capping the needle. She couldn't keep it in her pockets. They'd see it for sure.

So she arranged toys and the kid-sized kitchen station near the bench where the guards sat. It was simple to keep the syringe with the toy utensils. She snagged one and put it on the table so she'd have an excuse to exchange it later.

She could give the injection without the guard feeling more than a small prick on his skin. Insulin didn't need a vein, just fatty tissue. If he was sound asleep it might not bother him at all. But she had a sharp toy ready as an explanation. She also moved the trash can closer to the bench...just in case.

They should be coming back into the room soon. She'd been wondering for far too long about life and what the next stage held for her. When all this was done and over, there wouldn't be any waiting. It was so much better to find out. To know.

Leaving Waco, leaving her friends, leaving Josh wasn't her first choice. Waiting wasn't, either. She had to stop being a scaredy cat and start living life. That meant handing in her resignation to Josh and telling him how she really felt.

Forty-eight hours ago she'd been ready to give her notice and walk away. Even if it broke her heart. Well, there was no doubt her heart would shatter now, but it was a resilient organ and she'd manage. She could walk away if Josh didn't ask her to stay.

The locks on the door turned. She dropped her head into her arms on the tiny table and calmed her breathing. She was physically exhausted from a lack of sleep, food and an abundance of adrenaline pumping constantly. Forcing herself to pretend to be asleep might just slow her physical state to let it happen.

Being bent in half like she was wouldn't let her stay asleep for long.

The same guard came straight to the table to collect the emergency kit. She barely saw him through her lashes, watching his silhouette turn off the lamps in the corners, and then sit on the bench.

First step…check.

Rest, rest, rest. She was going to need it to get to safety.

There wasn't a clock in the room and they'd taken her watch—another way to make her dependent on them for Jackson's care. But her body told her she'd been in the cramped position far too long and she hoped her guard was deep in sleep. She pushed her damp hair away from her face.

It was definitely beyond hot.

She took the toy spatula and stood, trying not to make any noise. She'd cleared her path, thinking this through earlier. No squeaky toys, nothing to trip over.

She kept on her toes, not allowing her boot heels to make noise against the linoleum floor. She exchanged the toy gadget for the syringe and removed the needle cover. Still no peep from the kids or their guard. She looked at him; he'd rolled the ski mask up his face, covering his eyes. The smooth chin meant he'd either just shaved or he didn't need to.

The covered eyes meant it would be easier to follow through on her plan. He'd have to move the mask before he could see where she was. She risked a lot by tugging a little at his black T-shirt, but if she could stick this in his side...

Done.

This Mack, sitting on the bench, turned and grunted. He didn't wake. She replaced the cap, threw the syringe away like all the other supplies from earlier and tiptoed to sit on the mattress with the kids.

It didn't take long before their guard moaned, then held his stomach like he was cramping. Before Mack could reach the door, he detoured for the garbage.

Tracey didn't hesitate. She couldn't let herself think about what would happen to the young man. He was a kidnapper. He'd threatened Jackson's life. She was going to make sure the little boy was safe.

No matter the cost. No matter who she had to knock out with insulin to do it. Even in the dim light she could tell he was sweating and disoriented. He was unsteady on his feet and faintly asked for help.

She wanted to. She had to cover her ears, she wanted to help him so badly.

Instead, she got the kids up and sat them in chairs. Jackson was a little woozy and put his head back onto the table. When the young guard began leaning to one side, she struggled with him to put him on the mattress. Then searched his pockets for a cell phone.

Nothing except the keys to the doors.

Before she scooted the twins out of the room, she checked out the other side of the door. No one was there. She ventured farther, listening before she turned each corner. No signs of the other men. She quietly headed back and saw both of their heads poking around the edge.

Backpacks on, they ran to meet her.

"Are we going home now?" Sage asked.

"First we have to play hide-and-seek. You can't giggle or tell anybody where we're at. Okay?"

Both their heads bobbed. Sage jumped up and down, smiled then got Jackson excited as well. "We get to go home. We get to see Daddy." They said in unison, jumping again.

"Please guys, it's really important for us to be quiet. Shh." She placed a finger across her lips and lowered her voice. "Quiet as church mice. Ready?"

They hurried downstairs, where she used the keys again to get out the front door. Austin Avenue?

They were in downtown Waco? It must be the wee hours of the morning, because this was an area of town that was open until two. She hadn't heard any party or loud music. No wonder they'd filled the room with toys to keep the kids occupied and silent.

Tracey ran. She hoisted Jackson to her hip, holding tight to Sage's little hand. "Come on, baby, I know you're tired, but we've got to run. You can do it."

Where to?

They had to be gone—out of view. Fast. Before someone discovered they'd left their room. She tried the sandwich shop next door.

Locked.

They'd all be locked. Everything closed in this part of town. There was nothing to throw at a window. No alarm she could set off without the kidnappers looking out their window and seeing her.

So close.

They were so close to freedom. If they could just find somebody...

Nothing but parking lots, a closed sandwich shop, more parking lots and the ALICO Building. Maybe there was somebody still there.

It was the dead of night and there were no headlights. No one around to wave down for help. They made it across Austin Avenue and then again across Fifth Street. A door banged open. She dared to look back for a split second. It was them.

"Over there," she heard one of the men say.

"Sage, honey, put your arms around my neck." She'd run for their lives carrying the twins. But where?

The parking garage would be open. She ran between the structures. Garage to her left, fire escape to her right. Fire escape? Then what? Climb twenty-two stories outside the tallest building in Waco with twin four-year-olds?

No. All she had to do was make it up one flight before they saw her. The building was split-level—they could hide on the level that was a parking lot. It was more logical to choose the garage door. She couldn't leave their fate to the off chance someone left their car unlocked and they could hide inside.

What then? Blow the horn until their captors broke the window and carried them back to their downtown dungeon?

It would have to be the fire escape. She set a lethargic Jackson on the stair side of the fire escape, helped Sage over and climbed over herself. They were between buildings where the voices of the men chasing them echoed. She didn't know if it could be done, but it was their only chance.

"Quiet as a mouse, kidlets, we've got to keep quiet.

Go ahead and start climbing, sweetheart." She adjusted Jackson on her back moving as fast as she could behind Sage.

One foot, then another. Four-year-old legs couldn't take stairs two at a time. Neither could a twenty-six-year-old with a four-year-old on her back. If she wasn't scared of falling down, she would pick up Sage and make the climb with both of them.

The shouts changed. No longer echoes from the street, they were directly below them. Tracey stopped Sage and slowly—soundlessly—pulled her to the side of the building. Maybe they'd get lucky. Maybe neither of the men would look up. Maybe they'd take the logical path into the garage.

Maybe luck was on their side. Looking by barely tilting her head, she watched as the men took off into the other building.

"More quietly than ever, baby girl. We can do this."

It took time. The one flight was actually a little more than that. Their luck ran out. Just as they made it to the roof so did the kidnappers. They yelled out to each other or at someone else, she couldn't be certain.

They were on the lower roof. She set the twins next to a door and looked around for something to pry it open. No junk in the corner. Nothing just lying around to pick up and bang against metal. She heard the men taking the metal fire escape two steps at a time.

Running to the Fifth Street side of the roof, she yelled, "Help! Someone help us!" There weren't any headlights, no one walking, nothing.

Then to the parking lot side toward the river. Someone might be hanging out closer to the water, but it was too far away. "Help! Somebody. Anybody."

Chapter Fourteen

The kids were cuddled together. All Tracey could do was join them. They couldn't tackle the twenty stories of fire escape stairs. Even if they did, there wasn't a helicopter waiting to whisk them off to safety.

The men chasing them heard her cries for help. She heard their shoes slam against the metal steps, then across the roof. She braced herself for punches or kicks. The repercussions of running away. Maybe now. Maybe later. But these men would strike out. She'd protect the kids.

She repeated the promise that they'd be all right as the men both angrily kicked her legs. These men would lose. Josh would find them. They *would* lose.

"Stop it! Don't hurt her!" the twins yelled, still wedged between her and the wall.

Their screams echoed in her ears as they were pulled from her arms. One of the men jerked her up by her hair while the other had a hand on each twin. They struggled. She could barely stand.

He dragged her to the edge of the building, threatening to throw her over the side. His hands went around the back of her neck, pushed her to the ledge. She dropped to her knees.

"I wish I could get rid of you," he spitefully whispered. "I'd leave you on that sidewalk along with the jerk who let you escape. Did you hit him with a stuffed unicorn?" He shoved her forward into the concrete barrier. "Get up and get hold of one of them brats."

Limping down the fire escape, she wondered if they'd care that their friend might die from the insulin injection. She carried Jackson, and poor Sage was in the arms of the man to her right.

The men constantly looked over their shoulders, but they weren't followed. No one drove by. No police were in sight. They weren't gentle, especially the blond who held a gun instead of a child and shoved her every third step she took.

"He might just kill us for this. If anybody sees, we're dead. We need to get out of here, fast."

"So we don't tell him, right? He'd just get angry," the man carrying Sage answered. "She sure ain't going to tell him. Mack will never know they got loose. Besides, we got 'em back, didn't we? And we still have another twenty before we're supposed to leave and…you know."

Leave?

Yes, he'd cocked his head toward her. So what did he mean? Leave them or leave with them, taking them to a new location? Or maybe they planned to leave them here after killing them?

Once again she wished that she'd been brave or lucky enough to leave earlier, before the bars on the street had closed. Food trucks were normally one of the last things to leave the now-empty parking lot.

"You need to call 911 for your friend," Tracey told the men, trying to gauge their humanity. "He's very ill and needs emergency care"

"So he's sick. He'll get over it." Gun in hand, he shoved her through the outer door.

Would they call 911? If she admitted why he needed help they'd know for certain that she'd planned her escape instead of taking advantage of their guard being sick. Ultimately, she didn't want the weight of his death on her shoulders.

"I injected him with insulin and he's going into hypoglycemic shock." They ignored her as they entered the building they'd just escaped from. "Can't you drop him at the clinic with a note? He may die."

"That's on your head, lady. You're the one that gave it to him and he was stupid enough to let ya."

They pushed her into the toy room, Sage right behind her. The one holding the gun stuck the barrel under her chin and moved close to her face. His minty breath a stark contrast to the threats. "You listen to me, lady. Stay in line or we're getting rid of you no matter what Mack says."

Then bolted the door.

"Oh my!" She cried out before realizing she needed to control herself for the kids.

"What's wrong, Trace Trace?" Sage asked.

Jackson didn't say anything. He went to the mattress, saw it was full with the young man she'd injected and lay down next to the wall using a teddy bear for a pillow.

"When can we go home?"

"Soon, honey. Soon." She pulled the little girl into her arms and rocked her by shifting her weight from foot to foot. Her long hair was tangled again. She'd finger-comb it after breakfast.

"Did Daddy forget about us?"

"Oh no, baby. He loves you and is doing everything he can to get you back to him."

It took only a few minutes to get Sage to drift off to sleep. She adjusted the children on a blanket and

used the secondhand animals to make them comfortable and feel safe.

The young guard wasn't comatose. He roused a little,
making her heart a little lighter. He was clammy with
sweat, so she used the water from the water bottle to
dampen a couple of doll dresses and wiped his brow,
trying to make him more comfortable. She would never
be able to do that again knowing that the outcome might
mean somebody would die.

Sitting still in the predawn hours she remembered
something odd about their captors…she knew what
they looked like. While chasing her, they'd left their
masks behind. She could identify them. This development couldn't be good.

It was her fault for trying to escape. But she had been
right about telling Josh the whiskey was in the center of
the house. At least she knew they were definitely in the
heart of Waco. She prayed that he'd be able to find them.

That line was getting old. Of course she'd hope for
that. But she couldn't focus on it, either. She'd do her
job and think of another way out of this room. Her life
wasn't a series of rescues.

She'd walked away from all that when she turned
twenty-one. "Heck, I even changed my name to avoid
it." *Pick yourself up and get your head on straight,
Tracella Sharon Cassidy Bass.* That was her grandmother's voice talking from her overly pink bedroom.
Ha! Years ago Grandma Sweetie had declared that her
pieces of advice would come in handy. But Tracey bet
even Sweetie wouldn't have imagined this scenario.

She looked at the man in the corner. He was just a
man now. Not a creep, not an abductor with a gun—just
a young man who needed help. No one deserved to die.

And she'd help as best she could. She turned the water bottle upside down and got the last drops onto the cloth.

After she'd cooled their guard's forehead, she decided to talk with the other two guards. She knocked on the door trying not to wake up the kids. Then she knocked a little more forcibly.

"What?" one of them shouted through the wood.

"We need more water."

"Not now."

"Even another bottle for your friend?" She tapped on the door, attempting to get an answer.

"Lady, you need to shut up so we can figure this out."

"There's water in the tan bag you took from me." They'd even taken the kids' backpacks with their toys.

"Yeah, like we're giving that back."

"You have to. It has Jackson's insulin and supplies."

"Isn't that what you stuck in Toby—I mean Mack? One of them insulin needles, right? And you said he could die. So no way. I ain't letting you have it back. Needles are dangerous, man."

There was arguing. Raised voices. Lowered voices.

"Don't matter anyway. We're supposed to head out."

"Are you…are you leaving us? Please unlock the door before—" She tripped backward as the door was pushed open. The gun took her by surprise. When it was pointed at her head, street gangster style, she could only raise her hands and say, "Don't shoot."

"We ain't shooting you, lady. But we don't trust you neither. Get the kids. We're leaving."

"Where are you taking us?"

"Does it matter?" the blond holding the gun in her face said.

"To the airport. He dead yet?" asked the other as he hurried to the corner where the kids were.

"Shut up, you idiot," the blond man insisted. "First you use Toby's name. And dammit, thanks to him," he pointed at the ill man, "she's seen our faces."

She remembered what Josh had said. The kidnappers would feel safe as long as their identities were secret. Would they kill her and the kids now that they weren't? "He, uh, still needs a doctor, but I think he'll be okay."

"That's good I guess."

"No it's not," said the blond, waving the gun like an extension of talking with his hands. "What if somebody finds him? What if he talks?"

"Do we shoot him then?"

"What? You can't— He's unarmed and helpless." Tracey would have pleaded more but the men looked at each other as if she was crazy.

Maybe she was, since they were obviously ready to shoot her and the kids. Now they were going to taking them to a new place? Or could it possibly be...

"Is this an exchange at the airport? Who told you to bring us?"

"We don't do names, lady. We just do what we're told, and then we're gone."

"So there's no reason to kill him." She pointed to the unconscious guy. "You can just leave him here."

"We don't have time, man. If you want to plug him, go ahead. My hands are full." The second man pulled a sleepy Jackson into his arms.

The blond one lifted Sage. She squirmed and pushed at his shoulders. "I want Trace Trace."

Then she began to cry. For real, not a fake cry to get her way. She was genuinely scared of the man who held her and had a gun pressed against her back.

"Here, let me take her." Tracey held out her arms

and Sage threw herself backward, nearly falling between them.

The children were old enough to understand guns. Even at four and a half the twins knew about tension and that guns were dangerous. Their father was a Texas Ranger and had weapons in the house—inside a lockbox and gun cabinet—but they'd already had lectures about how they were weapons and weapons were dangerous.

Sage had watched the gun being waved around. She'd heard the discussion about shooting someone. She could tell things weren't right no matter how many toys were in the room.

"Let's get gone," the blond said. "Mack's expecting us to be there."

Tracey didn't want to draw their attention to the man in the corner, so she grabbed a toy bear for Sage to latch onto and left their backpacks. There were spare crackers and juice in the emergency kit that could tide them over until they received food.

They had almost reached the back door when she asked the blond, "The tan bag with his supplies. Where did it go?"

"Get in the van." He shoved her forward to the back stoop.

"We have to have that bag."

"You ain't jabbin' me with anything."

"No, we can't go without it. Jackson needs it."

"Should have thought 'bout that before you made Toby sick." The second guy put Jackson in her arms after she put Sage in the van.

"Where do I sit?" Sage asked, following with a huge sniff from her tears.

No seats. The panel van had nothing but a smelly old horsehair blanket.

"What an adventure, Sage. You and your new bear friend can help me hold Jackson."

She put the bear on the metal floor and Sage sat cross-legged next to it, then dropped her head onto her hands. Jackson woke up, rubbed his eyes and moved next to the bear, imitating his sister. Sage pursed her lips and Jackson mimicked or answered. Sometimes the twin language was hard to interpret.

The van door closed and they pulled out of the parking lot. It was still before dawn on Sunday morning. Too early for anyone to have noticed them being moved along by gunpoint. A lot of people went to church in Waco, but not *this* early.

Even if someone saw them sitting on the floor of the panel van, no one would think anything suspicious. All they could do was cooperate.

"Trace Trace?" Jackson nudged her leg. "I'm tired and hungry. Where are my snacks?"

"We'll have to wait for breakfast, big boy."

Jackson threw himself backward and stiffened his body. His small fist hit her bruised jaw. She clamped down on the long "ouch" that wanted to escape. It wasn't his fault and she refused to upset him more. When his blood sugar began to get low he became angry and quarrelsome. It was one of the first clues that his levels needed to be adjusted.

"Jackson's always 'posed to have crackers," Sage told her. "He's starting to get a little mean, Trace Trace."

"I know, honey, but they got left with the toys."

Sage leaned closer putting her hand close to her mouth, indicating she didn't want the men to hear her. "Is that man really going to die?"

"No, baby. His sugar's a little low right now, but he's going to be fine."

"That's good."

Tracey held tightly to the sides of the van and the kids held tightly to her. Fortunately, it wasn't a long ride to the Waco Regional Airport. This place wasn't huge by any means. She'd flown home from here several times before she'd turned twenty-one.

Maybe knowing the layout of the airport would be an advantage. If she was given a chance to run, she'd know where to go. But had the Macks hinted at an exchange. Her mind was racing in circles trying to figure it out.

After a few minutes she realized they weren't going to the airport. At least not the one in Waco. The twins fell asleep quickly enough with the rocking motion of the van.

The two men didn't speak to give her additional clues. She couldn't really see scenery out the back window, but it was mainly the black night sky and an occasional streetlamp. She tightened her arms around the kidlets, closed her eyes and concentrated solely on not being scared.

Very scared.

Chapter Fifteen

Kill Tenoreno? Mack wanted him to kill Tenoreno? The person pulling the strings didn't want their leader out of the country? Or who did they bring him here to kill? Less and less about this operation was making sense. He kept coming back to why him and why kidnap his kids? If he could determine the answer to that complicated question, then he might find the solution.

Why tell him to kill the prisoner? Why did they want Tenoreno dead? Why did they bring Josh to pull the trigger? A political nightmare for one. They'd prosecute him and persecute the Texas Rangers. He was thinking too far ahead. The problem was now.

"I'll need a weapon." He was handed a Glock. He fingered the weapon, wanting to pull it on Mack, knowing the man would never hand him a loaded gun. "I prefer my own. It's in the bag you have in the van."

In-Charge Mack shook his head. "Let me say this out loud. Kill me, kill my men, we kill your family. The men holding your kids don't care if they get a call to shoot or get a call to let them go. Understand?"

"Understood."

Thing was, Bryce would be waiting in that hangar, protecting Tenoreno. He wasn't just going to let Josh walk in and shoot anyone. Company F was prepared for an attack to hijack a plane, not massacre everyone. The Mack gang loaded and checked the machine pistols. A lot of men were about to be killed unless he did something.

Or just did what they wanted.

"Your plan doesn't make sense. You can't be certain I won't point this at the wrong person." He aimed the Glock at Mack's head. Three of the leader's men immediately pointed machine pistols at his.

"Hold on, give the Major time to accept the inevitable."

"And what would that be?"

"Mack." In-Charge pointed to the man to his right. "Dial."

Josh aimed his barrel at the night sky. "Point taken."

"You are a useful tool to get us inside the plane…for the moment. Just don't push me again."

Mack waved off the guns and took a step closer to Josh. "Between you and me, I didn't like this plan. Never liked depending on the emotional state of an anxious father. Give me solid logic."

He clapped Josh on the back, took his Glock and removed an empty magazine.

"Then you don't expect me to kill Tenoreno."

"I never depend on anyone with the exception of myself." Mack handed him the gun, nodded to the guy with his phone out and went about his business.

Josh was just a way to get into that hangar. A way to get on that plane. Why? He was tired of asking when the answer was simple—wait and find out.

"They're a couple of minutes out, boss," Laughing Mack said.

In-Charge Mack faced Josh, having to tilt his head up to look at him. "I know what you're thinking. How many of us can you take out if you jump one of the men and take his weapon? But you still have a problem." He folded his arms and looked around him. "Which one of us is supposed to call and check on your girlfriend? Which one of us has the power to tell them to pull the trigger or let them go?"

Damn.

"Now that's all settled. This is where you pull your weight, Major." Mack motioned for his men to come closer. "How many men and where are they located?"

Josh was taller than most of them there. Ten men to be exact. Ten men armed with automatic machine pistols. It didn't matter if they were accurate or not. Just aim close to a human, most likely they'd hit part of him.

Mack waited, his attention on Josh with an expectant look on his face.

"They'll make the prisoner transfer inside the hangar. Less exposure that way. Most likely four men—two rangers, two prison guards. The guards will leave, then the plane. You made this fairly public. They'll be expecting some sort of attack. Additional men might already be waiting."

"So we go in guns blazing and take everybody out," Knife Mack declared.

"Then you don't need me." Josh took a step back toward the van, both hands in the air. He didn't know if any of the guns around him had ammo. But he did know how to use that knife. He just had to get hold of it. "Mind making that phone call before you're all slaughtered?"

"We can get the jump on those guys," one of them said.

Their voices blended together as they spoke over each other. At their backs, Josh could see headlights on the road to the airport. Tenoreno had arrived. But Josh's main focus was on the real Mack. And his focus was on Josh.

The leader lifted a hand. All the conversation stopped.

"Only one person has to fire a weapon. That means only one person needs to get close enough, but we'll take two. Along with the Major."

Tracey had described this man's eyes as frightening. Josh understood why. Black as the dark around them. A color that broke down the walls you thought protected you. Maybe that was a little melodramatic, but true.

The stare was a test. Not just of willpower. It was a test to see who would be giving the orders and who would be taking them. Josh was a leader. It was something that he'd recognized in himself years ago. A skill that mentors had helped him hone. He understood that look. He could also turn his off and allow Mack to believe he'd won.

"I've already told you that I'd do anything to protect my kids. It doesn't matter what happens to me. But what guarantees do I have that my family is going to be okay?"

"You have my word, of course."

"We both know that doesn't mean much to me."

Mack laughed, threw back his head and roared, again halting the conversation of his men. "I knew there was something I liked about you." He turned and waved the men into different directions splitting them into smaller groups that would surround the building on foot. "Put him in the van."

Knife Mack shoved Josh against the bumper. His hand landed on top of his bag, where a smoke grenade and a tracking device were hidden. He just needed to activate the tracker.

"Whoa, whoa, whoa." In-Charge Mack held up his hand. "We still need this guy. Ride up front with me, Major."

Josh was escorted up front, an empty gun tossed in his lap. Empty. The last twenty-four hours had been disturbing to say the least. Sitting here, though, was a bit surreal.

He was in a van with the man who'd kidnapped his family. About to crash through a gate and storm a facility that his friends and coworkers would be defending. When had everything gotten so turned upside down?

"Hopefully this will be really simple," Mack instructed. "We pull up. The Major talks his way to Oaks, Mack takes him out and we take the plane before anyone's the wiser."

"Oaks? Aren't you after Tenoreno?"

"Two for one. We need them both."

Knife had just given him his first piece of useful information. They wanted Oaks and thought he'd be escorting Tenoreno. It sort of made sense now.

"He might not be there, you know. Oaks. There's no guarantee." The gate flew open and their panel van continued toward the hangar. "You could have done all this on your own. You could have taken me out. You didn't need my kids." He was tired of dancing around the truth. "Nothing I do is going to keep you from killing me and...hurting my family."

"You're a sure thing, Major Parker," he said in almost a sad voice. "Smart, too. I always enjoy working with smart people. And I don't think your men are going to just shoot you. You're our element of surprise. Kind of like a flash bang grenade that cops use."

Or maybe that was the answer—he was a sure thing. A sure way to get into the hangar, find Tenoreno and run. Seconds passed in a blur as they screeched to a halt in front of the only open airplane hangar. Handguns were aimed at his chest as he stepped onto the ground.

The other two men stayed in the van with the engine running. It wouldn't be long before eight additional men would be circling the building. They had enough fire-power to wipe out everyone on the perimeter before they knew what happened.

"What's the deal, Captain?" Bryce stepped from the back of the hangar. "Trying to make an entrance?"

"I wasn't driving." Josh looked around at his men from Company F. He dropped his handgun—totally worthless anyway—then raised his hands. "There's a couple of guys in this van who want Tenoreno."

"There are a lot of people who want Tenoreno. Sorry."

"They've got the place surrounded, Bryce. Whatever you were planning, it won't work."

"If they're here to hijack the plane they won't get far."

"Change of plans. They say they're here to kill Oaks. Is he on the plane with Tenoreno?" The original plan to overpower Mack's men and discover where Josh's family was being held was a bust.

"Tell the men to drop their weapons," Mack said from the darkness of the van.

"You know they won't do that, but you could lower yours," Bryce answered.

The Rangers were wearing vests. Ready for the shots Josh should have planned to fire with the weapons he had loaded with blanks. But he couldn't. They wouldn't give him his weapon. Knife Mack jumped out of the van next to him, raised his machine pistol, pointing it at Josh's head.

In-Charge Mack left the driver's seat and stood in front of the panel van. When the Rangers made a move, he stopped them by firing a burst into the ceiling. "Hold it! All of you stay where you are."

"You know I don't want to ask this, Bryce, but they've got my kids. Lower your weapons and don't get us all killed."

Bryce led the way, placing his handgun on the concrete and kicking it barely out of his reach. He squinted, questioning Josh as he sank to his knees. This was *not* the plan they'd discussed yesterday. The one that said it was better to ask forgiveness than permission. They were supposed to overpower these guys, not the other way around.

"Up against the wall, on your knees, hands on your head. Where's Oaks? I don't see him," In-Charge Mack demanded.

"Still in Waco. They were afraid he might get caught up in the moment. Maybe shoot the star witness," the pilot told him.

The first to give up his weapon and the first to give them information. Sort of unusual, but Josh didn't want to jump to the conclusion that the pilot was working with the kidnappers. You could never tell how people would react under stress.

"Get on the plane." Knife Mack shoved the pilot, then shoved Josh toward the others getting on their knees.

"Secure them, tell the others we're a go for phase two. No reason to panic. We knew this was a possibility." Mack shot beams of hatred toward the plane.

Them? Phase two?

"Join your men, Major."

"What's phase two? You have Tenoreno. Oaks didn't get in the way. You're done here. Just tell me where my kids are or call for their release."

"You are right not to trust me, Major. Looks like we'll have to hang on to them a while longer." Mack smirked.

"The perimeter is crawling with cops." Knife Mack retreated from a window.

The pilot fired up the engine.

"We'll be out of here in a minute. The others will take care of this mess."

Shotguns against machine pistols. How many would be hurt? Would he watch the men on their knees be slaughtered with a single blast? Whatever playbook Mack or Tenoreno had, it wouldn't be discovered here. His family would still be in trouble.

But maybe there was another way.

Josh's head cleared. He instantly knew what had to be done.

"Take me and let my men go. They get in that van and drive away. I give you my word I won't do anything on the plane. I could convince Oaks to meet us."

"Not a chance," Bryce argued. "Headquarters won't go for that. We're not leaving you."

"Nice play, Major." Mack was twenty feet away giving instructions to his right-hand man, then he boarded, turning once inside. "There's only one problem. As soon as I let your men go, they'll warn Oaks that we're coming. Take out the trash, men."

"This is my choice, Lieutenant." He lowered his voice for Bryce, "You know what to do once that plane is airborne. Take these guys out and warn Waco we're coming. Give the signal."

Knife Mack started toward them with crowd-control handcuffs.

"Now, Bryce. Give the order to attack."

Chapter Sixteen

The Rangers outside the hangar made their move. It might have been the last minute before the Macks reached the building, but they were prepared. Most of the gunfire was outside. Bryce rolled, taking cover farther away from the plane, shouting orders for the others. They took their hidden weapons and attacked.

Josh had extra drive that no one else in the hangar did—his need to save his kids and Tracey. His goal was to get on the plane and Knife Mack was the only person in his way.

Josh pushed the adrenaline he was feeling, channeling it to a rage he'd never experienced. All the while gauging that Knife Mack was raising the barrel of his machine pistol. "Get out of my way!"

In a well-practiced gym move—one he had never used in the field—Josh ran and jumped. Both of his booted feet slammed into the chest of his opponent. Josh was prepared to fall hard to the concrete floor, rolling when he hit, keeping his eyes on his opponent. Knife Mack shot backward.

Relentless fire bursts. Shouts. The engine starting. All the noise added to his rapid heartbeat. He heard or felt Knife Mack's "oomph," slamming hard into the wing of the plane. Still, the man got up quickly and moved toward him again.

Josh reached out, grabbed the man's arm and used his forward momentum to spin him into the fuselage. He banged his elbow hard into the man's chin. Then pounded his fist twice into the man's solar plexus attempting to knock his breath from him. He jerked the machine pistol from the man's shoulder, holding the strap across his neck.

Knife Mack didn't stop. Pushing at Josh's hands, he shoved hard enough to force Josh to stumble backward. Josh drew upon a hidden burst of energy thinking about the smiles of his children. He hit Knife Mack with all his strength. The man fell and slid into the back wall, rattling the metal shelves.

Bryce put a knee in Knife Mack's back and yanked his wrist to his shoulder blade.

Josh took in the surroundings. Three of the Macks were defending the runway for the takeoff but Rangers were flanking and about to overrun. Another couple of Mack men were face down in the dirt next to the taxiway.

Josh's only hope was pulling away from the hangar. The Cessna was a single prop engine so there weren't any blades to get in his way. He ran.

"No!" Bryce yelled behind him.

No choice. Josh was running out of time.

Time? Hell, he had seconds. The plane was turning to line up for takeoff.

One more burst of energy and Josh caught the open door. He grabbed whatever he could and pulled himself through as the plane turned revved its engines.

"Very impressive, Major."

In-Charge Mack sat sideways in the seat, holding his

machine pistol six inches from Josh's nose. The kidnapper could have pulled the door shut. He could have fired the weapon, shooting Josh. Instead he'd allowed a ranger on board.

Now he extended a hand.

Josh ignored the assist and pulled himself into a seat, shutting the door while the engine roared to full life. He was still alive, on the plane and stuck with a half-ass plan for what he should do next.

Keep himself alive. Get his kids and Tracey released. That was the goal...now he needed steps to reach it. "Is the pilot one of your guys?"

"I believe his name is Bart." Tenoreno, sitting in the seat behind the pilot, raised his voice, competing with the engine. "A new employee. Unlike Vince."

Josh had never met Paul Tenoreno in person. He'd seen the file. Photos of crime scenes. Surveillance pictures Oaks had accumulated off and on for over a decade.

"Vince? Deegan?" Josh couldn't remember the list of crimes attributed to this man, just that it was long. As a criminal, it seemed Vince had avoided pictures. It wasn't a good sign when he took off his ski mask, revealing his face. "I think I'll stick with Mack."

Tenoreno shook his chains. "Can we dispense with these?"

Mack tossed the keys across the aisle to Tenoreno's lap. The organized crime leader didn't look as intimidating in his state-issued jumpsuit. But he still behaved like a man used to having his orders followed.

The restraints were quickly unlatched, dropped and Mack transferred them to Josh.

"Gun." Tenoreno held his palm open and Mack dropped a Glock onto it after pulling it from his belt.

The keys flew back, landing against the shell of the plane and sliding to the carpeted floor. Mack left them there, staring at his employer as he transferred to the copilot's seat.

The confidence that the kidnapper had blustered was no longer apparent. His shoulders slumped. His face filled with hatred. His body language suggested he was tired, but he deliberately kept the gun barrel pointed at Tenoreno's seatback much longer than he should have.

"Change of plans, Bart," Tenoreno said, barely loud enough to be heard over the engine noise. "How much fuel did you manage?"

"I have enough to take you to the rendezvous. You didn't buy anything else. That's as far as this baby and I will take you."

"Unsatisfactory. Come up with a new location not far from Waco."

"That's not the deal," the pilot insisted.

"Your deal is whatever I say it is." Tenoreno pulled the slide to verify ammo was in place.

"What the hell are you doing? Are you seriously going to shoot him while we're in the air?" Mack shouted, sitting forward on his seat.

Tenoreno shot him a shut-up look. "Where are we landing, Bart?"

"Hearne."

"Get us there." Keeping his weapon trained on Bart, Tenoreno looked at Mack. "Call your men with the new location."

"That's taking an unnecessary risk. My men can easily bring Oaks to you later. How do you plan—"

"Do it! We'll exchange him and his kids."

Josh crushed his teeth together to keep from interjecting. He'd played right into Tenoreno's plan more than once. Mack removed a satellite phone from the bag at his feet and made the call.

"I want Oaks discredited and dead. He's supposed to be chained back there, not Parker." Tenoreno spoke to Mack who shrugged. "You've gotten sloppy, Vince. There are too many people involved. Too much has been left up to chance."

"I follow orders. It wasn't my plan that went wrong,"

"I suppose it was my idiot son, then. Why didn't kidnapping his kids work? Didn't the Rangers replace him with Oaks?" He pointed to Josh.

"That part of the plan worked fine." Mack smiled as if he'd regained the confidence he'd lost for a moment. "Maybe they thought Oaks would kill you himself if he was on a plane with you."

"Ha." Tenoreno put the headset on and turned to the front of the plane. Mack and Josh sat silently next to each other until Mack leaned forward and added the ankle restraints, locking Josh to the plane.

"I never underestimate the power of emotion. Especially that of a father. I told my employers that, but they insisted on this ridiculous revenge plan. Wouldn't listen to me." Was he bragging that he had predicted Josh's behavior?

"Smart advice for someone dumb enough not to follow it." They could talk without either of the other men hearing. "You know this exchange this isn't going to work. Right?"

"You Rangers are so full of pride that buying you off isn't an option. Fortunately, killing you is."

"You kidnapped my kids so you could kill Oaks?"

"No, Major. We did all this to free Paul. The only way to get Oaks off his back is to kill him." Mack pointed the gun at Josh. He raised and lowered the barrel as if it had just been fired. "You see, you guys just don't stop. We can buy off other agencies, bribe or blackmail some types of guys...like Bart. But Rangers? None of that works."

"So you're telling me that if the Texas Rangers had a history of corruption, my kids would be safe at home?"

"Kind of ironic when you look at it that way." Mack leaned back in his seat, machine pistol in his lap.

There wasn't any reason to keep a close eye on Josh. He wasn't going anywhere cuffed hand and foot. No chance to attempt anything.

"Before I waste my time trying to convince you I'm not important, tell me why you let me board. And don't say it's because you wanted to see if I could make it through the door."

"I've got to say that I admire the way you don't give up. You're here because I can use you for a hostage. Nothing more. Nothing less."

"Use me all you want. Just make the call that will let my kids go." Josh swallowed hard.

"We both saw the mess back at the airport. It won't be long before the Rangers are calling Oaks and the entire state is after us. I have some leverage with you here."

"I'm a nobody. They won't negotiate because of me."

"We'll see." Mack dropped his head back against the headrest and closed his eyes. At this point, Josh shouldn't and didn't trust anyone except himself to save his children. Except Tracey. He trusted Tracey. For one moment, it was nice to imagine what she might have been about to tell him. One moment when he hoped she knew exactly how he felt about her.

Chapter Seventeen

They pulled to a stop and Tracey felt the van settle into a parked position. She kept her eyes down, pretending to be asleep. She sneaked a peek out the windows. It looked the same as the rest of their ride. The sun was just dusting the treetops and highlighting the surrounding fields. Whatever was going to happen, it didn't seem like there was anyplace close to hide.

The two Macks looked at the phone, said things under their breath and got cautiously out of the van. Tracey rose quickly and looked out all the windows. They were at a small airport. One smaller than Waco and not large enough to have a terminal or control tower.

The van was parked a long way from any building or aircraft hangar.

"Listen to me, Sage. There might be a chance that you can run and hide without these men seeing you. If you can, you do it. Don't look back. This is important. Just run as fast as you can. Okay?"

"By myself?"

"Yes, baby." She lifted the little girl to look out the back windows. "You see those hay bales across the road?" She pointed. Sage nodded. "Can you run that far?"

"Is it important?" Sage whispered.

"Yes, baby. Very important. Somebody will find you. Promise."

"I want to go home," Jackson insisted. "I don't feel like running. I want to eat colors 'cause it'll make me run faster."

Tracey looked closely at Jackson's eyes. She hadn't monitored his blood sugar levels in several hours and had none of the necessary tools now. She had to completely rely on her experience of the last year.

Acting out, anger, lethargy, not making sense with his words—those were all sure signs that his blood sugar was dropping. She got up front as quickly as possible. Why hadn't she thought of that first? There weren't any keys in the ignition, but she locked both the doors.

"Sage, lock the back and the side doors. Quick!"

The van rocked back and forth a little when Sage moved. She made it to the side door while Tracey searched for a spare key or food. Nothing but ketchup packets and trash.

The van moved again, but this time it was from the rear door being yanked open.

"I told you she was up to something."

"It didn't matter. I had the keys to get back in." Blond Mack dangled them like candy in front of her.

Tracey huddled with the kids again, not trying to explain herself or reason with them. They were tugged from the vehicle. Tracey held Jackson on her hip and he put his head on her shoulder.

"You sure that's them, man?"

"You think there's more than one plane sitting on this out-of-the-way runway?"

"Then what are they waiting for?"

The men whispered behind her. Maybe they were

using her and the kids as a shield. She didn't know. She held Jackson's forty-four pounds tight against her and wanted to pick up Sage. Instead she held tight to her hand and the little girl held the secondhand bear against her own little chest.

There was no movement from the white Cessna.

"What's going on?" she asked. "Who's in the plane? Do we have to get on board?"

Her thoughts were considering the worst-case scenario. The one where awful things happened in an isolated basement where no one could find them. The bodyguards suddenly seemed like a really good idea.

Neither of the men answered. Neither of the men moved.

"I got a creepy feeling about this, man. You get me?"

Tracey thought it was the blond guy talking, but it didn't matter. They both were armed and the only place close where she could protect the kids was back inside the van.

She'd never make it carrying Jackson, who was more lethargic than just a few minutes ago. He needed food and she didn't know how much.

"What does the text say?"

"I don't care what it says anymore. Get back in the van."

It was definitely the blond Mack giving the orders. She could tell that they faced each other and had a phone between them. She inched Sage toward the corner of the van, ready to make a run for it. She desperately wanted her hunch about this to be right.

A hunch that told her Josh was on that plane waiting to see if she and the kids were released. But that would mean someone—like the FBI or police or Rangers—was here somewhere, waiting.

The men continued to argue behind her and she loosened her hold on Sage. She arched her eyebrows, questioning if she should run, and Tracey nodded. She looked so young and yet so much older than two days ago. Tracey didn't have to guess if she understood the danger—she did. Josh's little girl squeezed her hand, then tiptoed along the length of the back of the van and ran.

The arguing stopped. Tracey turned around, keeping her hand behind her back. Hoping the two Macks would think Sage was hiding there. She stared at the men, one arm cramping from holding Jackson, the other waving his sister to safety.

"Where's the girl?"

"She's right—"

They both took a step in Tracey's direction. Blond Mac's hands were out to take Jackson from her. She turned but only made it a couple of steps. The van doors were still open. Blond had a hold of Jackson; the other guy pushed her inside the van, climbing in on top of her.

She couldn't see if Sage made it across the road. Based on the cursing and slamming fists against the van, then the running to get in the driver's seat, she assumed Sage was out of sight.

Thank God.

THEY HAD LANDED about five or ten minutes earlier. Mack had been surprised and Tenoreno had been rather pleased. Neither had said anything loud enough to let Josh determine what was going on. But it had something to do with meetings and putting them at greater risk.

Tenoreno was in the copilot's chair and Mack was busy sending an in-depth text. Neither paid attention to the activity at the van. The plane was far enough down the runway to make the van visible to Josh. He yanked against the chains when Tracey and the kids had been wrenched from it. He managed to cap his panic when he saw his little girl run. He didn't want to draw attention to her.

"Did your heart stop there for a minute?" Bart the pilot asked. "I know mine sure did. That's this guy's kid. Right? Man, you've got a brave little girl."

Josh nodded. He might have gotten out a yes or confirmation grunt, but he couldn't be certain. As soon as the relief hit that the men weren't following Sage and she might be safe, the anxiety had doubled as Jackson and Tracey were pushed back inside the van. Tracey hadn't run. He'd seen Jackson's form. He was practically limp in Tracey's arms. Something was wrong with his son.

"What are you talking about?" Tenoreno shouted as Sage disappeared behind a hay bale. "Tell them to go get her. Why didn't you say something when she ran?"

"Man, I didn't sign on to hurt any kids. Disengage the transponder, fly the plane, get my payoff. Sure. Hurting kids was not included and won't be."

"If we didn't need a pilot, you'd be dead now." Tenoreno turned an interesting shade of explosive red.

"We don't need the girl. We didn't need additional hostages on the plane. I tried to tell you that."

"This is not a debate. You work for me."

Tenoreno screamed his lack of control. Bart shrank a little more toward the pilot's door. Mack's body stiffened as he deliberately sank back into the leather seat. The muscle in his jaw twitched. He let the machine pistol's barrel drop in line with his boss's head. Accident or deliberate?

Josh didn't want Mack to open fire. Not when he

didn't have a weapon and no control over the men still holding Tracey and Jackson.

"It doesn't matter now. Here they come. Open the door, then tell the men to bring the woman on board."

Josh couldn't see who was inside the darkened windows. Mack did as he was instructed—opened the door and called his men on the phone.

If he made it through this, someone might eventually ask him what he'd hoped to gain by allowing himself to become a hostage. Originally there'd been a lot of adrenaline involved. But it came down to being there for his kids. He couldn't let anyone else make decisions that involved their lives. And if that put his at risk.

So be it.

Chapter Eighteen

"This isn't going to work." George was compelled to voice his thoughts one last time. "There's only one reason they'd want you here, Captain Oaks. Paul Tenoreno wants to kill you."

"We have a sound plan."

"Hardly. It's our only plan. Might be a good one for Tenoreno. You get out of the car, they shoot you. Period. They have no reason to release any of the hostages."

Crouched in the backseat of a small sedan wasn't the most comfortable place George had ever held a conversation. It definitely wasn't the worst, either. At least he wasn't shoved in the trunk like last year. He shook the random thoughts from his mind and concentrated.

Aiden Oaks had parked the car next to the Cessna. His plan to accommodate the kidnappers and escaped prisoner hadn't included the FBI. George was coordinating the teams surrounding the airstrip.

Of course, the entire jumping-in-the-car-at-the-last-minute thing had caught him slightly unprepared. He was only carrying his cell phone and Glock. The ammo he had in the magazine was it. The team was communicating through a series of group texts.

"No one asked you to ride along," Aiden said.

"No, sir, you didn't. I have a lot of experience with

kidnappings and abductions. Did you know that, Captain?"

"I wouldn't say you've had any experience with this kind. Those kids are still in danger because the men who outrank me wouldn't allow me to escort Tenoreno's flight. He's a vindictive son of—"

"I know why we're waiting, but what do you think they're waiting for? Is the van with Tracey and Jackson still sitting on the road? Damn, that was a brave move Tracey made, sending one of the kids to safety."

The cop who picked her up had her safely in his squad car.

"Good thing the Hearne PD picked up Sage as she ran to hide behind the hay. Sweet thing argued that she had to stay there and wait on her daddy." Aiden chuckled. "Van's been creeping up behind us at a snail's pace. Everybody seems to be in a holding pattern. Are the men in place?"

"Three more minutes, sir."

Just before they'd arrived in Hearne to rendezvous with Tenoreno, he'd kicked the rearview mirror off the windshield. It was propped on the backseat headrest so he could see the plane. The door opened but he couldn't make out anything inside.

"Van's speeding up. I'm getting out and leaving the door open for you, Agent Lanning."

"We have eyes on Parker. He's handcuffed and manacled to the seat behind the pilot. Tenoreno is in the co-pilot chair." The team kept him up-to-date with a text. "You have your handcuff key ready?"

"Got it," Oaks said as he swung his legs from the car. He left the door as a bit of protection between him and the plane.

George dialed Kendall's number, ready to get the advance started with his men. He'd pass along information, but his phone was on silent, just in case the perps got close enough to hear him. Then he angled the mirror, attempting to find any guns pointed in their direction. They knew from looking through the windows that at least two hostiles were aboard, maybe three.

The Rangers in Huntsville had stated that only the kidnapper who gave the orders was on board. Bart Temple, the pilot, already had an open investigation about his suspicious activities. The report from the airplane hangar suggested that he had supplied information and had voluntarily gotten on the plane.

"Air traffic has been diverted. We have a helicopter standing by in case we need it."

The van squealed to a stop.

"Where are you going?" a man shouted.

George turned the mirror. "One man, armed with a Glock. Nervous. Anxious. Unpredictable. No eyes on Tracey or the boy."

"Move to the door, Oaks," a voice inside the plane said.

"I ain't no rookie. Release Parker and the other hostages."

"The Major is cozy and staying where he is."

"Then so am I." Oaks sat on the seat.

George knew what the captain was doing. It didn't make it any easier to wait on the kidnappers' next move.

Tracey screamed and George could only imagine what the kidnappers had done to elicit her reaction. Damn, he hated being blind. He whipped the mirror around to see the driver pulling Tracey past the steering wheel. Soon they were joined by his partner, who carried Jackson.

"The kid looks ill. I repeat, the kid looks ill and won't be able to run on his own."

"Hey, you guys in the plane." The driver pushed the barrel of his handgun under Tracey's chin. "Or inside the car. Whoever cares about this woman! You better give us a way out of here or she and the kid are going to get it."

"Yeah," the one cradling Jackson said. "We want our own plane. Or you can kick these bastards out and we'll take this one."

"I can get another plane here. Why don't you give me the kid to show good faith?" Oaks tried to negotiate.

"Oh no. No way! We keep both of them." They argued.

The man holding Jackson started waving his handgun, then smashed it against his own forehead, proving that he was losing it. If he touched the kid, nothing would hold George inside the car.

Everyone on the team hated unpredictable kidnappers. The ones who began to panic. The ones who were sweating buckets, were probably high as a kite and who made everything about his job high risk.

"That's a shame." Oaks raised his voice to be heard over the Cessna's engine. "We have a sweet private jet not too far away. We could have it here in ten minutes."

"Call 'em!"

"Sorry, can't do that until I have a hostage."

"Man, I just want to be gone." He pushed Jackson into Tracey's arms and climbed back into the van.

"Ron, what are you— Hey! Hey!" he screamed into his phone as the door swung halfway shut. "We're getting on that plane no matter what you say!"

He placed his gun at Tracey's throat and started her moving, carrying Jackson toward the plane.

Whether it was their intention or not, they'd parked the van partially in the path of the Cessna. To reach the open door, they had to walk close to the sedan. The men now calling the shots, hidden on the east side of the buildings, sent instructions.

"Captain, if there's an opportunity to rescue Jackson, McCaffrey wants us to take it."

"Are they seeing what we're seeing?" Oaks asked in a low voice. "The kidnappers are panicking. We can't startle these guys."

George wasn't certain if McCaffrey had a good grasp on the situation or not. He could hear the chatter in the background. Hear the arguing over what the best move might be. When the best-case scenario came up, he thought they'd back up his plan.

Jackson looked unconscious and unaware that he was being carried to the plane. Tracey stumbled because the remaining captor's gun was still at her throat and pushing her chin upward. George watched behind him with the help of the mirror. Feeling as helpless as Josh Parker.

The phone buzzed on his chest with another message from his partner. McCaffrey was about to blow a gasket because he hadn't burst out of the car and done anything. George rolled to his side, hiding behind the dark-tinted windows for a better view.

The two men were met at the plane door with a machine pistol. "Send the boy up. Then the woman."

"You dirty rotten son of a bitch! You ain't leaving us here to go to jail." The man holding Tracey turned in circles, always bringing her between him and any of the men who might have a shot.

"Take me." Captain Oaks moved slowly from behind the car door with his hands in the air. "Leave the kid in the car and take me. They'll let you on the plane if you bring me."

George was ready to spring into action. "That is not the plan."

JOSH LOOKED THROUGH the open door and saw Tracey stumble. Whatever was being said outside, he couldn't hear because of the yelling in the small plane.

"Give me the gun so I can shoot him myself." Tenoreno held out his hand, expecting Mack to drop his weapon into it. The older man climbed between the front seats and stuck his hand out again.

"Buckle in, Paul. Bart, get this plane in the air."

"Oaks is standing right there, dammit." Tenoreno pointed. "Shoot him."

"So are the FBI and more Rangers. Even if you can't see them, they have to be here. Oaks isn't stupid. He wouldn't come alone."

Mack was right, but Josh wasn't going to agree with him. He kept his head down and his mouth shut, continuing his search for something he could use to free himself. Unfortunately, the plane had been checked for that sort of material before transporting a prisoner.

"I want him dead. It's the reason we're here."

"I could have taken care of this. I had men in Waco ready to do the job after they got rid of the hostages." Mack explained. "But you had to detour and involve the kids again, making everybody on edge."

"Those incompetent jerks." Tenoreno pointed to the men holding Tracey.

"Someone has confused them." Mack pointedly looked at Tenoreno. "Now they believe they've been double-crossed. Their position is kind of natural."

"Don't take that tone with me, Vince. I know where your kid lives."

Vince, Mack, whatever the hell his name was, didn't like Paul Tenoreno. His knuckles turned a bright white, fisted as they were around the machine pistol grip. The plane shifted slightly to the side as someone climbed up the steps.

The blond guy who had been holding Tracey backed onto the plane—slowly, sticking his foot out behind him while he wrapped one arm around someone's throat. Josh had to pull his legs and feet out of the way. He didn't want the man to fall and choke... Aiden.

A shot of relief hit Josh. He didn't want anyone else on the plane, but knowing Tracey wasn't gave him a little hope she and Jackson might make it out of this situation alive.

"Good to see you alive, son," Aiden said to Josh as the new guy shoved him onto the empty seat.

"Captain Oaks." Tenoreno was halfway between the seats.

"Fancy meeting you here, Paul," Aiden taunted. "You okay, kid?" he asked Josh in a lower voice.

Tenoreno's fists hit both of the seat backs. "Shut up before I shoot you dead. Your blood would be splattered against this white leather in a heartbeat if we didn't need to leave."

"You don't trust that they'll let you?" Aiden taunted.

The result was another beet-red rise in Tenoreno's color. The man definitely didn't have control of his temper. And Aiden definitely knew what buttons to push. Tenoreno slammed Aiden forward.

To Josh it seemed that Aiden sort of threw himself forward, then he knew why. He dropped a handcuff key into his hand. His eyes must have grown wide with surprise because Aiden frowned and shook his head.

Josh recovered and tried to shrink into the seat. Let Aiden have all the attention and he could free his feet and hands pretty quickly. Or at least he thought he could.

The plane dipped slightly again as someone began climbing the steps. The second man was pushing Tracey up, and in her arms she held Jackson.

Escaping was complicated before. Now it was closer to impossible. Was he willing to risk a machine gun blast through the plane with two people he loved occupying seats?

Tenoreno continued to yell. "Get us out of here!"

Bart started the engine. Josh held out his arms to catch his son as Tracey handed him through the opening, before falling to her knees on the carpet as the plane jerked forward.

"Wait! No!" the man on the bottom step fell away.

"Pull the door shut, Tommy, so we can get going," Mack ordered.

Tommy laughed at the man—his partner three minutes ago—being left behind on the runway. He reached for the rope to pull in the steps and the slam of Mack's weapon firing hit Josh's ears. Gunpowder filled his nostrils before he turned his head and caught a glimpse of Tommy falling through the door.

Mack leaned across, fired his weapon again—presumably at the man he'd left behind. Then he pulled the stairs up and secured the door.

"Damn. What now?" Bart yelled.

It seemed like Josh had constantly asked himself the same question again and again for the past forty hours…

Chapter Nineteen

Jackson had barely been noticed by anyone on the plane since they'd tossed him back to Tracey. The sudden firing of the gun had made him scream. She was certain he hadn't seen any part of the cold-blooded murder. She'd had his face buried against her shoulder. His hands had already been over his ears.

"Just stay still and keep your eyes closed," she whispered to him.

She desperately wanted to be next to Josh, or better still not on the plane at all. But they were, and they'd survived another hour.

"Get us in the air, Bart, old buddy." Mack grabbed a pair of handcuffs. He pointed to an older gentleman sitting across from Josh. "Put those on Captain Oaks. And loop the seat belt through them so you can't get up and retrieve a gun."

After he had Aiden's hands locked into place, Mack took the open seat and buckled up. They kept taxiing to the end of the runway. The plane turned around and not only was the van still there, a row of patrol cars and SUVs were side by side, cutting off half the tarmac.

"Same question, second verse," the pilot said. "What now?"

"Can't you run them over with this thing?" the man

sitting up front said, like a minion who didn't really think.

After her time in the van, she realized these men were more like lost boys than criminals. Young men who got used by people like Mack. She couldn't let herself have too much sympathy. If it came down to it, she'd choose the Parkers every time.

"Let's try some diplomacy. Paul, get on the radio." Mack raised his voice to be heard over the prop engine.

She recognized his voice. That was the man who had hit her Friday. It seemed a lifetime ago, but she would never forget. He was the In-Charge Mack, the man who'd given all the orders.

Sitting practically in the tail of the plane, she had a clear view of everyone except the pilot. The fidgets of the men in restraints. The toe tapping of Aiden Oaks. The cavalier words that didn't match the tense, upright stiffness that Mack's body shouted.

And Josh. His glances kept reassuring her that it would work out. He'd come up with a plan. Then he caught her eye and sharply looked at her lap. There was only one seat belt for both her and Jackson. As inconspicuous with her movements as she could be, she buckled the seat belt around her waist.

She'd use her last ounce of strength to hold on to Jackson if something happened with the plane. She was prepared. Tenoreno picked up the microphone to radio the FBI, who was certain to be listening.

"Tell them about our situation. We're taking off or someone's dying. Starting with Daddy Dearest." Mack pointed the gun at the back of the copilot's seat.

"What are you talking about? Is this a joke? You work for me. Or—" Realization hit Tenoreno. "Who hired you? My son will pay you double to escort me to safety."

"Your son is the one who wants you gone. As in forever, never coming back. It would have simplified everything if I could have killed you in Huntsville. Or even right now. But Xander insists on seeing it happen." He kicked the empty seat across from him. "You stupid old man. Did you really think he would forgive you for killing his mother?"

"You've got Special Agent in Charge McCaffrey." A voice boomed through the radio.

"They're threatening to kill me. You have to save me. It's your job! Don't move the vehicles! Don't clear the runway."

"Who is this? What's going on in there? Stop the engine and exit the plane."

Mack placed the barrel next to Tenoreno's temple. The man in the orange jumpsuit tried to squirm aside, but there was no place for him to go. Tracey covered Jackson's ears and eyes.

"Trace Trace, that's too tight."

"That's unacceptable. Didn't you see him shoot one of his own men? He's not bluffing. He won't negotiate." Josh tried to shout loud enough for the agents to hear him.

"He's not going to back down," Aiden shouted at the same time.

Was Josh's fellow ranger talking about Agent McCaffrey or Mack? Josh looked first at her, then in the direction of Mack. She could see the murderer's jaw tighten. The muscles visibly popped.

"If you don't do anything, then you've just killed us." Tenoreno laughed like a crazy man.

"Do you think I'm going to fall for that? If you're

the one holding our people hostage, you won't get far. We have helicopters in the air waiting to follow you to any destination. We know there's not enough fuel on board to get you out of the country. Surrendering now is your only option."

"I don't think he's joking." Tenoreno sat forward looking out the windows.

Aiden seemed more uncomfortable. He'd moved his hands from above his head to closer to the top of his shoulder. "Why set up this elaborate prison break if you just wanted him dead?"

"He's about to pull the trigger." Tenoreno's voice shook into the radio.

Was Mack about to shoot? Tracey couldn't tell. One message had been crystal clear—Josh wanted her wearing the seat belt. And now it looked like they were going to take off.

"To hell with this standoff," the pilot shouted.

He pushed what she assumed was the throttle because the engine roared louder and they moved forward. Fast.

As the plane gained speed, she looked out her window and saw men with guns pointing in their direction. But in a blink they had pointed toward another target. There was gunfire—tiny pops to her ears which drowned in the airplane engine's hum.

The young man she'd dubbed as Simple Mack. The one left alive on the tarmac was firing his weapon. Not at the FBI, he was shooting at the plane. They were dangerously close to the SUVs before dramatically dashing into the air.

The bouncing up and down stopped, but the dipping didn't. Tracey loved roller coasters, but now there were no rails connecting her seat to the earth. It was several seconds before they stabilized in the air. And several more before anyone released their breaths.

Jackson was in her arms. No seat belt. If they crashed, would she be able to hold on to him? *No.* The takeoff was just a couple of bumps and she'd nearly lost the death grip around his waist. She had no more illusions about keeping Jackson safe. He was kicking and crying out and hitting her with his small fists.

"Keep that kid quiet."

"It's the diabetes." She knew that. He didn't realize what he was doing and after his blood sugar stabilized he wouldn't remember his actions. It hadn't happened often, but since it had, the family recognized the signs.

There was a lot of tension surrounding them and a lot of noise, even though she could hear better after popping her ears. Josh and Aiden seemed to be communicating by looks. They were going to do something. She just didn't know what or when.

She quickly rose a little and switched the seat belt from around her waist to tighten around Jackson's. It was a close fit to sit on the edge of the seat next to him pressed against the side of the plane. He didn't like it at all.

"Please, kidlet. We've got to do this to keep you safe," she said next to his ear, scared to death that he'd lift the latch and not be safe at all. She worked with him to get his ears popped and relieve some of the pressure.

"What now, Mack?" Josh asked.

"Don't you mean Vince Deegan?" Aiden smiled. "Yeah, I know who you are. Jobs like this aren't normally your forte. You're more of a…bully. Aren't you?"

From her new position, she could barely see the front of the plane. She heard a jerk on Josh's chains. She could imagine that he wanted to stop Aiden from antagonizing the man holding a machine gun. She hated not knowing what was going on. It made the fright level just that much higher.

"Bart, take us to the landing strip. Somebody's waiting." Mack's attention was on the front of the plane. Maybe on the pilot or Tenoreno.

He seemed to have forgotten that she wasn't tied up or restrained—with the exception that it was a tight fit between the seats. She reached forward, touching Josh's arm. He didn't whip around, but took a look at her slowly around the edge of the seat.

She leaned closer to him and said, "I can do something."

"No," Josh mouthed.

"Daddy! Daddy!" Jackson kicked the seat, and Tracey. "Take me home."

"It's okay, Jack. Everything's okay. I bet you're tired. Maybe try to take a nap." Josh said it loud enough for Jackson to hear. One sincere look from his father and he was leaning his head against the side of the plane.

But the outburst caught Mack's attention, causing him to look and stare at her.

Did he realize she wasn't secured? It was the first time that she hoped she appeared insignificant in someone's mind. And maybe that's how he saw her—insignificant or not a threat—because he turned his attention back to his phone.

Josh looked around the edge of his seat again. He winked. She smiled back in spite of the anxiety speeding up her heartbeat. She wasn't alone. He was there and he was not helpless.

Jackson's breathing evened out. She liked it better when he was awake. Even if the diabetes turned him into a tiny terror, she knew he was awake and not slipping into a deep sleep or diabetic coma. They didn't have long before Jackson was going to be severely ill.

At the risk of Mack noticing her lack of binding, she called out, "Where are you taking us?"

"Yeah, Vince, where are you taking us?' Tenoreno echoed.

"Not far."

"That agent said they're tracking us," the criminal said from the front, his tenor-like voice carrying to the back of the plane.

"We got rid of the transponder. You!" Mack lunged across the short distance between seats.

Tracey heard his fist hit Aiden. She heard him searching through pockets and patting him down. She could see the ranger's hands tighten on the seat belt, heard him release a moan of pain.

"How are they following us?" Tenoreno screamed.

"They don't need much but their eyes. The FBI wasn't bluffing about a helicopter." The pilot pointed to the right side of the plane. All heads looked. Tracey's view was blocked by a compartment of some sort but she could tell the pilot was telling the truth.

"If the FBI knows where we're going and can tell when we land," she said, leaning forward to be heard, "how did you plan on getting away?"

She was genuinely confused.

Mack's dark eyes, which she'd memorized the moment he'd raised his fist to hit her, went dead again. He was filled with blackness that looked so empty... so soulless. "I didn't."

"What the hell does that mean?" Tenoreno asked.

Tracey saw the concerned look on Aiden's face and knew it was mirrored on Josh's. She squeezed back in next to Jackson, dabbing some of the sweat off his forehead. There was nothing for her to give him. No juice, no water—nothing. All she could do was hope.

It wasn't long before the pilot circled an even smaller runway from where they'd left. The engines ebbed and surged as he lined up to set the plane on the ground.

"This isn't going to be pretty, people." The pilot gained everyone's attention. "Those gunshots must have hit something important and the controls aren't handling like they should. So grab something steady. It's going to be a bumpy ride."

Aiden, handcuffed to the seat belt, settled more firmly into his chair and braced a long leg on the seat across the short aisle. Josh couldn't brace himself at all, not manacled to the floor.

"Can't you unlock his feet?"

"Dammit, Mack. Let her have a seat belt."

Tracey's heart raced. Good or bad. It shouldn't matter what side you were on when a plane was about to crash. Mack didn't acknowledge them. He fingered the phone, then put it in his pocket.

There was nothing to grab. She sank between the seats and braced herself between the bulkhead and the closet. As she did, Mack noticed and didn't make a move to stop her or let her move to the open seat in front of him. Jackson was unconscious. None of the shouting woke him up. At least he wouldn't be scared out of his mind like she was.

"I love you," Josh said as the plane dipped and shot back to gain altitude. He didn't have to say anything. She'd known he loved her as soon as he'd held her hand in the bodyguards' rental car. That moment had changed everything for her.

Seconds later the plane bounced against pavement

and was airborne again. She kept her eyes glued to Jackson.

It wouldn't be long. Sage was safe. At least there was that.

"Hold on tight, baby." Only Jackson could have heard her, but she said the words for Josh, too.

Chapter Twenty

Josh braced himself as best he could. Mack was finally sitting straight in his seat and not watching his every move. There hadn't been an unobserved moment to retrieve the handcuff key from where he'd hidden it—between his cheek and teeth.

Once on the ground, they'd need the weapons that should be stored in the small closet next to Tracey. He couldn't give Mack time to recover from the rough ride or realize what was happening. He had to be ready. He had to be fast.

Spitting the handcuff key into his hands, he twisted his wrists until he could reach the latch. Key inserted, turned, one hand was free. The plane's power surged, trying to gain altitude, pressing his body into the seat. He fought gravity and leaned forward to release his ankles from the manacles.

"This is it!" Bart shouted, cursing like a sailor.

Josh sat up. There was no time to grab and hold Tracey like he wanted. Then it was apparent that Bart didn't have control. The plane was on its way to the ground. Crashing.

"Hold on, Tracey. We're going to be okay. Just hold on." He could see her boots in the aisle next to him.

He wanted to comfort his son. There was just no way to be heard.

Nothing was fake about what the plane was doing. There was a radical shimmy when the wheels touched down again.

Noise from every direction assaulted him. At first there were huge vibrations, bounces and slams. He thought that was bad until the plane made a sharp pull to the right, tipped, and he knew they were flipping. His neck felt like it snapped in two from the concussion of hitting the ground.

Stunned. He hung upside down, unable to see around him. Then he realized he couldn't really see his hand heading to his face, either. Stuff was floating in the air. Smoke or steam—he couldn't tell.

"Josh! Josh! You still conscious?" Aiden called.

"Yeah, I'm… I'm okay." His ears were still ringing.

Mack seemed to be unconscious next to him. His arms were hanging about his head.

"Tracey? Jackson?" No sound from either of them.

"The kid's still buckled. The girl looks like she's out cold."

Pulling his heavy arms back to his chest, Josh stretched his legs so he could push his feet against Aiden's seat.

"Hold on, Josh!" Aiden yelled. "I'm pinned in here just as tight as a bean in a burrito. My leg's busted up and caught between these things. Can you get out the door? Or see the machine pistol?"

"Give me a sec."

Bent in half and still a bit disoriented, his mind refused to adjust and accept that the plane was upside down and not just him. He managed to unclip his seat belt. There wasn't room to fall. It was just a jolt. The windows had shattered and the space around him had shrunk.

"Tracey? Jackson? Can you hear me?" He could finally see her, boots pointed toward him, lying on the ceiling. He shook her legs as much as he dared. He couldn't get his shoulders through to the area behind him. His seat was wedged in the way.

"Josh, you need to get the gun, son."

"Yeah." He did *know* that he needed to find the weapon. Logic told him that. But his heart wanted to free Tracey and Jackson first. They were both hurt, or worse.

Mack was hanging from his waist, seat belt still in place, arms swaying with each move that Josh made. He looked around on the ceiling—no weapons.

A pounding at the front of the plane made him jerk around. He hit his head on something fixed to the floor. There was a small triangle of space left where he could see the instrument panel. He carefully got closer, trying not to cause Aiden more pain.

The pilot was strapped in but it looked like his injuries were severe. Tenoreno kicked his door and it was almost open. Josh saw the gun. The strap was caught and it hung just out of his reach near the pilot.

Tenoreno stared at him and followed the direction he was reaching. An evil grin dominated his face. He moved like he was no longer in a rush. He casually lifted the machine pistol, moved the radio cord farther from the opening, then kicked the door a final time.

It sprang open and Tenoreno escaped. Josh pushed on the seat back until beads of sweat stung his eyes. It wasn't budging.

"Josh?" Aiden spoke softly, as if he were in pain. "Try the other door, son."

Crouching, he checked Tracey, giving her a little shake. He reached up and felt a pulse at Mack's throat. Then he checked the door next to his seat. Jammed. Their side of the plane had settled mostly in the field.

His head was beginning to clear a bit. His vision along with it. He checked Aiden, who had passed out. He had lost the handcuff key in the crash, but could get Aiden free with a knife. To get to Tracey and Jackson, he'd need a crowbar or tools to release the seat back. And to get either of those things he needed out of the plane.

"Hello?" a voice from the outside called. Knocks on the outside of the plane. More voices. And light. Lots of light as the door opened.

"Are you all right?"

"I'm fine but there are injured people and a child. Have you got a knife?" Josh asked the man who was at the door on the far side of Mack. Josh's ears were ringing badly and making it difficult to hear. He was catching every other word or so and letting his mind fill in the rest of the answer.

As much as he wanted to sit and let someone else take care of things, his son needed him. Tracey needed him. He wouldn't quit.

"My daughter, Jeannie... Hand me the knife. I think we can get everyone out. Paramedics are on their way."

"Let me get inside here." The man kept the knife.

Without too many words, they worked together and released Mack. The rescuer climbed out and Josh passed Mack through the door to him.

"Make sure you use these." Josh tossed the handcuffs that had been around his wrists a few minutes earlier. "Anchor him to something so he can't get away."

"You can come out," the man helping said. "I can free them."

"Not leaving until they do. You'll need me in here." Josh began moving debris, trying to get to Jackson and Tracey.

The stranger had seen what tools they needed to release the others, retrieved them and they went to work. "Start moving the dirt from the pilot's window," the man instructed someone who had just arrived.

This time another teen jumped in with him, rocking the plane just a bit.

"Where are the rescue crews?" Josh asked.

"We're in the middle of nowhere here," the teenager answered.

"They're probably another fifteen minutes out." The man moved carefully to Aiden. "Your friend has a broken leg, let's get this wreckage off him."

"The boy first," Aiden said.

"Boy?"

"My son's in the back along with Tracey. He has diabetes. They're both unconscious."

The man didn't need more of an explanation. He went to work removing the seat blocking Tracey. It was a tight fit and Josh felt in the way until they got some of the bolts removed and the seat needed to be held in place. His shoulder kept the seat on the ceiling while they finished and moved it in front of the door.

"Tracey?"

Josh needed to be in two places at once. But he let their rescuer check Tracey while he released his son.

"How long have I been out?" Her voice was breathy and tired. "Where's Jackson?"

"He's okay." Josh looked at his watch. "It's been seven minutes since the crash."

"It might be the diabetes keeping him knocked out."

The man called to someone outside the door to come get Jackson. Josh handed him to another stranger and leaned down to get Tracey. Her eyes opened.

"I didn't find anything broken," their rescuer said. "Can you climb out of here?"

"Is it over?" she asked, looking at Josh.

"Tenoreno's out there somewhere," Aiden answered behind him. "Watch yourself."

Josh looked at the Ranger Captain. "I'll be back to help. Just let me check on Jackson."

"You stay with your boy. These guys can handle me."

Josh helped Tracey through the door. She was already at Jackson's side by the time he was halfway out.

"Do you think it's too high or too low?" Agent Barlow asked, running around the tail of the plane.

"He hasn't eaten today, but he's been getting the basal dose so that should—" She turned Jackson on his side, checked where his insulin port should be. "The cannula is still here but no tubing and no insulin pump. So now there's a chance it can be clogged. The ambulance may have one."

Tracey took the information a lot more calmly than he did. He was feeling that intense uncertainty again. But watching Tracey thoroughly check his son brought him stability and reassured him. "He's going to be okay. They've called an ambulance. They'll have what we need."

"Jackson." She shook his shoulder. "Can you hear me? Wake up, baby." Tracey pulled up one eyelid and then the other to check his response. Jackson moaned.

"His skin is clammy to the touch," Josh said, knowing that they didn't have much time. "Where's the ambulance? They can test his level and will have a glucagon shot. That should bounce him back."

"We can't wait on the ambulance. We need honey." Tracey searched the people. "Does anybody have honey in their car!" she called out. "He needs his blood sugar brought up fast."

A woman ran from the other side of the plane. "I have what you need at the house. Our grandson is diabetic. I sent someone to fetch it."

Josh had been absorbed in helping his son and hadn't noticed that there was a small group of buildings about a football field away. Sky High Skydiving was written on the side in big bold letters.

"No! Wait!" Out of breath, a teenager stumbled into Josh. All he could do was shove a bottle of honey and a blood testing kit at Josh's chest. "This will work faster."

Josh popped off the top to open a honey bottle and handed it to Tracey. She squeezed the honey onto the tip of her finger and rubbed Jackson's gums, tongue and the inside of his cheeks.

The people who had gathered around were being moved back. Agent McCaffrey's voice was in the background giving instructions to another agent.

"Don't be too low...don't be too low," Tracey chanted.

Tracey went through all the steps they'd done several times a day in the last year. When this all began Friday afternoon, he couldn't remember the date he'd been to the hospital with Jackson. He knew it had happened, but his mind had just gone blank.

The memories and feelings came rushing back like a jet taking off. His son had looked a lot like he did now. Tracey had held him in her arms. He'd had a hard time talking and staying awake.

Everything a year ago had happened so damn quick. Jackson had gone from a healthy little boy to almost dying. He was an amazing kid who bounced back and took it all in stride. Diabetes was a part of his life—their lives—and he never let it stand in his way.

The details crowded his thoughts, trying to block out everything else. Four days in the ICU while the doctors slowly, carefully brought Jackson's electrolytes, potassium and blood sugar into balance. If they did it too fast, he'd die. If they did it too slow, he'd die.

The memory recreated the raw fright of that drive to the hospital emergency. His heart was pounding faster now than it had throughout the past two days.

He'll be okay. He has to be.

"What's she doing?" an onlooker asked.

"Trying to get his blood sugar up." Kendall Barlow answered for them, then knelt next to Josh and Tracey. "I wanted you to know that Sage is safe. We took her to a hospital near Hearne. She's a brave little girl and is talking up a storm about what happened. If you're uncomfortable with that…"

"You're sure she's okay?" Josh asked.

Agent Barlow patted him on the shoulder. "No reason to worry. Rangers arrived to escort her home. Bryce Johnson said he won't be leaving her side. I'll call and have him bring her to Round Rock."

"Round Rock?"

"It's the closest hospital. Agent McCaffrey gave the order for our helicopter to evacuate you guys." The agent stood and withdrew her weapon. "Can he be moved?"

Josh saw the weapon out of the corner of his eye. He scanned the area around them and saw Mack being loaded and handcuffed into the back of a truck. He didn't want to move Jackson until the digital reading came up, but they were about to be sitting ducks.

"What's going on?" Tracey asked from the ground. "His reading is only at forty. I'd like to see if we could get some juice. I'd hate to be in the air if he doesn't bounce back."

"We should take cover. Tenoreno escaped when we crashed. He grabbed the machine pistol before he got out of the plane."

"Does Jackson need juice or is he stable to make a twenty-minute flight to the hospital?" Kendall asked. "Or do we need to take him to the house?"

"No, we can't risk it. Not unless we can get him to drink something, get his levels a bit higher. This kit doesn't have glucagon." Tracey stood with Jackson in her arms. Josh reached for him but she shook her head. "Tenoreno is out there, isn't he? Do you think he'll try something?"

She'd lowered her voice so none of those watching or helping get Aiden and the pilot out of the plane could hear.

"Agent Barlow, I don't suppose you have an extra weapon for Josh? He's a better shot than I am."

Kendall reached down to her leg, unstrapped her backup pistol and handed it to him.

He nodded his thanks. His mind suddenly became clear, remembering something that had bothered him about their landing. "How did our pilot know where he was heading?"

"What are you saying?" Kendall turned in a defensive circle, keeping her back to Josh. "Like they meant to come here all along? This rough landing strip is a legitimate skydiving school. You sure? Why land at a field with no planes that could get fugitives to Mexico?"

"Dammit. Not Tenoreno. It's Mack who knew where he was heading. He was hired to bring Daddy to the vindictive son. Not set him free."

Josh searched the perimeter of the field again and nodded as they headed toward the buildings to the west. Tenoreno was out there—both father and son. The plane crash had been less than ten minutes ago and a man could get a long way on foot in that length of time. But Josh's gut told him that their escaped prisoner was close.

"So you think Xander Tenoreno wants his father dead?" Kendall seemed as surprised as he'd felt earlier. "And he's here waiting to kill him?"

"Is it such a far-fetched idea that the son would want revenge for his mother's murder? Or even to keep the power he's had since Paul was locked up?" He kept Tracey and his son close between him and the agent leading the way. "Maybe we should see if Mack's awake and find out."

Josh trusted Tracey's judgement about his son. He also trusted his own again. He shook off the insecure blanket he'd draped around his shoulders for letting these events happen. Jackson stirred a little, still displaying symptoms of low sugar, but he was a strong kid. He'd make it.

And Josh was a Texas Ranger because he was good at his job. He'd seen the hatred Mack—or Vince Deegan—had for Paul Tenoreno. It was possible Xander could hate him that much, too.

Chapter Twenty-One

Agent McCaffrey nodded to them, standing guard at the plane as the volunteers continued to free the men. Tracey carried Jackson, protected by Agent Barlow and Josh. Whatever her armed escort was discussing, her only concern was getting Jackson to safety. That meant to get him stable, then on that helicopter to Round Rock.

For the middle of nowhere, there were a lot of people gathered under a shed where Agent Barlow stopped. Parachutes. They were packing parachutes for skydiving.

Tracey could see the FBI helicopter on the opposite side of the road. Mack now sat in the back of the truck next to the helicopter. One of his hands was secured to a rail along the truck bed. The pilot was armed with a shotgun, standing guard.

"Ma'am, you mentioned you had juice?" Josh asked the woman who seemed to be the owner. "Is it in the house?"

"Yes, I've sent someone for it," said the woman who'd arranged for the honey and testing kit. "Do you want to take him inside?"

Tracey sat on a stool, balancing Jackson on her legs. She shook her head not wanting to be out of sight of the helicopter.

"No, thanks. We'll head out as soon as Tracey says." Josh kept turning, searching for something or someone.

She could tell that he was anxious but not just for Jackson's welfare. "I can wait on the juice if you need to talk with that man, especially if they might come back and hurt the kids again."

"The FBI can take care of it."

"Looks like they're a little short-handed. Go on. You can tell the helicopter pilot we'll be ready in five minutes." She was confident it wouldn't be long before Jackson was his normal self. Looking down the hill, they were loading the injured ranger on board. "You need to make sure everything's safe. I can wait on the juice."

"I'll be right back." He kissed Jackson's forehead.

Then he brushed his lips against Tracey's and ran to catch up and interrogate Mack.

Agent Barlow was behind her getting names and asking why each person was there. Jackson kicked out and Tracey almost lost him from her lap.

"You could lay him here. If he's not allergic, this is all fresh hay." A young woman stretched a checkered cloth over a loose bunch. "None of the animals have been near it yet. I just set it out this morning."

"Thank you." Tracey moved to let Jackson stretch out.

"Is he okay?"

"I think he will be. Do you live here?" Tracey wiped Jackson's forehead, now dry and cool. Definitely better.

"Oh no, this is a skydiving school. I'm taking lessons and help out with the animals. They're so adorable."

Tracey didn't normally have bad vibes about people. And after the past two days, she didn't really trust the one she felt from this woman, who seemed to be nice. There shouldn't be anything "bad" about someone trying to help a sick little boy get more comfortable. And yet...

Tracey stood. "You know, he is better. We should probably join Josh." She bent to pick him up, but stopped with a gun barrel in her ribs.

"Wow, you caught on real quick," the woman whispered. "Now, we need to leave the kid and back out the other side of this place. Got it? And if you make a move, then somebody else is going to be hurt."

Where had she come from? No one seemed to be alerted that she was there. It was barely dawn for crying out loud. So why wasn't anyone surprised that she was leaving?

When exactly was this sick nightmare going to end?

"I'll come with you." Only to keep anyone else from getting hurt. Tracey tried to get Agent Barlow's attention. No luck.

The woman holding the gun waited for the agent to walk to the opposite side of the structure. She giggled as they walked around the corner and through another shed with long tables.

The gun continued to jab her ribs as the woman picked up her pace and forced Tracey to the far side of all the buildings. They darted from a huge oak tree to a metal shed. Then another. Then another. This side of the skydiving facility couldn't be seen from the plane crash or where she'd left Jackson.

"They're going to know something's wrong. I wouldn't leave Jackson like that. Not voluntarily."

"We don't care if they come looking for you. The more they look, the more they'll flush Paul from his hiding place," a man in his midthirties answered from behind a stack of hay.

The twentysomething woman, actually about the

same age as Tracey, sidled up next to the man and lifted her lips for a kiss. And, of course, she lifted the gun and pointed it in Tracey's general direction.

"Why in the world do you think you need me to help you find your father? You are Xander Tenoreno. Right?"

It was hard to be scared. Too much had happened in the past two days—she'd barely been conscious half an hour. She'd changed or she was just plain tired. The reason was unimportant, but these two didn't really seem threatening to her.

"You know… I might have a concussion. Even though I feel totally fine." She crossed the lean-to and plopped down on a hay bale. "Or I might be quite confident that Josh won't take long to find me. But I am going to wait. Right here. You can do what you want. I'm waiting."

She was the one who sounded a little scary. Sort of delusional or exhausted. Maybe it was shock. Once she sat, she realized her entire body was shaking and her mouth had gone completely dry.

Xander Tenoreno acted like he was ignoring her, as if she wasn't important. But she'd been watching men and their body language closely for hours. And his was tense, ready to pounce if she moved the wrong direction.

"This is ridiculous," Tracey continued. "Your father is long gone. Probably stole a car and headed out while everyone else was running to the plane crash."

"You can shut up now." The chick—she'd lost the right to be referred to with respect—pulled the rather large gun up to her shoulder again. "Xander knows what he's doing."

Tracey nodded and began looking for a weapon or for something to hide behind when the shooting started.

Wow. She really did feel like help was on the way.

Josh wouldn't let anything happen to her. She was more concerned about both of them being separated from Jackson. He needed juice and was barely coherent enough to swallow.

Xander took out a telescope that fit on top of a rifle. He searched the fields and turned his body in a semicircle. He paused several times but didn't do anything except remove his arm from around the woman.

"Why not just let your father go to jail for the rest of his life?" She was legitimately curious. But it also occurred to her that if he was distracted, Josh would have an easier time taking him by surprise.

"My father wasn't going to jail. He wasn't even going to stand trial." He cocked his head to the side. "He was headed to Austin to make a deal. Screw me and our business over so that he could what? Get away with murdering my mother. That's what. His deal would have put him in witness protection. I have a right to take care of this the way I see fit."

Now she was scared.

"WHERE'S TRACEY?" JOSH SAT Jackson upright and made sure he could swallow some juice. A little dribbled down his chin, but he didn't choke. He'd give him a couple of minutes and then repeat the blood test.

"I thought she followed you. I checked the west side of the house, came back and she wasn't here." Kendall placed her palm on Jackson's cheek. "His color is better. Are you ready to transport now?"

"I…" He looked at his son, looked around for Tracey, then stared at the armed pilot. "Something's wrong. She wouldn't leave him alone like this."

They asked the family members and the instructor if they'd seen anything. Their answers were no.

"Maybe you're overthinking," Kendall said.

"Call it in."

"We only have three agents here, Josh. We can't cover each of these buildings until backup arrives."

"She could be dead or miles away from here by then."

"Ma'am?" He tapped on the shoulder of the home owner. "You said your grandson has diabetes, so you're familiar with it?"

"Oh yes, I'm sorry that we didn't have everything your wife needed."

Josh didn't correct her. Moving forward was more important. "Do you mind sitting with Jackson?"

"No. I'd be glad to."

Josh walked away and caught the end of Kendall's phone conversation.

"He's not going to stay put. Tenoreno's out there, sir. I can at least find out where." She hung up and faced him. "Do people always go out on a limb for you, Josh?"

"Not sure how to answer that, but I am grateful."

"Excuse me, you asked about the woman in the plane." A teenage girl holding a dog waited for an okay to finish. "Shawna's gone, too."

"Shawna?"

"She's taking lessons and wanted to feed the animals this morning."

"Has she ever wanted to do that before?" Kendall pulled out her cell again.

"No. Today's the first time."

"Do you have a picture of Shawna and a last name?" Kendall asked.

He battled with himself over whether he should go. Jackson needed him, but so did Tracey. His son was able to swallow. It wasn't his imagination that Jackson's color was better.

"Kendall, I need you to climb out on another limb for me." Her eyebrows arched, asking what without saying a word. "Five minutes and you take Jackson to the hospital."

"But he's—"

"My gut says yes he's better, but I have to be certain. I can't choose one person I love over the other."

"Better idea. You get on the chopper and I'll do my job and track down where Tracey is. Go. Take care of your kid."

While Kendall got the information necessary for her report or an APB on the missing woman, Josh looked for an exit route. Not because he was trying to ditch the FBI agent. If he could find the best route to leave the shelter, he might be able to find Tracey.

"Can I borrow your phone?" Josh asked and the young man nodded. "That's your mom sitting with my son over there, right? Can you tell her to call this," he shook the phone side to side, "if Jackson's condition changes?" He nodded again.

The boy went to his mother, pointed at Josh. He had to try to take care of them both. He'd track down Tracey. When he was gone, Kendall would take his son to the hospital. He focused.

Where would he… There. To keep out of sight they would have headed toward a tree with a tractor parked under it. It was the only place from that side of the shelter. He ran that direction and sure enough, his line of sight to the helicopter pilot was obscured.

He zigzagged across the property using the same logic. If he couldn't see anyone behind him, they probably didn't see him. Then it wasn't a matter of where he'd come from but what was right in front of him.

Tracey.

Along with Xander Tenoreno.

Tracey didn't seem in immediate danger. He could get Kendall or McCaffrey, surround the man ultimately behind the kidnapping of his kids. He felt the emotion building. He shouldn't burst in there with no plan to rescue the woman he loved.

The lines between logic and emotion blurred as he debated which path to follow. Xander looked through a scope toward the far tree line. Josh moved close enough to hear the conversation.

"Predictable. I knew he'd head for a vehicle after walking away from the plane. A shame I wasn't ready for the crash, but that surprise caught me off guard and I missed."

"It's okay, baby."

The girl, Shawna, who had been at the shed earlier, wrapped her arms around Xander and he shrugged her off, uncovering something on a hay bale. Yeah, it was a rifle. Mack had been telling the truth about Xander wanting to kill his father.

The decision about leaving had been made. The son was scoping the dad like it was deer season. Josh didn't have good positioning, he didn't have backup and he only had a peashooter revolver.

What could go wrong?

"Step away from the rifle. Hands on your heads, then drop to your knees." Josh revealed where he was and stepped from behind an animal feeder.

"Well if it isn't Major Joshua Parker here to save the girl again." Xander fingered the rifle trigger. He was not dropping to his knees with his hands on his head.

The girl got closer to his side. She didn't bother listening to Josh, either.

"Don't be an idiot, Tenoreno. I'm not going to let

you hurt anyone. Even your own father." Josh stepped closer, but not close enough to give Xander any advantage. Swinging the rifle around to point at Tracey or himself would be harder at this range.

"She has a gun," Tracey informed him as she slipped off her seat on the hay.

"And she knows how to use it." Xander shifted and the gun was in his hand. "But I know to use it better."

"Give it up. You're not getting away from here."

"Funny thing about revenge, Josh. I'd rather see my father suffer for what he did. He murdered my mother. All she wanted was to live somewhere else. Someplace where he wasn't. After forty years with him, she probably deserved it."

"So you kidnapped Jackson and Sage, and set up this entire game to get back at your daddy?" Tracey moved another step away from Tenoreno.

Josh could tell she was heading for the back side of the lean-to. All she needed was a distraction. "All this because you have daddy issues."

"Seriously? You think I'm going to fall for a question like that?" Xander aimed the gun at Tracey. "I'll let my girlfriend keep your girlfriend occupied while I take care of my business."

"You know I can't let you pull that trigger."

"You're not on the clock now, Ranger Parker. You can let me do anything you want."

"Thing is…he doesn't want to." Tracey answered for him, her shoulders rising with every frightened breath she took. "It doesn't matter how deviant you are or who your father murdered." She pointed to Josh. "That man is a good man. He'll give his life to protect you both. You'll never understand what makes him decent."

Josh's heart swelled. No two ways about it, she loved

him. His hands steadied. His feet were firm and fixed. He was ready for whatever came next. But she was wrong. He loved her and would protect her before doing anything else.

Xander ignored them and put his eye to the scope again.

"I'll say this one more time. Drop the gun, kneel and put your hands on your head." It was a small backup revolver. "I have six shots. That's three for each of you. No warnings. Center mass. I won't miss."

"Xander? Baby, what do I do?" The weight of the big gun or the nerves of the young woman caused the gun to wobble in her hands. Xander ignored her, too.

Shawna looked from Tracey leaning on the hay, to Josh pointing a gun at her. After he didn't answer or acknowledge her, she didn't look at her boyfriend. The gun dropped from her hands, she fell to her knees and began crying.

For a couple of seconds Josh thought it was over. He wanted to be back with Jackson and Sage. He wanted to talk about everything with Tracey. He wanted all this to become a memory.

Xander Tenoreno pulled the trigger. Josh squeezed his.

Shawna screamed. Tracey fell to the ground.

Josh leaped across the space separating him from Xander. Encouraged by the love he'd heard in Tracey's words and scared to death that something had just happened to her. Shawna was up and running but she was someone else's problem. Tracey needed to find the gun that had dropped from the woman's hands. The man fired and she'd hit the dirt herself, not certain what would happen.

Josh was fighting Xander. She was sure he felt like

he needed to eliminate the threat. The man was crazy. He'd shot his father in front of a Texas Ranger.

Where's the gun? Where's the gun?

Tracey scooted on her hands and knees looking for the silver steel in all the dirt and pieces of hay. Her head was down and she looked up only to see Josh winning the battle.

She got knocked backward when Xander tripped over her. Josh came in to land a powerful blow to the man's abdomen.

"Give it up." Josh watched as his opponent fell backward.

Tracey didn't need to search for the gun anymore. It was over. Xander Tenoreno didn't get up. He was done. Knocked out cold by the time Kendall and the other agent got to the lean-to.

"We heard shots."

"I'm not sure, but Paul Tenoreno might be at the other end of where that rifle is pointed."

"You okay?" Tracey asked. "Can you make it back to the house?"

Josh took a deep breath and stood up straight, wincing. "As long as you're here…I'll be fine. Let's go get our boy."

"Tenoreno junior's wound isn't serious. We'll ride with the emergency unit and transport him and Vince Deegan to Round Rock." Kendall joined them at the helicopter as they watched a now alert Jackson let the pilot settle a headset on his ears.

"And Tenoreno senior?" Josh asked.

"We were too late. Bullet hit the lung."

"I didn't think he'd do it."

"You aren't the murderer, Josh."

"Aiden and Jackson are set and ready. Unfortunately, the pilot didn't make it. There's room on the helicopter for one of you. Who's going?" McCaffrey asked, tapping Josh on the back of his shoulder with whatever papers he had in his hand.

It was his son. His place was beside him. Tracey didn't hesitate, she gently pushed Josh forward. "I'll find Sage and be right behind you, even if I have to steal a car to get there."

Josh stepped on board, watching her, acting as if he was about to say something.

The corners of Tracey's mouth went up and down. She couldn't keep a smile as the door began closing, separating them. She lifted her hand, then covered her mouth to hold back the tears.

"Hold it." Josh pushed the door aside and held out his hand. "She's with me."

They all moved out of his way and an agent got off, not bothering to argue. Once again he showed everyone around them that she wasn't *just* the nanny.

Chapter Twenty-Two

Bouncing back from the low blood sugar levels was a breeze for Jackson. What they hadn't realized was that his right ulna had been cracked in the plane crash. He'd been so out of it at the time that he didn't begin complaining until much later in the day.

Instead of sending them home to sleep in their own beds, the FBI put them in a hotel suite in Waco. They claimed it was easier to protect them there. And since it didn't matter where they slept, Josh agreed. They were all together. Exhausted but very much alive.

"Didn't they catch all the people involved?" she'd asked him once McCaffrey had gone.

Josh had pulled her into his arms and kissed her briefly. "They're playing it safe. Think of it this way, no cooking. No commuting back and forth to your place."

And no talking about how—or if—their relationship had changed. The suite had two bedrooms. She had to admit that room service and not making her bed had huge appeal.

Sage drew pictures that were full of Jackson's favorite things and asked for a roll of tape so she could cover the walls. There were a couple of times where she ran to the bed where Jackson was on forced rest and Tracey thought there might have been a hint of twin talk. Just long looks where they were communicating, but no words were exchanged.

They were back to their regular twin selves.

Whatever happened between Jackson and Sage, they didn't share it with her, but they did involve their dad. Josh had stepped into the hall for several phone calls she assumed were official Ranger business.

Tracey went to bed after watching Josh hold his kids close, tucked up under each arm. A beautiful sight. His look—before he'd fallen asleep—had invited her to join them, but it wasn't time. Not yet.

One day soon, they'd talk about the way they felt. Right now, they all just needed rest and assurance that nothing else would happen.

Day two of their protective custody, under a Ranger escort, Tracey took Sage home to clean up and grab art supplies. She thought Josh would want something clean to wear and headed to his bedroom when she caught Bryce coming from there.

"Oh, hi." He turned sideways in the hall so she could pass. "I was just grabbing him… He asked me to pick up—I even remembered his toothbrush."

He lifted a gym bag. She assumed it was filled with Josh's clothes and she didn't need to worry about picking anything out. But Bryce looked extremely guilty. What was up with that?

"Okay. So I'm just going to grab Sage some snacks, then we'll be ready to head back. Is anything wrong?"

"Nope. Nothing's wrong."

"I got Jackson's stuff." Sage came from their bedroom and Bryce scooped her up to carry her downstairs, making her giggle all the way down.

Everything shouted that the man was lying. She'd let Josh deal with whatever that was about. One short stop by her place and they were ready to head back to the hospital.

"Sage, honey, can you wear your headphones for a little while?"

Bryce waited for the little girl to comply, then her escort took a long breath. "That doesn't bode well for whatever you're going to ask."

"I need to know what's going on. Has something else happened? We're being guarded twenty-four-seven and you're acting very suspicious." Not to mention Josh's compliance with everything Agent McCaffrey suggested.

"Nothing that I know about. It seems that Xander Tenoreno bribed the pilot. They aren't making a big deal about that because he died."

Even with Bryce's assurances, Tracey has a feeling something was being kept from her. Everyone was acting so…different. Bryce drove into the parking lot and she saw the two men who had been her bodyguards standing at the front entrance.

"Oh, that's just great! Just when I thought everything was settling back to normal my uncle strikes again."

"You want me to get rid of them?"

"No. I can do it. Will you take Sage back to Josh?" She walked up to the guard who had at least spoken to her and stuck her palm out. "Your phone, please."

"No need for that, miss. Your uncle's inside. We're waiting for him here."

The demise of the Tenoreno family, the dramatic recovery of the twins. All of it made good television and press for the state and the Rangers. But all of it put the Bass family in the limelight, too. She'd expected a phone call from her uncle, not a visit.

She entered the lobby, expecting an entourage to

be surrounding Carl. He sat in the corner alone, a cup of coffee on the table next to him. He acknowledged her, she overheard some business lingo and expected to have to wait.

"There she is. I've got to go. Call you back later." Carl dropped the phone into his pocket—totally an unusual move for him. "You look tired, darling. Getting enough rest? Do I need to secure the entire floor so you can get a decent night's sleep?"

"I'm fine. It's been pretty hectic lately. So what do you need? If it's about the reporters, my name change is public record—there's nothing I could do about them finding out our family history."

"Same Tracey." He pulled her shoulders, drawing her to his chest for a hug. "But you're all grown-up now, right?"

When he released her, she took a couple of steps back, looking at him. "What's going on?"

"I needed to see that you were okay. Completely okay. And here." Wallet now in hand, he reached inside and took out a check. "Spend it on whatever you need. Buy a new electric fence or a security system or even bodyguards for a while. No, don't argue. You've discovered there are some seriously bad people in the world. Those kids need to be protected. Oh, and I'm here because I was invited."

He wrapped her hand through the crook of his arm and escorted her to as if it was Buckingham Palace. She might actually enjoy being an adult around him, but why would he say he'd been invited? By whom?

Carl stepped aside just before they reached the door to the suite. Bryce handed her a handmade princess hat Sage had decorated that morning. "I think you're supposed to put that on."

She followed instructions and entered. The room was overflowing with friends and relatives. Everyone was wearing either a crown or a princess hat.

"My lady." Carl placed her hand on his and took two steps.

The room was silent, people practically held their breath. Asking what was going on would ruin the entire effect. Carl joined Gwen's parents, who were steadying Sage and Jackson on chairs next to Josh. Both children had towels draped around their shoulders as if they were acting out one of their stories. Sage even had the wand they'd made together months ago.

Josh formally bowed. He raised his eyebrows and carefully took her hand.

"I was hoping for a moment alone before this happened," he whispered, "but I got outvoted." Josh cleared his throat. "Before we have an audience with the Prince and Princess Parkers, you need to know that their father—"

"The king," the twins said together.

"The king, loves you with all his mind, soul and heart. So…Tracey Cassidy…" He dipped his hand in his pocket and knelt on bended knee.

"Would you marry us?" they all said together.

Josh opened his palm where a sparkly diamond solitaire was surrounded by multicolored glitter. She cupped Josh's checks and kissed him with her answer as he stood.

Everyone began clapping.

"That means yes!" the twins shouted.

Epilogue

Two weeks later

"Let me get this straight. All you have to do is wait around until you're thirty years old and you get control of your own money. That sounds like a plan. You're already set for life," Bryce told Tracey. He had one arm around the waist of his girlfriend and the other wrapped around a bucket of Bush's chicken strips.

Tracey nodded like the ten other times she'd answered the question for Josh's men. Josh thought she'd lose a gasket if she discovered Bryce was teasing a fellow silver-spooner. She needed rescuing and this time he didn't need a gun.

"Did he tell you that I had to collect that rock and get it to the room before you?" Bryce said, pointing to her ring. "So you really don't have to work—"

"She does if we want to eat." Josh jumped in and stole the chicken from his computer expert. He whisked Tracey away to a corner of the kitchen not occupied by a ranger or significant other. "Sorry."

"You said you wouldn't tell anyone."

"I didn't." He shrugged. "They are investigators, you know. They all worked on different possibilities of who had the kids even when they were told to stand down.

It's just one of those things that happens at my office, Mrs. Parker."

He took a chicken tender from the box. Gone in two large bites. She laughed.

Life still hadn't settled into something resembling normalcy. Maybe it never would. Maybe normal didn't exist. But here they were—husband and wife. Had he been romantic? He couldn't wait that long. He'd asked. She'd replied, "Yes. Let's not wait."

So they hadn't.

Two weeks later, the Company was throwing them a surprise party. Tracey's uncle had flown Gwen's parents in the previous week. They all encouraged them to have the courtroom ceremony while they were visiting.

"Don't you think you should put the chicken on the table with the rest of the food?" Tracey asked, making a lunge for the box.

He plucked another tender and shoved it in his mouth. "We could feed a starving nation with what's on that table. They aren't going to miss this little bit of bird."

"Bryce will. You should have seen his face when you stole it from him."

"Ha. You should see yours now that you can't reach it."

"Oh, I don't want the chicken. I want your hands free. I'm getting kind of used to them touching me. But if you'd rather hold deep-fried chicken, then…" She shrugged and spun out of his arms.

"Okay, okay. You've made your point." He followed Tracey to the table, where she picked up two plates and filled them with munchkin-sized portions.

"I thought Gwen's parents were taking the kids to dinner?"

"They said they'd take them for chicken and since it's here—"

"You feel kind of weird letting them leave the house?" Josh took the plates from her hands and set them on the bar. "I get it. I'll take it up and explain."

"I'll go. They're really nice and I think they'll understand."

"Yep. And you're right." He wrapped his arms around her body and pulled her to him for a kiss.

The door opened and Josh watched from a distance as Aiden Oaks entered. White hat in hand—at least the hand that wasn't holding a crutch, blue jeans ripped up to the knee, leg in a cast, badge over his heart. "May I come in?"

"Sure."

"Need a beer?"

"Here, take this chair." The men of Company F made their commander comfortable.

Aiden swung the crutch like a pro and made himself comfortable. Josh squeezed Tracey's hand and kissed her for luck. That uncertain future might be resolved in the next couple of minutes.

"Hello, Captain."

"Major." He adjusted the crutch to lean on the chair and hung his hat on top. "How are the kids, Tracey?"

"Physically they're great. We're working on the kidnapping slowly. But I think we're all getting back to normal."

Josh threaded his fingers through hers. She knew why Aiden was there. Most of the conversation had stopped. There was the lull of a baseball game in the background. They'd all been expecting a decision on his reprimand at any time. Maybe it was appropriate that they get the news tonight.

They were celebrating the start of a new life.

"A couple of decisions came down the pipe today. Xander Tenoreno's been indicted on racketeering, kidnapping and everything else the attorney general's office could come up with. An operation to free the families of men who worked for him was successful. And before you begin clapping, the thing you've all been wanting to know…" he paused while the crowd came closer. "I'm returning the reins of Company F to Major Parker."

Cries of laughter and relief echoed through the house from the men and women surrounding him. Claps on the back and congratulations should have distracted him, but all he could see was Tracey's joy.

Their relationship had begun with a tragedy, and then adversity had brought them closer. His bride had the right to ask him to walk away from the Rangers after the kidnapping. Her uncle had told them he'd make arrangements for her to access her inheritance. Unlike what he'd told Bryce, neither of them needed to work.

Seemed like all he wanted to do was make up for the time they'd been waiting on each other to make decisions. He knew how much support he had from her. Seeing it now, all he could do was pull her to him and kiss her.

One kiss that turned into a second and a third. It might have gone further, but a couple of fake coughs started behind him.

"Do we have to stay upstairs, Daddy?" Sage crooked her finger several times, then just waved her hands for him to bend down so she could whisper in his ear. "What am I supposed to call Trace Trace now? Grandfather told me she's our stepmother. Is she going to get mean and grow warts like in all the stories?"

Josh laughed and picked up his little girl. "What do you want to call Trace Trace?" he asked, using the kids' nickname.

"Can it just be Mommy?"

His eyes locked with the woman who'd been there with him through the darkest part of his life. Her eyes brimmed with tears ready to fall. "I think she'd like that."

Tracey nodded her head, quickly whisking the tears from her cheeks before letting Sage see her. "Hey, kidlet. That sounds like a perfect name. No one's ever called me that before. You two will be the first."

Cast banging on the rails, Jackson flew down the stairs and into her arms. "They said we needed to ask, but I knew you'd like it."

Tracey kissed both of their cheeks with lots of noise. "I don't just like it. I absolutely adore it." Her eyes locked with Josh's. "Almost as much as I love all of you."

And just like kids that subject was settled and they ran back to their grandparents on the stairs. Their grandmother declared there was enough food to feed all five companies of Rangers. He felt Tracey's sigh of relief as she relaxed within his arms. The kids went up and Gwen's mother came for their dinner.

Before they handed her the plates, she gathered them both close for a hug, then wiped away a tear. "I want you to know how happy we are for you. We had begun to wonder if Josh was ever going to ask you after what he said last Christmas."

Tracey looked confused. "What did he say?"

His mother-in-law pushed forward. "Josh told us how he felt and that he wanted to remarry. You were a blessing to our Gwen, Tracey. If she can't be here to raise her children, I know she'd be happy you will be. Welcome to our family."

Tracey looked happy as they watched his mother-in-law return upstairs. "I meant to tell you about that."

"Did you change your mind or something?"

"Obviously not. I thought I should probably ask you on a date first. I intended to on your birthday," Josh whispered.

She twisted around to face him. "Get out of town. Really? What changed your mind? Get a little too tipsy instead?"

"I wasn't tipsy. Just lost my nerve."

"You? The man who ran and jumped into the small door of a plane with machine guns firing all around him?"

"Yeah, I know, hard to believe. But a wise man once told me never to ask a woman a certain question you didn't know the answer to. I thought I did. Only to realize the only thing for certain I knew was that I loved everything about you. But you might not necessarily feel the same."

She swatted at him as if he was totally wrong. He knew better. He'd messed up her birthday and he'd messed up the romance. He'd spend the rest of his uncertain future making it up to her.

Every day was precious. They knew it better than most. And he wouldn't take life for granted.

"Do you think those two will even notice that I've moved in?"

Josh seized the opportunity of her upturned face to kiss her again. Slowly, gaining the notice of their surprise guests and family. He came away with a smile on his face.

Happy. Satisfied that Tracey, Jackson and Sage were the normal he wanted.

Josh whispered his answer so only his wife could hear. "There will be a heck of a lot of sleepovers to explain if they don't."

* * * * *

FRIENDSHIP ON FIRE

JOSS WOOD

Prologue

Callie...

As she'd done for nearly thirty years, Callie Brogan kissed her daughter's sable-colored hair, conscious that nothing was guaranteed—not time, affection or life itself so she took every opportunity to kiss and hug her offspring, all seven of them.

God, no, she hadn't birthed them all. Levi and the twins—Jules and Darby—were hers. The Lockwood brothers—Noah, Eli and Ben—were the sons of her heart. Biologically, they belonged to her best friend and neighbor, Bethann Lockwood, who had passed away ten years ago. Dylan-Jane, well, DJ was another child of her heart.

The life Callie had lived back then, as the pampered wife of the stupendously wealthy, successful and most powerful venture capitalist in Boston, was over. Her beloved Ray was gone, too. She'd been a widow for three years now.

Callie was, *gulp*, alone. At fifty-four, it was time to reinvent herself.

So damn scary...

Who was she if she wasn't her kids' mom and her exuberant, forceful husband's wife?

At the moment, she was someone she didn't recognize. She needed to get to know herself again.

"Mom?"

Callie blinked and looked into Jules's brilliant eyes. As always, she caught her breath. Jules had Ray's eyes, that incredible shade of silver blue, incandescently luminous. Callie waited for the familiar wave of grief, and it washed over her as more of a swell than a tsunami.

Damn, Callie missed that man. His bawdy laugh, his strong arms, the sex. Yeah, God, she really missed the sex.

"Mom? Are you okay?" Jules asked, perceptive as always.

Callie waved her words away. She considered herself a modern mom but telling her very adult daughter that she was horny was not something that she'd ever do. So Callie shrugged and smiled. "I'm good."

Jules frowned. "I don't believe you."

Callie looked around and wished Noah—and Eli and Ben—were here. Eli and Ben had excused themselves from Sunday lunch; both were working overtime to restore a catamaran. And Noah was in Italy? Or was it Greece? Cannes? The boy used jet travel like normal people used cars.

Would Noah ever come back home to Boston? The eldest Lockwood boy wasn't one to wear his heart on his sleeve but his stepdad's actions after Bethann's death had scarred him. He had far too much pride to show how wounded he was, to admit he was lost and lonely and hurt. Like Bethann, he saw emotion and communicating his fears as a failure and a weakness.

Noah's independence frustrated Callie but she'd never stopped loving the boy…the man. Noah was in his midthirties now.

Her own son, Levi, sat down on the bigger of the two leather couches and placed his glass of whiskey on the coffee table. "Right, Mom, what's the big news?"

Callie took her seat with Jules next to her, on the arm of the chair. Darby and the twins' best friend, DJ, book-ended Levi.

Jules rubbed her hand up and down Callie's back. "What is it, Mom?"

Well, here goes. "Last Tuesday was three years since your dad died."

"We know, Mom," Darby murmured, her elegant fingers holding the stem of her wineglass.

"I've decided to make some changes."

Jules lifted her eyebrows, looking skeptical. Jules, thanks to Noah's desertion and Ray's sudden death, wasn't a fan of impetuous decisions or change. "Okay. Like…?"

Callie looked out the picture windows to the lake and the golf course beyond. "Before you were all born, Bethann's father decided to turn Lockwood Estate into an exclusive gated community, complete with a golf course and country club. Your dad was one of the first people to buy and build on this estate and this house is still, apart from Lockwood itself, one of the biggest in the community."

Her kids' faces all reflected some measure of frustration at the history lesson. They'd lived here all their lives; they'd heard it all before. "It's definitely too big for me. The tenants renting the three-bedroom we own on the other side of the estate have handed in their notice. I'm going to move into that house."

Callie could see the horror on their faces, saw that they didn't like the idea of losing their family home. She'd reassure them. "When I die, this house will come to you, Levi, but I think you should take possession of it now. I've heard each of you talk of buying your own places. It doesn't make sense to buy when you have this one, Levi. The twins can move in here while they look for a property that suits them. This house has four bedrooms, lots of communal space. It's central, convenient, and you'd just have to pay for the utilities."

"Move in with Levi? Yuck," Darby said, as Callie expected her to. But Callie caught the long look her daughter exchanged with her twin sister, Jules, and smiled at their excitement.

Callie knew what was coming next…

"DJ could move into the apartment over the garage," Jules suggested, excitement in her eyes.

She loved this house; they all did. And why wouldn't they? It was spacious, with high ceilings and wooden floors, an outdoor entertainment area and a big backyard. It was close to Lockwood Country Club's private gym, which they all still used. The Tavern, the pub and Italian restaurant attached to the country club, was one of her kids' favorite places to meet, have a drink. The boys played golf within the walls of the pretty, green estate where they were raised, as often as their busy schedules allowed.

It was home.

"I don't want to live with my sisters, Mom. It was bad enough sharing a childhood with them," Levi said.

He was lying, Callie could tell. Levi adored his sisters and this way, he could vet who they dated without stalking them on social media. Levi's protective streak ran a mile long.

"It's a good solution. This way, you don't have to rent while you're looking to buy and, Levi, since I know you and Noah sank most of your cash into that new marina, it'll be a while before your bank account recovers."

Callie wrinkled her nose. Levi probably still had a few million at his fingertips. They were one of Boston's wealthiest families.

Levi shook his head. "Mom, we appreciate the offer, but you do know that we are all successful and you don't need to worry about us anymore?"

She was *Mom*, Callie wanted to tell him. She'd always be *Mom*. One day they'd understand. She'd always worry about them.

"Are you sure you want to move into the house on Ennis Street?" Jules asked.

Absolutely. There were too many ghosts in this house, too many memories. "I need something new, something different. Dad is gone but I'm still standing and I've made the decision to reinvent my life. I have a bucket list and so many things I want to do by the time I turn fifty-five."

"That's in ten months," Darby pointed out.

Callie was so aware, thank you very much.

"What's on the bucket list, Mom?" Jules asked, amused.

Callie smiled. "Oh, the usual. A road trip through France, take an art class, learn how to paint."

Jules sent her an indulgent smile. God. Jules would probably fall off her chair if Callie told her that a one-night stand, phone sex, seeing a tiger in the wild, bungee jumping and sleeping naked in the sun were also on her to-do list. Oh, and she definitely wouldn't tell them that her highest priority was to help them all settle down...

She wasn't hung up on them getting married. No,

sometimes marriage, like her best friend's, wasn't worth the paper the license was written on.

Callie wanted her children to find their soft place to fall, the person who would make their lives complete.

But, right now, Callie wanted Noah home, back in Boston, where he belonged.

How was she supposed to get him to settle down when he was on the other side of the world?

One

Noah...

Noah pushed his hand into her thick hair and looked down into those amazing eyes, the exact tint of a new moon on the Southern Ocean. Her scent, something sexy but still sweet, drifted off her skin and her wide mouth promised a kiss that was dark and delectable. His stupid heart was trying to climb out of his chest so that it could rest in her hand.

Jules pushed her breasts into his chest and tilted her hips so that her stomach brushed his hard-as-hell erection...

This was Jules, his best friend.

Thought, time, the raucous sounds of the New Year's party receded and Jules was all that mattered. Jules with her tight nipples and her tilted hips and her silver-blue eyes begging him to kiss her.

He'd make it quick. Just one quick sip, a fast taste. He wouldn't take it any further. He couldn't. He wanted to, desperately, but there were reasons why he had no right to place his hand on her spectacular ass, to push his chest into her small but perfect breasts.

One kiss, that's all he could have, take.

Noah touched his lips to hers and he fell, lost in her taste, in her scent. For the first time in months his grief dissipated, his confusion cleared. As her tongue slid between his teeth, his responsibilities faded, and the decisions he'd been forced to make didn't matter.

Jules was in his arms and she was kissing him and the world suddenly made sense...

He was about to palm her beautiful breasts, have her wrap her legs around his hips to rock against her core when hands gripped his shoulders, yanked his hair.

Surprised, he stumbled back, fell onto his tailbone to see Morgan and his dad looking down at him, laughing their asses off. His eyes bounced to Jules and tears streaked her face.

"Bastard!" Morgan screamed.

"That's my boy," Ethan cooed. "Blood or not, you are my son."

And Jules? Well, Jules just cried.

Another night, the same recurring dream. Noah Lockwood punched the comforter and the sheets away, unable to bare the constricting fabric against his heated skin. Draping one forearm across bent knees, Noah ran a hand behind his neck. Cursing, he fumbled for the glass of water on the bedside table, grimacing at the handprint his sweat made on the deep black comforter.

Noah swung his legs off the side of the large bed, reached for a pair of boxers on the nearby chair and yanked them on. He looked across the bed and Jenna—

a friend he occasionally hooked up with when he was in this particular city—reached over to the side table and flipped on the bedside light. She checked her watch before shoving the covers back, muttered a quick curse and, naked, started to gather her clothes.

"Do you want to talk about it?" she asked.

Hell, no. He rarely opened up to his brothers or his closest friends, so there was no chance he'd talk to an infrequent bed buddy about his dream. Without a long explanation Jenna wouldn't understand, and since Noah didn't do explanations, that would never happen. Besides, talking meant examining and facing his fears, confronting guilt and dissecting his past. That would be *amusing*...in the same way an electric shock to his junk would be *nice*.

He tried, as much as possible, not to think about the past...

Noah walked over to the French doors that opened to the balcony. Pushing them open, he sucked in the briny air of the cool late-autumn night. Tinges of a new morning peeked through the trees that bordered the side and back edges of the complex.

He loved Cape Town, and enjoyed his visits to the city nestled between the mountains and the sea. It was beautiful, as were Oahu or Cannes or Monaco. But it wasn't home. He missed Boston with an intensity that sometimes threatened to drop him to his knees. But he couldn't go back...

The last time he left it nearly killed him and that wasn't an experience he wanted to repeat.

Noah accepted Jenna's brief goodbye kiss and walked her to the door. Finally alone, he grabbed a T-shirt from the chair behind him and yanked it over his head and, picking up his phone, walked onto the balcony, then perched lightly on the edge of a sturdy morris chair.

The dream's sour aftertaste remained and he sucked in long, clean breaths, trying to cleanse his mind. Because his nightmares always made him want to touch base with his brothers, he dialed Eli's number, knowing he was more likely to answer than Ben.

"Noah, I was just about to call you." Despite being across the world in Boston, Eli sounded like he was in the next room.

Noah heard the worry in Eli's voice and his stomach swooped.

"What's up?" he asked, trying to project confidence. He was the oldest and although he was always absent, his hand was still the one, via phone calls and emails, steering the Lockwood ship. Actually, that wasn't completely true; Levi buying into the North Shore marina and boatyard using the money he inherited from Ray allowed Noah to take a step back. Eli and Ben were a little hotheaded and prone to making impulsive decisions but Levi wasn't. Noah was happy to leave the day-to-day decisions in Levi's capable hands.

"Callie called us earlier—a for-sale sign has gone up at Lockwood."

"Ethan's selling the house?" Noah asked.

"No. He's selling everything. Our childhood home, the land, the country club, the golf course, the buildings. He's selling the LCC Trust and that includes everything on the estate except for the individually owned houses."

Noah released a low, bullet-like curse word.

"Rumor has it that he needs cash again."

"Okay, let me assimilate this. I'll call you back in a few."

Noah sucked in his breath and closed his eyes, allowing anger and disappointment to flow through him. Ten years ago he'd taken the man he called Dad, a man he adored and whom he thought loved him, to court. After his mom's death he discovered that the marriage that he'd thought was so perfect had been pure BS. The only father he'd ever known, the man he placed on a pedestal was, he discovered, a serial cheater and a spendthrift.

Stopping Ethan from liquidating the last of Lockwood family assets, passed down through generations of Lockwoods to his mom—a legacy important enough to his mom for her to persuade both their biological dad and then their stepdad to take her maiden name—meant hiring expensive legal talent.

Noah ran his hand over his eyes, remembering those bleak months between his mother's death and the court judgment awarding the Lockwood boys the waterfront marina and the East Boston boatyard and Ethan the Lockwood Country Club, which included their house, the club facilities, the shops and the land around it. Ethan was also awarded the contents of the house and the many millions in her bank accounts. All of which, so he'd heard, he'd managed to blow. On wine, women and song.

Fighting for his and his brothers' inheritance had been tough, but he'd been gutted by the knowledge that everything he knew about his mom and Ethan, the facade of happiness they'd presented to the world, had been a sham. A lie, an illusion. By cheating on his mom and choosing money over them, Ethan had proved that he'd never loved any of them.

Why hadn't he seen it, realized that his dad was actually a bastard, that every "I love you" and "I'm proud of you" had been a flat-out lie? Faced with proof of his father's deceit, he'd decided that love was an emotion he couldn't trust, that marriage was a sham, that people, especially the ones who professed to love him, couldn't be trusted.

And Morgan's actions had cemented those conclusions.

The year it all fell apart, he'd spent the Christmas season with Morgan and her parents. Needing something to dull the pain after her parents retired for the night, he'd tucked into Ivan Blake's very expensive whiskey and dimly recalled Morgan prattling on about marriage and a commitment. Since he'd been blitzed and because she'd had her hand in his pants, he couldn't remember what was discussed...

The following day—feeling very un-Christmassy on Christmas morning thanks to a hangover from hell—he'd found himself accepting congratulations on their engagement. He'd tried to explain that it was a mistake, wanted to tell everyone that he had no intention of getting married, but Morgan had looked so damn happy and his head had been on the point of exploding. His goal had been to get through the day and when he had Morgan on her own, he'd backtrack, let her down gently and break up with her as he'd intended to do for weeks. He'd had enough on his plate without dealing with a needy and demanding girlfriend.

Yet somehow, Ivan Blake had discerned his feet were frozen blocks of ice thanks to his sudden engagement to his high-maintenance daughter. Ivan had pulled him into his study, told him that Morgan was bipolar and that she was mentally fragile. Being a protective dad, he'd done his research and knew Noah was a sailor, one of the best amateurs in the country. He also knew Noah wanted to turn pro and needed a team to sail with, preferably to lead.

Ivan had been very well-informed; he'd known of Noah's shortage of cash, his sponsorship offers and that there were many companies wanting to be associated with the hottest sailing talent of his generation.

Ivan had known Noah didn't want to marry Morgan…

He'd said as much and that statement was followed by a hell of an offer. Noah would receive a ridiculous amount of money to sail a yacht of his choice on the pro circuit. But the offer had come with a hell of a proviso…

All Noah had to do was stay engaged to Morgan for two years, and Ivan would triple his highest sponsorship offer. Noah's instant reaction had been to refuse but, damn…three times his nearest offer? That was a hell of a lot of cash to reject. It would be an engagement in name only, Ivan had told him, a way for Morgan to save face while he worked on getting her mentally healthy. Noah would be out of the country sailing and he only needed to send a few emails and make a couple of satellite telephone calls a month.

Oh, and Ivan had added that he had to stay away from Jules Brogan. Morgan felt threatened by his lifelong friendship with Jules and it caused her extreme distress and was a barrier to her getting well.

A week later he'd forgotten that proviso when he kissed the hell out of Jules on New Year's Eve…the kiss he kept reliving in his dreams.

Not going there, not thinking about that. Besides, thinking about Jules and Morgan wasn't helping him with this current problem: Ethan was selling his mom's house, his childhood home and the land that had been in his family for over a hundred and fifty years. That house had been the home of many generations of Lockwoods, and he'd be damned if he'd see it leave the family's hands. His grandfather had built the country club and was its founding member. His mom had been CEO of the club and estate, had kept a watchful eye on the housing development, limiting the estate to only seventy houses to retain the wide-open spaces.

Think, Noah, there's something you're missing.

Noah tapped his phone against his thigh, recalling the terms of the court settlement. Yeah, that's what had been bugging him...

He hit Redial on his phone and Eli answered. "In terms of the court settlement, Ethan has to give us the opportunity to buy the trust before he can put it on the open market."

"I don't remember that proviso," Eli said.

"If he wants to sell, he has to give us three months to buy the property. He also has to sell it to us at twenty percent below the market value."

Noah heard Eli's surprised whistle. "That's a hell of a clause."

"We had an expensive lawyer and I think it's one Ethan has accidentally on purpose forgotten."

"Then I'll contact our lawyer to enforce the terms of the settlement. But, No, even if we do get the opportunity to buy the trust—"

"We *will* get the opportunity," Noah corrected.

"—the asking price is enormous, even with the discount. It's a historic, exceptional house on a massive tract of land. Not to mention the club, the buildings, the facilities. The golf course. We're talking massive money. More than Ben and I can swing."

Noah considered this for a moment. "We'd have to mortgage it."

"The price to us should be around a hundred million," Eli said, his tone skeptical.

"We'd need to raise twenty percent." Under normal circumstances he would never be making a financial decision without a hell of a lot more due diligence. At the very least, he'd know whether the trust generated enough funds to cover the mortgage. He didn't care. This was Lockwood Estate and it was his responsibility to keep it in the family.

"Ben and I recently purchased a fifty-foot catamaran which we are restoring and that's sucked up our savings. We'll be finishing it up in a month or two and then we'll have to wait a few weeks to sell it. Even if it does sell quickly, the profit won't cover our share of the twenty-million deposit. Do you have twenty mil?"

"Not lying around. I invested in that new marina at the Boston waterfront with Levi. I'll sell my apartment in London, it's in a sought-after area and it should move quickly. I'll also sell my share in a business I own in Italy. My partner will buy me out. That would raise eight million."

"Okay. Twelve to go. Ben and I have about a million each sitting in investments we can liquefy."

Thank God his brothers were on board with this plan, that saving Lockwood Estate meant as much to them as it did to him. He couldn't do it without them. Noah ran through his assets. "I have three mil invested. That leaves seven. Crap."

Noah was silent for a long minute before speaking. "So, basically we're screwed."

Damn, his head was currently being invaded by little men with very loud jackhammers.

Eli cleared his throat. "Not necessarily. I heard that Paris Barrow wants to commission a luxury yacht and is upset because she has to wait six to ten months to get it designed. If you can put aside your distaste for designing those inelegant floating McMansions as you call them, I could set up a meeting."

"What's the budget?"

"From what I heard, about sixty million. What are your design fees? Ten percent of the price? That's six mil and I'm sure we can scrounge up another million between us. Somehow."

Noah thought for a moment. He had various projects in the works but none that would provide a big enough paycheck to secure the house. Designing a superyacht would. At the very least he had to try. Noah gripped the bridge of his nose with his forefinger and thumb and stepped off the cliff. "Set up a meeting with your client's friend. Let's see where it goes."

"She's a megawealthy Boston grande dame, and designing for her would mean coming back home," Eli said softly.

Yeah, he got that. "I know."

Noah disconnected the call and stared down at his bare feet. He was both excited and terrified to be returning to the city he'd been avoiding for the past ten years. Boston meant facing his past, but it also meant reconnecting and spending time with Levi, Eli and Ben, DJ, and Darby.

And Callie. God, he'd missed her so much.

But Boston was synonymous with Jules, the only person whom he'd ever let under his protective shell. His best friend until he'd mucked it all up by kissing her, ignoring her, remaining engaged to a woman she intensely disliked and then dropping out of her life.

She still hadn't forgiven him and he doubted that she ever would.

Jules...

Jules frowned at the for-sale sign that had appeared on the lawn of Lockwood House and swung into the driveway of her childhood home—and her new digs—and slammed on the brakes when she noticed a matte black Ducati parked in her usual space next to the detached garage. Swearing, she guided her car into the tiny space next to it and cursed her brother for parking what had to be his latest toy in her space.

Jules looked at the for-sale sign again. She was surprised that the Lockwood boys would let the house go out of their family but, as she well knew, maintaining a residence the size of the houses on this estate cost an arm and a leg and a few internal organs. Jules shoved her fist into the space beneath her rib cage to ease the burn. She'd spent as much time in that house as she had her own, sneaking in and out of Noah's bedroom. But that was back in the days when they were still friends, before he'd met Morgan and before he'd spoiled everything by kissing her senseless.

It had been a hell of a kiss and that was part of the problem. If it had been a run-of-the-mill, *meh* kiss, she could brush it aside, but it was still—*aargh!*—the kiss she measured all other kisses against. Passionate, sweet, tender, hot.

Pity it came courtesy of her onetime best friend and an all-around jerk.

Jules used her key to let herself into the empty house. It was still early, just past eight in the morning, but her siblings would've left for work hours ago. Thanks to efficient workmen and an easy client, her Napa Valley project had gone off without a hitch and as a result, she'd finished two weeks early, which was unexpectedly wonderful. Since winning Boston's Most Exciting Interior Designer award five months ago, she'd been running from one project to another, constantly in demand. For the next few days, maybe a week, she could take it a little easier: sleep later, go home earlier, catch her breath. Chill.

God, she so needed to chill, to de-stress and to rest her overworked mind and body. Despite her business-class seat, she was stiff from her late-night cross-country flight. Jules pulled herself up the wooden stairs, instinctively missing the squeaky floorboards that used to tell a wide-awake parent, or curious sibling, she was taking an unauthorized leave from the house.

Parking her rolling suitcase outside her closed bedroom door, and knowing the house was empty, Jules headed for the family bathroom at the end of the hall, pulling her grubby silk T-shirt from her pants and up and over her head. Opening the door to the bathroom, she tossed the shirt toward the laundry hamper in the corner and stepped into the bathroom.

Hot steam slapped her in the face. A second later she registered the heavy and familiar beat of the powerful shower in the corner of the room. Whipping around and expecting to see Darby or DJ, her mouth fell open at the—God, let's call it what it was—*vision* standing in the glass enclosure.

Six feet four inches of tanned skin gliding over defined muscles, hair slicked off an angles-and-planes face, brown eyes flecked with gold. A wide chest, lightly dusted with blond hair and a hard, ridged stomach. Sexy hip muscles that drew the eye down to a thatch of darker hair and a, frankly, impressive package. A package that was growing with every breath he took.

Noah...

God, Noah was back and he was standing in her shower looking like Michelangelo's *David* on a very, very good day.

Jules lifted her eyes to his face and the desire in his

gaze caused her breath to hitch and all the moisture in her mouth to disappear. Jules swallowed, willed her feet to move but they remained glued to the tiled floor. She couldn't breathe. She couldn't think. All she wanted to do was touch. Since that was out of the question—God, she hadn't seen him in ten years, she couldn't just jump him!—she just looked, allowing her eyes to feast.

Noah. God. In her bathroom. Naked.

Without dropping his eyes from hers, Noah switched off the water and pushed his hair off his face. Opening the door to the shower cubicle, he stepped out onto the mat and placed his hands on his narrow hips. Jules dropped her gaze and, yep, much bigger than before. Strong, hard...

Were either of them ever going to speak, to turn away, to break this crazy, passion-saturated atmosphere? What was *wrong* with them?

Jules was trying to talk her feet into moving when Noah stepped up to her and placed a wet hand on her cheek, his thumb sliding across her lower lip. He smelled of soap and shampoo and hot, aroused male. Lust, as hot and thick as warm molasses, slid into her veins and pooled between her legs. Keeping her hands at her sides, she looked up at Noah, conscious of his erection brushing the bare skin above the waistband of her pants, her nipples stretching the fabric of her lace bra.

Noah just stared at her, the gold flecks in his eyes bright with desire, and then his mouth, that sexy, sexy mouth, dropped onto hers. His hands slid over her bare waist and down her butt, pulling her into his wet, hard body. Jules gasped as his tongue flicked between the seam of her lips and she opened up with no thought of resistance.

It was an exaggerated version of the kiss they'd shared

so long ago. This was a kiss on steroids, bold, hotter and wetter than before. Noah's arms were stronger, his mouth more demanding, his intent clear. His hand moved across her skin with confidence and control, settling on her right breast. He pulled down the cup of her bra, and then her breast was pressed into his palm, skin on skin. She whimpered and Noah growled, his thumb teasing her nipple with rough, sexy strokes.

Jules lifted her hands to touch him, wanting to feel those ridges of his stomach on her fingertips, wrap her hand around his—

Holy crap! What the hell? Jules jerked away from him, lifting her hands up when he stepped toward her, intent on picking up where they left off.

Jules slapped her open hand against his still-wet chest and pushed him back. Furious now, she glared up at him. "What the hell, Lockwood? You do not walk back into my life and start kissing me without a damn word! Did you really think that we would end up naked on the bathroom floor?"

"I'm already naked." Noah looked down at her flushed chest, her pointed nipples and her wet-from-his-kiss mouth. "And, yeah, it definitely looked and felt like we were heading in that direction."

Jules opened her mouth to blast him and, flummoxed, couldn't find the words. "I— You— Crap!"

Noah reached behind her for a towel and slowly, oh, so slowly, wrapped it around his hips. He had the balls to smile and Jules wanted to slap him silly. "So, how much does it suck to know that the attraction hasn't faded?"

Jules glared at him, muttered a low curse and turned on her heel and walked toward the open door.

"Jules?"

Jules took her time turning around. "What?"

Noah grinned, his big arms folded across his chest. "Hi. Good to see you."

Jules did her goldfish impression again and, shaking her head, headed to her bedroom. Had that really happened? Was she hallucinating? Jules looked down and saw that the fabric of her bra was wet, water droplets covered her shoulders and ran down her stomach.

Nope, she wasn't dreaming the sexiest dream ever. Noah was back and this was her life.

So this was her punishment for finishing a project early?

Unfair, Universe. Because all she wanted to do was catch a plane back to Napa Valley and Jules hunted for a reason to return to the project she'd just wrapped up. Jules ran through her mental checklist and, dammit, she'd definitely covered all her bases. The workmanship was exemplary, the client was ecstatic and his check was in the bank. There wasn't the smallest reason to haul her butt out of this house and fly back to California.

Balls!

After three months in California she'd desperately wanted to come home, to unpack the boxes stacked against the wall and to catch up with Darby and DJ, her best friends but also her business partners. Darby, her twin, was Winston and Brogan's architect. Jules was the interior designer, and DJ managed the business end of their design and decor company. She spoke to both of them numerous times a day but she wanted to hug them, to be a part of their early-morning meetings instead of Skyping in, to share an icy bottle of wine at the end of the day.

Jules scowled. It was very damn interesting to note that during any one of those many daily conversations one of them could've told her that Noah was back in Boston.

Five words, not difficult. "Noah is back in Boston."

Or even better: "Noah is back in Boston, living in our house."

He was tall and built and it wasn't like they could've missed him!

Jules sat down on the edge of her bed, her feet bouncing off something unfamiliar. Looking down, she saw a pair of men's flat-heeled, size thirteen boots. Lifting her head, she looked around her bedroom. A man's shirt lay over the back of her red-and-white-checked chair, a leather wallet and a phone were on her dressing table. No doubt Noah's clothes were in her closet, too. Noah was not only back in her life, he'd moved into her bedroom and, literally, into her bed.

Jules frantically pushed the buttons on her phone, cursing when neither Darby nor DJ answered her call. She left less-than-happy messages on their voice mails and she was about to call Levi—who hadn't shared the news either—when her phone vibrated with an incoming call.

"Mom, guess what I found in the house when I got home a little while ago?" Jules asked, super sarcastic. "Guess you didn't know that Noah was home either, huh?"

"Damn, you found him."

In the shower, gloriously, wonderfully naked. *Spectacularly naked and I must've looked at him like I wanted to eat him up like ice cream because, before saying a damn word, he kissed the hell out of me.* "Yeah, I found Noah."

"I told your siblings to tell you," Callie said.

Hearing a noise coming from her mom's phone, Jules frowned. "Where are you?"

"At a delightful coffee shop that's just opened up next to the gym at LCC," Callie replied. "Amazing ambience and delicious coffee—"

"And the owner is really good-looking!" A deep voice floated over the phone and was quickly followed by Callie's flirty laugh. Wait...what? Her mom was flirting?

"Is he?" Jules asked, intrigued enough to briefly change the subject.

"Is he what?" Callie replied, playing dumb.

Really, they were going to play this game? "Good-looking, Mom."

"I suppose so. But too young and too fit for me."

"I'll admit to the fit but not to the too young. What's ten years?" the cheerful voice boomed. "Tell your mom to accept a date from me!"

Well, go, Mom! Despite her annoyance at her family in general, Jules laughed, listening as her mom shushed the man. "Maybe you should take the guy up on his offer. Might be fun."

"I'm not discussing him with you, Jules," Callie said, and Jules was sure she could hear her blushing.

Since Callie normally shared everything with her daughters, Jules knew this man had her unflappable mom more flustered than she cared to admit. Now, that was interesting. Before Jules could interrogate her further, Callie spoke. "So, how do you feel about Noah being back in Boston?"

Sidewinded. Horny. Crazy. Flabbergasted.

Not wanting her mom to know how deeply she was affected by this news—hell, the world was Jell-O beneath her feet—Jules let out an exasperated laugh. "It's not a big deal, Mom. Noah is entitled to come home."

"Oh, please, you've been dreading this day for years."

Jules stared down at the glossy wooden floors beneath her feet. "Don't be ridiculous, Mother."

"Jules, you've been terrified of this day because you'll no longer be able to leave your relationship with Noah in limbo. Seeing him again either means cutting him out of your life for good or forgiving him."

"There's nothing to forgive him for." Okay, she had a couple of minor issues with that gorgeous, six-foot-plus slab of defined muscles. Things like him getting engaged to a woman he didn't love and kissing her on New Year's Eve while he was engaged. And then for remaining engaged to Morgan, disappearing from her life without an explanation—she was still furious that he dropped out of college without finishing his degree—and not trying to reconnect with her when he and Morgan had finally called it quits.

In the space of seven years, the two men she loved the most, her best friend and her dad, had dropped out of her life without rhyme, reason or explanation. Her dad had been healthy, too healthy to be taken by a massive heart attack but that was exactly what happened.

Jules doubted there was a reasonable explanation for Noah abandoning her and their lifelong friendship, for not being there at her dad's funeral to hold her hand through the grief.

Okay, maybe that last one wasn't fair; Noah had been in the middle of his last race as a professional sailor at the time.

"No more coffee for me, Mason," Callie said, snapping Jules out of her wayward thoughts.

She grabbed her mom's words like a lifeline. "Mason is a nice name. Is he hot? If he's too young for you, can I meet him?"

"He's far too old for you and not your type." Well, that

was a quick reply…and a tad snappy. Did her mom have the hots for Coffee Guy? And why not? It was time she started living for herself again.

"I don't have a type, Mom," Jules replied, and she didn't. She dated men of all types and ethnicities but none of them stuck. She didn't need a psych degree to know that losing the two men she loved and trusted the most turned her into a card-carrying, picket-sign-holding commitment-phobe.

"Of course you do—your type is blond and brown-eyed and has a body that would make Michelangelo weep."

She hadn't said anything about Michelangelo, had she? How did her mom know that? "Why do you say that?"

"I'm old, not dead, Jules. The boy is gorgeous."

Noah, wet and naked, flashed behind her eyes. *Goddammit.* Like she needed reminding.

"You need to deal with him, Jules. This situation needs to be resolved."

Why? Noah had made his feelings about her perfectly clear when he dropped out of her life. She'd received nothing from him but the occasional group email he sent to the whole clan, telling them about his racing and, after he retired from sailing, his yacht design business. He didn't mention anything personal, instead sharing his witty and perceptive observations about the places he visited and the people he met.

His news was interesting but told Jules nothing about his thoughts and feelings and, once having had access to both, she wasn't willing to settle for so little, so she never bothered to reply. For someone who'd had as much of his soul as he could give, she'd needed more, dammit…

"Mom. God, just butt out, okay?"

There was silence on the other end of the phone but

Jules ignored it, knowing that it was her mom's way of showing her disapproval. "Mom, the silent treatment won't work. This is between Noah and me. Stay out of it."

Jules rubbed the back of her neck, feeling guilty at snapping. Her mother had mastered the art of nagging by remaining utterly silent. How did she do that? How?

"Mom, I know you love me but I need you to trust me to do what's best with regard to Noah." Not that she had any bright ideas except to avoid him.

"The problem, my darling, is that you and Noah are so damn pigheaded! Sort it out, Jules. I am done with this cold war."

Jules heard the click that told her Callie had disconnected the call and stared at her phone, bemused. Her mom rarely sounded rattled and considered hanging up to be the height of rudeness. But as much as she loved her mother, she was an adult and had to run her life as she saw fit. That meant leaving her relationship with Noah in the past, where it belonged.

Jules looked up, waited for the lightning strike—her mom, she was convinced, had a direct line to God—and when she remained unfried, she sighed. What to do?

Her first instinct was to run...

Jules heard the bathroom door open and, hearing Noah's footsteps, headed down the hallway in her direction, flew to her feet. Grabbing her bag off the bed, she pulled it over her shoulder and hurried to the door. She pulled it open and nearly plowed into Noah, still bare-chested, still with only a towel around his waist. *Do not look down, do not get distracted. Just push past him and leave...*

"I'm going out, but by the time I return, I want you and your stuff out of my room," Jules stated in the firmest voice she could find.

"Levi said that you were away for another two weeks.

He insisted I stay here when he picked me up from the airport yesterday. I'll find a hotel room or bunk on the *Resilience*."

His forty-foot turn-of-the-century monohull that he kept berthed at the marina. The yacht, commissioned by his great-great-grandfather was his favorite possession. It was small but luxurious, and Noah would always choose sleeping on the *Resilience* over a hotel.

"How long are you staying?" She needed to know when her life was going to go back to normal. With a date and a time, the Jell-O would, hopefully, solidify into hard earth.

"I'm not sure. A month? Maybe two?"

Great. She was in for four to eight weeks of crazy. Like her life wasn't busy and stressful enough. Jules rubbed her forehead with her fingers. God, she did not need to deal with this now. Today. Ever. Seeing him created a soup of emotion, sour and sticky. Lust, grief, hurt, disappointment, passion…

All she wanted to do was step into his arms and tell him that she'd missed him so damn much, missed the boy who'd known her so well. That she wanted to know, in a carnal way, the man he was now.

Jules shook her head and pushed past him, almost running to the stairs. *Sort it out, Mom?*

Much, much easier said than done.

Two

Callie...

After a brief and tense conversation with Levi, Callie dropped her forehead to the table and banged her head on the smooth surface. Levi reluctantly admitted to her that none of them told Jules that Noah was back. Nor had they informed her that Noah was sleeping in Jules's bedroom at her old house.

Really, and these people called themselves adults?

Aargh!

The whisper of a broad hand skated over her hair and she lifted her head a half inch off the table to glare at Mason. With his dark brown hair showing little gray, barely any lines around his denim-blue eyes and his still-hard body, the owner of the new coffee shop looked closer to forty than to the forty-five he claimed to be. Yes, he was sexy. Yes, he was charming, but why, oh, why—in a room filled with so many good-looking women, most of them younger, slimmer and prettier than her—was he paying her any attention?

Mason slid a latte under her nose and took the empty seat across from her. Callie glared at him, annoyed that he made her feel so flustered. And, holy cupcakes, was that lust curling low in her now-useless womb? "Did I invite you to sit down?"

"Don't be snippy," Mason said, resting his ropy, muscled forearms on the table. "What's the matter?"

Callie thought about blowing his question off but suddenly she wanted to speak to someone with no connection to her annoying clan. "I'm arguing with my daughter." Callie sipped her coffee and eyed Mason over her mug. Because his expression, encouraging her to confide in him, scared her, she backtracked.

"She asked if you were good-looking, whether she could meet you. She's gorgeous, tall, dark-haired with the most amazing light silver-blue eyes."

"She sounds lovely but I have my heart set on dating a short, curvy blonde."

Callie looked around, wondering who he was talking about. His low, growly laugh pulled her eyes back to his amused face. "You, you twit. I want to take *you* on a date."

"I thought you were joking."

"Nope. Deadly serious."

Okay, this was weird. He seemed nice and genuine, but what was his game? "You don't want to date me, Mason."

"I've been making up my own mind for a while now and you don't get to tell me what I do and don't want." Mason's tone was soft but Callie heard the steel in his voice and, dammit, that hard note just stoked that ember of lust. Man, it had been so long since she'd felt like this around a guy, she didn't know what to say, how to act.

For the first time in thirty-plus years she wanted to kiss someone who wasn't her husband, to explore another man's body. The problem was, while he was a fine specimen for his age, she was not. Her boobs sagged, she had a muffin top and lumpy thighs. Despite her wish for sex, a one-night stand, that was more hope than expectation. And if she found the courage to expose her very flawed body to a new man, he wouldn't have the lean, muscled body of a competitive swimmer.

Mason made her feel insecure and, worse, old. There were, after all, ten years between them and, God, what a difference ten years could make. Age, the shape their bodies were in, and then there was the difference in their financial situations.

She was, not to exaggerate, filthy rich. Mason, she'd heard, was not. Did he know how wealthy she was? Was he looking for a, *ugh*, sugar mommy? What was his angle?

"Tell me about your daughter," Mason said, leaning back in his chair.

Yeah, good plan. When he heard about her family he'd go running for the hills. "Which one? I have two by blood, one by love. I also have four sons, one by blood."

Mason blinked, ran his hand over his face and Callie laughed at his surprise. "Do you have kids?"

"Two teenage boys, fifteen and seventeen."

"My youngest, Ben, is twenty-eight," Callie said, deliberately highlighting the differences in their ages again.

"You old crone." Mason sighed, stood up and pushed his chair into the table. He placed one hand on the table, one on the back of her chair, and caged her in. His determined blue eyes drilled into hers. "You can keep fighting this, Callie, but you and I are going on a date."

The Ping-Pong ball in her throat swelled and the air left the room. He was so close that Callie could see a small scar on his upper lip, taste his sweet, coffee-flavored breath.

"And while I'm here, I might as well tell you that you and I are also going to get naked. At some point, I'm going to make you mine."

Callie was annoyed when tears burned, furious when her heart rate accelerated. "I'm not... I can't... I'm not ready."

Mason's steady expression didn't change. "I didn't say it was going to be today, Callie. But one day you will be ready and—" he lifted his hands to mimic an explosion "—boom."

Boom. Really? Callie blinked away her tears and straightened her spine. "Seriously? Does that work on other women?"

"Dunno, since you're the only one I've ever said it to." Mason bent down to drop a kiss into her hair. "Start getting used to the idea, Cal. Oh, and butt out of your kids' lives. At twenty-eight and older, they can make their own decisions."

Callie scowled at his bare back as he walked away from her. Really! Who was he to tell her how to interact with her children? And how dare he tell her that he was going to take her to bed? Did he really think that he could make a statement like that and she'd roll over and whimper her delight? He was an arrogant know-it-all with the confidence of a Hollywood A-lister.

But he also, she noticed, had a very fine butt. A butt she wouldn't mind feeling under her hands.

Noah...

Noah would've preferred to meet with Paris Barrow at her office—did the multidivorced, once-widowed socialite have an office?—but Paris insisted on meeting for a drink at April, a Charles Street bar. Hopefully, since it was late afternoon, the bar would be quiet and he could pin Paris down to some specifics with regard to the design of her yacht. Engine capacity, size, whether she wanted a monohull or a catamaran. He had to have some place to start. Oh, and getting her to sign a damn contract would be nice—at least he would be getting paid for the work he was doing.

But Paris, he decided after couple of frustrating conversations, had the attention span of a gnat...

Noah pushed his way into the bar. Another slick bar in another rich city; he'd seen many of them over the years. Looking around, he saw that his client had yet to arrive, and after ordering a beer, he slid onto a banquette, dropping his folder on the bench beside him.

It was his second full day back in Boston and, in some ways it felt like he'd never left. After being kicked out of the Brogan house by his favorite pain in the ass, he spent last night on the *Resilience* and his brothers and Levi had each brought a six-pack. They'd steadily made their way through the beers while sitting on the teak deck, their legs dangling off the side of the yacht. No one had mentioned his abrupt departure from the house and he was glad. The last thing he wanted to discuss was Jules and the past.

Noah murmured his thanks when the waitress put his beer in front of him. Taking a sip, he wished he could make the memory of Jules standing in the bathroom, looking dazed and turned on, disappear as easily as he did this beer. He'd heard the door open and turned and there she was, shirtless in the bathroom, a wet dream fantasy in full Technicolor. Her hair was around her shoulders, her slim body curvier than before, her surprisingly plump breasts covered by a pale pink lace bra. He'd immediately noticed the darker pink of her pert nipples and her flushed skin.

Then he'd made the mistake of meeting her eyes.

Noah shifted in his chair, his junk swelling at the memory. Emotions had slid in and out of her eyes; there was surprise and shock, and it was obvious that nobody had told her that he was back in town. But those emotions quickly died and he'd caught the hint of hurt before appreciation—and, yeah, flat-out furious lust—took over. Her eyes had traced his body and he knew exactly what she was thinking, because, God, he'd been thinking it, too.

He wanted her…his hands on her long, slim body, his mouth on her lips, her skin, on her secret, make-her-scream places. Whatever they started with that one kiss so long ago hadn't died. It had been slumbering for the past ten years.

Well, it was back, wide-awake and roaring and clawing…

The impulse to kiss her, to taste her again had been overwhelming, so he had. And it was as good—no, freakin' spectacular—as he thought it could be. He'd thought about dragging her back into the shower, stripping her under the water and taking her up against the tile wall. He still wanted to do that more than he wanted to breathe.

He was so screwed…

"Noah? Noah?"

Noah jerked himself out of his reverie and looked up into Paris's merry blue eyes, her face devoid of lines. Standing up—hoping he wouldn't embarrass himself—he took her outstretched hand. She looked damn good for someone in her sixties, thanks to the marvel of modern plastic surgery.

Paris sat down opposite him and put her designer bag on the table. She ordered a martini, and after the smallest of small talk, she leaned back against the banquette, eyeing him. "So, I understand that you were once engaged to Morgan Blake."

Oh, Jesus. Noah kept his face blank and waited for her to continue. "I told her that you were designing a yacht for me—"

"Well, technically I'm not. Yet," Noah clarified. "You haven't signed the contract, nor have you paid me my deposit, so right now we're still negotiating."

Paris wrinkled her nose before opening her bag and pulling out a leather case. She flipped it open and Noah saw that it was a checkbook. Paris found a pen and lifted her eyebrows. Noah gave her the figure, his heart racing as she wrote out the check. Taking it, he tucked it into his shirt pocket before withdrawing a contract from his folder. Paris signed it with a flourish and tossed her gold pen onto the table. One payment down and he'd receive the bulk of the money when she approved his final design. "Now, can we talk about Morgan?"

"No."

Paris pouted. "Why not?"

"Because we need to talk about hulls and engines and square feet and water displacement. I'm designing the yacht, but I do need some input from you," Noah said, his voice calm but firm.

Paris looked bored. "Just design me a fantastic yacht within the budget I gave you. I hear that you are ridiculously talented and wonderfully creative. Design me a vessel that will make people drool. I don't want to be bothered by the details."

The perfect scenario, Noah thought, pleased. There was nothing better than getting a green light to do what he wanted. He just hoped that Paris wouldn't change her mind down the track and morph into a nitpicking, demanding, micromanaging client. But if she did, he would handle her.

Noah handed Paris her copy of the contract, wincing when she folded it into an uneven square and shoved it into the side pocket of her bag. She drained her martini and signaled the waitress for another. "So, about Morgan."

God. Really? "Paris, I don't feel comfortable discussing this with you. You're my client."

Paris waved his measured words away. "Oh, please! I'm an absolute romantic and a terrible meddler. I nose around in everyone's business. You'll get used to it."

He most definitely would not. "There is no Morgan, Paris. That ended a long, long time ago."

"Oh, I got the impression she'd like to pick up where you left off."

Okay, it was way past time to shut this down. "Yeah, my girlfriend might object to that."

Paris's eyes gleamed with interest. "You have a girlfriend? Who is she?"

He could've mentioned Jenna in Cape Town or Yolande in London, who were both beautiful and accomplished good friends he occasionally slept with. But another name popped out of his mouth, thanks, he was sure, to a hot encounter in a bathroom yesterday morning. "Jules Brogan."

Paris's eyes widened with delight. "I know Jules. She decorated my vacation house in Hyannis Port."

Oh, crap! Crap, crap, crap.

"She was named Boston's Most Exciting Interior Designer a few months back."

She was? Why had he not heard about that? Probably the same reason the family hadn't told Jules about his return. They didn't discuss either of them ever.

"She's your girlfriend?"

"We've known each other for a long time." That, at least, was the truth.

Paris's pink mouth widened into a huge smile. "She can do the interior decoration for my yacht. Aren't you supposed to give me an idea of the interior when you present the final design?"

Oh, hell, he didn't like this. At all. "Yes. But I have my team of decorators I normally work with in London," Noah stated, wondering how this conversation had veered so off track. Oh, right, maybe because he *lied*?

"I want Jules," Paris said, looking stubborn. Her face hardened and Noah caught a glimpse of a woman who always got what she wanted. "Do not make me tear up that contract and ask for my check back, Noah."

Je-sus. Noah rubbed the back of his neck. She would do exactly as she said. Paris wanted what she wanted and expected to get it. *No* did not feature in her vocabulary.

Noah leaned back, sighed and eyed his pain-in-the-ass client. "You're going to be a handful, aren't you?" he asked, resigned.

Paris's expression lightened. "Oh, honey, you have no idea. So, what should I tell Morgan?"

Noah groaned and ordered a double whiskey.

Jules...

Jules heard the muted sound coming from her phone and, without looking at the screen, silenced the alert. Eight thirty in the morning and today was, Jules squinted at the bottom right corner of her computer, Thursday.

The only way to stop thinking about Noah, and his wet, naked, ripped body, and the fact that he was back in her orbit, was to go back to work. Instead of taking the break she needed, she slid right back into sixteen-hour days and creating long and detailed schedules so that nothing slipped through the cracks.

Jules moved her mouse and today's to-do list appeared on her monitor.

The reminder of her 9:00 a.m. meeting with the girls was followed by a list of her appointments with clients, suppliers and craftspeople. Her last appointment was at five thirty, and then she had to hustle to make her appointment with her beautician, Dana, for an eyebrow shape and a bikini wax. She was not going to dwell on the fact that the bikini wax was a last-minute request.

It had nothing to do with looking good for a brown-eyed blond.

You keep telling yourself that, sweet pea.

Jules reached for her cup of now-cold coffee and pulled a face when the icy liquid hit the back of her throat. Yuck. Resisting the urge to wipe her tongue on the sleeve of her white button-down shirt, she pushed back her chair. Her phone released the discreet trill of an incoming call and Jules frowned down at the screen, not recognizing the number. As early as it was, she couldn't ignore the call; too many of her clients and suppliers had this number and she needed to be available to anybody at any time.

"Jules."

She recognized his voice instantly, the way he said her name, the familiar tone sliding over her skin. "Noah."

There had been a time when she'd laugh with excitement to get a call from him, when her heart would swell from just hearing his voice. But those were childish reactions and she was no longer the child who'd hero-worshipped Noah, or the teenager who'd thought the sun rose and set with him. He was no longer her best friend, the person she could say anything to, the one person who seemed to get her on a deeper level than even her twin did.

"What do you want, Lockwood?"

"We need to talk."

"Exactly what I said to you ten years ago," Jules said, wincing at the bitterness in her voice. After their kiss, he'd avoided her, ducked her calls. She hadn't suspected he was leaving until he came by her mom's house one evening to say goodbye. The kiss was never mentioned. When she asked to speak to him privately he'd refused, explaining that he didn't have time, that there was nothing to discuss. He and Morgan were still engaged. He was dropping out of college. He was going sailing. He didn't know how often he would be in contact.

Please don't worry about him. He'd be fine.

She'd been so damn happy to receive his first email, had soaked up his news, happy to know that he was safe and leading the race. He'd spoken about the brilliant sunsets, a pod of southern right whales, a squall they'd encountered that day, the lack of winds the next. Reading his words made her feel like they were connected again, that their relationship could be salvaged...

Then she noticed the email was sent to a group and that her mom, her siblings, his siblings, plus a few of his college buds, received the same message. Jules never received a personalized email, nor did she receive one of his infrequent calls back home. She'd been relegated to the periphery of his life and it stung like a band of fire ants walking over her skin. She still didn't understand how someone who meant everything to her had vanished like he was never part of her life at all.

"There's nothing to say, Noah. Too much water under the hull and all that. We're adults. We can be civil in company, but let's not try and resurrect something that is very definitely over."

"Oh, it's not over, Jules. We're just starting a new chapter of a yet-unwritten book," Noah replied softly. Then his voice strengthened and turned businesslike. "I do need to talk to you—I need to hire you."

Jules dropped her phone, stared at the screen and shook her head. "Yeah, that's not going to happen. Speaking of work, I'm late for a meeting."

"Do not hang up on me, Ju—"

Jules pressed the red phone icon on her screen and tossed the device onto her messy desk. Work with him? Seriously? Not in this lifetime.

The display room of Winston and Brogan doubled as a conference room, and most mornings Jules, Darby and DJ started their day with a touch-base meeting, drinking their coffee as the early-morning Charles Street pedestrians passed by their enormous window. Jules sat down on a porcelain-blue-and-white-striped chair and thought that it was time to redesign their showroom. It was small, but it was the first impression clients received when they walked through the door, and it was time for something new, fresh.

"Creams or blush or jewel colors?" Jules threw the question into the silence before taking a sip of her caramel latte.

Darby didn't look up from her phone. "Jewel colors. Let's make this place pop."

"Whatever you two think is best," DJ replied, as she always did. Jules smiled, her friend was a whiz with money but, unlike her and Darby, she didn't have a creative bone in her body. They made an effective team. Darby designed buildings. Jules decorated them, and DJ managed their money.

The fact that they worked so well together was the main reason their full house design firm was one of the best in the city. Oh, they fought… They'd known each other all of their lives and they knew exactly what buttons to push to get a nuclear reaction. But they never fought dirty and none of them held grudges. Well, she would if they allowed her to, which they never did.

Darby crossed her legs and Jules admired the spiky heel dangling off her foot. The shoe was a perfect shade of nude with a heart-shaped peep toe. So, she'd be borrowing those soon. Hell, they'd shared the same womb, sharing clothes was a given.

"Tina Harper, she was at college with us, is pregnant. Four months." Darby looked up from her cell and Jules noticed that her smile was forced. Her heart contracted, knowing that under that brave face her sister ached for what could not be. When they were teenagers, Darby was told that, thanks to chronic endometriosis, the chances of her conceiving a child were slim to none. Closer to none… It was her greatest wish to be a mama, with or without a man. And the way their love lives were progressing, it would probably be without one.

"Didn't she date Ben?" DJ asked.

Darby shrugged. "God, I don't know. At one point, Ben had a revolving door to his bedroom."

"Ben still has a revolving door to his bedroom," Jules pointed out, thinking of the youngest Lockwood brother. He was probably the best-looking of the three gorgeous Lockwood boys and he was never short of a date or five. She could say the same for her brother, Levi, and Eli and, she assumed, Noah.

Noah. Jules sucked her bottom lip between her teeth. As always, just thinking his name dropped her stomach to the floor, caused her heart to bounce off her rib cage. Remembering their half-naked kiss threatened to stop her heart altogether.

"So, how does it feel having Noah back?" DJ asked.

"He's back in your life, not mine," Jules replied, trying to sound casual.

She'd been interrogated by every member of her family so they could find out what had caused the cold war between her and Noah. Her stock answer, "We just drifted apart," resulted in rolling eyes and disbelieving snorts but she never elaborated. They periodically still asked her for an explanation. She knew Noah was staying mum because a) Noah wasn't the type to dish, and b) if he had, then the news would've spread like wildfire. The Brogan/Lockwood clan was not known for discretion. Or keeping good gossip to themselves.

Sometimes she was tempted to tell them that she and Noah had shared some blisteringly hot kisses just to see the expression on their faces. But then the questions would follow... Why hadn't they explored that attraction? Why couldn't they get past it?

It was a question that, when she allowed it to, kept her up at night. Why hadn't they dealt with the situation, addressed the belly dancing elephant in the room?

Ah, maybe it was because, shortly after kissing her ten years back, Noah flew Morgan to Vegas to, she assumed, celebrate their engagement. Their kiss, him dropping out of college, his engagement, him turning pro... He'd made every decision without asking her opinion. Okay, she understood that he wasn't obliged to check in with her but she had run everything past him and he did talk to her about his dreams, his plans. That Christmas season, Noah had clammed up and it felt like twenty-plus years of friendship had meant nothing to him…

That he and Morgan never married wasn't a surprise, nor was it a consolation. He'd wasted two years of his time, his money and attention on Morgan, but it was his time and money to waste. Still, Jules couldn't help feeling that his engagement was a big "up yours" to their newly discovered attraction. His lack of communication, blasé explanations and his lack of effort to maintain their friendship had severed their connection. Because she would never be able to fully trust him again, they could never be friends again.

And being lovers was out of the question. That required an even deeper level of trust she was incapable of feeling.

"Did you date anyone in California?" Darby asked her, pulling her attention off the past.

She had actually. "Mmm."

"Really? And…?" Darby asked, intrigued.

"Two dates and I called it quits. Since we live on opposite sides of the country, there was no point."

She always gave guys two dates to make an impression before she moved on, thinking that dating was stressful and who got anything right the first date? If they had potential, she extended the period, making sure that hands and mouths stayed out of the equation. Not many made it to twelve weeks and most of those didn't pass her was-he-a-better-kisser-than-Noah? test. Actually, none of them were better kissers, but the two who came close made it into her bed. One lasted another few weeks; the other went back to his ex-girlfriend.

She hadn't had a relationship that went beyond four months since college…and at nearly thirty she'd only had three lovers. How sad was that?

Yet, she continued to date, thinking that one day she'd find someone who made her forget about that nuclear hot kiss on a snowy evening so damn long ago. She had to find someone. There was no way she'd allow her best sexual memory to be of Noah Lockwood...ten years or four days ago.

"Maybe I should go back on Tinder," Jules mused, mostly to herself. But at the thought, her heart backed into the corner of her chest, comprehensively horrified. She didn't blame it, meeting guys on the internet was a crappy way to find love. Or to find a date with a reasonably normal man.

"Oh, come on," DJ retorted, calling her bluff. "Psychos, weirdos and losers. You don't need any of that."

"Says the girl who has sex on a semiregular basis," Jules murmured. Since college, DJ had an on-off relationship with Matt, a human rights lawyer, who dropped in and out of her life. It was all about convenience, DJ blithely informed them, and about great sex with a guy she liked and respected.

Jules wanted one of those.

"Please stay off the net, Jules," Darby begged. "You are a magnet for crazies."

Jules couldn't argue the point. All she wanted was to meet guys like her brother and Eli and Ben. Despite their grasshopper mentality when it came to women, the three of them—even, dammit, Noah—were interesting, smart, driven and successful men. They were honest and trustworthy—well, three out of four were—and she wanted a man like them and her dad. Was she asking too much? Were her brother and her friends the last good men left in Boston? And if she found that elusive man, would she ever be able to trust him not to hurt her long enough for her to fall in love? Or would her fear send her running?

DJ gently kicked her shin with the toe of her shoe and Jules blinked, lifting a shoulder at DJ's scowl. "What?"

"Why don't you take a break from dating for a while, Jules? You've been scraping the barrel lately. Whatever you are looking for, you're not finding."

Darby tipped her head. "What *are* you looking for?"

Jules stared out of the window. *I'm looking for a guy who makes me feel as alive as I do when Noah kisses me. I'm looking for a guy who will make me stop thinking about him, stop missing him, who will fill the hole he left in my life. I'm looking for someone who will make me feel the same way I did during that bold, bright moment the other day. Noah can't be the only man who can make me feel intensely alive... That would be cruel. No, there is someone else out there. There has to be...*

Noah was the only man who made her explore the outer edges of love and despair, attraction and loathing. Kissing Noah made her feel sexy and feminine and powerful beyond measure. But his actions when they were younger made her feel insignificant and irrelevant. He'd hurtled her from nirvana into a hell she hadn't been prepared for.

He'd dismissed her opinions, ignored her counsel, and those actions she could, maybe, forgive. But she'd never forgive him for destroying their friendship, for flicking her out of his life like she was a piece of filthy gum stuck to his shoe.

DJ clapped her hands, signaling that she was moving into work mode. Jules forced herself to think business. She had designs to draw up for a revamp to a historic bed-and-breakfast, craftspeople to meet to finalize the furnishings for a bar in Back Bay. Maybe she should stop dating for a while and immerse herself in work.

They had enough of it to keep them all busy for months, if not years.

"Profit and loss, expense reports... I need your receipts," DJ said, and Jules wrinkled her nose. "I need the cost estimates on the Duncan job."

"Ack," Jules said. She loved designing but hated the paperwork it generated. "Deadline?"

"Yesterday."

"Hard-ass," Jules muttered.

"I am," DJ replied, not at all insulted. "That's why we are in the black, darling. It's all me."

Darby and Jules laughed, knowing that DJ was joking. They were a team and each of them was an essential cog in the wheel. As always, they were stronger together.

Darby looked at her watch and stood up, nearly six feet of tall grace. Jules looked out of the window and lifted her hand to wave at Dani, the personal assistant they shared, Merry, their shop floor assistant and their two interns.

Her smiled faded when she saw who was standing behind them, six feet four inches of muscle wearing chinos, a blue oxford shirt and a darker blue jacket. His wavy hair was cut short and, like always, he was days beyond shaving that dark blond scruff off his face.

Through the display window, his eyes met hers and her stomach contracted, her heart flip-flopped and all the moisture in her mouth disappeared.

It seemed that Noah did indeed intend to talk.

Three

Jules...

Jules shoved her hands under her thighs and tingles ran up and down her spinal column. Darby and DJ turned in their seats to see who'd captured her attention and immediately jumped to their feet, their beautiful faces showing their delight at seeing him. Noah was, always had been, one of their favorite people.

Kisses and hugs were exchanged and while her sisters—one by blood and the other of the heart—and Noah did a quick catch-up, Jules allowed her eyes the rare pleasure to roam. Tall, broad, blond, hot...all the adjectives had been used in various ways to describe him, and Noah was all of those things. But Jules, because she'd once known him so well, could look beneath the hot, sexy veneer.

There were fine lines around those startling eyes and

a tiny frown pulled his thick sandy brows together. He was smiling but it wasn't the open, sunny smile from their childhoods, the one that could knock out nuclear reactors with one blinding flash. The muscles in his neck were tense and under the blond scruff, his jaw was rock hard.

Noah was not a happy camper.

Noah stepped away from Darby and DJ and their eyes met, the power of a thousand unsaid words flowing between them. Noah pushed back his navy jacket and jammed his hands into the pockets of his stone-colored pants, rocking on his feet. His eyes left hers, dropped to her mouth, down to her chest, over her hips and slowly meandered their way back up. Every inch he covered sent heat and lust coursing through her system, reminding her with crystal clear certainty what being held by him, kissed by him was like. Suddenly, she was eighteen again and willing to follow him wherever he led...

The thought annoyed her, so her voice was clipped when she finally remembered how to use her tongue. "What are you doing here, Noah?"

Noah pulled his hands from his pockets to cross his arms and his eyes turned frosty. "Nice to see you, too, Jules."

Darby, sensing trouble, jumped into the conversation. "Do you have time for coffee, Noah?"

Noah shook his head. "Thanks, hon, but no."

Jules linked her shaking hands around one knee. "Why are you here, Noah?"

"Business," Noah replied. He held out his hand and jerked his head to the spiral staircase that led up to the second floor, the boardroom and their personal offices. "You and I need to talk."

Jules didn't trust herself to touch him—he was too big and too male and too damn attractive. She didn't trust herself not to throw herself into his arms and slap her mouth against his, so she ignored his hand and slowly stood up. After taking a moment to brush nonexistent lint off her linen pants, and to get her raging hormones under some sort of order, she darted a look at Darby and then DJ, and they both looked as puzzled as she did. "Okay. I have some time before my conference call in thirty minutes."

She didn't have a call, but if dealing with Noah became too overwhelming, she wanted an out. Walking to the spiral staircase, she gestured for Noah to follow her. As they made their way up the stairs she could smell his subtle, sexy cologne, could feel his heat.

She was two steps ahead of him. If she turned around, right at that moment, they would be the same height and their mouths would be perfectly aligned. She could look straight into those deep, dark eyes and lose herself, feel his mouth soften under hers, find out whether his short beard was as soft as it looked, whether the cords of his neck, revealed by the open collar of his button-down shirt, were as hard as they looked.

She hadn't touched him long enough the other morning, and if she turned around, she wouldn't have to wonder...

Jules gave herself a mental head slap and carried on walking. How could they go from friends who'd never so much as thought of each other in that way to two people who wanted to inhale each other? And, dammit, how could she suddenly be this person who wanted to rip his clothes off and lick him from top to toe?

Jules groaned silently as she hit the top step and turned right to head for her corner office. Giving herself another mental slap, she reminded herself that she would rather die than give Noah the smallest hint that he still affected her, that she'd spent far too much time lately remembering him naked, imagining his hands on either side of her head, lowering himself so that the tip of his...

Oh, dear God, Brogan! Jules curled her arm across her waist and pinched her side, swallowing her hiss of pain. *Get a grip! Now!*

At her office door, Jules sucked in a breath and stepped inside her messy space.

Making a beeline for the chair behind her desk—she needed a barrier of wood and steel between her and Lockwood—she gestured him to take the sole visitor's chair opposite her. Steeling herself, she met his eyes and opened her hands. "So, business. What's up?"

Noah...

Noah sat down in the visitor's chair and placed his ankle on his knee, thinking that Jules's eyes were the color of a perfect early morning breaking over a calm sea. Light, a curious combination of blue and gray and silver. Looking into her eyes took him back to those perfect mornings of possibility, to being on the sea, where freedom was wind in the sails and the sun on his face.

If the dark hair and light eyes combo wasn't enough to have his brain stuttering, then God added a body that was long, slim and perfectly curved and, as he remembered, fragrant and so damn soft to the touch. Being this close to her, inhaling the light floral scent of her perfume, in the messy, colorful space filled with fabric swatches and sketches, magazines and bolts of fabric, Noah's lungs collapsed from a lack of air.

The urge to run was strong, away from her and the memories she yanked to the surface.

A decade ago there had been reasons to distance himself from Jules, including that clause written into his sponsorship deal with Wind and Solar. As a new year bloomed he'd grasped that his friend was no longer a child or a girl but a woman who he was very attracted to. They'd kissed and he knew they could never be lovers because they were such good friends. Two seconds later the thought had hit him that they could never be friends because they had the potential to be amazing lovers.

Walking away from her, shivering, into the falling snow, he knew something fundamental had shifted inside him and that there was only one thing he was sure of: their friendship would never be the same again.

Now and then, whether it was monster waves or his mom's death or Ethan morphing from a loving father into a money-grabbing bastard, Noah faced life head-on with his chin and fists raised. He had the ability to see situations clearly, to not get bogged down in the emotion of a life event. As tempted as he'd been to say to hell with everyone and fall into the romance of the moment—best friends kissing and being blown away by it!—he'd been smart enough to know that decision would come back to bite him in the ass.

Even if he'd been able to push aside his other problems back then—no money for the legal fights and his fake engagement to Morgan—he knew he was standing in a bucket on an angry sea. They couldn't be friends or lovers or anything in between. Her siblings were his and vice versa. They shared two dozen or more mutual friends and her parents were two of his favorite people. He and Levi had been talking about going into business together since they were in their early teens. He and Jules had been—were still—tied together by many silken cords, and if they changed the parameters of their relationship and it went south, those cords would be shredded.

If Jules hurt him, his brothers would jump to his defense despite the fact that they adored Jules; she was their sister from another mother. If he hurt Jules, her family would haul him over the coals... Either way, the dynamic of their blended family would be changed forever and he would not be responsible for that.

He could not relinquish the little that was left of the Lockwood legacy because of one kiss, a fantasy moment. He had to save the boatyard and the marina, and now the estate, if not for him, then for his two brothers. He owed it to his mom to keep Ethan's grubby, money-grabbing paws from what was hers and, morally, theirs.

"Are you just going to sit there in silence, or do I have to guess why you are here?"

Jules's snippy voice pulled him out of the past and Noah blinked before running his hand over his face. Right. He did, actually, have a valid, business-related reason to be there.

"Congratulations on your award as the best designer in the city, Ju," Noah said. Despite his frustration with the situation, he was extraordinarily proud of her. He'd always known she was an incredibly talented designer. But he hadn't expected her and DJ and Darby to create such a successful and dynamic business in so short of a time. People said that his level of success was meteoric, he had nothing on Jules and her friends. From concept to kudos in four years, they were a phenomenal and formidable team.

"Thank you," Jules replied, her voice cool. She rolled her finger, impatient.

Right, time to sink or swim. Noah preferred to, well, sail. "I have a job for you."

Jules's small smile didn't reach her eyes. "Not interested. I'm booked solid for months."

Yeah, he'd expected that. "I'm designing a superyacht,

a bit of a departure from the racing yachts I've developed my reputation on. My client is pretty adamant that she wants you to design the interiors."

"As interesting as that project would be, I can't take on another client, Noah. It's just not possible."

Jules leaned back in her chair and crossed her legs. Her eyes were now a cool gray and Noah knew she was enjoying having him at her mercy, being able to say no. Jules was taking her revenge on him for walking out of her life and, yeah, he got it, he'd hurt her. But the hell of it was that he needed her. He needed her now more than he ever had before.

Ignoring his need to save Lockwood Estate, his reputation depended on him persuading her to say yes. Noah opened his mouth to explain, to tell her how much rested on him gaining her help and cooperation but his phone rang, stopping him in his tracks. Grateful for the reprieve, he pulled his phone out of the inside pocket of his jacket and glanced down at the screen. A once-familiar number popped up on his screen.

The thought that there was no way she'd still have the same phone number as so long ago jumped into his mind. Then he remembered that he'd had the same number all of his life.

But why would Morgan be phoning him? Confused and shocked, he shook his head and tucked his phone, the call unanswered, back into his jacket pocket. He had nothing to say to his ex and never would.

"So, as fun as this nonconversation has been, I need to get back to work," Jules said, standing up and gesturing to the door.

Noah cursed softly and pushed an irritated hand through his hair. "Ju, we need to talk. At least, I need to talk—"

Jules placed both hands on the desk and glared at him, her eyes laser cold. "No, Noah, we really don't! You don't get to walk into my office demanding my time when you walked out of my life years ago, tossing our friendship without a word of explanation. How dare you think you can demand that I work for you when you treated me like I was nothing?"

Jules shook her head, her eyes glistening with unshed tears. "I mourned you. I mourned what we had. You abandoned me, Noah. You walked away from me and our friendship like it was nothing, like I was nothing." Jules circled her desk, headed toward the door and yanked it open. She rested her forehead on the door frame, and for the first time Noah realized how much he'd hurt her. Suddenly, his heart was under the spiky heel of her shoe.

No one knew, nobody had the faintest idea, how hard it was for him to leave Boston. On the surface it had been a pretty sweet deal, he'd been offered the money he needed and he had the opportunity for travel and adventure. He was twenty-three years old and the world was his playground. But underneath the jokes and the quips, his heart wept bloody tears. He was still mourning his mom, feeling helpless and angry at her death. He was gas-fire mad with Ethan for treating her like crap and lying to them.

His stability, everything he knew was in Boston: it was in the kind eyes and solid, unpushy support of Callie and Ray, in Levi and his brothers standing at his side, not talking but being there, a solid wall between him and the world. It had been in DJ's and Darby's hugs, in their upbeat, daily text messages.

It had been everything—her smile, her understanding, her kisses, her laugh—about Jules.

Leaving meant distance, walking away from everything that made sense. It had been frickin' terrifying and, apart from burying his mom, the hardest thing he'd ever done. Sailing that tempestuous, ass-cold Southern Ocean had been child's play compared to leaving Boston. And, because he'd just barely survived leaving once, he knew he couldn't fall back into the life he had before. He wouldn't allow himself to rely on Levi's friendship, Callie's support, his brothers' wall and Jules's ability to make everything both better and brighter. Because he couldn't survive losing any of it again.

Once was ten times too many...

Jules gestured for Noah to leave. "I have a call I need to take. Clients to look after."

Noah stood up and pushed his hands through his hair. Okay, this was salvageable. He would just tell Paris that Jules wasn't available, wouldn't be for some time. This wasn't a train smash. It was business. Paris would understand that. *It was business...*

In fact, it would be better if he and Jules didn't work together. Professional wasn't something he could be around Jules.

At the door, Noah stopped in front of Jules and bent his knees to look into her spectacular eyes. He wanted to explain, to banish some of the pain he saw there. "I never meant to hurt you, Jules."

Jules looked up at him and lifted her chin, her eyes flashing defiance. "But you did, Noah. And you still haven't explained why."

He didn't do explanations. Noah sighed, dropped a quick kiss on her temple—the intoxicating scent of her filling his nose—and before his hands and mouth did something stupid, he walked away.

It was only when he reached the sidewalk that his heart started to beat normally again, when his brain regained full power.

Noah stepped off the sidewalk to hail a cab. It was a good thing Jules have didn't the time—or the inclination—to work for him; she turned his brain to mush.

Jules...

The following Saturday, Jules picked up two breakfast rolls and made her way to the marina, where she knew she could find her brother, Levi. Despite them living in the same house, it had been ages since she'd spent any time with her older brother and she was looking forward to seeing him, but she did, admittedly, have an ulterior motive. She needed him to make a steel frame for a coffee table, and Levi, or rather the newly named Lockwood-Brogan Marina, owned a welding machine.

Along with his business degree, Levi also knew how to weld and the ham-and-egg sandwich was her way to bribe him. If Levi couldn't, or wouldn't, she'd ask Eli or Ben...

All three Lockwood boys and Levi had held part-time and summer jobs at the marina, and they all knew how to use their hands; Noah's grandfather had made sure of that. As a result, she and her sisters rarely had to pay for home repairs.

Besides, the boys had frequently made their lives hell: short-sheeting their beds, hiding their dolls, scaring the crap out of them. Making them work was payback.

Jules, dressed in a pink-and-red-patterned sundress and flip-flops, walked into the blessedly cool reception area of the marina and smiled at Levi's new receptionist, Meredith. The young blonde was talking to a middle-aged couple but she smiled before lifting her chin, silently telling her that Levi was in his office. Jules nodded her thanks, walked behind the counter and down the short passage to the end office, which had a spectacular view of the marina. Levi, dark-haired and blue-eyed, had his feet up on his desk and his tablet on his knees.

"Playing 'Angry Birds'?" Jules asked, tossing his sandwich into his lap.

"You know me too well." Levi placed his tablet on his messy desk and lifted the packet to his nose. He narrowed his eyes at Jules. "Ham and egg… What do you want?"

"A frame to be welded."

Levi unwrapped his sandwich, and after taking a bite, chewing and swallowing, he shook his head. "Eli is better at welding than me. Or, better yet, he can send one of his welders from the shipyard to do it."

"But that will take forever."

Jules perched on the edge of his desk, leaving her sandwich in front of him. If necessary, she'd bribe him with the second sandwich to get her frame welded today. She batted her eyelashes at him, knowing that he loved to be adored. "Please, Lee? You have a welding machine and you're—" she gestured to his tablet "—obviously not busy. The steel bars are already in your workshop at home."

Levi glared at her. "For your information, I was going over our financials."

The note of worry in his voice caught Jules's attention. "Everything okay?"

Levi was slow to respond, but when he did, his face carried no hint of his normal good humor. "Noah and I recently bought a majority share of the marina on the waterfront and are in the process of updating the facilities. We're asset rich and cash flow tight at the moment."

"But you're okay?"

Levi nodded. "I am. The businesses are. I'm not so sure about Noah. He's seriously stressed and I know it's money related. Did you know that he wants to buy the Lockwood Country Club Estate off Ethan?"

Jules frowned, confused. "Buy it? Why would he buy it since the Lockwood Trust owns it?"

"But Ethan owns the Lockwood Trust, not Noah and the guys. Ethan was awarded the estate when the boys took Ethan to court. How do you not know this?"

Because she never talked to or about Noah?

"Did you not wonder why Noah was staying with us, why he's sleeping on the *Resilience* and not at Lockwood House?"

"Well, I did, but—" Jules ended her sentence with a shrug. "I knew Ethan and Noah had a falling-out but not much more than that. So, what happened?"

Levi held up a hand. "Ask Noah. If he wants you to know, he'll tell you."

Jules's mouth dropped open. "You don't know either!"

Levi shrugged. "Noah doesn't talk much. You know that."

She really did. "So, what do you know?" Okay, she was curious, she'd cop to that.

Levi pushed a hand through his dark hair. "The guys need to raise a cracking amount of cash in order to get a mortgage to buy the estate off Ethan. In order to do that Noah needs to finish the design on the yacht he's working on but his client is being difficult."

"Noah always delivers. That's what he's known for, what he does." Noah was exceptionally good at what he did and was reputed to be one of the best racing yacht designers in the world.

"Well, this client wants something that Noah can't deliver and if he doesn't deliver, he won't get paid. If he doesn't get paid, he can't buy Lockwood House and the estate."

My client is pretty adamant that she wants you to design the interiors. Her heart and stomach dropped to the floor as Jules remembered Noah's words in her office. Her firm "no" had put his project, buying his family house and land, in jeopardy. *God, Noah.*

Levi continued to speak. "The client isn't listening and Noah's project is up the creek. Without her cash, he can't buy the estate. Without the estate, he doesn't get Lockwood House. And you know how much the house means to him."

Yeah, she did. All his memories of his mom were tied up in that house, in the country club she managed and the land she loved.

Levi balled his wax paper and threw it into the wastepaper bin across the room. He eyed the second sandwich. "I'll do your welding this afternoon if you hand over that sandwich."

Instead of tossing him the second sandwich, she scooped it up and headed for the door. "Hey! Where are you going with that sandwich?"

At the door, Jules turned. "Is Noah using Grandpa Lockwood's old office and is he there?"

Levi nodded. "Should be. He works longer hours than I do." He sent her his patented I'm-hungry-feed-me look that was difficult to resist. But Jules had other plans for her sandwich, so she left his office and headed for the spiral staircase at the end of the hall, the one that would take her to the conference room and Noah's office.

"I'm not welding your frame without the sandwich!" Levi's words trailed after her.

She didn't care. She had a bigger problem to fix.

Four

Noah, dressed in navy cargo shorts and a gray T-shirt under an open denim shirt, turned away from his architect's desk as she walked into his office without knocking. Standing in the doorway, she noticed his look of complete surprise before his face settled back into its inscrutable can't-faze-me expression.

"Jules. Good morning."

To hell with being polite, they were so far past that. "Why didn't you tell me that your project was in jeopardy?"

Noah lifted his broad shoulders in a weary shrug. "You're busy. I can't expect you to drop your other projects just because I asked. I thought my client was being unreasonable and that I could persuade her to consider other designers."

"Did you manage to do that?"

Noah tossed his pencil onto the desk and rubbed his fingers into his eye sockets. "Nope."

"So I'm it or you lose the project?"

Noah twisted his lips and finally nodded. "Basically." He lifted a hand. "Don't worry about it, Jules. I have other clients who have been begging me to design racing yachts. It's not a big deal."

Jules leaned her shoulder into the door frame. "But if you lose this project, you lose all your work and also the ability to buy back Lockwood House and everything else."

"Levi and his big mouth. I'll make a plan. If I don't buy it this time around, I'll wait until it comes back on the market and buy it then. For the first time since 1870 it'll leave Lockwood hands, but I'll get it back."

Jules saw the determination in his eyes. He would eventually take back his family's legacy but at what price? God, he'd already lost his mom and his home, was it fair that he lose this opportunity, too? Who knew when he'd get the chance to purchase Lockwood Estate again, if ever?

A management company ran the country club and estate but Jules couldn't bear the thought of another family owning and living in Beth's beloved and historic house; they might add on, rip it down, change it. No, a Lockwood deserved to live there or at the very least, the house should remain empty until one of the brothers decided he was going to move back in.

She hadn't recognized the consequences of her decision, because Noah hadn't told her, and she could kick him for that. If she'd known, she wouldn't have hesitated. This affected not only Noah but Eli and Ben, and her refusal to help felt like she was letting Bethann and her sons down. Yes, she was busy, but she could delegate work to her assistants and carve out some time for the project.

Jules walked into his office, dumped her bag onto his chair and placed the sandwich on his mostly empty desk. She couldn't eat; this was too important. But he might be hungry.

"Eat up, and when you're done, we'll go over the design brief."

Noah sent her a hard stare. "You're going to take the job?"

Jules rolled her eyes so hard that she was sure she could see her butt. "Of course I am."

"Why?" Noah demanded, his eyes wary.

"Because, as annoying as you are, you and that house are a part of my family, and family steps up when there's a problem. You need this job to be able to buy that house, and to raise the money to do that, you need me. There's no way that I am going to be responsible for the estate passing out of Lockwood hands. Bethann might start haunting me."

"It's a strong possibility and something I'm also worried about."

Noah looked down and, judging by the way his shoulders dropped, Jules knew he was trying to hide his relief. He hated anyone to see that he was worried, to think that he was weak. He liked the world to think that he was a tough-guy sailor, one who took enormous risks with aplomb, conquered high waves with a whoop and a yell, and he liked them to think that he did it with ease. Jules was the only person, apart from maybe her parents, who'd glimpsed the turmoil roiling inside of him.

But Jules, as always, saw more than she should and, standing in his office, in front of this delicious-looking man, she sensed the tension seeping from him, could taste his relief. And suddenly, weirdly, she wanted to put her arms around his waist, lay her head on his chest and tell him that it would be all right. That they would be all right. But, as much as she wanted to do that, she couldn't.

She'd trusted Noah once, trusted him with her deepest fears and feelings, her innermost thoughts. But he'd dismissed her, abandoned their friendship and ignored her.

No, she couldn't allow herself to be seduced by memories, to fall back into that space where the world was a brighter, better place with Noah in it. He was her client, sort of, and she had a job to do. This would be business and only business. She could never regain what was lost.

She'd work with Noah, give him her best effort but she'd never ever trust him again.

"Thanks, Jules. But before you accept, there's something else you should know."

That didn't sound good… Noah pulled in a deep breath before dropping his conversational grenade. "My client thinks that we're dating."

"Sorry?"

"She thinks you are my girlfriend, lover… Call it what you will."

Jules stared at him, her insides feeling like they were on a roller-coaster ride. His girlfriend? Why would his client think that? And why did the idea of being with Noah, tall, built and ripped, send shivers of…well, lust, up and back down her spine? What was wrong with her?

And, oh, Lord, being alone with him was an exercise in restraint. Yeah, she was still angry that he'd walked out on her, that he ignored her for years—no, she wasn't angry, she was hurt—but, worse than that, she was on fire, inside and out. Jules licked her lips and then swallowed, trying to get some moisture back into her mouth. Between her legs, an ancient drumbeat thrummed and her nipples pushed against the fabric of her pretty lace bra.

Just because Noah mentioned that someone thought that they were lovers. Ridiculous to the nth degree.

Jules dropped her eyes from his chest, allowed them to bounce off his muscled thighs before staring at the black and brown slate tiles that covered his office floor. She shouldn't be thinking about how attractive she found him. She had bigger problems than that to deal with. Like the fact that his client thought they were dating.

Uh…why would their client think they were dating?

Jules's eyes darted up to meet his, her eyebrows rising. "Want to explain how I went from being your designer to your girlfriend?"

Noah looked equally frustrated. "She was trying to set me up with…someone, so I said that I have a girlfriend. She asked who she was, your name was the first name that popped into my head."

Really? Surely he had a dozen names he could've thrown at his client. Noah was a good-looking, sexy, moderately famous and very successful guy. He had to have an encyclopedia-size black book of eligible candidates suitable to be his arm candy, so why did her name leave his lips?

"Because this is Boston, which is in some ways a ludicrously small town, she recognized your name and got all excited, insisting that she knew you and your work and that she wanted no one else to design her interiors."

Well, she'd made an impression on someone. A rich someone who had the money to buy a phenomenally expensive yacht. "As long as your client isn't Paris Barrow. I'm prepared to work with anyone but her."

Noah closed his eyes and Jules groaned her dismay. No! Why was the universe torturing her? She not only had to work with her oldest friend who now made all her hormones jump, but she also had to work with the client from hell? Paris wasn't mean but she found it hard to make a decision and stick to it. One day it was pastels, the next earth tones, a week later it was the colors of the Mediterranean. Wood, then steel, then ceramic, then a combination of all three.

Paris lived in her own world, surrounded by people whose mission in life was to make her happy. What Paris wanted, Paris got. Even if that meant changing her mind a hundred times.

She was a deliciously sweet, generous nightmare of epic proportions.

And, worse than that, she was incredibly nosy and horribly romantic. Married multiple times, widowed once, each and every one of her husbands was the love of her life. She was, so Jules heard, on the lookout for husband number six. Paris wouldn't be content with the idea of her and Noah just dating. Before she could blink twice, Paris would have them engaged and booking a church.

Jules tossed up her hands. "Uh-uh, no way. Not Paris Barrow, you're on your own."

Noah smiled, flashing white teeth. "Chicken," he murmured.

Jules hopped off her stool and slapped her hands on her hips. "She's like a walking, talking dating show! Everyone around her drops like flies when she comes into their lives."

Noah lifted an eyebrow. "Dead?"

Jules waved her hands to dismiss his words. "No! They fall in love, get married, get engaged. She's, again, a walking, talking bottle of fairy dust! And you told her that we're dating?"

"No, I told her that you were my girlfriend. One step up," Noah replied, very unhelpfully.

"Oh, God. She's going to harass us about the fact that we're not engaged, not married. Paris is a staunch proponent of buying the cow before you drink the milk."

Noah's low laugh danced over her skin. "I think you're making too big a deal about this, Ju. We pretend to be lovers, she harasses us a little, we resist. It's all good."

Jules sent him a dark look. "You have no idea what you're dealing with."

Noah folded his arms and his biceps pulled the fabric of his shirt tighter. Jules sighed, he had the sexiest arms she'd ever seen. Bar none. Noah's brown eyes turned serious. "Is our dating going to be a problem for you?"

For some reason Jules wanted to reassure him that there wasn't anybody in her life who caught her interest. Except him. Since he'd walked back into her office, into her life, she couldn't stop thinking about him, wondering how he tasted, whether his strength would be a counter to her softness, whether they'd be the perfect fit she imagined.

More than the physical attraction, there was a part of her that wished she could go back, to reexplore their closeness, to plumb his mind. She'd enjoyed the way he thought, his analytical brain, the tenderness beneath the suit of armor he wore. The combination of attraction and friendship was lethal. It could lead to more than she was ready for, for much more than she could deal with. No, she could not go back to what they had; it was dead. She couldn't risk having Noah in her life again and losing him.

It had nearly broken her once. There was no way she'd give him the power to do that again.

As for her attraction to him? She was a normal woman in her late twenties with needs, sexual needs, that had been long neglected. Noah was a gorgeous specimen and very capable of assuaging those needs. Her attraction to him was a simple combination of horniness and nostalgia and curiosity. It didn't mean anything; it couldn't mean anything.

He was a family friend, no more, no less.

A family friend with sexy arms, muscled shoulders and strong, strong legs. And a face that he could've inherited from a fallen angel.

Crap.

"Jules? Is your dating going to pose a problem to us working together? To acting like my other half around Paris?"

Jules blinked and shook her head, pulling her attention back to his question. "No, not at all. I'm not in a relationship with anyone."

"Okay, good. To keep things simple, I suggest that we never meet with Paris together, that one or the other deals with her, you on the interiors, me on the design."

Jules thought that he was onto something. There was no point in giving Paris any ammunition. And this way, Paris couldn't comment on their relationship. Or nonrelationship. Or, to put it another way, lie.

"That sounds like a plan," Jules agreed. "When does she want to meet with me?"

"As soon as possible, this week if we can arrange a time. Paris has a habit of forgetting meetings and darting off to Madrid or Mexico."

Yeah, she was familiar with the socialite's modus operandi. When Jules had designed her house, she'd have workmen waiting to start, waiting for Paris's final approval only to find that the blasted woman was at a spa in Monte Carlo.

One step at a time, Jules thought. "Let's start with what you imagine the interior of the yacht to look like."

"You don't want to get a brief from the client?" Noah asked, surprised.

"Normally I would, but Paris changes her mind on a minute-by-minute basis. Trust me, she's easier to handle if you don't give her the whole box of crayons to play with."

Jules walked over to her tote bag and bent over the side of the chair to pull a sketchbook from its depths and thought she heard a low groan from behind her. When she whipped her head around, she saw Noah staring at the floor, his clenched fist resting on his thigh. "You okay?" she asked, heading back toward his desk.

Noah's eyes flew up and Jules almost took a step back at the leashed power in his gaze. He rose, slowly and deliberately, and the air in the room disappeared. That power she saw on his face, in his eyes, was pure, undiluted desire. For her.

Holy hell.

The sketchbook slipped from her fingers as Noah's hands gripped her hips, as his masculine, fresh scent hit her nostrils and her chest banged against his. She couldn't stop her body's instinctive move to push her breasts into his chest, her hips aligned with his and… Yeah. There it was. Long. And hard. All for her.

Using her last few remaining brain cells, Jules slapped her hand against his chest, trying but failing to push him away.

"If you're going to be my fake girlfriend, I want one real kiss."

"Not a good idea, Noah."

"Screw good ideas," Noah whispered, his mouth descending to hers. His words whispered over her lips, and his eyes bored into hers. "Every time I've seen you since I came back, I've wanted to kiss you. It's bizarre but I keep wanting to check whether I imagined the power in our kiss. I don't sail much anymore, Ju, and kissing you is the closest I've come for months to feeling that same adrenaline."

God, how was she supposed to resist? He was all man, so sexy, and in his arms she was the woman she'd always wanted to be. Strong, sexy, powerful, feminine. But they shouldn't be doing this, it so wasn't a good idea...

Noah's mouth on hers kicked that thought away and all Jules could think about, take in, was that Noah was kissing her. He kissed like a man in his prime should, a man who was fully confident with who he was and how to make a woman feel incredible. He took and devoured, and just when she thought she might dissolve into a heap of pure pleasure, he toned it down, went soft and sexy, tender. He built her up, eased off, built her up again.

Sexually frustrating but soul-tinglingly wonderful. This...*this* was what she'd been missing from every other man who'd held her, kissed her. None of them made her core throb, her heart liquefy. No man before him made her feel intensely feminine, indescribably powerful yet, simultaneously, willing to be sheltered and protected. He made her feel everything she should.

Everything that she shouldn't.

She should step away and if he'd been demanding or insistent Jules might've done that, but Noah's hands didn't move from her hips, he didn't push his erection into her, didn't bump or grind. He just used his tongue and lips and, yeah, his teeth to maximum effect. Man, he was good.

Jules had no reservations about touching him, freely allowing her hands to sneak up under his shirt, exploring the thick muscles of his back, the ridges of his stomach, his flat, masculine nipples, the trail of hair that led down, down. She avoided his shaft, knowing that if she touched him there, if he touched her breast or between her legs, they would be making love in front of a clear window looking out to a busy marina.

But, damn, she was tempted…

Noah groaned deep in his throat, his mouth eased off hers and then his forehead was against hers, his eyes closed. "Crap," he muttered.

Crap indeed. Jules knew what he was thinking, he didn't need to voice the words. Like her, a part of him kept hoping that the attraction that had flared to life so long ago would dissipate at some point but… No.

It was still there. Hotter and brighter than before.

Noah's fingers dug into her hips. "Being your boyfriend and not being able to have the benefits of the title is going to be harder than I thought."

Because she was on the point of saying "To hell with it, let's get naked," Jules forced herself to step back and pushed her hand into her hair. "That shouldn't have happened. Nothing is going to happen, Noah."

Maybe if she kept saying it often enough the thought would sink into their stubborn heads.

Noah used one finger to push a curl off her cheek. "It just did, Ju. We can't deny that there's something bubbling here."

"I wasn't going to deny that. But we're not going there, Noah," Jules said, feeling that familiar wave of stubbornness sweep over her.

"Why not? We're adults. It doesn't have to mean anything."

Jules nailed him to the floor with a hard look. "Sex might not mean anything to you, Noah, but it does to me. It's not a way to scratch an itch, a way to pass some time." She shrugged. "I only share my body with men

I can trust, Noah. And, unfortunately, you're not that man anymore."

Jules ignored the flash of emotion she saw in his eyes, determined to ignore her inner voice that insisted that she'd hurt him, and bent down to pick her sketchbook off the floor. Holding it against her chest, she rocked on her heels. "I think we need some time to wrap our heads around the events of this morning."

She needed some distance from him, from the passion still swirling between them. "I'm going to go, but if you can send me the yacht's blueprints, I can put something together and we can thrash out a proposal to present to Paris."

Noah rubbed the back of his head and nodded. "Sounds like a plan."

Jules was grateful he didn't argue. "And when we meet again, it will be as professionals, Noah. This can't happen again."

It was Noah's turn to look stubborn. And frustrated. Jules could relate. "I can't just act like I'm not attracted to you, Jules, nor can I forget that you were once my best friend. I can't treat you like just a colleague."

Jules pulled her bag over her shoulder as sadness wrapped its cold self around her heart. "When you chose to walk out on us, on our friendship, you made anything deeper impossible, Noah. You neither gave our attraction, nor our friendship, a chance. I tried to salvage what we had, you didn't even meet me halfway. It was your choice, Noah, and you have to live with the consequences."

Jules, feeling sick and sad and, dammit, totally sexually frustrated, walked to the door. "I'll call you when I have something to show you."

Jules forced her feet to walk out the door, down the hallway. She just managed to throw a cheerful "'bye" to Levi and wave to Meredith. It was only when she passed through the access control gate and pulled her sunglasses over her eyes that she allowed a few annoying tears to escape.

She thought she was done crying over Lockwood, dammit.

Darby pushed her shoulder into the doorjamb and Jules met her eyes in the long freestanding mirror. Her sister was dislodging strands of hair from her messy bun every time her head moved. Dressed in low-slung sweats and a tank top, Darby shouldn't have looked so damn gorgeous, but she did. Her fraternal twin could wear a burlap sack and make it look like haute couture.

"So, another date?" Darby asked, her wide smile in place but her eyes showing concern.

"Nothing serious. Robert has been bugging me to have dinner with him for a while so I called him up and told him I was free tonight." She'd dated Robert the year before Noah left. He'd always been far more invested in their relationship than she was and Jules had hurt him when she'd finally called it quits. He was a nice guy, a kind, gentle man who'd been her first real boyfriend and her first lover.

"I thought you said you weren't going to go to dinner with him, that you didn't want him to think that there was any chance of you hooking up again."

That was before Noah returned and placed her heart, mind and body on a Tilt-A-Whirl. Jules refused to meet Darby's eyes. Hell, she was having trouble meeting her own. The only reason she called Rob was because she wanted to feel back in control, on firm footing and, because she was hoping for a miracle, a little part of her prayed that she'd look at him and magically fall in love with him. She knew Rob, knew how to handle him, what to expect. With Rob she'd be in control. He was safe and predictable...

Everything that Noah Lockwood wasn't. God, she was so pathetic.

Embarrassed at her behavior and her lack of maturity, Jules didn't answer her twin. She had to pull herself together, dammit!

Darby walked into Jules's bedroom and sat down on the end of her king-size bed, covered in blindingly white linen. Darby pulled her legs up and wrapped her arms around her knees, her slate-gray eyes curious.

"Where did you disappear to today?"

"I just needed some alone time."

After leaving Noah's office, Jules had needed to walk and then to run. Because she always kept a fresh set of gym clothes in a bag in the trunk of her car, she'd decided to head out of town to the Blue Hills Reservation to work out her frustration on a long trail run. After doing eight miles, she'd spent the rest of the afternoon sitting on the bank of the pond.

She'd kissed Noah. And she'd more than liked it. Holding her pencil in her hand, her sketchbook on her lap, she'd stared at the scenery, not seeing much beyond the blue sky and the forest. She was more interested in the movie playing in her head...his masculine, fresh-tasting mouth doing crazy things to hers, his strong body pressed up against hers, his warm male skin under her fingertips, the sounds of approval and desire he made deep in his throat. She hadn't been able to stop thinking about what they did, his hard body and what it all meant.

And when she couldn't think about that anymore, when those thoughts became too overwhelming, she allowed herself to wander back in time, to sitting on her parents' roof with Noah, talking about anything and everything. The goofy text messages they exchanged, the way their eyes would cut to each other as they shared a joke no one else was privy to. She was extremely close to Darby and to DJ but Noah understood her on a fundamental level they didn't.

What could these kisses, the intense attraction between them mean? Where was this going, what were they trying to be? Jules looked at her twin, unable to tell her sister—the person she shared everything with—how close she'd come to begging Noah to do wild and wicked things to her on the floor of his office. How she was both horrified and thrilled by the let's-get-naked-immediately thoughts that bombarded her whenever Noah stepped into a room.

"Jules, talk to me."

She couldn't, not today. Her feelings for Noah, her need and her resistance were too overwhelming to be discussed. But, because she was obligated to inform Darby of any developments in the business, and because it was a good way to change the subject, she could tell her about Paris. "I took on a new client today."

Darby looked surprised. "You don't have time for a new client."

So true. "It's Noah. His new client wants me to design the interiors of her yacht, is insisting upon it. My involvement has become a deal breaker so I said yes."

"I didn't think Noah could be pushed around."

So only Levi knew about the turmoil between Ethan and his stepsons? Jules wanted to explain the situation to Darby but it wasn't her tale to tell. She'd always kept

Noah's secrets—the few he shared with her—and always would. "This project is important to him."

Darby shrugged. "It's your call, Jules, but be careful of burning yourself out. You are working extremely long hours as it is."

Jules knew Darby was mentally measuring her stress levels, whether she'd lost or gained weight, whether she was as healthy as Darby wanted her to be. A college basketball player and a sports fanatic—she'd moved on from triathlons and was now into CrossFit—Darby was a health nut. Her twin no longer ate processed food and most carbs or drank coffee. She'd also stopped eating chocolate! Chocolate, for God's sake!

Jules didn't know how she got through the day.

"Blow Robert off, Jules, and come to The Tavern with us."

"That would be rude." And being in The Tavern would make her think of all the fun nights she'd spent there with Noah. Plus there was a good chance that Levi or his brothers would drag him to the bar tonight and she'd spend the evening trying not to beg him to take her to bed. The day had been long and hard enough as it was.

"May I point out that you only ever run away when you don't want to talk, and the only time you don't want to talk is when you are confused? And the only time I've seen you confused about a man is with Noah. So, did he kiss you or what?"

In the mirror, Jules watched herself turn a bright shade of tomato red. *Ah, crap.* How could she lie now?

Darby approached her from behind and wrapped her arms around her waist. Bending down, Darby rested her chin on Jules's shoulder. In the mirror, gray eyes met pure silver. Darby shook her head, a small smile touching her lips.

Darby was looking inside her and reading all her unspoken thoughts. "It's just an attraction, twin."

Darby squeezed her gently. "I'd believe that if there wasn't a whole lot of substance beneath the sexy. And you both have it in spades."

Five

Noah...

Being back in The Tavern was like revisiting his youth. Nothing about the upmarket bar had changed in the years Noah had been gone. The staff still wore white shirts, black pants and red aprons, there were still the same elegant black-and-white photographs of Italy from the '50s and '60s on the wall, and Dom, the head bartender, was still behind the bar, a little grayer, a little fatter, just as attentive. Noah recognized a few of the patrons and knew that, as Bethann's son, most recognized him. Grandpa Lockwood might've conceived the idea of the country club, but his mom had developed the estate's facilities and she built and designed the two restaurants, this bar, the gym and the handful of shops to serve the estate which now, cleverly, included a coffee shop serving light meals.

Being back at The Tavern with his brothers, Levi, DJ

and Darby was so normal and, damn, it was good to feel normal again, to be wearing faded blue jeans instead of designer pants, flat-heeled boots and a T-shirt instead of an expensive button-down and loafers. The bar inside the club had a stricter dress code—business casual—but this was a place for the residents to relax, to blow off steam. In here he wasn't the professional sailor or the yacht designer; there was no one he needed to impress.

Everything he enjoyed most—the cold beers, good music, easy laughter and companionship of people he'd known all his life—was in this room.

Well, except for Jules.

Noah took a sip of his beer and looked across the room, idly watching Dom pour red wine into a glass. He wanted to go back in time, to when Dom was younger, to before he understood Ethan was more concerned about money than his stepsons. He wanted to rewind to when Jules looked at him like he was a superhero, when he was young and blissfully unaware of the crap storm coming his way.

While it felt wrong for Jules not to be there, a part of him was grateful. Since kissing her this morning he'd been unable to concentrate, to focus. He'd tried to distract himself by having lunch with Eli and Ben, and Ben's latest blonde. He'd exchanged eye rolls with Eli at her baby-girl voice and take-care-of-me-big-boy attitude. Because they were in company, they avoided talking business and it was a relief to delay telling his brothers he was working with Jules. There would've been questions: Are you friends again? What happened to cause the great rift? Did you behave like a dick? What did you do to piss her off?

He'd have to have a conversation with them about Jules at some point. He might only be in Boston for a short period but none of them—because the Lockwoods were one of Boston's founding families and because Callie and Ray had been most A-listy of A-list couples—were low profile. Before one of them heard the red-hot gossip that he and Jules were dating, he needed to give them a heads-up and, at the very least, some sort of explanation.

Hell, they wouldn't have to wait to hear the gossip, put him and Jules within ten feet of each other and sparks flew. And that would raise more questions and speculation...

The best way to douse those sparks would be to avoid her, but that was impossible. Apart from the so-called fact that they were "dating," they were also now working together; he'd sent Paris an email confirming Jules's commitment to the project. While he was in Boston the next month or two, and because his friends and family were hers, they were going to be living in each other's pockets. And trying to keep his hands and mouth off her was something he didn't seem to be able to master. Kissing her wasn't nearly enough... Limiting himself to a few kisses was like giving a drunk the smallest sip of whiskey, waving the glass in front of his nose while keeping his hands bound to his sides.

Having Jules, kissing Jules and not being able to take it to its natural conclusion was a cruel and unusual punishment.

Speaking of punishments...he'd never grasped how much he'd hurt Jules, how much his departure had affected her. He'd been so caught up in his own grief, misery and, yeah, homesickness that he couldn't think about those he left behind. Apart from the odd email and phone call back home, he focused all his attention on the present, on winning his races, being the best damn sailor he could be. Emotional distance, the ability to step away from a situation and focus, became a habit. Those traits, and the need to keep busy, kept him winning races, as many as possible as soon as possible.

Winning, disconnecting, moving forward was an entrenched habit, but here in Boston he was battling to connect with his cool, rational, thinking side. He had Jules to thank for that.

Levi jammed the end of a pool cue into his side. "Can you, at the very least, acknowledge that I'm kicking your ass?"

Noah looked at the pool table and cursed. Only a few balls remained, and if Levi sunk those, he'd be handing over some cash. He was out of practice.

Levi bent over the pool table, eyeing his shot. Noah was surprised when he lifted his eyes to lock with his. "Anything I need to know about? You seem distracted."

He could lie but this was Levi. He could justify not telling his brothers—they were younger than him and this was none of their business—but Levi was Jules's brother. And a protective one at that. If he was going to open this can of worms, it had might as well be now.

"Just the past smacking me in the face." Noah lifted his beer bottle to his lips. "This life is very different from the one I've been leading."

"High-end clients and cocktails," Levi said after taking his shot, the five ball rolling into the far right pocket. Damn.

"Pretty much," Noah agreed. "This, a simple evening playing pool with my mates, is something I haven't done in years."

"Your fault, not ours," Levi said with his characteristic bluntness. "We were here."

He couldn't argue with that. Noah put his beer bottle onto the high table and rested his hands on the top of the cue. He needed to say this, had to get it out. "Lee, Jules and I—"

Levi held up a hand and his face turned dark. "Oh, hell, no! I don't want to know."

And he didn't want to spit the words out but he had to give Levi a heads-up, he owed him that much. But how to gently tell him that he wanted his sister with a ferocity that terrified him was turning out to be harder than he thought. He mentally tested a few phrases but none of them sounded right and all of them would end up with him sporting a broken nose. So he settled for simple. "Paris Barrow thinks we are dating—long story—but I should tell you that something is cooking between us."

Levi rolled his eyes. "That's the best you can do?"

"I'm trying to avoid a trip to the emergency room," Noah admitted. "So, yeah, that's all I can say."

Levi stared at him while he made sense of that statement. When he did, his expression darkened. "I need brain bleach." Levi bent over his cue again, stood up to speak and bent down again, frustration radiating off him in waves.

He stood up, tossed the cue on the table, dislodging the few remaining balls. "Crap, Noah! She's my sister and you are my oldest friend. I should punch you just for looking at her, but then you might piss off again and we might not see you for another decade!"

Underneath the frustration he heard anger and, worse, hurt. His absence hadn't only affected Jules, it had touched Levi, as well. And, he surmised, Eli and Ben and, to a lesser extent, DJ and Darby.

He didn't even want to know what Callie thought about his time away...

Levi's punch to his shoulder packed restrained power and rocked Noah back onto his heels. "Don't mess this up,

Noah. You hurt her and we'll have words. We're partners and that will make for a tough atmosphere. Be very, very careful, because one wrong move will have consequences."

He knew that. God, he wasn't an idiot.

"Thanks for spoiling the game and my mood, dude," Levi said and stomped off toward the bar.

Crap. *Good job, Lockwood.* His phone vibrated and when he pulled it out of his pocket, he read the name on his screen. Morgan. Dammit.

Hi. Where are you? Would you like to get together for a drink for old times' sake?

It took Noah two seconds to type out a solid, in caps NO. After pressing Send, he shut his phone down and slipped it back into the pocket of his jeans. Not now. Not ever.

He'd rather chew his wrists off than allow her back into his life. The fact that she was spectacularly beautiful and amazingly good at sex had confused his twenty-three-year-old brain and he'd stayed with her far longer than he should have. Jules had detested her from the moment they met and the feeling had been mutual. Trying to juggle his best friend and girlfriend had been a pain in his ass. But as time went on, the sex became wilder and Morgan became clingier, and Jules more disparaging about their relationship.

Fresh air wafted toward him and Noah turned to look at the open door. All rational thought evaporated as he took in Jules's teeny-tiny dress and ice-pick heels that made her legs look longer than should be legal. Black material skimmed her curves and fell from a round neck over perfect breasts, leaving those creamy shoulders and toned arms bare.

Not knowing whether he could take much more, Noah lifted his eyes to her perfectly made-up face, her extraordinary eyes dominating the rest of her features. Her mouth, frequently ignored because her eyes were so startling, was covered in a light gloss and he wanted to pull that plump bottom lip between his teeth. She'd subdued her hair into some wispy, complicated roll, and diamond studs glinted in her earlobes.

Mine, his body shouted. *Mine! Mine! Mine!*

Calm the hell down, caveman, his brain replied. *You don't believe in love, or commitment.* And, as he'd learned from his mom and Ethan, love made people act foolishly and lose control. He had no intention of following in their footsteps. He was more than happy to learn from the mistakes of others.

So, instead of walking over to her, throwing her over his shoulder and kissing her until she screamed with pleasure, he turned at the sound of amused female laughter and looked into DJ's lovely face.

DJ grinned. "Watching you two has always been one of my favorite forms of entertainment."

Jules...

Jules stepped into the always busy bar and instinctively made her way to the back right-hand corner, where the gang always made themselves at home. Yep, they were all there. Darby was leaning across a pool table, about to make an impossible shot, Eli was looking resigned at losing some more money to her, and Levi and DJ had their backs to the wall, beer in their hands. Ben was wedged between two blondes at the bar and he didn't look like he wanted, or needed, rescuing.

Same old, same old...

Jules wove her way between the tables, greeted a few regulars and smiled at Dom behind the bar. Then she looked back to the billiards area and her heart belly flopped when she noticed Noah standing in the shadows, looking hot. He was the reason she'd rushed through her dinner with the still-pleasant Rob, the reason she'd kept checking her watch. Noah was the reason she steered her car here instead of heading home. She was a pigeon and he was her homing device.

Because that thought annoyed and irritated her, Jules indulged her inner toddler and ignored Noah, pretending not to notice the way his broad shoulders filled out that designer T-shirt, the way his jeans clung to his muscular thighs and outlined his impressive package perfectly. Before Noah, her eyes had never dropped below a guy's belt. Jules's cheeks heated and she closed her eyes, mortified.

Only Noah could make her feel so out-of-control crazy.

As if he could feel her eyes on him, Noah swiveled his head and their gazes collided, a million unspoken thoughts arcing between them. Jules, because she could read him so well, managed to decipher a few heading her way. *I want you. I missed you. God, you're hot. This is complicated.*

Did he still have the ability to read her eyes? Would he be able to discern that she was terrified of what him returning to Boston meant, scared that he would hurt her again? Would he see her wishes that they could go back, that he would kiss her again, that he would show her how spectacular sex could be?

The flash of awareness in Noah's eyes told her that he received her this-is-crazy-and-we-should-stop messages.

They really should. Jules watched Noah approach her and desperately wanted to thread her fingers into that thick hair, feel that blond stubble against her lips, feel him rock himself against her core.

What they should do and what they were going to do were two vastly different things.

Noah...

Noah handed Jules a G&T, heard her quiet thank-you and leaned his shoulder into the same wall Jules had her back against. She smelled fantastic, but beneath her smoky eyes and expertly applied makeup, she looked frazzled. And exhausted.

Like him, she was working long hours and if she was going home to lie awake fantasizing about how they would burn up the sheets, he could sympathize. When he finally fell asleep on those long nights, he often woke up with a hard-on from hell, his mind full of her, throbbing with need.

God, he was so tired of solo sex.

"Darby looks like she's cleaning up," Noah said, trying to distract himself from images of Jules naked, under and on top of him. "When did she get so good at pool?"

Jules smiled and he saw the kid she used to be, fun loving and so damn naughty. "Darby dated a pool player in college and she spent hours being coached by him. She said it was the only way she could get any of his attention. As a result, she got really good at it. And Deej and I are really grateful for her skill."

There was more to this story. "Okay. Why?"

"Throughout college Darby hustled guys who assumed she was just a pretty face and her winnings always funded our bar bill. Some of her bigger bets also paid for a few beach and skiing weekends away." Jules took a sip of her drink and smiled. "As you know, Mom and Dad put us on a budget. If we wanted money to party and play, we had to work for it."

For all their worth, and it had been considerable, Ray and Callie believed in making their kids work for their money. His mom learned that from them, too; he and his brothers were expected to work at the club as golf caddies or, while he was alive, for Grandpa Lockwood at the marina. At the time he'd resented putting in the effort, but those long summers spent busting his butt taught him the value of hard work. He couldn't have achieved his sailing and financial success without knowing how to put his head down and graft. Jules wouldn't have built a business without it either.

If he ever had kids, it would be a lesson he'd pass on.

Except having kids, getting married—or getting married and having kids—wasn't part of his plan. Designing Paris's yacht, buying back this estate and leaving Boston was. Jules wasn't part of the plan either. Noah looked at his watch and saw that it was nearly midnight. He hadn't planned on staying this late and had work he wanted to complete tonight, but when Jules arrived, he knew he wasn't going anywhere. Standing next to her, breathing in her scent, was where he most wanted to be.

And staying later meant more drinks and he was pretty sure that he was close to the limit. Damn, he wouldn't be driving himself home tonight and that meant either asking one of his brothers for a lift. Except that Eli had left Darby to talk to a redhead in the corner and Ben was... Well, Ben was gone—so that meant he would be catching a cab.

Noah pulled his phone out of his back pocket and powered it up. After he plugged in his code, his phone lit up like a Roman candle on the Fourth of July.

"You're a popular guy," Jules said, and he heard the

snark in her voice. The possibility of her being jealous gave him an unexpected thrill.

Noah stifled a smile and scrolled through his messages. One from Paris, a few from his team back in London and four, five, seven from Morgan. "Crap on a cracker," Noah muttered, scowling.

"Problem?" Jules asked, lifting her finely arched eyebrow.

Having nothing to hide, he held up his phone so that she could see his screen and the various missed calls and notifications from his ex.

"Wow," Jules said, eyes widening.

"Yeah, did I tell you that the reason I named you as my girlfriend was because Morgan has put it out there that she wants us to get back together?"

Jules dropped her head and ran her finger around the rim of her glass. "Is that a possibility?" she asked quietly.

"I'd rather get smacked repeatedly in the teeth by a flying boom," Noah stated flatly.

There was that small smile, the one he'd been looking for. Jules lifted her head and he saw the relief in her eyes, and a hint of humor at his quick response. "So why does she think that's a possibility?"

"Because she's deluded?"

Jules smacked him on the arm. She thought he was being sarcastic or, worse, rude about Morgan's issues. He rubbed the back of his neck. "I wasn't joking. She actually is bipolar and she also has some other mental health problems. Her dad described her to me as being 'emotionally fragile.'"

He'd been thinking about calling it off when Morgan had had her first proper meltdown, staying in bed for two weeks, not eating or drinking or, God, bathing. She'd bounced back from that episode and he'd decided to give her some time to recover before he broke up with her.

But every time he distanced himself, she went into a decline and he genuinely worried for her. When she was healthy, she was a fun partner and, well, yeah, the *sex*. Her skill between the sheets was partly to blame—along with too much whiskey—for him agreeing to even entertain the idea of commitment.

Her father had worked fast, offering him exactly what he needed when he most needed it. Two years passed and when he was released from his sponsorship deal with Wind and Solar, the first thing he did was visit Morgan and formally end their engagement. Why he bothered, he didn't know since they were both leading very separate lives. But he did the deed and a week later Ivan sent him a brief text message stating that Morgan was in the hospital and that they both blamed him for her nervous breakdown.

He'd tried to let her down gently. He'd seen Morgan a handful of times over those two years they were supposed to be engaged and, within a month of him leaving Boston, their twice-a-week phone calls fizzled to once a month and then to one every couple of months.

He sent her the same emails he sent everyone else and Ivan paid for her to visit him in various ports as he raced, but those visits became, thank God, rarer and rarer. The cash kept coming in from Wind and Solar and he kept the few liaisons he had time for very low-key and trouble-free.

Amazing that, ten years later, when he was supposed to be so much wiser and mature, he was in another fake relationship, but this time with Jules. Maybe life was finally realizing a fake relationship was all he was capable of.

Jules, as he expected her to, looked shocked. "Wow. That's… Wow." It took a moment but then her natural curiosity and frankness reasserted itself. "I still don't understand why you became engaged to her. I know you didn't love her—" Jules's eyes dropped from his and he saw her swallow "—like that."

He'd never loved a woman, not like that. And he never wanted to. What could be worse than thinking someone loved you, lived and would die for you, only to find out that you'd been played for a fool and what you thought was love was something else? The concept of love was too nebulous, too open to interpretation.

Jules looked like she was waiting for an answer and Noah wasn't sure how to respond. Reticence was a habit he couldn't break, not even with Jules. Besides, his fake engagement to Morgan wasn't exactly something he was proud of but it had been the best choice at the time. "There were reasons, Jules. Can we leave it at that?"

Jules's chest rose and fell, and when she finally lifted her face to look at him, he saw profound sadness in her eyes. She opened her mouth to speak but then shook her head and remained silent. He shouldn't ask but the words left his mouth despite his best intentions. "What were you about to say, Ju?"

Jules scraped the last of the gloss off her bottom lip with her teeth. Then she bobbed one shoulder. "I was just thinking that we used to tell each other everything but then I realized that wasn't true. I used to tell you everything but you didn't reciprocate. You were very selective with what you wanted me to know and, as an adult, I can recognize that now. But it still makes me sad."

God, didn't she realize that he told her more than most, that she, at one time, knew him better than anyone else? "I did talk to you, Jules. As much as I could," he quickly added as a qualifier. "Besides, talking about boyfriends and how mean or unreasonable our parents were wasn't exactly life-and-death stuff."

"It was more than that and you know it," Jules protested.

Yeah, it had been but he couldn't think about that now. Because remembering made him want to go back to when his life was uncomplicated, to that time when his mom was alive, his father loved him and life was golden. His biggest worries were what amateur race to enter next, getting his assignments in on time, dating that cute blonde in his marine systems class.

"Whatever it was, we can't go back, Jules. We have to deal with the here and now," Noah said. God, he was tired and, yeah, sad. This was the downside to being back in Boston, hanging out with his family and people who knew him well. He couldn't insulate himself from emotion, distance himself when conversation turned personal.

It wasn't easy to do when he was talking to someone who'd lived across the road for most of his life. He'd desired other women, of course he had—he was in his thirties and had always enjoyed a healthy sex life—but there had never been anyone whom he thought about constantly, whom he, let's call it what it was, *obsessed* over. Even in his teens he'd never spent this amount of emotional energy thinking about a girl.

He was so completely and utterly screwed. And because he was on the point of saying to hell with it and throwing caution to the wind—and his obsession at her feet—he thought that it might be a good idea if he took his ass back to his boat.

Yep, Eli was on his way out with that redhead, so his only options were a taxi or to sleep on the couch at Jules's house. Not that he would sleep knowing that Jules was upstairs, in that comfortable bed...

An expensive cab ride it was, then.

Super.

Six

Jules...

Jules sat in Noah's visitor's chair and propped her bare feet up on his cluttered desk. Leaving her sketch pad on her knees, she dropped her thick pencil on top of the pristine paper and lifted her arms to gather her hair and twist it into a knot. She picked up a lime-green pencil from the small table next to her elbow and jammed it into her hair, working the pencil in to keep it all up.

She darted a look at Noah sitting at his high desk, black-framed glasses resting on the bridge of his nose. His brow furrowed in concentration as his hand flew between his notepad and a desktop calculator. Every now and again, he scribbled something on the plans spread out in front of him.

Hot damn, sailor. Or a hot sailor, damn. Both worked in Noah's case.

Seeing that Noah was concentrating on his blueprints, Jules pushed her hands under the large sketch pad and pulled her tight skirt up her thighs so that she didn't feel like she was sitting in a fabric tube. An improvement, she thought. Jeans or jammies would be miles better but she'd left the Brogan and Winston offices earlier that day to meet Noah and Paris at Joelle, a see-and-be-seen cocktail bar that was housed in one of the chicest boutique hotels in Back Bay. Possibly in the city. They'd thought that it would be better for Jules to meet Paris on her own but their client had declared them a unit and insisted on a "Team Paris" meeting. Her words, not theirs.

While Paris downed margarita after margarita, she and Noah tried to nail down Paris's wishes, expectations and desires for her yacht and its interior.

Two hours and four margaritas later, none of which had, sadly, passed their lips, they still had nothing. They were, however, handed a glossy invitation to a soiree Paris was planning at the end of the month. "Just a few friends, darling. Casual chic, be there by seven."

Through experience Jules knew *casual chic* could mean anything from ball gowns to beachwear, and seven actually meant later—much, much later. Everybody knew to add an hour or two onto Paris's stated time.

Jules tapped the point of her pencil against the white paper, leaving tiny dots on the surface. "She wants it to feel open but also cozy. Sophisticated but relaxed. But mostly, it has to look like it cost a fortune."

Noah lifted his head to look at her. Or rather, he looked at her after he eyed quite a bit of her exposed thigh. Jules thought about tugging her skirt down but then Noah would know that she noticed him checking out her legs, and he might also realize that she liked him looking at her legs. *Aargh!*

Noah straightened and lifted his arms in the air to stretch, pulling his button-down shirt across his ridged stomach and wide chest. Through the white cotton she could, if she stared hard enough, see his flat brown nipples. Jules couldn't stop her eyes from skating over his stomach, over his pleasing, and promising, package to look at his thighs covered by his gray suit pants. They'd be tanned and, as they'd been since he was fourteen, corded with muscle. Pleasantly furry.

Man, her old friend/new colleague was seriously *hawt*. As in smokin'.

And…none of this was helping her with her other problem, her real problem of not knowing what the hell Paris wanted.

Jules dropped her head back and groaned. "I need inspiration."

Noah stood and rested his hands on his hips. "How can I help?"

Jules lifted her head up and rubbed the back of her neck. "Did Paris say anything to you about the interiors when you first spoke to her about designing the yacht? Was there anything in those conversations that could steer me in the right direction?"

Noah thought for a minute. "Not really. She told me to design something that would make her friends drool. Gave me the budgeted figure and said to come back to her when I had some thoughts. I've managed to pin her down to some specifics—what she wants the boat for, cruising the Caribbean and possibly the Med, and for entertaining, which means big reception and deck areas. Her eyes glazed over when I mentioned anything to do with engineering or design." Noah frowned. "'Design a boat, here's a small deposit to get you started, make it spectacular.'

"I don't think she's very interested in sailing."

Jules laughed at his deadpan comment. "What makes you think that?" she quipped. "So, tell me about the boat."

Noah walked around the desk to her and perched his butt on the corner of his desk. "I sent you the blueprints. All the specs are in there."

"Yeah, but I have no idea what the boat actually looks like. Maybe I can take some inspiration from your design..."

"I didn't send you the concept drawings of the yacht?" Noah asked, sounding shocked by his inefficiency.

"Nope."

Noah frowned again before walking back to his drafting table and pulling a folder out from underneath his blueprints. Flipping it open, he removed a sheaf of papers and returned to his spot on the desk. Stretching out his long legs, he handed Jules the sheaf of papers, a hint of nervousness in his eyes. It almost seemed like Noah was seeking her approval, that he wanted her to like his work.

Strange, since Noah was the most self-assured man she knew.

Jules looked down and her breath hitched. Despite the roughness of the sketch she could see the fluid, almost-feminine lines of the yacht, the gentle curves, the sensuous bow. Moving on to the paper below, Jules tipped her head to the side. Noah took his rough design to his computer and the color printout in her hand looked like a real, already built yacht, just ten times more beautiful than the concept drawing.

Sleek, elegant, feminine...spectacularly well designed.

"Oh, my goodness, Noah, it's..." Jules couldn't think of an adjective that adequately contained how wonderful she thought his design was. She sighed, slumped back in her chair and looked into Noah's intensely masculine face. "It's… Wow."

"You like it?"

"Are you kidding me? It's gobsmackingly, shockingly beautiful. I have no words."

Pride flashed in Noah's eyes. "I like it."

"You should." Jules tapped her nail on the glossy paper. "You've put so much thought into the design, you know exactly what you want the interior to look like."

Noah nodded, so Jules picked up her sketch pad, found a clean page and picked up a bright pink pencil, prepared to make a list.

"I thought about echoing the fluidity of its lines with a feminine interior," Noah said, "but by *feminine*, I mean sleek and sexy as opposed to frilly and fancy."

Yeah, she understood. Long lines, gentle curves, no harsh edges.

"I'd like comfortable white furniture with pops of color. Bold pinks or oranges or reds, feminine colors but strong tones. There are a lot of windows to show off incredible views so we have to consider the sea an accessory."

Noah tossed more suggestions at her and Jules wrote quickly, struggling to keep up with him. Interesting textures, hidden flat screens, storage space. He'd thought about it all. He eventually ran out of ideas—thank goodness because her hand was starting to cramp— and gripped the edge of his desk with both hands, his intense eyes locking with hers. "Make it feminine, sexy but soft. Accessible but with a hint of mystery. Look inside."

Her head jerked up at his last sentence and the air between them turned thick and warm. "What do you mean by that?" she asked, unable to disguise the rasp in her voice.

Noah's intensity ratcheted up a notch and... *Zzzz...* She was sure that was the sound of her underwear melting. "I look at the yacht and I see you. Sexy, slim, so damn feminine."

"Noah." Jules pulled his name out into three, maybe four, syllables. It was a plea but she wasn't sure what she was asking for. *Please kiss me* or *please don't? Please stoke the fires and make me burn* or *please hose me down?*

"What do you want, Jules?"

Nothing. Something. *Everything.*

Jules was unable to answer him, and when a minute or two passed—or ten seconds, who knew because time was irrelevant—Noah surged to his feet. Tossing her sketch pad to the floor, he gripped her biceps, lifted her up, and up again, so that her mouth was aligned with his. Still holding her, his mouth touched hers...sweet and hot and sexy and... *Dear Lord.*

Jules wasn't sure how his arms came to be around her waist and how her skirt got high enough to allow her legs to wind around his hips. All she knew was that her core was pressed against his impossibly hard erection, her nipples were pushed into his chest and his mouth was turning her brain to slush.

She didn't want to be anywhere else.

For years she'd been kissing guys who made her feel something between mild revulsion and "mmm, this is okay" but nobody turned her into a nuclear reactor like Noah did. Nobody had ever made her feel she'd choose making love to him over dodging a missile strike or a tunnel collapse. If she got to touch and be touched by Noah, she'd take her chances.

Oh, man, she was in so much trouble.

Noah's hand ran up the back of her thigh, over the bare skin of her butt. "A thong. Nice."

It would be so much nicer if he got rid of that tiny scrap of material that called itself underwear. "Take it off." Jules spoke the words against his lips, dipping her hands into the space between his pants and his lower back, wanting to go lower, to feel his butt cheek under the palm of her hand.

Noah pulled back, his eyes intensely focused. On her, on making her his. She wanted that, to belong to him again, if only for this moment in time. "Jules…"

She knew what he was about to say and she didn't want to hear it. Yes, it was a bad idea. Yes, they'd only just reconnected. Yes, there was a lifetime behind them and they had no idea how to navigate the future. But she wanted this, wanted to know Noah before they reestablished their friendship. Because the yacht project had them spending so much time together, she couldn't keep him at arm's length, even if she wanted to. Which she didn't. She wanted Noah back in her life, the hole in her heart was finally closing. They were on their way back to being friends.

God, she hoped he knew there couldn't be more between them, that this night and a burgeoning friendship was all they could have. They'd make love, get it out of their systems and accept that they could never go beyond a casual friendship.

Because, as nice as it was to have Noah back in her life, she was never going to open up to him again in the way that she did when she was a child, then a teen. She'd trusted him once and he'd abused that trust when he left her, stayed away without so much as an explanation for an entire decade.

Noah was going to leave again; it was what he did, and this time she wasn't allowing her heart to leave with him.

But sex, pleasure—yeah, she trusted him with her body. If she wanted to know passion, and she did, then it had to be now, today. Tomorrow could take care of itself.

"I want this, Noah. I want you."

He opened his mouth to argue but Jules didn't give him a chance, she just molded her lips against his and slipped her tongue inside his mouth to slide against his. She heard his deep, feral growl, felt his fingertips push into the skin of her butt. When the thin cord of her thong snapped, she knew she'd won the small argument.

Or that Noah had let her win. She didn't care.

"One time," Noah muttered, pulling away from her mouth to push his lips against her neck. "One time and we get over this."

Jules nodded her agreement and briefly wondered if Noah knew she would agree to selling her kidney on the black market if it meant making love to him. She was under his spell...

Or for the first time ever she was finally experiencing the joy of really, really good foreplay. And if foreplay was this intense, sex itself was going to be fan-damn-tastic.

Suddenly she couldn't wait. She put a little distance between their bodies and attacked his shirt buttons, needing to see him, feel him. Whoops, button gone. Oh, well, tit for tat since her tattered thong was lying at their feet. Her thong was forgotten as Noah's hand ran up the inside of her leg, skating past her core, making her squirm.

Jules spread his shirt apart and placed an openmouthed kiss against the skin above his heart. Noah. God, she was making love to Noah. Suddenly scared, she rested her forehead against his chest, her hands on his belt buckle but making no attempt to divest him of his pants.

Was this a mistake? She was sure it was…

Noah's hand stilled. "Second thoughts?"

"Yes? No… I don't know."

"If you want to stop, we can pretend this never happened. Or we can carry on and pretend this never happened. Either way, in the morning this can all be a wonderful dream or a fantastic memory."

"Do you want to stop?"

Noah's strangled chuckle rumbled across her hair. "Honey, I have a sexy woman in my arms, the one I've fantasized about since I first tasted her luscious mouth a decade ago. That kiss changed everything and I've been wanting to kiss you, taste you there and everywhere, since then. Hell, no, I don't want to stop."

Jules looked up at him. "You thought about me?"

Noah used one finger to push her hair off her forehead and out of her eyes. "More than I should've. I imagined you naked and responsive and the reality is a million times better than the dream."

"How can one kiss change us?"

"God knows," Noah said, lifting his hand to pull her silk T-shirt out of the band of her skirt. His hand trailed over her rib cage before covering her breast, his thumb pulling the lace of her bra over her already aching nipple.

"Stop or carry on, Jules? Tell me now."

She wanted this. It was just one time and they'd forget it happened in the morning. Or was she deluding herself? When dawn broke, forgetting anything wouldn't be easy to do but she was willing to find any excuse, clutch any straw to be with Noah. To know him intimately.

Thinking that actions would say more than words, Jules gripped the edges of her T-shirt and slowly pulled the fabric up her torso, revealing her lacy white bra. She heard Noah's intake of air, and when she looked at him, his eyes were on her breasts. Using one finger, he gently rubbed one nipple before transferring his attention to the next.

"I guess that's a yes."

"A huge fat gaudy yes," Jules responded huskily.

Jules gasped when Noah grabbed her hand and pulled her across the room and into a space between the wall and his drafting table. Pushing her into the corner, he placed her back to the wall and undid the front clasp of her bra. Then both her breasts were in his hands and she groaned. "As much as I like that, want to explain why we are in this corner?"

"Windows. Marina. Can't see us here," Noah muttered, bending to suck her nipple. A hot stream of lust hit her core and Jules moaned. Noah couldn't use long sentences and she couldn't speak at all.

Lord, they were in a world of trouble.

To hell with it. Nothing was hurting now. And she wanted more. She wanted it all.

Jules reached for Noah's pants, undid his belt buckle and managed, somehow, through luck rather than skill, to flip open the button to his pants. Jules was very conscious of his erection under her hand and she couldn't resist running her fingers over his length, imagining him pushing into her body, slowly and, oh, so deliciously. She slid the zipper down and then pushed his pants over his hips, wrapping her hand around his shaft and skating her thumb across its tip.

Noah cried a curse and lifted her skirt to bunch it around her waist. They were half-undressed but they didn't care, nothing was more important than having him fill her, stretch her, make her scream.

"Condom," Noah muttered.

Protection. Yeah, that was important. Noah reached

behind him and patted the desk, grunting when his hands closed around his wallet. Pulling it to him, he flipped it open, digging beneath the folds. Eventually, he pulled out a battered foil packet that Jules eyed warily.

"That looks old."

Noah ripped open the packet and allowed the foil to float to the floor. "It'll do the job."

That was all she cared about. Jules tried to help him roll the latex down his length but Noah batted her hands away. Covered, his hand slid between her legs and Jules shuddered. *Oh, God, yes. There. Just like that.*

"Do you like that, sweetheart?"

"So good." Jules spiraled on a band of pure, undiluted pleasure and lifted her head, looking for Noah's mouth. He kissed her, hard and demanding. Noah lifted her thigh over his hips and plunged inside her. Feeling both protected and ravished, Jules had the sensation of coming apart and being put back together as Noah worked his way inside her, as if she were spun sugar and liable to break.

"Noah," Jules murmured, her face in his neck, trying to hold on. In another dimension, Jules heard the vibrant ring of his phone. Focused on what Noah was doing to her, making her feel—she'd never believed it could be this magical, this intense—Jules ignored the demands of the outside world, but when the phone rang again she tensed.

Noah clasped her face in one hand, using his thumb to lift her jaw so that their eyes clashed and held. "You and me, Jules. The rest of the world can go to hell."

Jules nodded as he pushed a little deeper, a little further and she whimpered. She wanted more, she needed every bit of him. "So good, No. You feel amazing."

"It's going to get better, Ju. Hold on."

"Can't. Need to let go… Oh, God."

Noah stopped moving. Jules whimpered and ground down on him, wanting to set the pace. Jules thought she heard Noah's small chuckle but then he was moving, sliding in and out of her, the bottom of his penis rubbing her clit and she was done. The world was ending and it was...

Stars and candy and electricity and fun and...

Mind-blowing. And emotional. Tears pricked her eyes and she ducked her head so that Noah didn't see the emotion she knew was on her face. This was only supposed to be about good sex, great sex, but here she was, trying to ignore that insistent voice deep inside claiming this was more, that it always had been, that she was a fool if she thought they could be bed buddies and brush this off.

This is Noah, that voice said, *your best friend, your hottest fantasy. He's not just some random guy who gave you the best orgasm of your life. He's the beat of your heart—*

No! No, he wasn't.

Those feel-good hormones were working overtime, her serotonin levels were making her far too mushy. She could not allow herself to allow the lines between sex and love to blur, to mix it up with friendship and good memories to make one confusing stew. Sex was sex; friendship and love had nothing to do with this.

She wouldn't allow thoughts of love and forever to mess with her mind. She was smarter than that.

Noah...

Sex against the wall with his onetime best friend. He was not proud. Noah ran a hand over his face, listening as water hit the basin in the bathroom adjacent to his office. He hadn't intended that to happen...

Liar, liar...

He hadn't been able to think of much else than touching Jules—tasting her, sliding into her warm, wonderful heat—since he'd returned to Boston. And since he was being honest, he could admit, reluctantly, that he'd told her the truth when he'd said that he'd often thought about doing that and more since their decade-old kiss. He'd sailed many oceans and had spent many long nights, waves rolling under the hull, imagining doing just that.

But not up against a wall. Not for their first time... That was all types of wrong.

Noah tucked his shirt back into his suit pants and ran his hands through his hair. He dropped to his haunches and picked up Jules's sketch pad, smiling a little at her girlie, swirly handwriting. He closed the book, picked up the colored pencils that had rolled off the table and placed them on his desk. What now? Where did they go from here?

Noah looked at the closed door and wondered what was going through Jules's smart head. Hell, what was going through his? Not much since he was still trying to reboot his system. All he was really sure of was that sex with Jules was the best he'd ever had and, yeah, he'd had his fair share. He'd been single all of his adult life and sex wasn't that difficult to find.

But that had been a physical release, some fun, something he enjoyed while he was in the moment but rarely thought about again. Jules, sex with Jules, was not something he was going to be able to dismiss as easily. Or at all.

Yeah, it happened at the speed of light—something else he wasn't proud of—but he had a thousand images burned into his brain. Her eyes turned to blue the wetter she became, her brows pulled together as she teetered on the edge. The scar on the top of her hand, the perfect row of beauty spots behind her ear. Her mouth, the combination of spice and heat, feisty just like she was. Her scent—he'd never be able to smell an orange again without becoming mast hard. She'd ruined citrus for him... or made it ten times sexier.

And, God, how was he supposed to work twelve inches from where he'd had the best orgasm of his life? Unless he moved his desk, his concentration would be forever shot. In the morning he'd move his desk to the opposite corner. There wasn't as much light and the view was crappy but he'd manage to get some work done.

Or maybe he was kidding himself. Just having Jules back in his life was a distraction he didn't need.

He needed her to complete this project... She was red-hot at the moment and was in the position to pick and choose her clients. Paris wanted her and only her.

Once Jules produced her portfolio of design ideas for Paris to look at—hopefully she'd fall in love with one of the proposals, and quickly!—Paris would sign off on the design and a hefty pile of cash would hit his bank account. He'd use that money for the down payment on the house. He already had a preapproved mortgage in place to tide him over until he sold his apartment in Wimbledon and George paid him out for his share in their yacht rental business in Italy.

Ridiculous that he had many millions in assets but, thanks to the timing of other investments, he was experiencing a temporary cash flow problem.

Up until fifteen minutes ago he was also experiencing a sex flow problem.

His phone vibrated on his desk, and Noah picked up the device, wishing the damn things had never been invented. He saw the missed call from earlier, frowned at the unfamiliar Boston number and saw that his caller had left a message. Dialing into his voice mail service, he lifted the phone to his ear, keeping one eye on the bathroom door.

"I cannot believe that you would embarrass me this way! Paris Barrow told me that you are seeing Jules Brogan! How dare you, Noah? Her of all people! Why didn't you just take out a banner ad stating that I meant nothing to you?"

Noah looked at the screen, cut the call and shook his head. Getting harassed by your ex was a very good way to chase away any lingering fuzzies. It was also a great way to kill the mood.

Crap. Ignoring Morgan, leaving her long text messages unread and not confronting her directly was not getting his point across. It didn't matter whether he was in a fake relationship with Jules or neck-deep in love with her or anyone else, what he did and who he did it with was nobody's business but his own. He was going to have to meet with his ex and explain to her, in language a five-year-old could understand, that his love life was firmly and forever off-limits.

Noah rubbed the back of his neck. Obviously his return to Boston had flipped Morgan's switch.

The door to the bathroom opened and Noah saw the resigned but determined look on Jules's face. Nothing had changed.

Having sex up against the wall—hell, having sex—was going to be a onetime thing.

Damn. Crap. Hell.

Jules rubbed her hands on her thighs before folding her arms, causing her breasts to rise. And, yep, his IQ just dropped sixty points back to caveman mentality. "So, that happened," Jules said, darting a glance at the corner. Judging by her trepidation, he expected to see that the wall had caught alight.

And how was he supposed to respond to that? Yeah, it happened. He wanted it to happen again... Next time in a bed.

"Not one of our smartest moves, Lockwood."

And here came regrets, the we-can't-do-this-agains. Jules lifted her tote bag off the floor and brushed past him to pick up her sketch pad and pencils. As he pulled in a breath, he smelled that alluring combination of sex and citrus, soap and shampoo. All girlie, feminine Jules in one delightful sniff. His junk stirred.

"I'm going to head home. It's been a long day."

It had but, thank baby Jesus, it ended with a bang. Noah gave himself a mental kick to the temple for the thought. It was asinine, even for him. He frowned, wondering when she was going to spit out what she was actually thinking...

This isn't a good idea. This can't happen again. Let's pretend I didn't get nailed against a wall and that it wasn't the most head-exploding, soul-touching sex of my life.

Jules half smiled as she held the sketch pad against her chest. "Let me work with what you gave me and hopefully I'll have a couple of sketches, sample materials for you in a couple of days. Will that work for you?"

What was she rambling on about?

He'd left stubble burns on her neck, her blouse was incorrectly buttoned up. Noah wanted to undress her, take her on the desk and then, when he was done, he'd dress her again. Properly this time.

Or maybe he'd just hide her clothes and keep her naked.

"Noah?"

Jules looked at him as if expecting an answer. What the hell did she say?

"Oh, God, you're getting weird. I didn't want us to act weird," Jules muttered, shifting from foot to foot. "Are you waiting for the other shoe to drop, the sky to fall down? Relax, I'm not going to ask what this means, whether we can do it again. I'm fully aware of your bam-wham policy."

Bam-wham... *What?*

"What are you talking about?" Noah was impressed that he managed to construct a sentence that had the words in the right order.

Jules patted his chest, much like his mom had to placate him when he was ten. "It's all good. No. That was something that had been building to a head for ten years and it needed to erupt. Now we can go back to doing what we do best."

"And that is?" And why did he sound like he had a dozen frogs in his throat?

Jules's smile was just a shade off sunny. "Being friends." Jules patted his arm this time and it took Noah everything he had to not react. "I'm out of here. I'll talk to you in a day or two, okay?"

Noah watched her walk out of his office and two minutes later, heard her run down the metal stairs to the ground floor of the building. Hayden, the marina's night manager, would make sure she got to her car safely so he could stay here and try and work out what the sodding hell just happened.

And, no, it most definitely was not okay.

Jules...

Ladies and gentlemen, the award for Best Actress goes to Jules Brogan.

Oh, why couldn't sex with Noah have been meh and

blah? Why did it have to be skin-on-fire, want-more wonderful? It had taken a herculean effort for Jules to turn her back on Noah and leave the office. Now at the bottom of the stairs leading to the reception area of the marina's office, she ignored the burning urge to retrace her steps.

She and Noah didn't have a future. They never had. He was only in town long enough to complete this project and within a few weeks, maybe a month or two, he'd be gone again. If she didn't keep her distance she would be staying behind, holding her bleeding heart in her hands. This time she wouldn't only be mourning the loss of her friend but also her lover.

She'd cried enough tears over Noah, thank you very much.

As more tears threatened to spill, Jules could only pray that Noah wouldn't follow her in order to continue their going-nowhere conversation. And situation.

She couldn't allow history to repeat itself; that was just stupid. They needed to keep their relationship perfunctory and professional. Two words that weren't associated with sex.

What had she been thinking... Had she been thinking at all? Their kiss so long ago had knocked them out of the friends-only zone and had, admittedly, rocked her world. How could she possibly have thought she could handle sleeping with him?

Then again, when Noah touched her, when his eyes darkened to that shade a fraction off black, her brain exited the room and left her libido in charge. Her libido that hadn't seen much action and couldn't be trusted to make grown-up decisions.

Jules waved off the night manager, who offered to walk her to her car, and stepped into the warm night.

Pulling in a deep breath, she waited for the night air to clear her head. Walking down the marina, reason and sanity returned.

Use that brain, Brogan.

She wasn't living in Victorian times; this wasn't a catastrophe. She was fully entitled to have sex with and enjoy a man, his skills and his equipment. This didn't have to mean anything more than it was: a moment in time where they did what healthy adults did. It was sex, nothing more or nothing less.

A fun time was had by all up against the wall.

She wasn't a poet, nor was she a liar... Jules sighed. Despite her brave words to Noah and her insouciant attitude, sex did mean something to her, sharing her body was a curiously intimate act. She never slept with men unless the relationship was going somewhere...and, because there hadn't been many contenders to feature in her happily-ever-after life, she was a shade off being celibate.

Sleeping with Noah had been an aberration, an anomaly, a strange occurrence.

Jules pushed through the access gate to the marina, turned to look back at the double-story office building and blew out a long, frustrated breath.

She couldn't sleep with him again. It was out of the question. He'd hurt her, disappointed her, and she couldn't trust him not to do that again. Erecting a wall between them was the smart, sensible course of action. It was what she had to do.

So why, then, did it take her five minutes to open her car door and another ten to start the car and drive home?

Seven

Callie...

Callie hugged DJ and Darby, and then pulled Jules into her arms, keeping her there for an extra beat, wishing she could ask Jules to stay behind, to demand that Jules tell her why she'd spent most of breakfast staring out of the window of the coffee shop, her thoughts a million miles away.

"Are you okay, baby girl?" Callie whispered in her ear.

Like she did when she was a little girl, Jules rested her forehead on Callie's collarbone. "I'm fine, Mom."

No, she wasn't, but this wasn't the time to push and pry. Not when there were so many ears flapping, Darby's, DJ's and also, dammit, Mason's. She'd introduced him to her daughters and he'd been courteous but professional, thank God. Points to him that he kept his flirting between them.

Enough of him, this was her time with her daughters and she wasn't going to waste a minute of it thinking about Mason. Callie's eyes flicked across the restaurant, saw that Mason was looking at her, and she shook her head. Distracting man! He wasn't, in any way that counted, her type. Too young, too good-looking, too... poor?

God, she was such a snob! She had enough money to last several lifetimes and it wasn't like Mason was penniless. He had a good business, looked financially liquid. She'd never judged men, or anyone, by their bank balance. Why was she doing it with him?

Because she was looking for any excuse, poor as it was, to keep her distance.

It didn't matter, nothing was ever going to happen between them! Irritated with herself, Callie stepped back and framed Jules's face with her hands, sighing at the confusion she saw in her eyes.

There was only one thing she could say, just one phrase that she knew Jules needed to hear. "Just keep standing, honey. Keep your balance until it all makes sense."

It had been Ray's favorite piece of advice, one he'd used his whole life. And, except for him dying when he was supposed to be retiring, it mostly held true.

"I needed to hear that, Mom." Jules managed a small smile. Then the smile evaporated and pain filled her eyes. "I miss him, Mom."

"I do, too, honey," Callie said, touching Jules's cheek with her fingers.

Callie walked her to the door, holding her hand. At the door she hugged her girls again and caught Mason's gaze over Jules's shoulder. His blue eyes were on her, a curious mixture of tenderness and heat. Damn that lick of heat spreading through her!

Jules stepped back and when she smiled, mischief danced in her eyes. "He's really good-looking, Mom."

That point had crossed her mind a time or two. Callie opened the door and ushered her brood outside. Shaking her head, she retraced her steps to her table, sat down and pulled her notebook out of her bag. Flipping it open to the first page, her eyes ran down her bucket list.

She'd moved to a new house in a different section of the estate so she could tick the first item off her list. She squinted at number two. Seeing tigers in the wild meant planning a trip. Was that still what she wanted to do?

"Learn a new skill? Bungee jump? Have phone sex?"

Callie heard the voice in her ear and when she whipped her head around, she found Mason's face a breath away, his sexy mouth hovering near hers. Callie wanted to scream at him for reading her private list but her tongue wouldn't cooperate. Then she felt his thumb stroking her back, while his other hand was on the table, caging her between his arm and his chest.

So close, close enough to kiss.

"Do you know how much I want to taste you right now?" Mason murmured.

"Y-you read... It was private," Callie stuttered, mortified. Her cheeks were definitely on fire. She'd mentioned sex! On her list! Now Mason knew she wanted some... Callie looked around the coffee shop, convinced that a million eyes—people she played bridge and tennis with—were all watching them, somehow knowing that she wanted to kiss Mason more than she wanted to breathe.

God, she was losing her mind.

"I'll tell you what's on my bucket list if it makes you feel any better," Mason replied, his hand moving up her back to cup her neck, the heat of his hand burning into her skin.

"You're probably just going to steal my ideas and call them yours," Callie muttered.

Mason's eyes flicked down to the list and Callie slammed her hand down on the page to cover her writing.

"I've traveled, thrown myself off a bridge on a rope, don't need another job. Wouldn't mind another trip some-where." He smiled and Callie's stomach flipped over. "I have had one-night stands, wouldn't recommend it."

Callie placed her face in her hands and groaned. "What are you, some sort of mutant speed-reader?"

Mason's laugh raised goose bumps on her skin. "Only a few items are on my list, Callie."

Callie scowled at him. "Do I even want to know?" She placed a hand on his shoulder to push him away but got distracted by the muscles bunching underneath his polo shirt. *Nice...*

Seeing that she was stroking him like he was expen-sive velvet, she yanked her hand away and, yes, dammit, blushed again. "Back up!"

Mason flashed her a smile and jerked her pen from her hand before picking up her notebook. Flipping to a new page, he pulled off the cap of her pen with his teeth and started writing.

He flipped the page back to her list, wrote some more and handed the book back to her. Callie looked down, no-ticing that he'd placed asterisks next to her "have a one-night stand" and "have phone sex" bullet points, drawing a line from both to what had to be his phone number.

Her face turned so hot she was sure that her skin was about to reach meltdown temperature. Mason skated his fingertips down her cheek before sending her a slow smile and turning away.

After a few minutes of resisting the urge to peek—she was embarrassed enough as it was—Callie turned the page and saw Mason's so-called bucket list. It was comprised of just three bullet points and a sentence.

Take Callie on a date.
Make her laugh.
Kiss her good-night.
See previous page for additional suggestions.

Clever, sexy man. A very dangerous combination.

Jules...

Since arriving at Whip, an exclusive cocktail bar situated in a boutique hotel on Charles Street, Noah had looked on edge. His jaw was tight and his eyes were a flat deep brown, suggesting that he was beyond pissed. But why? What had happened? What had she done?

"Are you okay?" she asked, jabbing her elbow into his side.

"Fine," Noah said through gritted teeth.

Jules sighed. Since their conversation the other night at The Tavern, Jules now saw their past a little clearer and remembered having to badger Noah to open up, to tell her anything. He was one of those rare individuals who internalized everything, preferring to rely on himself and his own judgment to solve his problems.

Unlike the rest of the clan, Noah had refused to openly discuss girls, college, his problems. The best way to get Noah to talk had been to join him on the back roof of Lockwood House and refuse to budge until he'd opened up. That was how she found out that his tenth grade girlfriend had dumped him, that he was going to study yacht design, how he was dealing with news that his mom had been diagnosed with pancreatic cancer.

But if she'd struggled to make him speak up on a thirty-foot-high roof back when they were friends, there was no chance of him opening up to her in a crowded room heaving with people who considered eavesdropping an art form.

Jules accepted Noah's offer to get her a drink from the bar and, standing by a high table, looked around Whip. She took in the deep orange walls, the black chandeliers, the harlequin floors. The decor was upmarket and vibrant... She approved. Just like Darby studied and commented on buildings, critiquing decor was an occupational habit for Jules.

Jules looked at Noah's broad back, saw that he would be waiting at the bar for a while and, feeling anxious, tapped her tiny black clutch bag on the table. By mutual, unspoken agreement, they'd given each other some space this past week, hoping to put some distance between them and their hot, up-against-his-office-wall encounter. She hadn't thought about him a lot, only when she woke up, ten million times during the day and when she went to sleep at night.

Jules sighed. Despite her busy days and her insane workload, the urge to touch base with Noah was at times overwhelming. A random thought would pop into her head and the only person she wanted to share it with was Noah. She'd be out and about, see an innovative light fixture or an interesting face and she'd reached for her phone, wanting to tell Noah about what she'd heard, done or seen.

A part of her thought she was sliding back into the habits of her younger self, to when she'd been in constant contact with Noah, but this was something more, something deeper. Every time she forced herself to cut the call, to erase the already typed message, she felt like she was stabbing a piece of her soul, like she was fighting against the laws of nature.

Not being connected to Noah was wrong. But her instinct for self-preservation was stronger than her romantic self, so she kept her distance.

But, God, her heart leaped when she opened the door to him tonight. It threatened to jump out of her chest when he placed a hand on her lower back to escort her to the classic luxury car he'd kept locked up in the underground garage at Eli's apartment. She'd gripped the door handle to keep from leaning sideways and touching her lips to his, from threading her fingers into his hair.

Jules tossed another glance at Noah's back. She really needed that drink and the soothing effects of alcohol, though a swift kick in the rear might be equally effective.

Noah was off-limits. Today, tomorrow, always. She rather liked having her heart caged by her ribs and not walking around in someone else's hand.

"Jules Brogan?"

Jules turned and smiled when a still-fit-looking older man with shrewd green eyes and silver hair held out his hand to her. Jules tipped her head, not recognizing his face.

"Ivan Blake."

Okay, the name sounded familiar but she couldn't place him. The connection would, she hoped, come to her in a minute or two. "I hear that you are Paris's interior designer."

"For her yacht, yes."

"And I understand that you and Noah are seeing each other?"

Now, what did that have to do with him? Since she wasn't prepared to answer him, she just kept quiet and looked around the room. "You don't know who I am, do you?"

"Should I?" Jules asked him, her voice three degrees cooler than frosty.

"I'm Morgan's father."

And a million pennies dropped. "Ah." What else could she say? I never liked your daughter, and I think she played Noah like a violin? "Is Morgan here?"

Because her presence would really make this evening extra interesting. And by *interesting* she meant freaking awful.

"She wasn't feeling well so she decided to stay home."

Thank God and all his angels, archangels and cherubs.

"She's been trying to reconnect with Noah and she feels like you are standing in her way," Ivan said.

Jules nodded to Noah, who was standing a head and sometimes shoulders above many men at the bar. "He's a big guy, Mr. Blake, I couldn't stand in his way."

"You're missing my point, Miss Brogan."

Jules allowed her irritation to creep into her voice. "You're missing mine. Noah is a successful, smart, determined man. If he wanted to reconnect with Morgan, I wouldn't be able to stop him. And tell me, Mr. Blake, when is Morgan going to stop having her daddy fight her battles?"

"Morgan is fragile."

Jules wanted to tell him that Morgan was also manipulative, but she kept silent. Wanting to walk away but hemmed in by the crowd, she had to stand there and keep her expression civil.

"Would you be interested in doing some work for me?"

Jules's eyes snapped up at the change of subject. Say what? "Are you kidding me? Morgan would disembowel you if you hired me."

"Not if you distanced yourself from Noah to give her a chance to win him back," Ivan said, his voice both low and as hard as nails.

"I don't need the work, Mr. Blake."

"But your sister does. She's been looking for a breakthrough project for a while, a way to put her name out there, to allow her to work on bigger and more exciting projects. She needs a chance and you could give that to her.

"I'm on the board of a very well funded foundation dedicated to promoting the art and artists of this city. The foundation has acquired a building not far from the Institute of Contemporary Art which we intend to demolish and replace with another smaller art gallery and museum. We're looking for an architect to design the space," Ivan continued.

Dear Lord, that was so up Darby's street.

"Walk away from him, just like he walked away from you, and I'll put in a good word."

Wow.

Jules frowned at him, feeling like she was part of a badly written soap opera. "You're kidding, right? People don't do this in the real world."

"Oh, they do it far more often than you think," Ivan said, a ruthless smile accompanying his words. "Just think about my offer. I'm prepared to give Darby a fair chance, maybe throw some design work your way."

"If I break up with Noah," Jules clarified, trying to stifle the bubble of laughter crawling up her throat. This was both too funny and too bizarre for words. He was offering Darby a huge project, a project that would catapult her career to the next level if Jules broke up with her fake boyfriend.

Again... Wow.

A part of her wanted to say yes; this man was offering her sister an opportunity of a lifetime. An art gallery and museum… Was he kidding? Darby would sell her soul to work on a project like that! Jules hesitated, conscious that she had yet to say no, that she *should* say no.

"Turning me down would be a bad business decision, Ms. Brogan. I can promote you and your sister, but the pendulum swings both ways."

And that meant what? He'd blackball and bad-mouth them? Jules tipped her head to the side and was surprised at the resignation she saw in his eyes. He didn't want to do this, act this way. The man was tired, emotionally drained.

"Why are you letting her push you like this?" Jules asked softly.

Ivan pulled in a deep breath, and sorrow and anger and fear mingled in his eyes. Ivan stared at her and was silent for so long that Jules didn't think he was going to answer or acknowledge her question. "Because," Ivan said, speaking so softly that Jules had to strain to hear his voice, "I'm scared that if I don't she's going to go a step too far."

Ivan ran his hand over his jaw and stepped back. "Let me know your decision, Ms. Brogan."

Before she could reply, tell him that she wasn't interested, Ivan Blake faded into the crowd, leaving Jules alone and wondering if she'd imagined the bizarre conversation.

"Have you seen Morgan?" Noah asked through clenched teeth.

Jules turned at Noah's voice and, not for the first, and probably not the last, time that night, noticed how good he looked in his black suit, slate-green-and-black-checked shirt and perfectly knotted black tie. Jules followed his eyes and saw that he was looking at Ivan Blake, his expression as dark as thunder.

He handed her an icy margarita and Jules took a sip. "She's not here, No. You can relax." His expression immediately lightened and his shoulders dropped from around his ears.

So his bad mood was due to his fear of running into Morgan. Now that made sense and it was something she could fully relate to.

"Thank God. And how do you know?" Noah replied, his hand wrapped around a tumbler of whiskey.

"Her father told me," Jules said.

"He spoke to you? What did he want?" Noah released a bitter laugh. "Oh, wait, let me guess. He wants you to break up with me."

No flies on her big guy. "Yep. How did you guess?"

"Because his daughter has been bombarding me with text and voice mail messages, begging to meet, to give her another chance."

Jules reached out, grabbed the lapel of his jacket and twisted the fabric in her fist. "You do that and I swear, I will drown you in the bay."

A small smile touched Noah's mouth and he removed his jacket from her fingers and smoothed down the fabric. "I'm not stupid. I got stuck in that web once. I'm not moronic enough to do that again."

"If she's hassling you, you need to tell her that, Noah."

Noah scowled. "I've been trying! I've asked her to meet. I even popped by their house but apparently no one was home. But I did catch movement behind the drapes of what was always Morgan's room."

"You know where her room was?"

Noah shrugged. "Sex." Ew. Jules shuddered but Noah

didn't notice. "She's been trying to get my attention for three weeks and now she won't talk to me, answer the door?"

"Of course she won't. She knows you're going to tell her something she doesn't want to hear. Instead, she sent her father to try and manipulate the situation."

He wore his normal inscrutable expression but Jules saw the worry in his eyes. "Would he be able to manipulate you?"

The urge to thump him was strong. "I'm going to pretend that you didn't ask me that."

"Sorry, but Ivan Blake has the ability to discern what people want or need and then push the right buttons to obtain his—or in this case, Morgan's—goal."

There was a story there and she'd ask him to explain, but first she wanted to go back a few steps, to get him to clarify an earlier point. Actually, thinking about it, it was still related to the topic at hand. "What did you mean when said you got caught in his web? As I said the other night, *you* stayed engaged to the girl long enough that she couldn't have been all bad."

"The sex was fantastic," Noah said, and Jules narrowed her eyes. He lifted up his hands in apology. "I was young and she was talented. But she was hard work."

"Again…you were together for nearly two and a half years! Why?" Jules demanded, knowing there was something she didn't understand, a huge puzzle piece she was missing.

Noah took a sip from his glass, his eyes never wavering from hers. "I never proposed to Morgan." What? Well, that was unexpected. Still, it didn't explain the long engagement.

Noah ran a hand through his hair and Jules noticed his agitation. Good, he should be agitated since he'd allowed whatever he had with Morgan—the supposedly fantastic sex, ugh—to get so out of hand.

"That Christmas Eve we had a discussion about commitment, but I was drunk and exhausted and don't remember much of it. I woke up the next morning, sporting a hangover from hell, to this wave of good wishes on our engagement," Noah said, pitching his voice at a level only she could hear. "Getting married was the last thing on my mind.

"Then, now and anytime since," Noah added, his words coated with conviction.

His statement was an emotional slap followed by a knife strike up and under her ribs, twisting as it headed for her heart. She shouldn't be feeling this, there was nothing between them but a long-ago friendship, a few kisses and hot sex. Still, something died inside of her and in that moment, standing in a crowd of the best-dressed and wealthiest Bostonians, she felt indescribably sad and utterly forlorn.

She'd never imagined that Noah would live his life alone. Like his mom, he had an enormous capacity for love, provided he thought you were worth the effort. Once, a long time ago, she had been worth the effort. But that boy, the one who'd trusted her in his own non-communicative way, had loved her, of that she was sure.

This adult version of Noah, tough, stoic, determined, didn't. And he would never allow himself to. The thought popped into her head that if he wasn't going to marry, then neither was she, but Jules dismissed it as quickly as it formed. His decision had no impact on her future plans...

She hoped.

Annoyed with herself, Jules opened her mouth to bring

them back to the ever so delightful topic of his engagement to Morgan. "So why stay engaged, No? Fess up."

Noah rubbed his hand over his jaw, and Jules wondered if he'd tell her the truth or fob her off. "So, there I was on Christmas morning, nursing a hangover from hell, and before I could make sense of what I was hearing, Ivan handed me a massive sponsorship deal. It was three times bigger than any offers I'd received before, included a new yacht, an experienced crew."

Jules struggled to make sense of his words. "But you were sponsored by Wind and Solar."

"Which he has a controlling but little-known interest in," Noah explained. "He made me an offer I couldn't refuse."

"To drop out of college, to run away?"

Noah's jaw tensed. "That's your perception, not mine."

"You left me with barely a word and definitely without an explanation. You abandoned me and our friendship. You also broke your promise to your mom to look after your brothers and to finish college," Jules hissed.

The color drained from Noah's face and Jules wished she could take her words back. It wasn't like Noah left his brothers alone and defenseless when he went away ten years ago; Eli was already in college and Ben was about to start his freshman year. They both had a solid support system in her mom and dad and Levi, and could turn to any of them if they needed help or guidance.

His brothers had been fine but he did leave them. As for finishing his education, his lack of a degree hadn't hurt his career at all, so who was she to judge? But it was just another promise he'd made that he'd broken...

We'll always be friends, Ju. There will never be a time that we don't talk. I'll always be there for you, Ju. You can rely on me...

She could and she had…until she couldn't. And didn't.

Noah drained his glass of whiskey. "Just to clarify… I finished my education. I didn't break that promise. I did my best to look after Eli and Ben. That was part of the reason I had to leave, why I had no choice but to take the—" Noah jerked his head in Ivan's direction "—as-shat's offer. I'm sorry I wasn't around, Jules, sorry that I missed your dad's funeral, that I couldn't hold your hand. But, Jesus, I was doing what I needed to do!"

"You're not telling me everything, Noah."

Noah stepped closer to her, trapping Jules between the wall and his hot, masculine frame. Her traitorous body immediately responded to his nearness, and her nipples puckered and all the moisture in her mouth and throat dried up. He was using their attraction as a distraction from their conversation but Jules didn't care. Her need to be kissed was the only thought occupying her shrunken brain.

She shouldn't kiss him, because kissing was one small step from sleeping with him again, thereby narrowing that emotional distance she needed to keep between them. Jules placed her hand on his chest to push him away but her actions had all the effect of a ladybug's.

"We're supposed to be lovers, Jules. Can you damn well act like it?" Noah muttered, dropping his head so that his mouth was a hairbreadth from hers. Jules sighed, forcing her body to relax.

"You drive me crazy, Noah."

"Ditto, babe."

Noah's mouth skated across hers in a leisurely slide, his lips testing hers. Jules wound her arms around his neck, her fingers playing with the surprisingly soft hair at the back of his head, wishing that she could run her hand down his back, over his butt.

Noah tore his mouth off hers and pulled back, lifting his hand to her face. Holding her cheek in his hand, the pad of his thumb glided across her bottom lips and she shuddered, the sensation almost too much to bear. "Yeah, I far prefer soft and sexy Jules to spitting and snarling Jules."

Jules opened her mouth to blast him but Noah spoke before she could, resting his forehead on hers. "Wind and Solar offered me a hell of a deal but it came with a huge price... I was caught between a rock and a hard place."

Oh, she wasn't going to like what she was about to hear.

"After Mom's death, I needed a lot of money very quickly. Blake offered me more than I needed, but the catch was that I had to stay engaged to Morgan for two years, enough time to get her mentally healthy."

Well, hell. Jules was trying to make sense of his words, this new information, when she saw their client, a champagne glass in one hand and delight in her eyes, approaching them. "I'm here! Let the party begin. Come, come, there are people I want you to meet! Oh, Julia, you look delightful! Come, come..."

Eight

Noah...

Jules—why did people assume her full name was Julia?—looked sensational, and that was a huge, irritating problem since Noah had this uncontrollable desire to pull her from the room, find a private space and rip that very delightful, extremely frivolous dress from her amazing body.

He didn't know if her blush-pink-and-black lace dress was designer or not—he so didn't care—but it suited her perfectly, being both quirky and sophisticated. She'd pulled her hair up into a sleek ponytail high on the back of her head and her makeup was flawless, with her face looking like she wasn't wearing any at all.

His childhood friend, gangly and gawky, was gone and the sexy woman she'd morphed into made all his blood run south. Grown-up Jules was sunshine and hurricane, calm seas and storm surges, the beauty of a tropical sunset and the tumult of the Arctic Ocean.

Like the many seas he'd sailed, she was both captivating and fascinating, with the power to both soothe his soul and rip it in two. Excitement pumped through his body and he felt alive. Rediscovering Jules was like setting off across the Atlantic Ocean, not sure what type of sea or weather conditions he'd encounter but damn excited to find out.

Noah allowed himself the delight of watching Jules, long legged and sexy, as she followed in Paris's wake. He hadn't seen her since she left his office ten days ago and it was nine days, twenty-three hours and thirty minutes too long. He'd spent most of that time with half his mind on his work and the rest dreaming, lost in memories of how she felt, tasted, smelled.

There was action in his pants and Noah thought it would be a very good idea if he stopped imagining her naked so he didn't embarrass himself. He knew of a quick way to deflate his junk, so he scanned the room, looking for Blake. He needed to speak to Morgan's father, make it very clear to him, so that he could explain it to his daughter, that he'd rather swim in shark-infested waters than hook up with Morgan again. He was sorry that she was a little rocky, slightly unstable, but she was no longer his problem.

Jules smiled and his heart flip-flopped. Damn Paris and her ill-timed interruption.

What was going through Jules's head? Did she hear and understand that he'd needed the money, that he hadn't had another option? That he did what he needed to do because he was between the devil and the Bermuda Triangle? But if she did think that he was a money-grabbing moron, then it was no one's fault but his own.

He wasn't good at opening up, exposing his underbelly. Communicating wasn't his strong point; he preferred action to words. Even his brothers didn't know the extent of Ethan's treachery. They didn't know about his many affairs, the incredible amounts of money he spent on girls just hitting their twenties.

He'd kept that from them, thinking that they didn't need to be burdened with that knowledge. In hindsight, he should've gone to Callie and Ray, asked for their help, their advice.

But looking back, he hadn't asked for help, shared what was going on because if he had, they would've seen how hurt he was, how out of control and messed up he'd felt. And if he'd fallen apart back then, he didn't think he would have recovered. And maybe that was another reason why he'd been prepared to accept Ivan's offer, since it had given him the option to run away, to put some distance between him and his mom's death, Ethan's betrayal, the need kissing Jules had evoked.

When he was sailing, he had to be fully present—his crew's safety was his responsibility—and he had to compartmentalize. Standing back from the situation, from the emotions, had allowed him to function and had become an ingrained habit.

He was finding that difficult to do with Jules now. She was constantly on his mind and not always in a sexual way. He found himself wondering about the weirdest things—did she still make her own granola, refuse to eat olives, make those face masks with oatmeal and honey?—and fought the impulse to connect with her during the day, just to hear her voice, see her smile.

And he wanted her back in his arms, naked and glorious, more than he needed his heart to pump blood through his body.

Noah rubbed the space between the collar of his shirt and his hair and caught Jules's concerned frown, the "Are you okay?" flashing in her eyes. She was worried about him, and her thoughtful expression suggested that she was still mulling over their conversation. There was no way Jules would leave that subject alone; she wouldn't be satisfied with the little he'd told her. She'd have questions...lots of questions.

He was still debating whether to answer them or not. He wanted to, for the first time in, well, forever, he wanted someone else's perspective, another opinion. No, hell...

He wanted Jules's perspective, her opinion. Wanted it but didn't want to want it...

This was why globe hopping, dropping in and out of people's lives was so much easier. Noah did up his jacket button, pushed his shoulders back and centered himself. Introspection could wait for later, right now he needed to socialize, to earn his crust of bread. And that meant discussing boats and sailing, recounting the highlights of his career and listening to amateur sailors as they tried to sound like they knew what they were doing.

Noah had played the game long enough. He understood the value of networking; it was extremely likely that a number of Paris's friends might have a spare fifty million for a new boat and he wanted them to think of him to design their vessel. Yeah, okay, designing an expensive yacht had been more fun than he'd expected. Building and designing boats, all types of boats, was his passion and rubbing elbows with potential clients was crucial for his business.

So get your head in the game, Lockwood.

Noah squared his shoulders, looked around the room to find Jules and saw her staring at the back of a silver-haired man, her eyes wide with distress. Noah instinctively made his way across the room, determined to reach her. Keeping his eyes on her, he was nearly at her side when a low voice calling his name halted him in his tracks.

No wonder Jules looked distraught. He didn't even need to look at the man's face, he knew exactly who'd caused his heart to stop, his blood to freeze. What the hell was his stepfather doing back in Boston? Just before leaving Cape Town, he'd checked to see where Ethan was and had been told that he was in Cannes. That he intended to remain there for the foreseeable future.

His stepfather, because he was a contrary ass, was exactly where Noah didn't want him to be: in Boston, breathing the same air he was.

Noah's fists clenched and he searched for and then connected with Jules's sympathetic gaze. She didn't know how or why he was at odds with Ethan but her loyalty was first and foremost to him. Her support was a hit of smooth, warm brandy after a freezing day on the water.

"Keep cool," Jules mouthed, holding out her hand. Noah gripped her fingers and nodded, grounding himself before turning around to face his stepfather.

"Ethan."

It seemed to Noah that the whole room was holding its breath, waiting to see how this encounter played out. Then he remembered that no one outside of his brothers knew of his war with Ethan. Noah was used to keeping his own counsel and Ethan wouldn't tell anyone that his stepson had instituted legal proceedings against him. The world only saw what Ethan allowed them to see, and that was the veneer of a charming, rich man-about-town.

His hid his snake oil salesman persona well.

"Hello, son."

Noah gritted his teeth. He'd once loved Ethan calling him son, loved the fact that blood and genes didn't matter to him so the *son* felt like a hit of acid. Funny how having his and his brothers' inheritance stolen tended to sour the adoration.

It took everything Noah had to shake Ethan's hand, to pull his mouth into something that vaguely resembled a smile.

"I thought you were in the South of France."

Ethan whipped a glass off a passing tray and smiled, his blue eyes the color of frost on a winter's morning. "I've been back for a month or so." Ethan sipped at his drink, not breaking eye contact with Noah. "As you know, I've put Lockwood Estate on the market."

Noah tightened his grip on Jules's hand. It was the only thing keeping him from planting his fist into his stepdad's face. "And as you know, I'm enforcing the clause that you have to offer it to us first, less twenty percent of the market value."

"My lawyer informed me. I find it tiresome having to wait." Ethan smiled the smile he stole from a shark. "If you don't manage to buy it within the prescribed time period, I'll still sell it to you."

"What's the catch?" Because there would be one, there always was.

"The marina. Give me the marina and twenty million and you can have the estate and all your mother's crap."

His mother's crap being the Lockwood furniture, the paintings, the silver. God, he wondered if there was anything left. Her jewelry, her collection of Meissen figurines?

He was going to kill him, he really was. While the house had sentimental value, the marina was a valuable asset and one that could easily be sold. And that was why

Ethan wanted it. Yes, the estate was bigger and more valuable, but it would be harder to unload. Ethan was doing what he did best, making life easier for himself. Jerk.

Ethan was exploiting Noah's love for Lockwood land and his family's legacy. It was a deal he could never, would never, agree to. Partly because he was done being exploited by his stepfather but also because Levi was now a full partner in the marina and wouldn't allow such a half-ass arrangement.

"Out of the question," Noah replied.

"Pity. I'd rather go broke than let you have the estate."

"Please, you're far too materialistic and vain for that," Noah replied, his harsh growl coming from deep within his throat. Red mist was forming in front of his eyes, and he was moments from losing it.

Punching Ethan would so be worth the assault charge…

"I have a plan B and if my life turns out the way I'm planning it to, I might take the estate off the market anyway. No matter what happens, I refuse to put another cent toward your mother's house. I'd rather watch it fall apart, board by board."

It was an empty threat, one that was verbalized purely to needle him since Noah knew the maintenance of the Lockwood house was paid for out of the profits from the country club and its facilities. There was no way the management company would allow the magnificent home to fall apart on the grounds of such an exclusive estate.

Noah tensed but Jules squeezing his hand kept his inscrutable expression in place. But, damn, it was hard.

Pulling her hand from his, Jules stepped between him and Ethan and smiled. Noah's protective instinct wanted her behind him but the quick shake of her head kept him from moving. She smiled but her eyes were deep-freeze cold. When she spoke, her voice held an edge he'd never heard before. Tough, compelling, hard-ass. "Uncle Ethan, it's been a long time."

Ethan's smile turned oily; the old man loved the attention of a pretty woman. The younger the better. That love of attention emptied his bank accounts faster than water ran from a tap. "I know that I should remember you, but forgive me, pretty lady—" *Pretty lady? Gag.* "—I don't... Wait! Jules Brogan?"

Jules nodded. "Hello."

Ethan flushed and ran a finger around the collar of his shirt. "I'm sorry about your dad."

"Not sorry enough to come to his funeral, though."

Ethan pouted. "Noah wasn't there either."

Typical Ethan, always trying to flip the tables and shift blame. "Noah was, if I recall, crossing the Indian Ocean at the time. What was your excuse for not being there for my mom, to support her when she lost the man who was your neighbor and friend for more than twenty years? The same woman who cooked for you and your boys for months before and after Bethann died, who took in your boys when they were on school breaks, who was more their parent than you were?"

"Uh..."

Noah wanted to smile at Ethan's red face, at the hunted look in his eyes. He saw Jules open her mouth to blast him again but seeing Paris approaching them, he gripped the back of her neck. Jules looked up at him and he shook his head, gently inclining his head in Paris's direction. Their hostess and client held a PhD in gossip and he didn't want them to star in her melodramatic account of their run-in with Ethan.

Noah's eyebrows flew up when Paris wound her arms around Ethan's neck before dropping a kiss on his temple. She grinned. "Surprise! My sweetie told me he hadn't spoken to you for a while, that you'd had a tiny falling-out so I thought this would be a perfect occasion for you two to kiss and make up!" Paris's eyes sparkled with excitement. "Ethan told me that he taught you to sail, Noah, and he's kindly offered to guide me through the process of designing and buying a yacht."

Noah's heart plummeted to the floor and nausea climbed up in his throat. Noah looked at Ethan and saw the malice in his eyes, revenge-filled amusement touching his mouth.

"Darling!" Paris said, dropping a kiss on Ethan's lips. "There is music so we must dance."

Ethan raised his glass to Noah and invisible fingers encircled Noah's neck and started to squeeze. "We'll speak soon...son."

Noah hauled in shallow breaths as they walked away, dimly hearing Jules's calling his name.

When he finally pulled his eyes to her face, he clocked her distress and concern. "Noah, are you okay?"

Noah shook his head. "Nope. Basically, what I am is screwed."

Jules...

Jules was still reeling from the unexpected encounter with Ethan—and she could only imagine how Noah felt. They'd left the soiree as soon as they could and the drive back to Lockwood was silent. Without a word, Noah opened her car door, escorted her to her front door and, in the dim shadows on the porch, stared down at her with enigmatic eyes.

She had a million questions for him, a need to dig and delve, to understand the past, but it was late and clarity wasn't what she most wanted from Noah right now. No, this wasn't about what she wanted but what she needed to give him...

A couple of times at Whip she'd looked his way and while he seemed to be talking, having a good time, she'd sensed that it was all one damn good performance. He played the game well but she could tell that Noah was played out, mentally and emotionally. For the first time she appreciated how hard it was for him to return to Boston and to face his past.

Jules glanced across the road to Lockwood House, looking hard and menacing under the cloudy sky. He'd come home to buy his inheritance back but dealing with his past had to be harder than he imagined. She'd assumed that his spat with Ethan had been just that, a spat, an old bull, young bull thing, something that would blow over. She hadn't really noticed that Eli and Ben didn't speak about their stepfather much; he was always out of the country, and because he was a sailor and yachtsman, she'd assumed that Noah had more contact with Ethan than they did.

That was a mistake. Noah loathed Ethan, and Ethan returned his antipathy.

Something fundamentally destructive had occurred to cause such unhappiness...

Noah placed a hand on the door above her head and looked down at her, his face as hard as the house over the road. "It's been a long and crappy evening, Ju, I don't want to talk about it or answer any questions."

"Fair enough," Jules replied, placing her hands flat against the wooden front door behind her. Arching her chest, she looked up at him, deliberately lowering her eyes. She knew what Noah wanted and it was the one thing she could give him, what she wanted—no, needed—as much as he did. To step out of their complicated lives and feel.

Warm skin, wet lips, heat…

Noah's voice was low but rough. "I want you. But you know that already."

"I do." Jules nodded, hooking her hand around the back of his neck. "And I want you, too. Take me to bed, No. Take me away to a place where our passion is the only truth."

"Nothing changes, Jules. As soon as I buy Lockwood, I'm still leaving," Noah stated quietly, still looming over her.

His blunt statement hurt, of course it did, but it didn't distract her from wanting what they both craved. "Kiss me, Noah."

Judging by his hard eyes and tense body, Jules expected to be hurtled to mindlessness by hard and fast sex. So his soft kiss, the tenderness in his touch, surprised her.

Noah bent his knees, placed an arm beneath her bottom and lifted her so that her mouth was aligned with his. Her feet dangled off the floor, but it didn't matter because Noah was holding her, exploring her mouth, seemingly desperate to taste her. Her breasts pushed into his chest and she shifted her knee, brushing against his erection.

Yum…

Noah allowed Jules to slide to the floor, silently demanding the key to the door. She licked her lips and shook her head, her brain stuttering. Noah released a frustrated sigh, reached for her clutch bag and flipped it open. His fingers delved inside and he withdrew the key, handing the bag back to her and stabbing the lock all in one fluid movement.

Impressive, since she wasn't sure how to spell her name. "How can you think, act? All I can think about is how wonderful you make me feel."

Noah gripped her wrist and jerked her inside. "I'm motivated. I've been imagining ripping that dress off you all evening."

Okay, that statement pierced the fog. But...no. As much as she wanted to get naked, this dress was too expensive to be a casualty. She slapped her hand on Noah's chest. "Do not harm this dress, Lockwood."

When he just smiled at her, Jules slapped him again to make her point. "Seriously, Noah. Don't do anything to this dress."

Noah held up his hands before his expression turned, and she saw determination, tenderness and a great deal of fascination in his face. He touched her cheek and his fingers trailed over her jaw. "You are so damn beautiful, Jules."

Jules touched her tongue to her top lip. When he spoke in that reverent voice, his confidence and cockiness gone, she saw Noah at a deeper level, stripped bare. She liked the softness beneath the bad-boy layer, the tenderness beneath his alpha facade.

She liked him. She loved him. And in ways she shouldn't.

Determined not to go there, not to think about that now, Jules closed the front door and linking her fingers with Noah's, led him up the stairs. She smiled as they both instinctively avoided the steps that creaked, staying to the side of the hallway to muffle their footsteps. They were adults but they were acting like her parents still occupied the master suite down the hall.

Jules led Noah into her bedroom, shut the door and kicked off her heels. Turning around, she looked at her man, taking a moment to watch him watch her. Deciding that her dress needed to go—because she didn't fully trust that wild look in Noah's eye—she reached under her arm and found the tab to the hidden zip, slowly pulling it down her side. The dress fell apart and Jules, enjoying this striptease more than she thought she would, slowly stepped out of it, draping it over the back of her chair. In the corner of her eye she caught her reflection in her freestanding mirror, saw her strapless, blush-colored bra and matching high-cut panties. Her underwear covered as much as her bathing suit normally did but she looked wanton, like a woman anticipating her lover.

And, dammit, she was.

Who would make the first move? Jules didn't know, so she just stood there as the tension in the room ratcheted upward.

Noah lifted one eyebrow, his face hard in the light of the bedside lamp she'd left burning. "You sure about this?" he asked quietly, his lashes dark against his cheek. "Because if we start, I'm not sure that I'll be able to stop."

"I'm sure."

"Then I'm damn grateful."

Noah shrugged out of his jacket, pulled down his tie and tossed both onto the chair, covering her dress with his clothing. Flipping open the button on his collar, he stepped toward her, the pads of his fingers skimming the column of her neck. Her collarbone, the slope of her breast. His gentle touch gave permission for the butterflies in her stomach to lift off. Him taking it slow was more erotic than deep, hot kisses and on-fire hands.

He was such a tough man, so self-contained, but his tenderness was a surprise, his need to draw out their lovemaking astonishing. But he'd speed up in a minute, and they'd go from zero to ballistic. There was too much chemistry between them to allow for a long, slow burn.

Noah held her head in both hands and his thumbs drifted over her eyebrows, down her temples and across her cheekbones.

"Kiss me, No."

Noah half smiled. "Shh. Don't think, don't rush, just feel. Enjoy me loving you. There is no hurry."

Noah didn't wait for or expect a reply, he just lowered his head and his mouth finally—finally!—skimmed hers. As they kissed along slow, heated paths of pleasure, she touched him where she could. She tried to open his shirt with hesitant, shaking fingers, and it seemed like eons passed before she managed to separate the sides of his shirt, allowing her hands to skate across his chest. She pulled her fingers through his chest hair, across his flat nipples, over his rib cage. She dragged her nails over his stomach muscles, feeling like a superhero when he trembled under her touch.

Through the fabric of his pants, she stroked the pad of her finger along his erection, from base to tip, and was rewarded by the sound of a low curse.

Needing more, Jules flipped open the snap on his pants, pulled down his zipper and released his straining erection. Using both hands to cage him, she arched her neck as Noah's mouth headed south, nipping the cords of her neck, sucking on the skin covering the ball of her shoulder.

Without warning, Noah spun her around, ordering her to put her hands on the wall. Following his lead, she gasped when his mouth touched every bump on her spine, barely noticing when her bra fell to the floor at her feet. Stepping close to her, his hands covered her breasts, his thumbs teasing her nipples into hard points.

"I want you," he said, dipping his head to her neck, sucking on that patch of skin where her neck and shoulder met.

Noah hooked his thumbs into her lacy panties and slid them down her legs. Then Noah's hands were on her butt, his fingers sliding between her legs, finding her most sensitive spot with ruthless efficiency. Jules lifted her arms above her head, rested her forehead on her wrists and began to pant.

One finger entered her, then another, and she climbed…reaching, teetering, desperate.

Noah chuckled, pulled his hand away to tease her breasts, slid his fingers across her flat stomach.

"Noah…"

Noah's chest pressed into her back, his erection flirting with her butt. "Yeah?"

"I need—"

"What, babe?"

Jules turned her head and torso and lifted her face, prepared to beg. His eyes, sparking with gold flecks, met hers and then his mouth was over hers, possessive and demanding. Wriggling so that she faced him, Jules hooked a leg over his hip and groaned when his erection brushed her curls, finding her sweet spot.

Pulling her backward, Noah half lifted and half dragged her to her bed, sitting and pulling her down so that her legs fell on either side of his thighs, as close as they could be without him slipping inside.

Noah pushed her hair off her face. "Babe, I need a condom and to get my clothes off. I'm not making love to you half-naked."

Jules moved against him, sliding her core up him. She smiled when Noah's eyes rolled upward. "Okay, in a minute."

Noah gripped her hips and lifted her off him, the muscles in his stomach and arms contracting. *Wow, hot.* Noah stood up, picked up his jacket and found the inside pocket. He pulled out a strip of three condoms, which he tossed onto the bed next to her hip. Jules flopped back on the bed and watched Noah strip, boldly inspecting him from the top of his now-messy hair to his big feet still encased in his shoes. He had a tattoo just above his hip and Jules sat up to take a closer look. After he removed his socks and shoes, she reached for him, allowing her fingers to skate over his ink, a nautical rope.

The knot of the bowline rested on his hip while the rope traveled across the very top of his thigh and onto his lower stomach. Jules appreciated the artist's work, the battered quality suggesting the rope was well used. "Do you miss sailing, No?"

Noah's fingers tunneled into her hair. "Not as much as I missed you."

Not sure how to respond, Jules stared up at him with wide eyes.

Noah pinned her with his gaze, his big body looming over hers. Her legs fell open and his erection nudged her opening. "I need you, Jules. I need to be inside you. To feel… Jesus, Jules."

Jules silently finished his sentence for him: *to feel complete.*

Jules wound her arms around his neck as he slid inside her, just once, skin on skin. Like him, she craved this contact, just for a brief second or maybe a minute, with no emotional or physical barriers. Then Noah pulled out, rolled a condom on and returned to loving her.

Which he did, as he did most things, extremely well.

Nine

Jules...

The next morning, when Jules stepped into her mom's sunny kitchen—Levi's kitchen because it was his house now—Darby grabbed her hand and hopped on one foot.

"Juju! News!"

Jules eyed the full coffeepot. Since Noah spent most of last night doing wonderful things to her that might be illegal in certain countries, she was exhausted. Her brain was fried and her energy levels were low. Speaking of, where was the man of the hour, of the past several hours? Her bed was empty, he wasn't in the bathroom and he wasn't helping Levi make breakfast.

Maybe he wanted to avoid facing her family first thing in the morning. God knew she did. But it turned out that she needed coffee more than she needed to avoid conversation.

"Guess who had a date last night?" Darby asked, hopping from one foot to the other.

Okay, she and Darby had the twin thing going on, but Darby could *not* know that she'd slept with Noah. No way. Turning her back on her sister, Jules ignored Levi's greeting and grabbed a mug from the cupboard above the coffeepot. Pouring some of the brew into her cup, she took her time turning around, hoping that they wouldn't notice the stubble burn on her jaw and her many-orgasms glow.

"Isn't there a rule in the Bible about talking about this stuff on a Sunday?" Jules asked.

Levi, who was melting butter for—thank you, God—eggs Benedict, glared at Darby. "Don't think so but I wish there was." Levi frowned at her. "Are we talking about you?"

"Me?" Jules slapped her hand on her heart. "Why me?"

She waited for Levi to say that he'd seen Noah walking out of her bedroom but Levi just shook his head and returned to his task of making breakfast.

Dammit. There was nothing to feel embarrassed about. She and Noah were consenting adults, but she didn't feel comfortable with the idea of her brother knowing that she and Noah... Jules shuddered. Too much to handle on little sleep and with no caffeine in her system.

Darby cocked her head. "You look exhausted, Jules. How much sleep did you get last night?"

Not much since she'd spent most of the night exploring the land of Noah. "It's been a long, long week and last night was difficult. Ethan was at Paris's cocktail party and he is going to be the liaison between Paris and Noah, helping her to make decisions about the yacht."

"Dammit," Levi grumbled.

"Why is that a problem?" Darby reached for an apple

before jumping up on the kitchen counter, her long legs swinging. "Ethan knows yachts. He taught Noah to sail."

Levi shook his head and turned back to the stove. Jules touched his arm and waited until he looked at her. "How much do you know about their falling-out?"

"Not that much. You know Noah. He's not great at communicating. I've gathered bits and pieces from Eli and Ben, stuff they've said over the years, but I don't know what happened, *exactly*." Levi shook his head. "And I'm not telling you, Jules. It's his story to tell."

His reticence wasn't a surprise. Levi wasn't a gossip.

"I have no idea what's going on," Darby complained, between bites of her apple.

"I'll tell you what I can when I can, Darbs," Jules replied. Wanting to get off the subject of Noah and his past—he'd hate to know they were discussing him—Jules tossed her a smile. "So, what's the big news?"

"Oh, God, gossip." Levi groaned. "Can this wait until later?"

"No." Darby pointed a finger at Levi. "It concerns our mother."

Levi stepped away from the stove and frowned at her. "What's wrong with Mom? Is she hurt? Why aren't you telling me anything?"

Levi went from zero to protective in two seconds flat. Sipping her coffee, Jules eyed her siblings over the rim of her cup.

"She's fine," Darby replied before a sly smile crossed her face. "In fact she's more than fine. I heard that she had a hot date last night. Dancing was involved."

Jules hoped it was with the coffee shop owner. Apart from the fact that he was sexy in an older guy/action hero–type of way, her mom hooking up with him would ensure a decent supply of coffee for a long time to come.

Yeah, it wasn't pretty but Jules was willing to encourage this relationship to feed her coffee addiction.

"She went clubbing?" Levi demanded, his expression turning dark.

Go, Mom.

"Where? What? With who?"

Levi looked like he was ready to blow. How could he not know that Darby was winding him up? "Darbs…" she warned.

"Okay, not clubbing. But she did go dancing at a salsa club and she was looking fine."

"How do you know all this?" Levi said, sounding skeptical. Jules shook her head. Darby had friends everywhere and she encouraged those friends to talk, okay, report back to her. She was like the human version of social media.

"A friend of a friend. She also had a dinner date the night before last."

Two guys? Way to go, Mom! Jules grinned but Levi looked like he wanted to rip someone's head off. "Who is he? Where does he work? What does he do? Do we know him? Seriously, I'm going to go over to her house and—"

Jules lifted an eyebrow, waiting to hear what he would do to their mother.

"—give her a stern talking to!" he finished.

Jules giggled. "Calm down, Rambo. She's allowed to have some fun."

"Fun is bowling or golf, not salsa and dinner dates!" Levi picked up some scallions and started chopping the hell out of them.

"Mom is allowed a life. She's been alone a long time. If she wants to get it on, good for her. At least one of us is getting some."

Levi dropped the knife and slapped his hands over his ears. "Shaddup, Darby. Seriously!"

Darby laughed, enjoying Levi's discomfort and her eyes met Jules's, inviting her to share the joke. *Mom's not the only one who is getting lucky...*

Darby heard her silent words and her smile faded, her eyes widening. Jules bit her bottom lip. She normally told Darby everything but she wasn't ready to discuss Noah with her and she wasn't ready to articulate what she was feeling. Mostly because she didn't know what she was feeling, except confused.

Darby glanced at Levi and, seeing that his concentration was back on the scallions, lifted her eyebrows. "Noah?" she mouthed.

Who else? Jules nodded and shook her head. She held up her hand, silently begging her sister to let it go.

Darby pouted before slumping back in her chair, defeated. *We will talk about this.*

I know. Just not yet.

Are you okay?

Yep. Just confused.

Darby waggled her eyebrows. *Tell me this, at the very least. Was he good?*

Jules placed her hand on her heart. *He was amazing.* "What's going on?"

Jules turned to see DJ standing in the doorway, her eyes bouncing from face to face.

"My mother is salsa dancing and dating two guys. I'm freaking out, and Jules hasn't had any sleep." Levi looked up from his task and pointed his knife at Jules, then Darby. "And Jules and Darby are doing their weird twin, silent communication thing."

DJ placed her hands on her hips, eyed Jules and her sister before turning her attention back to Levi. "Your mom deserves to have some fun, and Jules also, if I'm not mistaken, got herself some last night and that's what they were discussing."

Okay, so it might not just be a twin thing; it might be an I've-known-you-since-you-were-six thing. DJ moved to stand behind Levi's back and pointed her finger to the ceiling.

Noah?

Again, who else?

Was it good?

Why were they so concerned about Noah's prowess in the sack? Seriously?

"I can feel the air moving behind me, DJ," Levi growled. "Enough already with the sex talk. I don't want to know who is having sex, when. *Ever,*" Levi said before sending Jules a hard look. "Do I need to beat someone up for you?"

Jules quickly shook her head. "No! I'm good." Seeing the concern on Levi's face, she scrambled to find some words since Levi didn't do the silent communication thing. "I'm good. We're good. Everything is good."

Levi folded his massive arms across his chest. "Good."

Jules frowned at his sarcastic repetition of her word.

"Because I would hate to have to kick my best friend's ass. Speaking of, can you find him and tell him that breakfast will be ready in fifteen?"

Maybe Levi was better at the silent communication thing than she thought.

As she had a hundred times before but not for a long time, Jules climbed up the ivy-covered trellis that led up to what used to be Noah's bedroom within Lockwood House and wondered what she was doing. She wasn't ten or fourteen or even eighteen anymore.

A month after Bethann's death, Ethan had closed up the house and moved to the apartment they kept in the city. She remembered hearing her father and mother discussing his abhorrent behavior, his lack of respect, but being young and self-involved, she hadn't paid much attention to their hushed conversations. All she knew was that Noah was hurting and that their family, which had seemed to be rock solid, detonated with Bethann's passing and the reading of the will. Within three months of her death, Noah had left Boston and dropped out of her life.

Why hadn't she pushed and probed, demanded more information? In hindsight, it was easy to see how much Noah was suffering, to see how unhappy he'd been with Morgan, to discern that she wasn't given him the emotional support he needed. Sex with Morgan might've temporarily dulled the pain but sex wouldn't have dulled his grief, his fear.

But Jules knew why she hadn't dug deeper with Noah. She had been upset with him about his involvement with Morgan—jealous, maybe?—and frustrated when he pulled back into his noncommunicative shell. She'd been dealing with her own grief and frustration at not being able to connect with her friend, betrayed by the announcement of his engagement and devastated by his kiss.

Devastated, confused, emotionally battered.

But that was in their past and she had to deal with Noah as he was today, with the adults they both were. He wasn't a young man anymore and she wasn't a teen. They could, presumably, separate attraction from sex, love from friendship, curtail their wild imaginings…

She was a successful businesswoman, a confident woman…

Who was, technically, trespassing. Jules raised the sash window and flung her leg over the windowsill. Actually, there were no technicalities involved, she was definitely trespassing.

Jules dropped her feet to the floor and wasn't surprised to see Noah in his room, dressed in a pair of old, well-fitting jeans and a long-sleeved gray shirt, the sleeves pushed up to his elbows. Thanks to his recent shower, his blond hair looked a shade darker. She inhaled the dust and mustiness of a closed room but also soap and toothpaste and his special Noah-only scent.

Jules stood up straight, slapped her hands on her butt and looked at Noah. "Levi says breakfast is nearly ready."

Noah sat on the edge of what used to be his bed and frowned at her. "Not that hungry, actually."

Jules wanted to go to him, to drape her arms around his neck and snuggle in, but the expression on his face was remote, his body tense. Knowing that he wouldn't open up without some prodding—if he opened up at all—Jules sat on the edge of the sill and stretched out her legs. "Why did you break into your dad's house, No?"

"Ethan's house," Noah corrected her, his mouth tightening. "He stopped being my dad a decade ago."

"What happened, Noah?"

Noah stared at his feet, his hand draped between his bent knees. "My mom's will wasn't clear and there was room to maneuver. Ethan essentially tried to screw us out of our inheritance. When he was faced with the choice of inheriting millions or keeping his kids, he chose the cash." Noah stared at the hard, glossy wooden floor. He cleared his throat and when he continued speaking, Jules heard his voice crack with emotion. "He raised us. We called him Dad. Eli and Ben were toddlers when he came into our lives and he spent twenty-plus years being our dad. He was at every sport match he could make, at every play, prize giving. I thought he loved my mom with every fiber of his being.

"Two weeks after her death, I called him at the city apartment and a woman answered his phone, a very young-sounding woman. He was in the shower and she told me that she intended to keep him busy for the rest of the night, if I understood what she meant."

Jules fought the urge to go to him, but if she did he'd clam up and stop talking. She gripped the sill to keep herself in place.

"I confronted Ethan the next day and he laughed in my face. He told me to grow up, that the woman I talked to wasn't the first nor would she be the last. It was what men did, he said."

No, it wasn't. Her dad never cheated on her mom.

Noah's knee bounced up and down. "He then went on to tell me that he'd done his job—he'd raised us as Mom wanted him to do, and he was cashing in. The businesses, the house, the bank accounts, it was payment for being incarcerated in his marriage, his life, for the past twenty years."

Jules bit her lip at Noah's bleak tone. "If I behaved, let him take, well, everything, he'd continue paying for our education, if not, we could waft in the wind."

"Oh, Noah."

"I couldn't let him do that, not without a fight. I needed money to hire lawyers and Ivan gave me more than I needed, provided I stayed engaged to Morgan for two years. After a lot of legal wrangling, the judge gave us the marina and boatyard. Ethan got the cash and the estate. I needed to keep sailing to keep generating the cash to upgrade the marina and boatyard so that they could become profitable again."

"But you did it, Noah. You saved your grandfather's businesses."

Noah lifted his head to look at her. "The price was enormous, Jules. When I finally broke it off with Morgan she had a nervous breakdown and was admitted to some psychiatric facility. They blamed me, despite the fact that our relationship hadn't been anything more than a few calls and emails for months."

"They needed someone to blame, No, and you were handy."

"Maybe." Noah stood up and walked over to his desk, looking at the medals hanging on the wall, the sailing trophies still on the shelf. "Most people think that the opportunity to sail for Wind and Solar was a dream come true."

"Wasn't it?"

She could see the tension in his back in the way he held his neck. But when he turned around and looked at her, Jules saw the devastation on his face. "Leaving Boston was a freaking nightmare. Oh, the sailing was fun, visiting new places was interesting, but when I stepped onto that plane at Logan, I left everything behind. My mom was gone and I was still mourning her, trying to come to terms with her early, brutally unfair death. I lost my dad, too. I didn't recognize the man standing in front of me, taking us to court for *his paycheck*. I had to leave my brothers and hope like hell that they were sensible enough to stay out of trouble, and if not, to run to your folks if they found themselves in a sticky situation. I left my friends, not only Levi, but other friends of both sexes. I left you, the person who knew me best, and I left this weird thing between us, an attraction that blew in from nowhere and was left unexplored. I felt like I had my entire life ripped from me…"

"Which you did." Jules waited a beat before speaking

again. "You could've told me this, Noah, at any time. I would've understood because, dammit, I needed to understand."

Noah shrugged. "Time passed and as it did, the words grew harder to say."

Noah pushed his thumbs into his eyes and Jules wondered if it was because he didn't want her to see the tears there. Hers were about to overflow.

Noah folded his arms, looked up at the ceiling and, a long time later, looked back. The grief was gone and determination was back on his face. "There is no way I am going back there, Jules, back to that place where I felt lost and scared and alone. I've learned how to live on my own, be on my own—I can't do this happy-family thing…"

She didn't recall asking him to but…okay.

Noah looked around the room, his face hard. "This is just a house, these are just things. This is just land. My mom isn't here and by buying it I won't change the past, change what he did, the choices I made. Mom doesn't care whether it stays in the family or not—she's not here!"

Jules winced at the muted roar. "I'm killing myself, and for what? To design a boat for a woman who doesn't seem to care what I come up with or not? So that I can raise the money to buy a property I'm not sure I even want in a town that holds nothing but bad memories for me?"

Well, that stung.

"I could forget about buying the house and the estate. I could walk away. I have a client begging me to meet him on the Costa Smeralda, another in Hawaii, both wanting designs I could do in my sleep. I don't need to be here, Jules! I don't need this crap in my life! Sun, sailing and sex…with none of the drama!"

Jules nodded, pain punching tiny holes in her stomach lining and her heart. He didn't want a life in Boston and he didn't want her. He needed his freedom, she knew this... She'd always known this. So why did it hurt so much? Jules pushed her hair off her face and forced herself to look him in the eye, to confront her feelings. "I'm sorry you feel like that, No. I'm sorry that you think a life in Boston can't give you what you need."

"You don't know what I need, Jules!"

Yeah, she did, but getting him to realize that was an impossibility. But she'd try. At least once... "You need us, Noah, and you need *me*. You need to wake up with someone who loves you, who gets you, understands your past and who will always be on your side. You need to spend your days with your brothers and play pool with them in The Tavern and golf outside your front door. You need to have coffee and dinner with my mom and talk about your mom. You need to buy this house and you need to *stay*."

Noah frowned at her and she could see hope and frustration and fear going to war in his eyes. "Why do you say that?"

Because she loved him. She'd loved him every day of her life and she'd fallen in love with him again when she saw him standing naked in her shower. Her brain had just needed a little time to come to terms with what her heart always knew.

"Because if you walk away from this house, from Boston, from me, you're going to regret it every day for the rest of your life. You belong here, Noah. You belong with me."

Jules held up her hand, knowing he was about to make a hard rebuttal. "I get it, Noah. I understand how much it must have hurt leaving because I felt it, too. Not having you in my life was horrendous and I was determined that I wouldn't give you another chance to hurt me. But here I am, doing it again. Love is scary, Noah, but it's the one thing that should be scary! We shouldn't just be able to jump into love without thought. I know if you walk away again I'll be in a world of pain, *again*, but I can't divorce myself from what I feel because loving you is an essential part of who I am."

Jules stood up and made herself smile as she placed one leg over the windowsill. "If you leave, if you don't fight for this house, fight for your life, fight for me, you'll be an old man living with regret, unable to look yourself in the eye."

"I don't love you, Jules."

Such impetuous, defiant words. Jules closed her eyes, trying to hold back the pain. "Of course you love me, Noah. You always have. Just as I've always loved you. You're just too damn scared to admit it and even more terrified to do something about it."

Callie...

There was no way that Mason would hear that she'd been on two dates in the past week. While many of her friends frequented his coffee shop, she doubted that he made it a habit to quiz the elderly about their love lives.

And if he did, he shouldn't.

Her friends, the few who knew she was dating, wouldn't think to tell him. To them Mason was part of the service industry, not someone to gossip with. The thought made her feel ugly, petty and ashamed. She shouldn't even be coming here but she was as addicted to his gorgeous face as she was to his coffee blend.

Oh, who was she kidding? He could serve strychnine-flavored java and she'd be coming back for more. It was official: she was pathetic. Callie pushed open the door to the coffeehouse and cursed when her eyes flew around the room, instinctively seeking out the man she'd come to see. She'd blown off a round of golf this morning with Patrick and an invite to lunch with John. Her dates thought that their evenings had gone well but, apart from the salsa dancing, she'd been as bored as hell—and Mason was to blame.

Patrick and John were perfectly nice, urbane, success-ful men in their early sixties. Accomplished, successful and courteous, they were appropriate men for a woman of her age to date.

They were also deeply, fundamentally, jaw-breakingly boring. And they seemed, dammit, old.

"Stop frowning. You're going to get wrinkles," Mason murmured.

Callie turned her head to see him standing behind her, dressed in khaki shorts and an untucked, white but-ton-down shirt with the cuffs rolled back. He was car-rying a cup of coffee and a slice of carrot cake, and her mouth watered—at the sight of him and the dessert. She couldn't indulge; she had to try and keep her muffin top under some sort of control. Though she suspected that horse had bolted a long, long time ago...

"I already have wrinkles," Callie told him, sitting down at the nearest table and glaring at him.

"Hardly any," Mason replied, his eyes wandering over her face and down her neck. "In fact, you have the most gorgeous skin. Want some coffee?"

No, I want to stop thinking about you. I want to stop imagining what your hands feel like on my skin, your tongue in my mouth. I want to be able to date and not feel like I am cheating on my dead husband and you.

Callie sighed. "S'pose."

Mason delivered the coffee and carrot cake to a nearby table before returning to her side. He held her chin and lifted her head, blue eyes assessing. "Who pissed on your battery?"

He was so damn irreverent. "Don't be crude."

Mason's thumb skimmed her bottom lip. "Stop acting like you are 103. Spit it out, woman."

She should object to him calling her "woman," should tell him to go to hell. But his rough voice and the tenderness in his eyes just warmed her from the inside out.

Or more accurately, from that space between her legs and up.

Callie gestured for him to take the other seat. "Don't call me 'woman,' and don't loom over me. Sit if you want to but don't...*hover*."

Mason frowned, slid into the chair opposite her and rested his arms on the table. He didn't speak. He just looked at her with assessing eyes. Callie drummed her fingers on the table between them, wondering what to say. She couldn't tell him that she'd missed him, that she'd wanted to be with him, that eating out with another man seemed wrong.

"Cal? Talk to me."

"Jules, my daughter, is going through a rough time. She and the man she loves, who I think also loves her, can't find a way to be together."

Mason remained silent for a moment. "As a parent, I fully understand that you are worried but that's not why you are upset. Tell me the truth, the full truth." Mason stopped one of his passing waitresses, ordered a latte and turned his attention back to her.

"I wanted an espresso," Callie muttered.

"No, you didn't, and aren't I supposed to be the child in this nonrelationship?" Mason asked, his voice sounding tougher than she'd ever heard it. Callie flushed, sat back and tried to get her anger under control. None of this was his fault and her acting like an angry teenager wasn't helping.

"One of the reasons I like you, Callie, is that you appear to be a straight shooter. So, last chance, speak or shut up," Mason said, his eyes flat and his jaw hard.

Callie ran her thumbnail across the wooden table. "I went on two dates this past week."

Mason immediately stiffened. "Why are you telling me this?"

"Because they were very nice, very successful men of a certain age and they were—"

"I think I'm going to throw up," Mason interjected.

"—as boring as hell. I spent most of that time wishing they were you," Callie continued, ignoring him.

Mason's eyes lightened, darkened and lightened again. Callie fell into all that interest and emotion and, yeah, desire. "What are you saying, Callie?"

"I'm saying that I am a fifty-four-year-old woman who is not only just coming out of mourning, but menopause, too. I am a cocktail of hormones, insecurity and confusion. I am both terrified of having sex and equally terrified of not ever having it again. I've been a wife, am still sort of a mommy, but I've forgotten how to be a woman."

Mason ran his hand over his jaw, visibly shocked by her blunt speech.

"I want you but I don't want to want you. I don't want to disappoint you but I don't want to disappoint myself. I'm never getting married again—Ray was the only husband I'll ever have."

"Jesus."

If she stopped now, she'd never start again. "If you keep asking me, I might say yes to a date. I might even get up enough courage to put my overweight, very unsexy body in your hands and I might let you kiss me."

"*Might?* Screw that."

Mason pulled her to her feet and led her through the crowded tables toward the counter on the far side of the room. Callie tried to tug her hand away but he was too strong and, yeah, this was the most excitement she'd had since she and Ray made love in the hot tub—

The slap of Mason's hand on a swinging door dragged her from that memory—from the guilt rising in her—and she found herself in a tiny kitchen. Mason hauled her across the room and, keeping his hand around her wrist, flipped the dead bolt on the back door. Hot, humid air swirled around her as Mason guided her down the steps and, the next moment, her back was against the rough brick wall. Mason stared down at her, his eyes boring into her.

"Tell me now you don't want this and I'll back off."

Callie placed her hands on his chest and lifted her face up. "I do but I shouldn't—"

"Again, screw that."

Mason's hands captured her face and his mouth covered hers and plundered, sliding over hers like he owned it, his tongue twisting hers into submission.

This wasn't a boy's kiss but a man's, a man who knew what he wanted and how he intended to get it. There was no hesitation because Mason listened to her body language, saw the desire in her eyes. Impatient and determined, he wasn't the type to waste time, to hang around waiting for her to be 100 percent ready.

Turned out that he was right, she was ready. Her tongue knew what to do, her hands ran up his strong back, down his hard butt, skirted around to feel his flat, hard stomach. Since she was touching him, Mason obviously thought that a little quid pro quo was in order and his broad hand sneaked between them and covered her breast, immediately finding her nipple and rubbing it into a hard, tight point.

It felt natural to tilt her pelvis, to push against that long, hard erection...

His erection. His...

Erection.

God, she was kissing a man who wasn't her husband, who was so much younger than her, in the alley behind his coffeehouse. *Whoa, brakes on, Brogan.*

Mason, feeling her resistance, rested his forehead on hers. "Please don't regret this, Callie. You didn't do anything wrong."

Callie's hands fell to her sides as Ray's face flashed on the big screen in her mind. What would he think? What would her kids think? Her friends? Callie stepped away from Mason, who looked flushed and, oh, so frustrated.

"Then why do I feel like I have?"

"This again." Mason shoved his hands into his hair. "He's dead, Callie, and you're alive, still here, still sexy, still a woman. You didn't die with him."

"A part of me did, Mason!" Callie cried. "And the part of me that is waking up is still coming to terms with all of this!"

Mason's eyes flashed with irritation. "I'm not going to beg, Callie. Or run after you. Or wait forever."

Callie narrowed her eyes, suddenly furious. "That's such a man thing to say! Because it's not going your way, you issue a threat? Guess what, Mason? I'm not young enough or stupid enough or insecure enough to fall for that BS!

"This goes at my pace or it doesn't go at all," Callie added, furious.

Callie saw the regret in his eyes, the apology hovering on his lips. It had been a spur-of-the-moment statement, something she instinctively knew he regretted, but it gave her a damn good excuse to walk away, to put a whole lot of daylight and space between her and this man who'd dropped into her life and flipped it upside down.

"I'm not going to come back here for a while. I need time to think," Callie told him.

Mason nodded, clearly still frustrated but back in control. He gestured at the still-open door. "I'll follow you in shortly. I need some time."

"For what?" Callie asked the question without thinking and frowned at his raised eyebrows. Then Mason shocked her by grabbing her hand and placing her palm on his very hard penis. Through his shorts she could feel his strength, the sheer masculinity under her palm. She leaned forward, wanting to kiss him but Mason pulled back and dropped her hand.

He turned away, and when he spoke his voice sounded rough. And a little sad. "Go inside, Callie. I'll see you when and if I see you."

Walk away, Brogan. It was the right thing to do. She didn't want to, but Callie forced herself to pull open the door to the coffee shop, to step back into the cool kitchen.

Back to reality, where it was safe. But where it was also so damn lonely.

And brutally unexciting.

Ten

Noah...

Of course you love me, Noah, you always have. Just as I've always loved you. You're just too damn scared to admit it and even more terrified to do something about it.

Jules's words rolled around Noah's head as they had every minute for the past three weeks. He wanted to dismiss them, to shrug them off as a figment of her overactive imagination, but they ran across his mind on a never-ending ticker tape.

He wanted her, of course he did, she was everything he wanted, but he was too damn scared, comprehensively terrified of what it meant to go all in with Jules. Noah thought that he had just cause to be. He'd had everything at one point in his life; he'd had the world at his feet. A solid family structure, parents who adored him, pain-in-the-ass brothers who'd charge hell if he needed them to. Friends—good, close friends.

Then, like a cheap car slamming into the back of a heavy rig at high speed, his life had crumpled and crashed around him and his world as he knew it ended. Everything he knew, relied upon, was no longer there. The people he thought he knew morphed into strangers. His dad became his enemy, his girlfriend a means to an end, his friendship with Jules suddenly colored by a shocking dose of lust. Leaving his life behind hadn't been a choice. But walking away still hurt like the hot, sour bite of hell.

He didn't think he could cope with loving something— a person, his life, normality—and having it ripped from him again. But nor could he live a life that didn't have Jules in it. And he didn't want her as his friend...

Rock and hard place, meet the devil and the deep blue sea.

He loved her, of course he did. He'd loved the ten-year-old Jules who caught frogs and climbed trees, the fourteen-year-old with braces, the young woman he'd watched evolve into an adult woman. Then he kissed her and he saw a thousand galaxies in her eyes, felt the power of the universe in her touch. That hadn't changed: Jules was still, and always would be, the person who made his world turn.

Tides changed, the moon waxed and waned, and seas dipped and rose but Jules was his sextant, his North Star, his GPS.

Wherever she was, was where he wanted to be. But fear, cold and hard, still gripped his heart. God, he'd much rather be fighting a squall in the Southern Ocean than be caught in this emotional maelstrom.

Noah looked up at the rap on his door frame, happy for any distraction coming his way. Levi stood in the doorway, dressed in board shorts and dock shoes, his red T-shirt faded by sunlight. Noah noticed the six-pack in his hand, the bottles dripping with condensation. Hell, yes, he could do with one or three of those.

Levi walked into his office, tossed him a beer and sat down on his chair, his long legs stretched out in front of him. Noah cracked the top, took a long sip and rested the cold bottle on his aching head. "So, you need to make a formal offer on the Lockwood Trust in two days or the estate will go on the market," Levi said bluntly.

He was aware. "There's no chance Paris will sign the final design by then. Ethan won't let her."

"Has Jules completed her designs?"

Noah glanced at the folder holding Jules's sketches, the fabric samples, the wonderful mock-ups of the yacht's interiors. They'd been communicating via email for weeks but Jules still managed to do a stunning job and Paris, and anyone with taste, would love her designs. "She's done. So am I. Paris just needs to approve the designs."

"So when are you meeting her?"

"I haven't made an appointment to see her yet." Levi pulled a face and Noah shook his head at his friend's disapproval. "I know I should but I keep wondering what's the point? Ethan will shoot down everything I say, he'll demand a redesign and time will run out. I've been working on other projects but my fees won't earn anywhere near as much as what Paris cane pay me. Basically, I'm screwed."

Levi frowned before pointing the top of his bottle in Noah's direction. "Sorry, who are you and what have you done with Noah Lockwood?"

Noah sent him a blank look, wondering if Levi had had a few more beers before ending up in his office.

"Noah, one of the things that set you apart from other

sailors was your utter belief in yourself and the course you were on. You backed yourself a hundred percent and you never ever gave up. Where's that dude?"

Noah opened his mouth to blast Levi, to defend himself, but Levi spoke over him. "You always raced until the bitter end, sometimes you went across the finish line without realizing that you were done, that you had won the race, because you were so damn focused, because you fought, right up until the end. You still have a couple of days. Why the hell aren't you still fighting?"

"I…uh…" Crap, he didn't have an answer for that.

"My sister—the miserable one living in my house—and your future are deserving of all your effort, Noah, all your competitive spirit and every last bit of determination," Levi said, emotion bleeding through his tough words. He leaned forward, his intense gaze nailing Noah to his chair. "It's the Rolex Sydney Hobart Yacht Race, you and your closest competitor are in the Bass Strait and it's neck and neck. Are you going to alter course, or are you going to hold your nerve, and your course, and fight for the win?"

Adrenaline pumped through his system. He could taste the drops of seawater on his lips, the wind blowing in his hair. Wind catching his sails, he could hear the whoop of his teammates as his yacht sailed forward.

Keeping his eyes on Levi's, he drained his beer and reached for his phone. "I'm going to hold my course."

Levi nodded and the fire of frustration in his eyes died. "Thank God, I wasn't looking forward to kicking your ass."

For the first time in days, Noah smiled. "As if you could. Now, get lost. I've got a house to buy and a meeting to set up."

Levi ambled to his feet, snagging the plastic cage holding the beers. "And a girl to win?"

"Yeah. And a girl to win."

Levi looked concerned. "And if you lose?"

Noah lifted one shoulder and held his friend's eye. "I never lose, Levi. But there's a first time for everything and if that happens, I'll do what I always do…"

"And that is?"

"Stand in the storm, ride it out and keep adjusting my sails."

Jules…

I am not going to cry. That will not happen. This is business. Paris is a client and Noah is a colleague. You can do this. You have to do this.

Woman up, Brogan.

Jules placed her hand on the wall next to the elevator in the lobby of Paris's building and stared at the expensive marble flooring. Dammit, this hurt. Every cell in her body ached, her eyes were red rimmed from crying too many tears and from nights without sleep. She felt sick from the tips of her toes to her ears. God, even her hair hurt. She was fundamentally, utterly miserable.

Her fault, so her fault. She told herself not to fall for Noah again, she knew a broken heart was a possibility. Heartbreak, such small words for such a life-altering condition. Jules wished she could go back to her childhood, when skinned knees and broken arms hurt and were inconvenient but they healed, dammit. This…this gut-ripping, soul-mincing pain was going to be with her for a long, long time. And she knew she'd never be the same person again, she was irrevocably changed. Quieter, harder, a lot more lost and very alone.

This was now her life.

Jules looked down at the screen on her phone and glared at the prosaic, to-the-point message on her screen. Five o'clock meeting with Paris. Be there.

Noah's terse instructions were followed by Paris's address.

Jules hadn't spoken to Noah since leaving him in his childhood bedroom nearly a month ago. He didn't come back to the house for breakfast, and when he didn't contact her on Monday, or on any day that following week, she assumed that history was repeating itself and Noah was retreating from her bed and her life. She spent every moment she had working on her designs for the yacht—the sooner she finished with them, the sooner this would all be over—and couriered the finished designs and the sketches to Noah's office two weeks ago.

She'd yet to hear whether he approved, what he thought. She could be going into a presentation showing Paris sketches and designs Noah hated. Because she still had her pride, and that meant that she had a reputation to maintain, a job to complete and that meant— *grrr*—obeying his text message order. She'd never bailed on a project and didn't intend to now. No matter how difficult it would be to see Noah again, knowing he chose his fear over her, she would get into this damn elevator and finish the job.

If she didn't, she would never be able to look herself in the eye again. *Time to be brave, Brogan.* An hour, maybe more, and she'd be done. She could go home, pull a blanket over her head and shut out the world. And release all the tears that were gathering in her throat.

Jules left the elevator and walked down the long hallway, telling herself that this was it, this was the last time she would be seeing Noah for God knew how long.

Standing outside Paris's door, she worked her fist into her sternum, mentally tossing water on the fire in her stomach.

An hour, Brogan. You can do this. You have no choice!

Wishing she was anywhere else—she was exhausted and stressed and *sad*, dammit—Jules knocked on Paris's door and jumped when the door swung open. Noah stood there, strong and confident in his gray suit, white shirt and scarlet power tie. His hair was brushed off his forehead and he looked like he could stroll into any business meeting anywhere in the world and take control.

Jules met his eyes and frowned at the tenderness she saw within those brown depths, the flicker of amusement. He thought this was funny? His inheritance was on the line and her heart was hemorrhaging, and he was amused? Jules welcomed the surge of anger and clenched her fists, the urge to smack him almost overwhelming.

She hauled in a breath, then another, knowing that her face reflected all her suppressed rage. She was going to kill him, slowly and right there. A sympathetic female judge would understand, she was sure of it.

"You look like you are about to blow a gasket."

A gasket, an engine, input the codes to set off a nuclear strike. How dare he stand there looking rested and relaxed? Did he have any idea of the strolls she'd taken through hell lately?

"I— You— I'm… God!" Jules rubbed her fingers across her forehead. She couldn't do this, there was no chance. She was leaving, going home and crawling into bed before she fell apart completely. She wasn't brave and she definitely wasn't strong.

"I've got to go." Jules managed to whisper the words

and turned to leave. Noah's hand on her arm pulled her back to face him, and then his hands were on her hips and drawing her slowly and deliberately toward himself. When not even an ant could crawl between them, he brushed his mouth across hers, his tongue tracing the seam of her lips, before lifting his head.

Why was he doing this? Was he trying to torture her?

No more. She was done with this. Jules slid her fingers under his open suit jacket, grabbed the skin at his waist and gave it a hard twist.

Noah's eyes widened and she heard his pained gasp. "Ow. For what?"

"Do you know how much it hurts to kiss you, knowing that I might never be able to do that again?" Jules hissed, furious at the tears that clouded her vision. "That's not fair, Noah, and worse than that, it's cruel."

Noah rubbed the back of his neck, looking shocked and a little embarrassed. "Jules, babe, just hang on."

"For what, Noah? No, I'm done! I can't do this anymore. It hurts too damn much!"

Noah touched her cheek with his knuckle. "I'm asking you, one more time, to trust me. Please, Jules."

Jules shook her head, willing away the tears in her eyes. "I don't think I can, Noah. You've drained me of the little strength I had left."

"Dammit, Jules—"

"Julia? Oh, is Julia here?" Paris trilled from somewhere in the cavernous apartment behind them. "Noah! Is that Julia? If it is, tell her to come and have a glass of champagne and to show me her pretty, pretty work."

Jules closed her eyes, twisted her lips and, refusing to look at the man she wanted the most but couldn't have, turned on her heel and forced herself to walk into Paris's luxurious apartment.

Noah...

Noah was regarded as one of the best sailors of his generation, one of the top money earners in the sport. He was a decent businessman, successful and wealthy. A good brother and friend. None of that meant anything, everything was stripped away, and he was now just the man who'd made Jules cry.

Never again. He was done with that. From this moment on, Jules and her happiness were his highest priority, making sure that she'd never have cause to doubt him again, his lifetime goal. And, because he didn't want her to suffer longer than she had to, Noah injected steel into his spine and followed his woman into the overly decorated lounge of Paris's apartment.

Ethan was at the meeting, just as he'd expected and banked on him to be. Noah had given their encounter a lot of thought so he had a plan. Taking control of the presentation—knowing that Jules needed something to anchor her—he suggested a virtual tour of the yacht. He quickly connected his laptop to Paris's big-screen TV and, thanks to some very high-tech computer software, showed Paris what he and Jules envisaged for the yacht, inside and out. Pity their client couldn't feel the waves rolling under the hull, taste the salt on her lips, but that being said, it was still kick-ass tech.

As he'd requested, Paris and Ethan kept their comments until the end, allowing him and Jules to complete their presentation before they were bombarded with questions.

"It's beautiful." Paris sighed and clasped her hands. "Utterly marvelous. What shall I call her?"

"Whatever you like." Noah smiled but it faded when he darted a glance at Jules and saw her blank face.

"Before your rhapsodizing gets out of control, my dear, I should like to point out that there are some very crucial design flaws in what Noah has presented," Ethan said, his voice pitched low. No, there weren't. How could Paris not hear the malice in his voice, see the spite in his eyes?

And so it started.

Placing his ankle on his knee, Noah cocked his head. Ethan met his eyes, not for one minute believing that Noah would rake up the past. It was a fair conclusion for him to reach; generally, Noah would rather bleed to death before asking for a bandage, help or even a plaster. Well, not this time. There was too much at stake.

"There are no flaws in the design," Noah said, his voice calm. "Ethan is just saying that to irritate me."

Paris frowned. "Nonsense! He's your stepfather. He raised you. And he's just trying to make your design better and to look after my interests."

Noah shook his head, conscious of Jules's eyes on his face. "Ethan never looks after anyone's interests but his own, Paris. He doesn't want you to sign off on the design, because if you do that, then he has to sell Lockwood Estate to me, at twenty percent below the market price. He'd lose twenty million if that happens."

"That's not true," Ethan bit out, turning an alarming shade of red.

Noah dropped his leg, leaned forward and opened a folder, pulling out a copy of the judgment. He pushed it across the table in Paris's direction. "Proof." Noah reached across the table and took Paris's hand in his. Damn, he didn't want to hurt her but when it came to choosing between her happiness and Jules's, between saving his inheritance and kicking Ethan out of his life forever, he would. Besides, she and Ethan had only been together a few weeks; she was as much a victim of his machinations as he was.

"Paris, I like you. You're a pain in the ass to work for, but you have a warm heart, a romantic heart. I think you are wonderfully charming and witty but you *are* a woman of a certain age."

Paris narrowed her eyes at that statement and Noah ignored her, along with Ethan's growls of disapproval. Noah forced himself to articulate the words. "Ethan doesn't date woman your age, in fact he rarely dates anyone over the age of twenty-five." *Dammit, just spit it out!* "The only reason he's dating you is because you are rich and he's broke."

"I am not! This is slander! How dare you?"

"Noah—"

Noah ignored Jules's quiet warning and flicked a quick glance at Ethan, looking apoplectic with rage. He pulled out another stack of papers and put them in front of Paris. "Photos of his last ten girlfriends, copies of his credit report—he owes money all around town."

Paris looked down, flicked through the papers and when she lifted her head again, her eyes were flint hard. *Gotcha, you bastard.*

"Those are bogus—you can't prove anything. Paris, it's not true. He's been lying to you, too… He and Jules aren't romantically involved, he just said it to appeal to your softer side," Ethan shouted.

Noah cursed when doubt flew into Paris's eyes. Deliberately not looking at Jules, he held Paris's gaze and waited for the question. If she didn't believe him, he was sunk. He'd lose the house, his time and the money.

He could live with losing all three but, God, if he lost Jules…

"Are you and Jules not romantically involved?"

Noah had to answer her honestly, knowing that nothing else but the truth would get him through this quagmire. "There's nothing romantic about Jules and I," he replied, sighing when he heard the harsh note in his own voice and Jules's gasp.

Okay, not off to a good start. He rubbed his hand over his head, ordering his tongue to cooperate. "*Romance* implies something ephemeral, wishy-washy, fleeting. Jules and I have known each other too long and too well to settle for such a weak description of our relationship."

Paris tipped her head to the side. "So how would you characterize it?"

Well, hell, he was going to have to say it after all. And with an audience. Okay, then. Noah shifted his gaze from Paris's face to Jules's, her light eyes surprised and, yes, terrified.

Join the freakin' club.

"She's been my best friend all my life, my rock, my true north. She's the reason the moon pulls the tide, why the earth spins, the reason my sun sets and falls.

"Yes, we started off by faking something that we thought wasn't there, not knowing that it was, that it has always been a part of me, of us."

Jules clasped her hands together, her face devoid of color, her eyes begging for more. Something to banish the last of her fear, something that would restore her trust. Noah kept his eyes on her face but directed his words at Paris. "Sign off on the yacht or don't, Paris. Yeah, a part of me will be sad at missing out on reclaiming the house and land that's been in my family for generations, but I'll live with it. What I can't live without, what I refuse to live without, is Jules. I'd live in a freakin' cardboard box if it meant being with her. She's my..." His voice broke when he saw the tears in Jules's eyes. He swallowed and bit the flesh on the inside of his cheek to keep it together. Were her tears a good sign? Bad? He couldn't tell.

He forced himself to speak again, this time speaking to Jules directly. "You're…everything, Jules. You always will be, I promise."

Jules lifted her fist to her mouth, the tears now running down her face. What did they mean? Did he still have a chance? God, he hoped so. When they were alone he'd drag more out of her. Things like "Yes, let's give us a chance" or "Okay, we can go out on a date." He was intelligent enough to know that he'd hurt her—again—and that she'd take her time forgiving him, that she'd have to learn to trust him all over again.

He could live with that. After all, he wasn't going anywhere for a while and when he did he was coming straight back to Boston.

Paris cleared her throat, pushed the stack of papers incriminating Ethan away from her. "Out."

Noah thought she was talking to him but then realized that she was looking at Ethan. "You have a minute to leave my home. If you do not do so in that time, I will not only have you ostracized from polite society, I will tell every rich young lady I come across that you have impotence issues."

Noah turned to smile at Jules and his breath hitched at the flicker of hope he saw in her eyes. He pushed his chair back, intending to go to her, to pull her into his arms, when Paris gripped his wrist. Her fingernails pushed into his skin. "Oh, no, you don't. You are going to keep your hands off her until we've gone through your design in detail. Then I'll sign off on the design and write you a check."

Noah groaned, Jules whimpered and Paris looked from him to Jules and back to him, resignation in her eyes.

"Oh, all right, then! Contract signing and check but I'll expect you both back here tomorrow to talk about my beautiful, beautiful yacht. Will you two have sorted yourselves out by then?"

Noah, still unsure, darted a glance at Jules, who had yet to speak. "Hopefully."

Jules pulled a tissue out of her bag, wiped her eyes and hauled in a breath. Then her eyes focused and she nodded at the folder in front of him. "Let's get this done, Noah."

So, what did that mean? And where the hell did he stand?

Jules...

Noah decided that the closest place they could find privacy was on the *Resilience*, and unlike what happened in movies, they didn't run down the sidewalks of Boston, pushing past people to get to the marina. Silently, they took the elevator to the ground floor, where they caught a taxi to the marina. At the access gate, Noah plugged in his code, escorted Jules through the turnstile and to the far quay where his magnificent J-class yacht was berthed, her tall mast making her easily recognizable.

It felt like she was having an out-of-body experience—had Noah really told her, in front of people, that he loved her? It was so surreal, like it was the best dream ever. God, she really hoped she never woke up. Jules slipped off her shoes, sighing when her bare feet hit the teak deck. She headed to the bow, where she sank down and dangled her feet off the edge of the yacht.

Jules lifted her head and saw Noah looming over her, looking unsure. She patted the space next to her and Noah shrugged out of his jacket, pulled off his tie and dropped them to the warm deck, immediately lifting his face to the sun.

"Did you mean it?" Jules asked quietly, searching his eyes for the truth.

Because he knew her so well, he didn't need clarification on exactly what she was asking. He nodded. "Absolutely." Noah flipped open the cuffs on his shirt and started to roll them up. "You were right, you know. About me loving you, that I always have."

She could barely hear his precious words over the sound of her own heartbeat... Dare she believe this was really happening?

Noah managed a smile, his eyes intense as he tucked a strand of hair behind her ear. Immediately the wind blew it across her mouth again.

"Do you...love me? Back at Lockwood House, you told me you did but that could've changed in the last three weeks."

She saw his fear of being rejected and her heart lurched. This was Noah as she'd never seen him before: humbled, vulnerable, uncertain. *This mattered, she mattered.*

Jules touched his cheek, ran her hands over his thin lips. "My first memory was you picking me up when I fell. I think Darby pushed me off the swing. You helped me up and I looked at you and I felt...whole. My three-year-old heart recognized you... I'm not putting this well." Jules stumbled over her words. "I've spent the last ten years looking for something I always had, something that I only feel when I'm with you. You are what I need in my life, No, the only thing I need. It's more than love. It's..."

Noah finally smiled at her. "Right."

Yeah, it was. Being with Noah was where she was supposed to be, being his was what she was meant to do. They had their careers and their interests and their friends, but they were destined to be a unit. She and Darby might've shared a womb but she was convinced she and Noah shared a heart.

Noah's mouth skimmed hers but he pulled back when desire flared. "Can we do this? Be together?"

"We can do anything, No. Yeah, your work is mostly overseas but we can work around that." It would be hard but he was worth it. He was worth *everything*.

"My client consults are overseas. My work doesn't have to be. Technology pretty much allows me to work anywhere, and most of my correspondence with my freelance staff is done online. I'd still have to travel but I could easily make my base here in Boston."

"Is this where you want to be?" Jules asked him, unable to disguise the tremor and hope in her voice.

"Jules, you are where I want to be," Noah replied, sounding confident again. "Your business is here, your clients are here. If I want to be with you, and I do, then Boston is where I'll be." He held up his hand when she opened her mouth to speak. "And, yeah, of course I'm moving here to be with you but, as you pointed out, my brothers are here, Levi, my businesses. Added bonuses."

The sun was shining, the air was fresh but her lungs felt constricted; she couldn't breathe. This was her fantasy, the best news she could get and she was on the verge of passing out. The cliché about being careful what you wish for drifted through her head.

Jules sucked in some air, waited for her head to clear, before using both hands to hold back her hair. She wanted to look at Noah, see his eyes when she asked him her next question, the one she had to have an answer for.

"Can I trust you? Will you promise not to wander off with my heart again?"

Noah scooted closer to her, his hand covering the side

of her face. "My heart is yours, babe. It always has been. You know that."

"As mine is yours," Jules said.

Noah pushed a curl behind her ear. "I need to go to Costa Smeralda to meet with an oil sheikh who wants me to design a state-of-the-art yacht. No longer content to have oil wells and hotels and race horses, he now wants to sail competitively. I thought you could come with me and we could have a preengagement honeymoon."

Jules's mouth curved. "So, we are getting married?"

Noah's mouth slid across hers in a kiss that promised her forever. "Damn right we are. But right now you need to kiss me."

So Jules did. In fact, they kissed for so long and with so much abandon that numerous complaints were laid at the receptionist's desk against the couple who were, as one elderly sailor stated, "oblivious to the world."

It took a minute of Levi calling their names and one shrill whistle to pull them apart.

"Get a room!" Levi told them, looking up at them when they peered over the hull of the boat. Their dopey, radiant faces told him everything he needed to know.

"Lee, we've decided to get married!" Jules shouted, incandescently happy.

Levi placed his hands on his hips and smiled. "Honey, that decision was made for you twenty-plus years ago by Mom and Bethann. You've just taken your time to get with the program."

Jules and Noah exchanged broad smiles. It was probably true but neither of them minded.

"Congrats, guys. But enough public displays of affection, okay?" Levi asked. *"Please?"*

Jules laughed, shook her head and looked at Noah as

Levi turned away. "Love you, Noah." She couldn't say it enough, she had ten years of lost time to make up for.

"I love you more, babe. So, do you want to go belowdecks?" Noah said as he stood up, holding out his hand.

Jules placed her hand in his and allowed him to pull her up and into his chest. Yes, of course she did. On land or sea, being with him was the only place she wanted to be.

Epilogue

Callie...

One down, four to go, Callie thought, thinking of the call she'd received from Jules an hour earlier. She stood in front of the front door to Mason's coffee shop, frowning at the closed sign. It was after five; Mason closed at four thirty and he'd already be on his way home.

It was better that he was gone, she wasn't even sure why she was there. Callie rested her hand on the cool glass and remembered feeling and sounding as giddy as Jules did when she and Ray announced that they were in love, that they were getting married. It was all so new; she'd been a virgin, he'd only had one other lover. They were each other's first loves, their *only* loves. She didn't know how to love anyone but Ray and didn't think she could.

He'd been a wonderful husband, a considerate lover, an excellent father. They'd traveled, raised their kids, socialized. And she still loved him with every breath she took. He'd been her world, still was. Oh, she'd been to grief counseling and knew she could be idealizing Ray and their relationship, it was what everyone did. But they'd had fun, dammit, and it was as good as she remembered.

Her attraction to Mason, the crazy, heat-filled dreams, her fantasies of his broad hands on her skin, touching her in the places that only Ray knew, filled her with guilt and she felt like she was cheating on her husband. Her lust for this younger, *hotter* guy was tearing her in two.

And the affection she was feeling, the connection that arced between them, burned a hole in her stomach. She had no right to feel this way, to be both terrified and excited at seeing Mason…as well as annoyed and irritated and turned on. Even in those early days with Ray their attraction hadn't burned so brightly. It had been a steady flame instead of a bonfire.

She loved her husband, she *did*. So why, when she was supposed to be so happy for her daughter, so excited for her future, couldn't she stop thinking about this denim-blue-eyed man? Why could she still taste him in her mouth, feel his hand on her breast? Why did she ache between her legs?

And, this made her blood run cold, what compelled her to run to him, oh, so desperately wanting to share her wonderful news? Why was he the first person she wanted to tell?

It couldn't work, it would never work. She was Callie Brogan, still in love with her husband and Mason was the coffee shop guy.

The door under her hand moved and Callie lifted up her tear-soaked face, her eyes colliding with his. His hand encircled her wrist and he gently pulled her into the empty shop, chairs on tables, a mop and bucket in the center of the floor. He wiped away her tears with his thumb before gently pulling her into his arms, his hand holding the back of her head.

"Hey, honey, what's the matter, huh? What can I do?"

"Nothing. Uh…my daughter is in love and getting married." Callie managed to hiccup through her tears and, burying her nose in his flannel shirt, she sank into him. "I'm so happy, and I just wanted to tell you."

Stroking her back, Mason buried his face in her hair and, somehow, knew what she needed him to do.

He just held her.

* * * * *

LET'S TALK

Romance

For exclusive extracts, competitions and special offers, find us online:

f MillsandBoon

X @MillsandBoon

◎ @MillsandBoonUK

♪ @MillsandBoonUK

Get in touch on 01413 063 232

MILLS & BOON

THE HEART OF ROMANCE

A ROMANCE FOR EVERY READER

MODERN

Prepare to be swept off your feet by sophisticated, sexy and seductive heroes, in some of the world's most glamourous and romantic locations, where power and passion collide.

HISTORICAL

Escape with historical heroes from time gone by. Whether your passion is for wicked Regency Rakes, muscled Vikings or rugged Highlanders, awaken the romance of the past.

MEDICAL

Set your pulse racing with dedicated, delectable doctors in the high-pressure world of medicine, where emotions run high and passion, comfort and love are the best medicine.

True Love

Celebrate true love with tender stories of heartfelt romance, from the rush of falling in love to the joy a new baby can bring, and a focus on the emotional heart of a relationship.

HEROES

The excitement of a gripping thriller, with intense romance at its heart. Resourceful, true-to-life women and strong, fearless men face danger and desire - a killer combination!

From showing up to glowing up, these characters are on the path to leading their best lives and finding romance along the way – with plenty of sizzling spice!

To see which titles are coming soon, please visit

millsandboon.co.uk/nextmonth

Afterglow Books is a trend-led, trope-filled list of books with diverse, authentic and relatable characters, a wide array of voices and representations, plus real world trials and tribulations. Featuring all the tropes you could possibly want (think small-town settings, fake relationships, grumpy vs sunshine, enemies to lovers) and all with a generous dose of spice in every story.

♪ @millsandboonuk

⊙ @millsandboonuk

afterglowbooks.co.uk

#AfterglowBooks

For all the latest book news, exclusive content and giveaways scan the QR code below to sign up to the Afterglow newsletter:

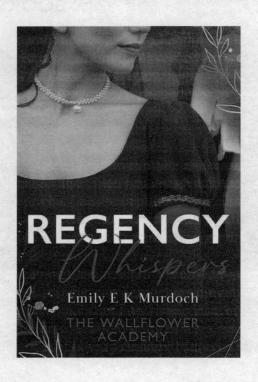